Riders
on the
Orphan Train

Alison Moore

Designed and published by:
Roadworthy Press
Fayetteville, Arkansas

Cover art: Gary Weidner
Author photo: Russell Cothren

A chapter of this novel titled "The Orphan Train" appeared in the short story collection, *The Middle of Elsewhere,* by Alison Moore, Phoenix International Press, 2006.

Library of Congress Cataloging-in-Publication Number:
2012950765

ISBN-13 978-0615684550
ISBN-10-0615684556

In memory of Lee Nailling
Orphan Train Rider to Texas

Other books by Alison Moore:

Small Spaces between Emergencies
Synonym for Love
The Middle of Elsewhere

Acknowledgements

I would like to thank these organizations for their generous support:

The National Endowment for the Arts, Texas Institute of Letters, Humanities Texas, New Mexico Humanities Council, Harry Ransom Center, Humanities Research Institute/University of Texas at Austin, National Orphan Train Complex Museum and Research Center, Orphan Train Heritage Society of America, Inc., Louisiana Orphan Train Rider Museum, and the Children's Aid Society of New York.

I owe a great deal to the following Orphan Train Riders who shared their stories with me: Lee Nailling, Art Smith, Howard Hurd, Fred Swedenborg, Alice Ayler, Colonel Leonard Winget, Bill Oser, Alice Bernard, Mary Maresh, and the countless family members I have met at Orphan Train reunions and presentations of the multi-media program that my husband and I perform, *Riders on the Orphan Train*. I'd also like to thank all the museums, libraries, and universities that hosted our program.

To Mary Ellen Johnson, mentor, friend, and source of inspiration. She was the founder of the Orphan Train Heritage Society of America, Inc. in Springdale, Arkansas, and has been enormously helpful through the years in helping to raise awareness of this little-known part of our history. Without her dedication to the Orphan Train Riders and their descendants, this book would not have been possible.

Very special thanks to:

Michael Adams, who always believed in this book. Janet Kaye for editorial advice and moral support. To Nan Cuba and Bob Ayres, fellow Warren Wilson Program for Writers grads, and Olive Mondello, and Jean Salvato, who read portions of the novel in progress. To Tom Wilkerson, Gary Widener, and Adelaide Adamson, who helped design and produce this book. To Dennis Samuelson, long-time friend, tireless researcher, and developer for the facebook page, and Dee Dunlap for the web sites. To Harold Dupre, Kay Bernard, Philippe Charlot, Tom and Vicki Bell, Richard Walker, Muriel Anderson, Amanda Wahlmeir, Susan Sutton, Vic Remmer, and Truda Jewitt for research assistance and encouragement.

To all the friends who gave me room, literally, to write. Collectively, they create a map of support: Jane Fountain (Johnson City, Texas), the Ucross Center (Ucross, Wyoming), The Writers Colony at Dairy Hollow (Eureka Springs, Arkansas), the Mulholland Family (Fayetteville, Arkansas), the Dobie/Paisano Fellowship at the University of Texas at Austin, Eric and Peggy Luplow (Truchas, New Mexico), Mike Fitzmorris (Tucson, Arizona), Peggy Hitchcock, (Paradise, Arizona), Mt. Sequoyah Retreat Center (Fayetteville, Arkansas), Jane Murray (San Angelo, Texas) and Betty Moore (Terlingua, Texas).

To the three patient canines, Maggie, Punkin, and Buffalo, who sat at my feet while I wrote and revised.

To fellow musicians on the same wavelength: David Massengill, Robin and Linda Williams, and Tim O'Brien. And everyone at the Kerrville Folk Festival.

Last but not least, to my husband, musician and songwriter Phil Lancaster, partner in the multi-media program *Riders on the Orphan Train*. Fifteen years on the road together has created a story I never could have imagined on my own.

Maud
December 15, 1916

Halfway to America an Irish girl dreams of Egypt. Instead of the Statue of Liberty greeting her as she's imagined for so long, the pyramid of a pharaoh with an all-seeing eye stands guard at the entrance to the harbor. It's on the dollar bill, after all. The eye regards her with little interest, perhaps a certain disdain. It blinks, once. The shutter closes, as if it's seen all it needs to. She's just another one of those migratory creatures, foreign and ravenous, about to devour everything in sight.

A sudden silence shakes her, and she finds herself, not in the deserts of Egypt, but tangled in the sheet of her cold bunk on the *Carpathia*. The engines have shut down, the spinning propellers stalled. The ship drifts— she can feel it—a monstrous, flat iron pressing down heavily upon the wrinkled Atlantic.

She shifts in the narrow bunk, slides off the edge of the thin mattress that reeks of the hope of thousands who have made this passage before her, including those *Titanic* survivors, four years ago, though she doubts they were put in third-class. Her coat, for she sleeps in her coat for the warmth, catches on a sharp spring, tearing on the way down, past the bunk where Munirah, from Syria, sleeps. The Arab girl has not been well, had developed a fever two days ago. She moans softly. Perhaps it's not from the fever, but a dream of her betrothed in Brooklyn. Below her, an old Italian woman from Brindisi sleeps clutching a bundle of sausages and a crucifix. Another woman, seasick since the start, from somewhere unpronounceable in the Ukraine, holds a samovar in a pillowcase, protecting the fetus that swims inside her. Or perhaps the fetus is inside the samovar by now, needing greater armor. The crossing is dangerous. German submarines could sink their ship at any time.

The women, when they do sleep, snore the same no matter how they talk. Greenhorns, they're called, no matter what country they started from.

Maud makes her way through the tiers of mothers, of daughters, of sisters stacked like tinder inside the steel hull riding heavy and low upon the water. The *Carpathia* is an ark out of the Old World with the last of everything crammed inside. She had expected to hear only English, but this ship was nearly filled by the time she embarked in Cobh with passengers who had begun the voyage earlier in Liverpool. Passenger ships were curtailed with the war in Europe, and the *Carpathia's* normal ports of call had been cancelled. Some had come all the way to Liverpool from Madrid, Marseilles, even Istanbul. There were Italians and Turks and Serbs and Jews, whirling dervishes, an albino from Finland and a ventriloquist from Genoa. Brides-to-be from Krakow and a few old maids from western Ireland. All trying to run the gauntlet to America.

She is Maud Farrell, eleven years of age, heading toward her father. He's in New York praying for her safe arrival. His eye, when it is not concerned with focusing the lens of a camera, will be on the calendar for the day his only daughter will arrive. He will take her to 256 Elizabeth Street where her supper will be set upon a table: New York steaks, rare. Potatoes from Idaho, not Ireland. The regal, elegant name of the street lures her westward in spite of this voyage with its sickness and sleeplessness and all the worry about the war. She's hopeful, still.

Maud climbs the stairs through the lower decks into the freezing air. The sight that confronts her takes her breath. Above the four stacks, a canopy of the Northern Lights undulates over the Atlantic. Below it floats a meringue of ice. The bergs groan and calve in the ink-dark water. There is no difference between sea and sky and the stars have sheared away from some greater star like shards of ice. Everything splinters: the families and countries they left behind. Above all of it, that banner of improbable color unfurls like a flag of an undeclared country. The Northern Lights shift and crackle; they snap like a vast sheet strung on a line of stars. Deserts and pyramids, even the war in Europe, seem very far from here.

More than half her life ago, her first glimpse of that more exotic part of the world had imprinted itself deeply within her. It's no wonder she dreams of Egypt now. Her father woke her, threw a cloak over her nightdress, and took her by the hand to Gortadoo to see his magic lantern show of the Seven Wonders. He had stretched a sheet between two poles, a gray square, until the magic light shone upon it. When the Great Pyramid of Cheops filled the screen, she'd walked straight toward it. She stopped, staring at the screen and her shadow rose as tall as the great pyramid itself.

The crowd behind her shouted to get down in front, but she stood there, mesmerized. Her mother had gone away a year before, and to Maud, it seemed entirely possible her mother had stepped through this very screen; she might well be able to follow her there. Despite her efforts, she only managed to push against the cloth once before the pyramid rippled and then slowly dissolved.

Before two more summers came to a close Maud would be packed off to Killarney. Surrendered to the custody of the Sisters of Mercy Industrial School and their terrifying methods of soul-saving while her mother wandered loose in the world—to England, it was said, with a Protestant poet. She left nothing, not even a note behind. Her father escaped his humiliation by hiding under a cloak, literally, by becoming a portrait photographer (it was rumored he photographed some women in the nude). He went to ply his trade in the more permissive country of America. And now, Maud finds herself at a longitude approximately halfway between the two.

When she returns to her bunk, a group of women have gathered around Munirah. Maud moves closer, sees the blue letters she often spoke about, postmarked from Brooklyn, now clutched in her fist. Maud holds the other, un-fisted hand. The fever has fully taken hold of Munirah and she calls out his name, Mohammed, like a heated breeze from deep inside her.

Before the night is out Munirah is gone; all these women from Arabia and Europe with their remedies and herbs cannot cure her. The ship's English doctor listens for her pulse through a stethoscope, peels back her eyelids and pronounces her cause of death as meningitis. He barely touches her. She is that cold already. It took him that long to get down through all the decks, his watch ticking on first-class time.

Maud steps back and watches as the women from Munirah's country bathe her, wrap her with great tenderness in a white linen tablecloth. They do not try to take the letters from Munirah's hands. They carry her up the narrow metal stairs to the deck.

Maud stands perfectly still when the captain says the common prayer that has nothing to do with Munirah. It could just as easily be Maud, wrapped up for the hereafter, clutching letters from the West full of promises. It could be her, sliding down that rough plank into the freezing, indifferent ocean.

A loose edge catches on a splinter so that the

shroud unwinds, spinning the girl down. Everyone watches, horrified as this naked, brown girl slips from the cloth and hits the water face up. Maud pushes past the captain, past the women that washed her, and yanks the cloth free from the plank until it floats down to cover her and settles partway over her body, leaving the brown nipples exposed. The blue letters scatter over the sea, floating like petals of hydrangeas before they go under. The ship doesn't even slow down. In a few seconds it's beyond, the wake of its passing stirring the immigrant Arab girl, folding her into the sea.

≋

Tonight, the ship is stopped. Not by the untouched body of a young Muslim girl with a fever, but by ice. Lots of it. A gauntlet, sharp and cold and threatening. Maud watches it slide along the hull, scratching its long, illegible name in the black paint like a bully writing blasphemy on the churchyard wall. And now they might be sailing right over the wreck of the *Titanic*, the memory of the place deeply imprinted in *Carpathia's* hull.

The sea is filled with the bones of those who perished. Including her mother. She'd gone down on the *Sussex*, a ferry between England and France, attacked by a German U-boat. That event turned abandonment to tragedy—if she hadn't been killed, she might have come back, after all. But even in death her whereabouts is unknown. Her body was never recovered from the sea.

It's bad, all of it: Munirah's death and awful burial at sea, the memory of her mother, the dream of the eye in the pyramid closing on everything, the ice, the scratch on the ship, like the mark of the quarantined. Would they even be allowed into America? Would they even make it that far? Are there U-boats below, the heart of this ship in its sights? The Kaiser could change his mind any minute and rescind the moratorium on unrestricted submarine warfare.

Out of the corner of her eye something moves. Munirah, revived by water, climbing over the railing, incredulous about being left behind? Her mother, surfacing slowly with open arms? Maud turns. More shapes appear. Six of them emerge from the iron stairs wearing white robes, peculiar hats. They must be the Whirling Dervishes that had made their way across Europe from the Middle East. All they did was sit down on the deck ever since the ship set sail, refusing the slop that passed for stew, passing a steady supply of their own hard boiled eggs between them. Now these dervishes stand on the stern, faces lifted to the sky. Their white robes, like long, thick skirts, are luminous, tinged pink and green from the *aurora borealis*. Tall hats thrust like stove pipes into the air. In silent agreement they form a circle and lift their arms. They move together, becoming one body, many arms raised toward the twisting, crackling sky. Then something possesses each, moves each man into a tighter and tighter spin, the white robes unfurling until they all blur together, dissolve in a spinning halo of light.

The ship drifts slowly westward through the ice, scratched but not torn open, propelled, perhaps even protected by this eerie prayer. Is it for Munirah? Maud hopes so. She also hopes it's for the memory of everyone who perished below in this time of war.

Maud inches her way along the rail, pulled toward the dance by centrifugal force. She has no white robe. Only a torn coat. She has no word for this kind of praise. All she knows of Mary pales in the face of this God made of wind and whirling heat. She can feel this heat even in the freezing December air, the last cold grasp of a Europe at war not yet ready to let them go.

A bell rings. Twice. From the sky? Or is it the first

mate signaling the engine room? The whirling of the dervishes winds down. With a great shudder the ship wakes; the propellers tear at the water. The furled robes fall back into ordinary folds. Below, stripped-to-the-waist Irish stokers heave coal into the fiery boilers. Maud comes back to the world, the one where the magic lantern goes out and there's a blank screen of a strange, new country stretching before her, not to the east, but west. A country with mystery in its money and hungry people giving up everything for the promise of freedom, to claim a place there, no matter the cost.

The dervishes file past her. They walk now, one foot in front of the other, their feet not winged but encased in rather ordinary shoes. They silently descend the stairs to the deck below.

≋

It's five in the morning. Cold. Colder. Maud wonders if she'll ever be warm again. She clings to the railing on the deck, straining for the first sign of her up ahead as they pass through what she just heard someone call The Narrows. Land, finally.

Liberty has been talked about ever since they left Queenstown, argued about. The number of points on her crown. The height from bare foot to tip of the torch held aloft. The real meaning of the broken chain at her feet. The unbreakable promise of her name. Now all the din has come down to whispers. She's out there somewhere near. She's who they pray to now, no matter what god they started out with. The green lady lifts the light by the golden door for them all.

When they'd first set sail, Munirah had told her that the statue was originally meant to stand at Suez, veiled. But she said Egypt could not afford this woman and the Frenchman who designed her took his plans West. Took off the veil, but kept the light.

Maud's father had sent her a photograph he'd taken of a groundbreaking ceremony on Staten Island with the Statue of Liberty in the background. In the foreground of the photograph, a group of Indians stood next to President Taft. But best of all was a young boy, his back to the camera, blurred by motion, reaching to shake the hand of one of the Indian chiefs. It was a ceremony, her father had written, for the dedication of a new statue of the Vanishing American holding a bow and arrow in one hand, his other hand held up in greeting. Maud looks for this statue, too, but does not see it anywhere in the harbor.

Munirah should be here to see Liberty. She's a sight that makes people weep; so Maud has heard in the fragile envelopes her father sent back to her in Ireland. The sisters in Killarney always held her father's letters out to her with great disdain, as if the paper itself was contaminated with Yankee blasphemy. Western Ireland had a proud tradition of resisting the pull of immigration, but even that was changing. Her father had much to say in the letters with their thrilling stamps. "Forget whatever photograph of Liberty you've seen," the letters say. "Black and white doesn't do her any justice. It's like seeing God, God as a woman standing tall, not bent over by labor. Liberty is larger than Mary and not near so melancholy. She represents the future, not the past. You, dear girl, are the future of America." He'd enclosed a photograph he'd taken of the statue. Maud didn't flinch at the shocking comparison that came from her father. Secret letters from a secret father. Until the one about Liberty was found by accident in the laundry by another girl who passed it on to the Mother Superior. Maud stood before the grim tribunal, the damning letter on the table. She was asked to denounce her father's sacrilege and tear the photograph in two. Instead, she boldly stated that the letter was addressed to her and was none of their concern. She was commanded to hold out her hands, palms up in front of her. She held out her arms but refused to surrender her palms to them. A switch sliced the air, landed on the back of her hands, her wrists, her arms, leaving marks she still has. She paid for every sentence, and it took awhile for her hands to stop hurting enough to pick up a pen and answer. Meanwhile, they tore the photograph for her.

Soon after, news of the German attack on the French ferry *Sussex* arrived, delivered by the priest, Father Mallory, from Dunnequin. He had a newspaper article with the passenger list. Her mother's name was on it, but Maud saw no mention of her lover's name: Michael Leary. Maybe she was leaving him. But she was not on her way back to Ireland; she was headed for France. Perhaps her lover was fighting in France, at Verdun. Maud grieved, but this grief was not as great as the first, the night she tried to follow her mother into the magic lantern show and felt the consummate despair of reaching for the unreachable across the sands of Egypt.

The loss of her mother gave her some reprieve from scrutiny and punishment. In an odd way, death seemed to reward her. She was given special privileges: visits to the library replaced her duties in the laundry. She read the works of Rudyard Kipling insatiably beneath a green table lamp until someone had to come and get her for supper. Sister Irene, who had a collection of classical sheet music, allowed her to play the piano. She already knew a little. Her mother had begun to teach her on the piano in the school where she taught. She always had liked Chopin. She never did much care for Brahms.

Before the year was out a steamship ticket in a paper jacket imprinted with a picture of the Statue of Liberty was delivered personally by Father Mallory. He told her the ticket was from her father. And so she sailed to America, away from danger of all kinds, furiously prayed for by the Church she left behind.

Maud can hardly stand the wait now, not just to see Liberty, but to get off the *Carpathia*, to have her feet on solid ground again, no matter what condition her shoes are in. To *arrive*. She strains to see through the fog. By now, the rest have been roused, dragging their blankets and bundles from below deck. The ship passes the Lightship Ambrose, but it's little more than a votive candle on its spindly legs set atop the signal vessel. A lonely bell tolls slowly from the wake of the *Carpathia's* passing.

Everyone holds their breath, wrapped against the cold, pressing forward, waiting for Liberty to show herself. How can she be hidden by bad weather? How can Liberty be lost in fog? When they see her, they know they will be safe.

"There," someone says, a little doubtful.

"Where?" someone else replies.

"Isn't that her?"

It's terrible that they can't tell for sure. She should be unmistakable. People are crying now. From exhaustion or relief, Maud can't tell which. Liberty or not, they're here. But there is a faint green glow, like a smear in the harbor. Maybe she is veiled, after all.

"It's the torch, isn't it?" a man says anxiously.

"Has to be."

"Step to the center of the ship," a voice calls out over a bullhorn. The *Carpathia* remains listing to starboard with the weight of so much anticipation. Nobody moves. Some people get down on their knees as they drift past the island where Liberty stands. Liberty is lost, at least the solid presence of her holding the light for Maud's grand entrance. What she has instead for her arrival is a misty apparition, and it seems the power of the nuns has intercepted this necessary welcome, obscured the secular sentry that lured so many from the

Church and cast them upon what was considered the unbridled temptations of a brash and lawless country.

The ship plows through the fogbank, and it isn't until they're within shouting distance of Manhattan that they see anything. Spires. Towers piercing the fog. A jagged, slate-colored mountain range of a building poking through with the lights going out. One tower in particular has a crown, a frightful mansion atop a stilt, and on top of that, a great beacon throwing light in all directions like the all-seeing eye on the pyramid with its eerie, omniscient scrutiny. And New York seems to her less like a city in heaven than a façade, a place where people wait, not for opportunity, but for their fate to be decided upon by powerful, invisible strangers.

Here it is: America. Maybe the nuns were right.

In the nine days it's taken to cross, almost twice as long as anticipated due to foul weather, she's slept, or tried to, on the top bunk when the weather was too raw to stand on deck, which was mostly, and stared at the ceiling constructing a picture in the chipped and sweating gray paint scratched by knives and fingernails of those who'd crossed before her. Through the graffiti of boredom she tried to make her own picture: of a gleaming Liberty lighting her way, and then her father waiting for her on the pier. Bands playing. Streamers flying. The sun itself would be so much brighter in the New World, as if the blazing star had been reborn out of the gray pall of Europe, glad for such a vast, new horizon to shine upon.

She would descend the gangway into the arms of the only person in the world who could rightfully claim her until she became herself again, the gray days of waiting, the predictions from the nuns of abandonment by a wayward father dripping off her like water running off a seal.

Already the picture needs revision. It seems almost childish in the face of this gray, unwelcoming city.

They're early and it's still dark. But there is no war here. Not yet, anyway. And so the sun should be shining. The fog hasn't had a chance to burn off. It's as if they're being smuggled in. And her father? For the first time it occurs to her that he might not even be here. He had a bad habit of disappearing into pubs. In Gortadoo he wasn't hard to find. But here? Maybe Father Mallory had bought the ticket for her out of pity. He'd been a good friend of her father's, after all, a bearer of both good news and bad. He'd given her the address of St. Elizabeth Church near the old Castle Gardens. But she won't be needing that.

"More greenhorns," she hears an officer say to a man in a launch that pulls alongside. "Had to toss an Arab overboard."

"Immigration boss," a boy next to Maud says. "They'll do the first- and second- class people right on the ship. Third Class goes to Ellis Island where they can look us over longer. They turn your pockets inside out, sure. And your eyelids, too," he says, wincing.

"How do you know?" She's heard about the trachoma, the dreaded button hooks to peel back the eyelids with to look for the presence of the disease, so he must be telling the truth. She's just testing him, is all.

"I been here before," he says. Maud turns to get a good look at him. He can't be more than sixteen or seventeen. His cap is turned sideways in what her father would admiringly call a "to hell with you salute." Around his neck, a red scarf, like the kind drivers of motorcars wear, knotted at the throat. Despite the tatters it's a rather elegant, outlandish accessory for someone traveling steerage.

"Thought I'd have another go. Two years now since I got turned away. A big H chalked on my back, for the heart. I was breathin' too hard going up the stairs. That's how they tell who's sick. Who's worth keeping. You look sharp when you climb those stairs.

Whatever you do, don't cough. And don't be acting crazy or you get an X. He shoves his hands deeper into his pockets. "And if you got some job lined up, don't breathe a word of it. They don't want contract labor in the United States of America."

"Why not?"

"They're afraid the Irish will be takin' the jobs from the natives. But if they get in the war and start sending their own, they'll be needing us."

She doesn't really like listening to this now. According to him, America sounds more like a place of rules and petty concerns than opportunities. Natives. Aren't they Indians? Do they *need* jobs? She thought they rode on horseback over the Great Plains and hunted buffalo for their suppers without any extra help from anyone.

Dawn doesn't break. It leaks. Light, if you can call it that, only thickens the fog. A gray, clammy stew, stirring. The *Carpathia* is towed. Towed! Tethered to a tug like a groaning, lumbering ox following a pugnacious bulldog.

The covered gangways are quickly set against the ship's side as soon as stevedores tie the ship to the pier. A waiting crowd presses forward holding overlapping umbrellas. A line of taxis idle along the cobblestone street, puffing clouds of smoke from their tailpipes.

First class passengers stream out of the ship, cleared for entry. Just like the boy said. They're greeted by relatives, whisked into motorcars and taxis and horse-drawn carriages while the luggage is identified by a purser and brought to them on a cart by an African.

Maud is nearly pushed away from the railing by people straining to get a clear view of those waiting below. She hangs onto the railing hard and it's so cold her hands stick to the steel.

The boy who spoke to her earlier says, "Don't waste your time looking. Whoever comes for you knows not to come here. We'll be hours, days maybe at Ellis. You're met at the island, not here. These people here are only waiting for first class." He lights a ragged, hand-rolled cigarette. The smoke from it joins the gray air above him. "When I come in before it was summer and so many were waiting to go to Ellis that we had to stay on the ship for two days in harbor to get our turn. Five thousand a day was coming through then. People was trying to swim ashore they were so crazy with waiting but only got picked up with a big hook from the customs agents in a launch."

She can easily imagine the people jumping ship only to be fished out of the water on a great hook and thrown flopping into the police boat like flounder.

"What's your name, then," Maud asks. He could be useful. A guide, of sorts.

"John Tyrone."

"From?"

"Mayo, God help us. You?"

"Maud Farrell from Kerry." She's not going to say anything about the Sisters of Mercy Industrial School in Killarney. That's over now.

"Good thing your last name isn't Burgermeister; you'd never get in. You on your own? A little young aren't you?" He doesn't wait for an answer. "You're tall enough to say fourteen and be believed, if anyone asks, if you need to go to work. But to get off Ellis you have to be spoken for, by family that comes to get you. Who's bringin' you here, then?"

"My father. He's a photographer." It's been a long time since she's called him Da. It strikes her then that she has so few memories of him and in a way, he seems more like a suitor who has sent for her, not a father. Someone with a camera, not a daughter.

"Lucky you. My Ma's working in a cloak factory," he says. My Da was underground with the transit. Building the IRT underground railway, last I knew." He stubs the cigarette out on the railing, pockets the rest for later. "He's probably gone West by now. Where's your Ma, then?"

"In the Channel. The *Sussex.*"

He puts a hand gently on her shoulder. "Dear God. And America didn't lift a finger then, either."

She doesn't know why she's telling him the truth. Maybe telling it will make it more real than the newsprint. This is the first real sympathy she's gotten, too late, really, for the toughening that happened involuntarily like a carapace forming over too-tender skin. Her mother, a victim of the war, a target because she was on a ferry between two countries.

A whistle blasts from a ferry sidling alongside. John Tyrone grabs her shoulder and says, "You hold onto me. They'll be ready for us now. We'll get on the ferry first." Maud grabs her suitcase and he shoulders his way through the crowd, pulling her behind him.

The crowd turns like cattle in a stockyard, trying to funnel their way down the gangway with bundles wider than the walkway itself. Cooking pots and candlesticks clank together inside the sacks that don't have featherbeds to soften the clamor.

The ferry is little more than a barge, a squat thing next to the ship and with no canopy over it to keep off the rain and mist. Black smoke belches from its stubby stack. The word *Magnolia* in grimy gold letters gave up its gleam long ago. A bored captain leans out the window in the wheelhouse, smoking. A line of officials guards the gangway from the rest of the pier so they can't get away.

Maud takes literally two steps on the mainland. That's all. Long enough for her name to be found next to a number on the manifest and a tag with that number pinned to her coat. Twenty-six. She hopes it's a lucky one.

John Tyrone guides her across the uncovered

wooden gangway straight to a spot on the stern. "It won't be so cold here," he says. He lights up what's left of his smoke, picks a fleck of tobacco from his tongue and carefully pushes it back into the butt end.

The ferry lists to port side now with all the weight stepping onto it but levels out as the people boarding find places out of the wind. The bow fills last. With a doleful blast of its whistle the ferry backs away from the pier, turns slowly with its load and heads back into the harbor, accompanied by a flock of scolding gulls above the stern. Maud was hoping that birds in America would be different. These are the same old gulls they had in Gortadoo. Greedy and hungry and shrill.

"What will you be wanting with America, Miss Maud Farrell?"

For so long her only goal was to come to America. Now that she's here she'll need another one. "To be a singer. To play my own piano."

"Can you sing, then?"

"My mother did. My father says I got it from her."

"Penny opera?"

"No. I sang in the pubs when I was five. He'd set me on the bar and ask for ballads. But I'd like to know real opera. I listened to recordings on a gramophone with my mother."

"No Irish opera that I know of."

"Should be."

"That's a big idea for a ten-year-old. You are ten, aren't you? Or an eight-year-old with grand ideas."

"Eleven!"

"Well, why not? You could pass for fifteen, easy, tall as you are. You can be an opera star and I can be president. Who can stop us?"

She smiles. She can't remember the last time she did so.

"What do you want with America?" she asks.

"Everything."

RIDERS ON THE ORPHAN TRAIN

"Such as?"

"Such as a cattle ranch in Texas. I been looking after sheep my whole life, watching 'em nibble their way up and down the low hills. In the West there's mountains and so much tall grass the cattle rip it up in great big mouthfuls. Fat, they are. And expensive. Shoulder to shoulder with the buffalo. And I'll have a steak dinner from one of my own herd every weekend at a hotel where someone will be playing her own piano!" He waves his arms to indicate the expanse of it all. He can hardly stand still, describing it. He stops, looks at her, dead serious now. "And some young lady singing Irish opera in a fancy dress and all, making everyone sit up and listen and be proud to be Irish in the West of America." He pinches the end of his smoke. Just the paper left now.

West? This *is* The West, she thinks. Anywhere farther is unimaginable.

The ferry shudders through the harbor. Gulls, silent now, coast on the wind without flapping. John Tyrone tosses the last bit of the burnt-out smoke into the air. A seagull swoops low to catch it, and then drops it into the water.

Ellis Island looms ahead soon enough. Four spires crown a massive brick and limestone building the size of a grand castle, with arched windows high up. Farther on, Liberty finally shows herself and from this vantage point, she's little more than a small figurine perched on a pedestal. Whatever light she holds has been extinguished now that it's day. But a sorry excuse for a day. Hardly more than dingy, as if the light of America were rationed somehow, saved for a long, indeterminate future, hoarded in Washington, maybe, given to those in first class who were accustomed to such brightness all their privileged lives.

John Tyrone says nothing now, his advice used up. Maybe that's all he knows. Maybe things have changed since he was last here and he's figured that out already. She isn't sure he'll be much help once she gets onto this island, once she starts climbing the stairs. After all, he was turned away once. Is his heart any better this time around? She pictures the giant staircase, broad at the bottom, split in two near the top. To the right go the lucky; to the left go the damned with H's and X's on their backs. Nuns, no doubt, wait to receive them and save their wretched souls.

Broken oyster shells litter the beach of this island and rattle like broken crockery when small waves wash over them. The waterline leaves a ragged hem of brown froth as it slides back into the harbor.

"That's the gauntlet, there," John Tyrone says, nodding toward a crowd of people lining the path beneath an enormous awning.

The passengers from the *Carpathia* stream slowly off the ferry carrying their baskets and bundles. They inch toward the entryway, desperate to get out of the cold wind. Just before they reach the threshold the numbers on their tags are sorted in groups of thirty by an official. "That's how many of us fits onto one of their pages," John says. His number, she notices now, is 35. He'll be in a different group going in. They pass a table with piles of thick slices of bread, cups of milk. Her first food in America.

"I'll find you in the Great Hall," he says. "Listen for my name. They'll call it out. And don't leave your bag with the left luggage. Hold onto it. And Maud, have you got twenty-five dollars?"

She nods. A gold piece and five dollar bills sewn into the hem of her coat.

"They'll want to see it," he says. "You have to have money to get in now, so you won't become a burden, a public charge."

Maud quickly rips out the hem of her coat, puts the money in her pocket. But the coat looks awful now—first the tear from catching on the spring in her bunk, now the ragged hem. She looks like a beggar, a wretch from an industrial school, not somebody's awaited daughter.

She clutches her small suitcase, the leather scratched off the corners already, and makes her way toward the door. She looks up. Two limestone eagles glare down at her, clutching shields with stars and stripes. They look like they'll swoop down any second and pluck out the eyes of anyone who doesn't appear to measure up.

Inside the entryway she's faced with a mountain of bundles and trunks. People who know they can't carry them set them down, adding to the pile, holding fast to their claim tickets. Surely this small island will sink with the weight of the luggage alone. At the end of this room, as big as a mine tailing, the slate stairs rise. John Tyrone hadn't been kidding. She looks up. Leaning over the railing on the landing above, men in uniforms scrutinize them. Up they go, the immigrants, a dark wave rising. Maud is careful not to cough, not to stumble. A woman in front of her struggles with a clanking bundle, gasping for air near the top of the stairs. She's breathing so hard she starts to cough. Immediately, a medical examiner who has no doubt been following her painful progress from the very first step pulls her aside. He turns the woman around and marks a "C" on her back with a piece of blue chalk. A man with a cane is marked with an "L." Maud follows these letters, hearing people behind her wonder out loud what they mean. She doesn't know what these specific letters mean, but they're not good. A chalked letter on your back is a bad grade; there are no A's. All of these letters are marks of failure, not merit.

She stands in front of a white-coated doctor sitting on a little raised platform. He tells her to press her fingers down on the table. She presses down hard.

"Pink," he says. "Good." The next doctor asks her to read something and hands her a book of stories by O. Henry and she reads a paragraph about a foolish woman who believes she is wearing diamonds.

A matron steers her toward an elderly woman just ahead of her with an H on her back. "Ladies, in there," she says, pointing to an open room. "We want to listen to your hearts, if you still have them." Maud catches a glimpse of a woman in her chamise examined by a nurse. A good thing Maud doesn't have an H because they'd take her shirtwaist off too and see the marks on her arms and hands. And what letter would they have for her then?

Maud joins a line moving slowly toward another man in uniform. What she sees first is the pregnant woman with the samovar, big as a house, her face lifted, looking up toward the ceiling, as if a great mural were there to be regarded in awe. She holds her shawl about her with great dignity. But there's nothing on the ceiling to be seen and her dignity is short-lived. Maud sees the button hook peeling back the woman's eyelid. She jerks but does not cry out. The button hook is withdrawn but the woman does not look down right away. She's still gazing, it seems, at something above her as the doctor wipes the hook on a handkerchief. He takes out a piece of blue chalk and writes "E" on her back, below it, a "T." A nurse tells her she'll take her back to the baggage hall to claim her things. The woman looks relieved. She's passed. Then the nurse says, "You'll have to wait in the detention area for a ferry to get another ship back to your country."

"Country?" the woman says. "I come here. America my country now ."

"You're contagious," the nurse says. "We can't have that here."

Contagious. As if everyone she looked at would die. And the baby in her, it must be turning over right now, knowing it's got to cross that ocean all over again.

She staggers forward, this woman who a moment ago drew her shawl around her proudly. All the infirmities start to show: a limp that she'd obviously hidden coming up the stairs. Doubt drags the proud shawl off her shoulder. Higher up, above the "E" is a "Pg" that had been mostly covered. Who knows what she'll be returning to—her house in flames? Her family slaughtered? Her entire country in ruins?

She's shunted to a corner where a stricken group stands huddled together. Maud watches her halt in her steps as she sees what she's being relegated to: damaged goods. All the ones with chalk marks. Several X's. One on a man whose eyes are crossed. The others on two dwarves and a tall woman who cannot stop laughing.

And then it's Maud's turn to have her eyelids turned inside out. For the first time on this trip, she's completely terrified. The man in the uniform inserts the cold buttonhook under her lid. She blinks rapidly trying to expel this foreign object while a strange man with terrible breath peers into her helpless, wide-open eye. She wants, more than anything, to yell, but she stands still. This is the last station of the cross here at Ellis. But then there's the other eye, worse since it knows what to expect in advance of the hook. The man pulls her eyelid back with his fingers first and then slips the hook in, hard. Then, it's over. Nothing marked on her back. Her eyes aren't even red from crying like half the people here. She knows how to hold on to her tears. Her tears would have satisfied the nuns but she did not give them; they were hers to withhold. But now her eyes sting from the shame of medical scrutiny as if the naked soul, always safe behind the iris, had been shocked and tricked into exposing itself.

She makes her way to the stairs and leans over the railing to see if she can see John Tyrone. She's worried that she might have missed him. But it's easy to spot him, near the top now with his rakish hat and his red scarf. He's not even breathing hard; he practically bounds up the stairs, or would if there weren't so many people trudging in front of him. As soon as he gains the top step he calls out, "They moved the stairs! They used to be right in the middle of the room!" and a doctor in a gray suit pulls him aside. The doctor points to the hat, tugs on the scarf. Then he turns him and marks an X on his back.

John Tyrone cranes his neck to see what mark has been made. He has to take off his coat. His face— Maud can barely look—flushes red with anguish and indignation. "I'm not a lunatic!" he cries, and the doctor narrows his eyes and nods as if that outburst just proved his initial diagnosis.

John Tyrone stands there, his mouth open in disbelief. He's been marked. Again. There is no worse mark to get. He may as well be insane. It's his flamboyance that's culled him from the herd and marked him now, as eccentric, unfit for this orderly country. Or an anarchist. Or maybe that he announced for all to hear about the stairs being moved, a dead giveaway that he'd already been turned away once.

"This is America!" John cries, trying to rub the blue X off his coat before he puts it back on. He looks, one by one at the faces in the circle beginning to form around him. He keeps turning, in that small circle, looking for someone. The doctor, nervous now, tries to grab him, but he only turns faster, shouting, "What is it you're all so afraid of?"

The Italians and the English, even the dervishes, the Turks who'd danced on the *Carpathia* watch him in silence. The pregnant woman with the contagious eyes. The dwarves with the X's that take up their entire backs. Everyone watches John Tyrone go mad, afraid he might reflect on them all.

Maud pushes her way to the inner circle around

him. He stops when he sees her, dizzy and reeling, and holds out his hand. It trembles there in the stirred-up air between them. With everything in her she wants to take it, to hold that hand that helped her. But would it mean a blue X on her, too, a cancellation of herself and all she's come for? How can he ask it of her?

The sight of that hand beseeching her is more than she can bear. She reaches forward, too late. Two officials tackle him and he hits the tiled floor, howling.

"Go on, then!" John cries. But it's not to the men who wrestled him down. It's to Maud, and the ones without letters whose good health and good manners have gotten themselves a place in America. It's the fracturing of a dream, and this fragment of outrage that flew off of him lodges into her skull like shrapnel and stays there.

Somehow she's passed through the gauntlet. They did not see her suspect soul, her wayward father, the fatal desire of her mother. The strife of the Old World etched in her face. Here, in the cold cavern of the Isle of Tears she longs for heat and sunlight, that firm sense of walking forward through the golden door. On the other side she will spin herself free of shameful history. She will revise herself in her own good time.

She keeps going, past the men with chalk and the doctors with their button hooks and the eyes of the marked detainees toward the Great Hall, the vestibule to Purgatory with windows and a view. Waiting. In an hour, or two, or four, of working her way through the maze of cattle chutes, someone will call out John Tyrone and there will be silence. They will call Maud Farrell. And she will answer.

Ezra
December 27, 1916

Ezra Duval stands on the balcony of the tenth-floor apartment in the Hotel Chelsea. There's a floor for each year of his life. Carefully, he opens the folded newspaper he picked up in the lobby. The news is terrifying these days, the war in Europe coming closer with each morning's headline. He's afraid that his father could be drafted, sent to France to fight, that Ezra's eleventh birthday, just ten months away, will be beside the point in the face of so much danger and devastation. And then what will become of him? He's been a half-orphan since the day he was born. His father is the only thing that keeps him from disappearing into an orphanage.

And where is his father tonight? Late. Always late. Always elsewhere in his attention. But alive.

Ezra turns the pages past the news of the war, looking for something to keep his imagination from conjuring images of trenches and rifles and fallen horses and fathers dying far from home.

He looks down from the balcony, at the newsies and the singing girls making their way to the piers. From this perspective, Ezra gains a certain necessary omniscience; he could be the narrator of the story around him. But ten floors in the air give him no distance and although he is at liberty to come and go, the tenuous future and the frightful past hold him hostage his own free country.

He turns back to the newspaper where an article on page two grabs his attention. The *Carpathia* has made its last voyage to New York as a passenger ship and will be outfitted for war by the British Navy. Once, it carried the survivors of the *Titanic* here.

He remembers the *Carpathia*. He remembers that night, four years ago, all too well.

Ezra had been awakened by a great commotion in the street below. Taxis pulled up and passengers were assisted at the curb. Ezra had opened the window and even ten floors up he could sense the confusion. These people had no luggage. It was raining and they had no umbrellas. Some ran for the door, others simply stood in the rain until someone, a cabbie, the doorman, led them by the arm into the lobby of the hotel.

He had closed the window, called out for his father. Nothing came out of the dark, not a voice, not a person, living or dead, filling the doorframe. Suddenly he felt very frightened. In a panic he left the apartment in his nightshirt, ran down the hall to the elevator.

Something was very wrong. Henry, the night elevator man, was not at his station. Ezra closed the brass gate himself, pushed the letter "L" and descended to the lobby. Mr. McGarragh, the night clerk would have an answer. As the outer doors of the elevator opened he had the fleeting sensation of what it must feel like to be an animal about to be loosed from a cage. He stayed there in the elevator, his finger on "L" to keep the doors from opening again.

The lobby was crowded; no one paid him any attention. There was chaos at the desk, no one really in charge except the harried Mr. McGarragh, trying to help this sudden influx of unexpected guests. A young woman sitting on a chair shrouded in a man's overcoat looked up at Ezra, her face a mask of shock. She stood up and walked like a somnambulist toward him, reaching her hand through the gate. Then she opened the gate and pulled him into the lobby, going down on her knees to clasp him to her breast. She wept. Wept! Ezra watched the faces of the others, a hush coming over the entire entourage except for the woman's weeping and saying the name "Daniel" over and over again. Feeling these desperate arms he himself began to cry for this was what he had imagined in excruciating detail so many times: reunion, his mother, not dead but returning from some long voyage in which she'd searched everywhere for him. There were people in this audience who wiped their eyes, some who simply stared until an older woman stepped forward, her ample figure pinched by a dress designed for someone half her size. She placed her hands on the weeping woman's shoulders, shaking her, saying, "Dorothea, no. No, child. This isn't Daniel." Dorothea's grip slowly loosened and she pulled back enough to look at him. Her face searched his and he felt her arms let go of him. He watched the miracle dissolve in her eyes—she was that close. The pupil seemed to widen, swallowing the green that surrounded it until the black circle like a sun in eclipse darkened with total despair. She hung her head and rocked back and forth on her knees as the older woman knelt, unsteadily, to hold her, saying, "I'm sorry. I'm so sorry." Ezra stood there barefoot in his nightshirt and looked helplessly at his audience. Finally, Mr. McGarragh came over to him.

"Ezra. These people just came in on the *Carpathia*. They were rescued from the *Titanic.*"

Ezra looked at the survivors again and everything made terrible sense. He knew all about the *Titanic*. The mixture of shock and panic, the ill-fitting clothes, the chaotic arrival without luggage all added up. Exhausted, they waited for keys to rooms where they could collapse in privacy and cry.

Somehow it felt possible, fantastically possible that his father's absence that night was a result of his going down with the *Titanic* into the frozen sea, even though logic, pushed to the sidelines, told him his father was in Brooklyn, working, as always, in the museum.

His father came through the lobby doors as the first reporters arrived. Flashes exploded from cameras, questions were shouted out to the survivors. Gerald Duval found his son standing in a nightshirt as if he had come in on the *Carpathia* with the rest of them.

His father did not rush to him and clasp him close and say his name, but he did place his hands upon his shoulders. He steered him toward the elevator and said not a word as they ascended and walked to the door that Ezra, in his haste, had left open. He was put to bed and actually kissed on his forehead. He remembers the neon "E" of the hotel sign outside the window of his bedroom, flickering, unable to stay on or completely go out, as if it wanted to tell him something else but could not quite remember what it meant to say.

Tonight, the letter "E" on the hotel sign level with Ezra as he stands on the balcony flashes on and stays on. Below the E is L, below the window but still visible. He'll spell his way back to the world. L is for Lorraine, his mother, whom he can barely even imagine, let alone remember. His father has said more than once and always in anger that she would still be alive today if she hadn't insisted on having a child. But he can't think about death any more tonight. After all, it's almost a brand-new year.

When he steps back inside the apartment he can hear, on the floor above, the French painter Claire du Lac stretching a canvas. He hears the tap, tap, tap through the floor where the canvas is being tacked to its frame. He concentrates, imagining strands of Claire's loose, dark red hair swinging into the hammer's trajectory. He thinks he can hear her swear in French and in the pause of hammering that allows for her hair to be pinned in place, another sound filters through the floor—a scratch—a cigarette lit with a wooden match on the rough edge of the frame, as she pauses in her labor. It's all so reassuring. He's still here. Right here, in the last few days of 1916.

Ezra's attention slips away toward his father, still across the river, in Brooklyn, poring over bones from crypts in the basement of the museum. For the one hundredth time this week alone Ezra wishes his father were studying *him*. That *his* story could be as fascinating as the lost boy-king of Egypt. But Ezra has no sensational story. He's right here, visible, roiling with images in which the past and present mix so freely. If it weren't for this hotel that teems with vivid ideas of painters, playwrights, and poets in their prime, it would be difficult to stay grounded in the present for more than a few minutes at a time.

The residents hold salons in various apartments. Cook spaghetti feasts. Give toasts with Italian red wine to the labor unions, Ezra Pound and the shy ghost of O. Henry leaning in the doorway for a listen in on all the stories being told. They call Ezra "The Sentry" because he keeps watch. He counts the comings and goings of the residents and transients through the entryway nine more floors below. Above the lofts on the top floor with their grand windows letting in the light of so much inspiration, his friend Otto, the painter, lives in the pyramid apartment.

Next to Otto's pyramid is a garden where he keeps a coop for pigeons among the potted trees. Earlier, Otto had been up there tending to them, showing Ezra how to swing the lure.

Ezra wishes he had a carrier pigeon right now. He could send a message. To whom? President Wilson? No, to his father. The pigeon could tap on the basement window of the museum. His father would look up, perturbed by the bird's insistent tapping, go to the window to shoo it away, notice the tiny scroll tied to its neck with a red string. The message would be written in symbols he would have to decode, reminding him of the lateness of the hour, the imminent ending of the year. In his narrative, his father would come home immediately and burst into the room, look at his son by the window and say, "My true treasure is here. All along it was here!"

But Ezra has no carrier pigeon of his own. His father is still in Brooklyn, thousands of years away.

Claire du Lac resumes her tapping. A code to call Ezra back. If he listens closely enough he can almost understand. He taps twice on the wall to answer.

∿∿∿

On New Year's eve, Ezra stands without his father on the rooftop of the Chelsea with the other residents to watch the first minute of 1917 explode in fireworks.

Mr. Grossman, a seven-foot-tall vaudeville actor from the fourth floor, raises Ezra up high, sets him on his shoulders, and dances on the rooftop, turning Ezra in a circle to see all of it—the new year, the beautiful shining city, the sky filling with continuously blooming light from some invisible source below.

Claire du Lac lifts a bottle of foamy champagne, pours it into Senda Marquez's glass and kisses her on the mouth. The four musicians from the Gaiety who share an apartment on the second floor strike up a rousing tango while the actress who is really a man dances with her Negro lover—a shockingly provocative shimmy. Ezra feels himself enveloped in an alliance with the eclectic. For a moment, he feels sorry for his father's solitary fixations, missing this luminous moment for the dream of a dimly-lit glimpse into a pharaoh's plundered tomb. The grand finale of the fireworks fills the sky.

The war is across an entire ocean. His father, oblivious to all except Egypt, is only a river away.

≋

Claire du Lac walks Ezra to school today after the holiday in unseasonably warm weather. He feels escorted by a queen of some unpronounceable country in her outlandish attire—a sequined robe over a man's tuxedo, a gold-tipped walking cane and a cigarette in an ebony holder. Her cinnamon-colored hair is loose, flowing about her narrow shoulders. The children at the school, always ready to taunt, are silenced by her presence. She is unequivocally beautiful, especially when she smiles, which she does liberally, especially in the company of children. She gives both a bow and a curtsy as she lets go of Ezra's hand. The other mothers in the dark skirts and pale shirtwaists and stiff hats with hair constrained by pins and combs stare, divided between disapproval and cautious fascination. But Claire does little to endear Ezra to his classmates or their legal guardians. They keep a wary distance. He isn't taunted or bullied, but neither is he included in their games, and in the bare yard at recess he spends his time alone reading the novels of Zane Grey.

Today, a girl he recognizes, Jenny Ferguson, lingers on his periphery, coming closer until she steps up and announces that she wishes she had such an interesting mother. "Mine smokes, too, but not with a holder."

Ezra doesn't say anything. For the moment he likes being thought of as a boy with a mother. With Claire as that mother, he could be so much bolder.

Jenny Ferguson glances at his novel approvingly. "I'm going out West at the end of the school year. My father trains horses for the motion pictures," she says proudly. "Reilly's stables at 31st near 10th. He's been in

California and now we have a ranch near Los Angeles. He wants my mother and me to come straight away. I'm just here temporarily."

Ezra closes his novel. He looks at her face framed by a page boy haircut of straight blond hair. Her duster seems so blatantly yellow in the sea of dark winter coats. She's in the next grade up from him, a little older. Right now she seems much more worldly than he is.

"I'm temporary, too," he says, not quite sure what he means by temporary but feeling a certain solidarity with the word, a strong feeling, now that he thinks of it, that it could also easily apply to him.

"Where are *you* going?" she asks.

"Maybe Egypt. Or Utah," he says, only because it was in the book he was just reading.

She glances at the cover of the book, looks at him curiously. "What for?"

"My father is an Egyptologist," he says. "He wants to go there."

She looks uncertain. "I meant Utah. My father trained the horses for the Sheik of Araby but that was really made in Nevada. At least the desert part. What will you do in Egypt? Will you live in a pyramid?"

"No. Probably in a hotel." And he can see it so clearly—another hotel where all he will do is look out the window and wait for his father to return. The only difference is that the electric sign will probably be in hieroglyphics and when he looks out the window there will be nothing but desert as far as he can see broken by a long line of overloaded camels. There will be no residents like those in the Chelsea. Riding a horse in a western motion picture sounds like a better prospect. Given a choice, he thinks he'd like to be an Indian, to dispense with saddles altogether, to yell as he gallops over the mountains of Utah while the naïve, un-prepared pioneers run for their lives.

He invites her to come to the Chelsea after school

for Mexican hot chocolate in Claire du Lac and Senda's apartment, and it isn't until he sees Jenny's shocked appreciation that he understands how unusual it is to live in a hotel.

With her, it's thrilling to stroll through the lobby with its grand fireplace and paintings. He waves to the day clerk behind the desk, Mr. Dupre, and asks for his key and his father's mail then proceeds to the elevator where Charlotte, the daytime elevator operator, slides back the brass gate to admit them.

"My house only has a set of stairs. This is like being inside a watch," she says as the whirring of the gears and pulleys, the rhythmic clicks of the passing floors fills the small cubicle.

Ezra sorts through the mail. He holds up one envelope made of watermarked, ivory paper. The return address is from a Lord Carnarvon in London. He recognizes the name; his father has mentioned him more than once.

"Is that the king?" Jenny asks, looking over his shoulder at the envelope.

"They have a queen now. This is a really rich man that hires people to look for kings. Dead kings. The ones in the pyramids."

"I think it's creepy," Charlotte says. "Crawling in those tombs. I wouldn't do it for a hundred dollars."

He laughs, surprising himself. "I wouldn't either," he tells her.

The elevator opens onto the top floor. They go down the hallway to the end, passing several doors. Behind one, a violin is clearly heard, its descending scale broken abruptly by a heated admonition in a foreign language.

"Hungarian," Ezra says. "Two brothers. They play in an orchestra. For the opera at the Grand." He feels as confident as a guide in a museum, leading people through the strange and wondrous halls with helpful facts and esoteric information.

Ezra knocks on Claire's door. Music can clearly be heard—a woman singing to a guitar. The music stops abruptly and Claire opens the door, stepping back with it, providing a frame for the tableau within: Senda, sitting on a pillow on the floor, a bright embroidered shawl about her shoulders. She holds a guitar. Claire steps out from behind the door in a sequined caftan, her hair wrapped up in a blue silk turban. Senda rises from her cushion, black harem pants ballooning around her as she stands.

"*Cherie*," Claire says, kissing Ezra not just once but three times—first one cheek then the other, then the first one again.

Jenny watches this greeting, wide-eyed, impressed.

"This is Jenny," Ezra says. "From school."

"*Enchanté*," Claire says, taking her hand.

Jenny answers, "Delighted, I'm sure."

"*Chocolát?*" Claire asks.

But Senda is already in the kitchenette, pouring heated milk from a pan into glasses containing the chocolate powder. She inserts a wooden implement into the glass, and then rolls the stem between her palms rapidly, as if she's trying to make a fire, creating a contained turbulence by frothing the milk and chocolate together.

"I am pleased," Claire says to Jenny, "to see Ezra bring such a fine friend from the school. He is too much with adults here."

"Neither of us gets picked for the games at school," Jenny says. "But I don't want to play." She turns to Ezra. "Do you? They're for children."

"No. I never did. Not really."

Jenny nods solemnly, as if she understands. And maybe she does. Maybe that's why she's here, with him.

Senda hands her a glass.

"This is really good," Jenny says, sipping the

chocolate slowly.

"It has *almendras*. Almonds. Also cinnamon," Senda says. "I like this word. I like to say it: cinnamon. *Cinnamon*. It is like a song inside a single word? It sings with itself." She lifts her glass, inviting a toast. As the glasses clink Ezra feels a rush of pleasure seeing the delight in Jenny's eyes, her readiness to have her glass meet and touch all the others.

Senda leans toward Claire, putting her glass to Claire's lips and Claire in turn reaches across to Senda with her glass.

Jenny watches them. She steals a glance at Ezra who's watching, too. Jenny reaches across the cushion, and he's so intent on this glass coming to him, the pressure on his lips, the taste, so much sweeter coming from her that he forgets to reciprocate until she reminds him. And now, as he watches her partake from his belatedly offered glass, he feels a pull, a new one, a sense of belonging. He knows if she had not pulled her hand away he would have taken much more than a sip. He would have drunk it all, that sweet dark milk with the song inside in one continuous swallow.

He wants to show Jenny the garden on the roof, but she says she has to go. "I'm already late," she says. "But I'd like to go up to the roof, or someplace else, with you another time."

He says goodbye to her in the elevator when he gets off on his floor. She says she wants to ride by herself the rest of the way. He runs to the balcony in the apartment, waits for her to appear from the double doors to the street.

What's taking her so long? The old ladies having their tea in the lobby at this hour are probably making a fuss over her, asking her their interminable questions, forgetting the answers as soon as they hear them. But there she is now, her yellow duster a bright spot moving along the gray pavement. Ezra calls out to her, but his voice is lost in the sound of a passing trolley. She stops, turns, looks up. Did she hear him or sense him there, leaning over the balcony waving as the hotel sign comes on? The light throws him immediately into silhouette, a dark filament barely interrupting the light. She waves to him, and it's thrilling, to be seen, to be signaled to and to be illuminated at this exact moment. To be connected. It's as if his world has just expanded beyond what he can imagine. He has a friend, a friend of his own. The world widens, beyond his body and the balcony which holds him, to the busy street below and the river it leads to at either end. The Grand Opera House, the park near the Hudson Guild where motion pictures are shown on certain summer nights on sheets strung between trees. All the places he'd wandered, lonely and awkward, afraid to venture further, always returning to the Chelsea, the hotel and the people that are his home. Now that city beyond the hotel might be navigated in the company of a friend.

But for how long? She said she was temporary.

He enters the apartment, closes the balcony door. He stacks the day's mail neatly upon the table to wait for his father's return. He sits at the table to do his lessons, setting aside the "New Riders of the Purple Sage" for later, like a sweet dessert after the bitter appetizer of arithmetic.

Again and again, the envelope from London on the top of the pile pulls him from long division and times tables. He finally picks it up, turns it over. It feels important, its substantial ivory paper flaunting itself among the flimsy envelopes containing bills, notices. He puts it down but can't stop looking at it. It's just asking to be read. But he can't risk tearing it; he will have to steam it open.

Once the kettle on the gas burner sends forth a plume, he holds the envelope's seal over the spout. It doesn't take long—maybe English glue is less sticky or has lost its grip on the long journey over the sea. He turns off the kettle then carefully lifts the envelope's flap. He's done this before and so has gotten over whatever guilt he might have about such surveillance.

His father is a mystery to him, and so Ezra is compelled to discover him in the only way he can. So far, nothing much beyond receipts from a supply house in Chicago for a telescope, a bill from Siegel Cooper for a steamer trunk, letters from his brother, Michael, in Staten Island asking for money. He used to hope he would discover letters from his mother, that she had not died after all and had only fled to a more interesting life in Denver, but there never were. This envelope promises something altogether different. He pulls out the single sheet of ivory paper, opens its crisp fold. Along the top, embossed gold letters proclaim Lord Carnarvon and his London address. Chelsea. Not a hotel. Below in grand penmanship:

Mr. Duval,

Preparations are underway for Carter's expedition to Luxor in October. He has indicated a need for your exemplary qualifications as set forth in your letter and references of 10 January. I have corresponded with the curator of your museum and find your qualifications eminently suitable for this endeavor. In exchange for your extended leave of absence I am offering your museum a number of items from Carter's earlier finds in Luxor. Pity the Americans have not the same passion for this kind of exploration. Be that as it may, Carter is most keen for your collaboration and expertise and the many preparations necessary before we embark. To whit, your passage will be booked on the Aquitania as soon as you cable me your earliest possible departure.

Awaiting your timely arrival,
George Edward Stanhope Molyneux Herbert
5th Earl of Carnarvon

Ezra can barely get the letter back in its envelope. His hands are shaking and he has a terrible time getting the flap to reseal. He puts the letter back on top of the pile then sits down at the table. He can hardly keep track of the thoughts racing through his head. He'll be moving, first to England, then Egypt. School may not even be over. Jenny could still be here.

Otto Heller knocks on the door—his secret knock: three short, two long. He's bringing Ezra his supper. When Ezra opens the door Otto has a rolled canvas under one arm, a sack under the other. In his hands, two glasses of egg cream. On his head, a bowler hat with a blue and yellow feather from a macaw given to him by his paramour, as he calls her—a cigarette girl at Cavanaugh's named Louise who lives in Far Rockaway.

Ezra is so relieved to see Otto, to be distracted from his thoughts that he stands there simply appreciating him until Otto has to say, "Do I come in or do we eat in the corridor?"

"No, please. I mean, come in." Ezra relieves him of the egg creams and carries them to the table, spilling a little from each. The letter is still there. He puts it on the bottom of the pile. He doesn't want to look at it a moment longer.

Otto sets the sack on the table. "Louise got us some beef stroganoff. Also, some borscht. And a steak that was sent back by some fellow from Boston who claimed it was incinerated goat rather than grilled bovine. Such mistakes are to our benefit. But first, I will show you my latest masterpiece that will never make an exhibition." Otto unrolls the canvas. The view from the roof down toward 23rd Street with the letter H from the sign, the potted palms, and the clutter of chimneys from all the roof tops that look like odd-sized pegs on a vast board.

"It pleases you?"

"Yes, very much."

"Of course. You see this bit of yellow? That is your paramour, walking. I added her in just this afternoon. Now it's complete."

"She's my friend," Ezra says.

"Even better. Paramours can be unpredictable. This I will have in my own exhibition. To hell with juries and critics. They give only two choices to independent thinkers: submit or rebel. So, I rebel. You will come—bring her. Her name?"

"Jenny."

"Ah, Juliette. And you are Romeo, here on your balcony. The tables turn in America so easily. Everything changes so quickly. We here in Chelsea are abandoned as the Great Ship of Commerce sails slowly north. There is even talk of the Eden Museé opening again only this time in Coney Island. Can you imagine? Soon we will be looking out from our lonely tower toward Times Square, an island of lights as we toss on the waves of the backwater of Broadway. The Great White Way beckons from 34th Street, and here on 23rd we grow accustomed to lengthening shadow. That is why that bright spot of yellow took my attention. And see what direction Juliette goes?"

"West?"

"Yes. West. The sun waits for us to accompany her on her journey."

"What is East?" Ezra asks, thinking of Egypt where he will soon be exiled.

"The East. It is the past. The sun may rise there but it does not stay long."

"Will you go West—to San Francisco?" Ezra asks.

"No. My place is here. I must paint the last fallen cart horse. Prostitutes drying their hair on the roof. A fire at the piers. The alleys. The darker palette. And you, Ezra, will you be a cowboy, perhaps?"

"I'm afraid not."

"Why not?"

"I think my father might have other plans."

"And what might those plans be?"

"To go to the past."

"Ah, yes. Of course. The great mysteries of the East. We can't all abandon them. But he would take you with him?"

"Of course."

Otto's face softens. "Of course," he says. "You could stay here with us..." Otto begins, but doesn't continue for some time. "Ezra, I will tell you a secret. I see you reading all the time. You go to that world of the West and you are completely where the author takes you. But for you, that will not be enough. You must have your own book. A special book to write in. What you see, yes, but most important, what you have to look for. No one can take this from you. No one. Only you will read it. Only you will know exactly what it means. There is great benefit not to mention complete privacy in having your own secret language."

Otto cuts into the charred steak revealing a pale pink interior. "Ha! The fool from Boston who likes his steak still bloody. This is perfection. Here—take this first piece."

But all Ezra can do is pick at it. If he is hungry, the hunger is muffled by his mind working like a printing press, churning out the same thoughts over and over. This could be the last meal he has with Otto. That spot of yellow on the painting may be the only evidence Jenny was ever here. The E on the hotel sign will have to go on and off without him.

Leave the Chelsea? How can he leave Claire and Senda and Mr. Roy, the bellman, Mr. McGarragh and Mr. Dupre at the desk? The never-ending parade. And Jenny? He had just admitted her into his world. The hotel is his home, his yard the roof garden by Otto Heller's pyramid apartment. In this rooftop yard he helps to care for the potted palms, the pigeons. The scent of fresh oil paints exude from canvases on warm days when the French doors are flung wide open; the sashes tangle in the philodendron when the wind blows, which is most afternoons in the spring. How can he leave? How can he not be present for Claire's coded tapping as she stretches canvas? Senda's *chocolát*? Otto's leftover dinners and new painting? The arguments of the Hungarian brothers? All this: gone. Exchanged for what? A distant place where he knows no one, where the New York skyline will be replaced by an arid wasteland. And if his father is so distracted here in New York, Ezra can only imagine what would happen in Luxor. Ezra will turn to dust in the dry air, waiting. Every last speck of him will disappear.

Maud
1916/1917

The cacophony of Ellis Island is deafening. Where is her father? Maud scans the faces on the other side of the cage reserved for young women and children with no sponsor. A young man holds up a sign in Arabic, at least it looks like Arabic. Munirah's betrothed? With worry in his eyes he scans the cage and does not find who he is looking for.

Where *is* her father? To even ask the question is to admit his absence, that there is no one here of her flesh and blood to be claimed by. Maybe, like John Tyrone, her father has an X on his back—not here, but in the city itself. In Gortadoo, he had a reputation, she knew. What he called art, others called pornography. Even here, the eye on the dollar keeps a close watch. Maybe the land of freedom doesn't have enough freedom to go around.

"Likely to become public charges." She's heard that same phrase before. There's no letter on the coat for that. It's not a disease, it's a damnation. In Ireland, countless children are public charges and most, like herself, not even orphans. Just poor or unwanted. Abandoned, but safe from all temptations. Safe from

Protestant vultures who would swoop down upon any unbaptized soul.

A woman arrives, very official looking in a white apron over a dark dress, white cuffs with protectors. Spectacles. She says in English first that it's late, nearly four o'clock, that they must spend the night here.

"But where are the beds?" Maud says.

The woman laughs. She can still do that after working in a place such as this. "Not here. In the dormitory, upstairs." Then she says something in another language to a miserable group of children in the corner. Italian? They're still clutching the pieces of bread given to them in the first line off the ferry, sliced in a shape they've never seen. They're afraid to eat. Or, they're holding onto it. After that kind of voyage, food is precious. You don't know how long until the next meal. Better to wait until you're starving.

A young girl Maud's age sits by herself, a headscarf tied tightly beneath her chin, her booted feet braced around a bundle on the floor. The matron asks her a question in yet another language. It sounds quite like Russian—Maud heard it on the *Carpathia* when the woman with the samovar spoke, which wasn't very often. The odd cadence comes back to her now.

The girl nods. The woman speaks again to this girl, who immediately begins to cry as if hearing her native tongue from this stranger is the last straw. Maud listens to the matron, impressed at her fluencies. It's like being able to play several instruments, being let in on the secrets of the world by knowing the codes to various countries. She's always taken speech for granted. Now, she sees it's the key to freedom itself, being heard and understood. And more than that, the freedom to say what she thinks out loud without punishment.

They're so close. The City of New York is just across the water and they can only look at it through the cage window. It's no more than a picture on the wall like the portrait of President Wilson.

The Great Hall is empty now, the last of the lucky going out the door to the ferry. The clerks close their manifest books and rub their eyes. They laugh over the day's more appalling cases, the impossible names and how to pronounce them. They put on their hats and coats and leave. Leave! They're going home to suppers, to their own beds, to their wives and children.

The hope that's carried her across the ocean, through the gauntlet of U-boats that could sink them, through the lines of inspection, even past the horror of losing her one new friend, her guide, John Tyrone, to the arbitrary X, now drains from her. This is it. The grand entrance, the reunion with her father: locked in a cage with other children who can't understand a word she says. The matron is her only link—and theirs—to the languages they speak, to understanding what they must do next. And they have to share her.

Where is that matron now? Gone on the ferry with the rest, forgetting them in their cage with no water left and only those slices of bread they'll probably be fighting over in the morning.

More people come through the door, taking off their coats and hats. Their matron appears from behind another door and speaks to a woman just arriving, points to her charges in the cage. The new woman nods. She opens the cage, beckons the children to follow her and they do—up a set of stairs in the corner of the building, their boots making an incredible amount of noise, echoing off the tiled walls so that they sound like a hundred, not a handful.

"Where is it you'll be taking us, then?" Maud calls out to her.

The matron stops, looks over her shoulder.

"Irish?"

Maud nods, grateful to be recognized, but wary.

"Late bloomer, you are. Mostly Bohemians and

Italians and Jews and Russians these days. Some years ago now, a group of orphans came from Russia with saber marks on their faces and hands. We'll probably see something like that again, any day, only it won't be wounds from sabers."

The other children listen, left out of this conversation. Maud steals a glance at the Russian girl who has no marks, at least not any that she can see. But then even the most blatant marks can be hidden. The matron resumes her daily climb and once again the common language of shoes scraping on slate resumes. They reach a landing and beyond it, a long hallway of closed doors. The matron stops at the second one, opening the door onto a smaller version of steerage. Rows of iron bunks three deep fill the room. But there are clean sheets and pillows. Just like the annual inspection day at St. Joseph's in Killarney. Officials from Dublin came and saw clean linens, real cutlery, new clothes, actual toys. It all got locked up into cupboards again as soon as the inspectors left, satisfied that the State's money was well spent and not wasted on frivolity.

Maud makes for the bed nearest the window to claim it with her suitcase, drawn by the red of the sunset to the west. Somehow, the weather has broken while they waited in the cage. And now the green lady with the torch emerges, shining, though Liberty is still so far away.

The matron comes over to the window and stands next to her. She can't be *that* much older than Maud. Definitely less than twenty.

"When they first brought her she was in pieces in crates for a year. Her head was in one with the crown sticking out, her foot in another."

In Maud's mind, Liberty took up the entire deck of a ship built expressly for the purpose of transporting her, her raised hand with the torch rising over the bow. To think of her being cobbled together, made in pieces, not whole, and put into packing crates is a great disappointment. And unseemly as well.

"So here's your first history lesson that won't be in a book. The French give it in good faith and the Americans just shrug. They can't manage to scrape up the money for a pedestal, said she should have come with her own. Not until that Russian girl Emma Lazarus, God rest her, wrote that poem and shamed people to open their pockets. Still, the rich sat by and it was average blokes sending in nickels what did it. Emma never did live to see it, was sick when she passed through the harbor."

To Maud, the broken chain around her Liberty's bare ankle that she's seen in pictures now seems like the physical result of breaking out of packing crates. Her great, green foot kicked her way out into a place that took so long to receive her.

"Did you know she was meant for Egypt, first?" Maud asks.

"I heard that, but hardly believed it. But then it's probably not in the history books either."

She's come so far and it's not far enough. There's so much farther to go. There's a whole country to America, not just New York. John Tyrone talked about Texas. Maybe her father is on his way there and no matter how far she gets he will always be disappearing over the next hill. Maybe it wasn't the priest or her father but the nuns who bought her ticket to teach her a lesson. They sent her off to the ultimate punishment and humiliation. She's tired and these are the thoughts of exhaustion. She can't help but sigh out loud.

"Long day," the matron says. "Long life already. Come to supper then."

Maud, as hungry as she is, leaves the window reluctantly. As long as she can see Liberty there's hope. But turn away for an hour and she might be gone again, swallowed by fog, taken apart and sent back in packing crates to France or Egypt. And if Emma Lazarus could write a poem and move a mountain, what might she herself put down on paper that her father could not fail to recognize? He might not know her face but he would surely know her handwriting. But the walls here are thick with names, messages in other languages. How can she not be overwhelmed by them? How does English even stand out? Her voice is a better bet. He used to stand her up on the bar at the pub in Dunequin to sing "The Parting Glass" after he'd had a few pints and had an audience to listen to his grand schemes for opening a photography studio. If he'd had enough to drink, he'd cry as she sang. If she stopped, he would lift his head and beg her to continue. This power to make a grown man cry had scared her at first. She was only five at the time, and didn't understand that the source of his tears might have been the memory of her recently departed mother. But she could not help but try to move him, again and again. It's a memory of an intimacy greater than any. It comes back now, here, because she has no bearings, only this song that once moved him to tears. And she can't sing it loud enough now for him to hear across the water.

The matron opens a door onto a vast dining room with rows and rows of people already eating. Cutlery clangs on real china plates.

She sits down. Someone passes her a plate with boiled meat and potatoes and bread. There's a bowl of fruit in the center. At the next table, they're eating herring, and bananas, of all things. At this time of year. Nothing is right. She stares at the food on her plate, the coffee steaming from a cup just now set in front of her by a man in white clothes and an apron. There is a place for her here, at this table. What's been set before her is a banquet, not the bread soaked with blood from the butcher's shop and baked to the color of iodine in St. Joseph's oven.

Tomorrow her father should be here, waving when her name is called again. They will cross the last bit of water to Elizabeth Street, to a table he's prepared for her. She won't tell him of the other crossing, the ice and the Northern Lights; she'll leave out the burial of Munirah at sea, the dervishes dancing over the bones of the drowned. It's the only part of her life he won't know, that she hasn't put in a letter. And she will finally see what she's already read about in his letters: the map of America on the wall along with framed photographs of the Brooklyn Bridge. The hat he bought on Division Street with his first commissioned portrait, the rose bush on the fire escape he got from a cart on Ludlow. And the piano he was saving for. Will it be there? Will there soon be photographs of her to put on the wall as well? The future lies untouched before her like the food on her plate, growing cold.

The meal over, the waiters take the plates away to wash. She grabs an orange from the bowl. The Italian children furtively put their bread in their pockets.

Back in the dormitory the matrons take them to the washroom to scrub everybody clean and check for lice. Afterwards, the children's clothes are thrown into a trash bin. She takes her coat back when she's sure no one is looking. She knows what comes next. The first night at St. Joseph's her shorn hair and clothes were burned together in a barrel as if she were a witch.

When she looks down at her naked self in this bare shower room she's horrified to see several dark hairs springing from her sex. After these hairs, breasts and her monthly can't be far behind. It's too soon, too soon for all of it.

〰〰〰

Morning. There is another morning.
"Maud Farrell."

"Yes, sir."

"That is your name?"

"Yes."

"Passage on the *Carpathia* from Liverpool?"

"I got on in Cobh."

"Queenstown, then." He writes it down. "Place of birth—the English name, not the Gaelic?"

"Gortadoo, Parish of Dunurlin. County Kerry."

"Ireland."

"Yes, the same." A young woman writes all this down on a long sheet of paper for him.

"The ship's manifest says your sponsor is your father, Michael Farrell, of 256 Elizabeth Street."

"The same."

"And where is Mr. Michael Farrell?"

"He should be here."

"Sadly, he is not. We are trying to contact him. You'll have to wait. Do you understand?"

"I speak English perfectly well but I don't understand any of this."

"A young girl simply cannot enter this country unaccompanied."

"But I have twenty-five dollars."

He looks up, the pen for the moment stopped. "That's hardly the point, young lady."

"But they said—"

"It isn't the money. You could have a hundred and still need a sponsor."

"I can work."

"I'm sure you can. I'm sure you will. That is not the point either."

"What *is* the point, then?"

He slaps the pen down on the ledger. It rolls from the book and stops an inch from the edge of the table. Maud stares at it, willing it to fall. It doesn't.

"White slavery is a very unfortunate concern in this country. Young innocent girls like you are taken…"

The matron coughs. He doesn't finish the sentence. "You'll simply have to wait. We'll call for you."

"I've waited here already for days. What am I to do now?"

"There's a playground on the roof. Perhaps it will warm up this afternoon. And no running in the halls."

"I'm not a child," Maud says. And she isn't. Not anymore. It's been quite a while since she's acted like one, of any age.

"Come with me," the matron says and leads Maud out of the room. "Well then," she says when the door is safely closed behind them. "You've got cheek, I'll say. You'll probably need it."

They stand leaning on the balcony overlooking the Great Hall. Below, lines of people move slowly through the chutes. The din is overwhelming, a boiling stew of languages. The shouted names from the podium at the end of the line are mostly unpronounceable. Swinging doors open onto a crowd of relations in heavy coats and hats. She watches the Italian children with the bread bulging in their pockets push through that door, escorted by a man who must be their father, or at very least, an uncle. They rush into the arms of grand-mothers, cousins, all weeping with joy.

Tears of all kinds—that's the prevailing language here. The joy of the claimed, the anguish of the detainees. She looks down on them in their cages, waiting. They look up. She knows that look, has felt it upon her own face. From where she stands, she hears tears of rejoicing, sees the door that says "Push to America." And they do. Push. There is no easy walking through. Maud grips the railing. She searches for her father by the rows of desks. Hats of all kinds, beards— would he have one?—glasses, shawls, fantastic costumes full of embroidery and ribbons. Fat, thin, none of them him.

The mass of people move through the chutes like

food through an intestine, a dark progression of evolution itself. The Great Hall is really an ark run aground; it's raining. Animals with tags become people only when their names are called. There may not be class here but there is a hierarchy, a pyramid, bottom-heavy, small and exclusive at the top.

Three enormous windows with at least a hundred panes each look in on the scene, wide-eyed and astonished at this endless procession. Liberty stands in the harbor, frozen, unable to put down her light, to stop the flow.

Maud looks across the great teeming hall to the opposite balcony where others like her pass the time by watching the endless tide. And there, almost directly opposite her is John Tyrone. No hat or scarf, his fine head of hair shorn. But it's him. She lifts her arm to signal him. He doesn't raise his head. He's looking at the scene below, hypnotized by it as if he's seeing something through a microscope, the squirming of protozoa inside a single drop of water.

A man in uniform taps him on the shoulder. Then he raises his head and just before he turns he sees Maud's frantic signaling. It's all she can do to walk, not run down the halls to the other side of the gallery. She gets there just as he's about to enter a Board of Inquiry room. "Got a hearing," he says.

There is no time to say anything else. The door closes behind him. She sits down on a bench in the hall. She waits.

Before long a woman in uniform comes by with a large basket and stops in front of her. Bottles of milk clink against cups. A mountain of thin stacked crackers, "Uneeda" stamped on each and every one, wait to be selected and eaten.

Maud takes two crackers and a cup of milk. The woman moves on. By the time she's eaten the second cracker, nibbling in tiny bites along the edges to pass the time, the door opens and John Tyrone comes out, a yellow card with a cross on it in his hand. He holds it up proudly.

"My ticket to freedom!" he says.

"I'm so glad," Maud says. "Really." She is. And she isn't. She was hoping he would have to wait also, until she is released. But no, he's proved himself sane somehow, erased the X. It didn't take long. At least he got a second chance.

"Where's your Da?"

"I don't know."

"He'll turn up, sure."

Maud nods, but she's not sure. She only hopes so. And even that is fading.

"He won't be able to forget you," John says. Those words go straight into her ears, down into the pit of her stomach and cause it to clench. It's not hunger. It's more like a yearning for what he said to be true, to feel the truth of it as well as she knows her own name. But the sadness slides toward shame. Her father isn't here. She should know not to count on anyone for anything.

John Tyrone holds out his hand. She takes it, gives it a firm shake. "Good luck to you." And then he's gone, down the stairs, past the throng to the head of the line, to the desk where he's duly recorded in the ledger. She watches it all. But just when he's going through the swinging doors he turns, looks back in the general area of where she's still standing. He waves once more. Then the doors open wide as he pushes with both hands and steps into the open air, into a light flurry of snow melting in the harbor.

≋

At the far end of the dining hall tonight, there's a Christmas tree with lighted candles and a band just now starting up. A banner saying Happy New Year 1917 in six different languages hangs from the far wall. New Year. She hadn't even thought about that, and for some reason, it seems as if time itself has just passed the point of no return. If she'd arrived earlier things might be different. But now it's almost another year and whatever had been planned is erased from that calendar. 1916 is almost behind her.

There's a gift by her plate, a book by the shape of it. She unwraps it. "Huckleberry Finn." She's never heard of him.

Later, after lights out, she looks through the window above her bed to the skyline of the city and the fireworks crowning it. The other children, hearing the popping of the explosions, crowd around her, crying.

"It's all right," she says, for it's what must be said. "It's beautiful, not dangerous. It's only a new year." And it is, though they might think that soldiers have followed them here. She looks at their frightened faces and knows whatever horror she's survived is nothing compared to the relentless reverberations of war.

The song that made her father cry does the opposite as she sings it here. The voice of anyone singing in any language is a miracle. It's the music, not the song that soothes until there is only the sound of children, breathing before a window, fogging the panes, clearing a circle to see through, and an Irish girl singing as the last night of 1916 comes to a close.

≈

The days blur together, but what divides them is orderly enough: meals at precise times, washing up, lights out. The shower, such a novelty at first, is now only hot rain beating down upon her. At least there is no laundry to be done, day after day. The only thing to break the monotony is to return to Huck and Jim on their raft, to read slowly, make it last. Once in a while she goes up to the roof to see the snow, to feel it on her face, to look out toward Liberty and appeal to her. Liberty stands, looking the other way, raising her torch for yet another ship coming into the harbor.

The matrons know Maud by name now. They give her extra crackers. More books to read that they think are suitable for girls. But it's Huckleberry Finn, in particular, that she begins to read all over again the instant she finishes it. If she had a raft, she could escape, cross the harbor and look for her father on her own. She'd probably do a better job of it than the Powers That Be. But the kindness of these matrons surprises her. She doesn't know how to take it— kindness for the sake of kindness. It's astonishing. Free.

In her worst moments she sees Ellis Island as the place where she lives now, a huge, echoing castle with at least a thousand visitors each day, uninvited, who don't know her. There's a howl building inside of her. She let it out once, on the roof when there was no one else there—she doesn't want to risk an X. But her voice just got tossed around by the wind. What she really wants is to lean over the balcony and tell everybody to go home and leave her in peace. But all she can do is hold onto herself a little longer. How long can they keep her? Surely there's a limit to detention in America.

On a rare day with sun she goes up to the roof again to feed crackers to the gulls. They've come to expect her and they fight raucously for every crumb. Ferries come and go, and the barges that bring in the big steamers leave a trail of black smoke as they shove the immigrant ships up the Hudson into their berths.

The matron pushes the door open against the wind and calls to her.

"Maud, come quickly. They're calling for you."

Maud drops the rest of the crackers and runs for the door.

"Is he here?"

"All I know is they're calling for you downstairs."

The matron—Leticia is this one's name—escorts her to the front of the line, presents her to the grim inspector.

"This is Maud Farrell?" he asks.

"Yes," Leticia answers for her.

He turns to Maud. "Your brother's here."

Brother?

She searches the faces behind the wire screen trying not to look too startled. And there he is. Not her father. John Tyrone touches a finger to his lips.

"Do you know him?" the inspector asks.

"Of course," she says. She's shaking now. Here he is, holding out his hand. What will it mean if she takes it? Giving up on her father completely? Where else will he find her in that enormous city across the water except here, the port of entry? Three days ago the man from the Board of Inquiry called for her to appear again to tell her that Michael Farrell no longer lived at 256 Elizabeth Street. That they were trying to find him by calling all the hospitals and prisons, putting advertisements in all the newspapers, even the *Jewish Daily Forward* where such notices were often posted. But there has been no word. And now, as if knowing this— perhaps John Tyrone has read these notices himself— he shows up to smuggle her out of Ellis Island.

She takes his hand. There is no other. She doesn't even hear the inspector's questions to John very clearly about his employment, his lodgings. He has some papers to back up whatever he's saying. Leticia is handing Maud's suitcase to her brand-new brother.

"Welcome to America, Maud Farrell," the inspector is saying, stamping her card, writing her name, at last, in the book. With both hands Maud pushes the door open to America. But something frays, a rope coiled tight inside her, the holding on to the defiant hope in the face of so much to the contrary. It's not what she thought would happen at all.

"We fooled 'em, didn't we?" he says. "Serves 'em right. It was easier than I thought. I got my payback."

She nods, manages a smile. And now what? she wants to say. Is this just a prank, getting even with those who detained him? Or is he one of those white slavers with a fresh, desperate recruit? Or just a person of her own country, doing what he can to help? Her family, who had always seemed so small, just got larger. The Irish. She belongs to them as surely as if Ireland is her surname in this new, jumbled map of the world.

〰
〰

They step off the ferry at Battery Park and work their way through a gauntlet of hawkers in at least five languages shouting about rooms, jobs, cheap restaurants. Hebrew Societies. Hungarian Leagues. And a chorus of jeers. The natives, throwing every slang word in the book at them, naming them according to their own lights. Sheeney. Guinea. Kike.

A girl stands there singing by herself, holding out her hand. A boy no more than three years old is selling matches. An older boy with a bundle of newspapers and torn knicker pants and a cap pulled sideways on his head smokes a hand-rolled cigarette. A blind man sells pencils. A horse shits as it pulls a cart full of rags, the green clods steaming in the cold air of the fifth day of the New Year.

John Tyrone is saying he's found a place for her in a settlement house, whatever that is, as they climb onto a streetcar. There's no room to sit so she stands, clinging to the brass pole in the aisle. The wheels grind along the tracks.

"I'm off to Texas," he says.

"What?" It's hard to hear what he's saying.

"Texas. A job with the Southern Pacific Railroad,"

he shouts. She doesn't ask anything else; she's still trying to assimilate the idea of Texas. A place of wide open space seems improbable here in the midst of a roiling throng of people and vehicles and animals and buildings that block out the sky. After the cold gray of Ellis, the sheltered, strictly ordered world that required nothing of her but waiting, Texas sounds like heaven. American heaven where anyone who wants to can go.

They get off at Allen Street and start walking. The ground shakes with the passage of trains underground. And the ones in the air, overhead on the elevated tracks make a terrifying noise. "All I have to do is get there," he shouts.

A few more steps and he's out with it. "Do you still have your twenty-five dollars?" he asks. "I'll pay you back."

Her heart tumbles into her left foot. He's not taking her any farther than here. He expects to be paid for getting her out. There's nothing free, nothing to know anymore except that everything here has a price, especially freedom.

She reaches into her pocket and without a word puts the money in his hand. She owes him a great deal more than this money. It doesn't matter now. But he's handing back the five dollar bills, keeping the twenty. He hands her suitcase to her as if she's just redeemed its pawn.

"Good luck to you then, Maud Farrell."

John Tyrone is swallowed up by the pushcarts and the cries of the newsies and vegetable sellers and the songs of singing girls. The uproar of commerce, cacophonous, brash, rude, fills in the wide-open space he left behind.

She doesn't ring the bell on the door in front of her. She sits on her suitcase right on the step. She can howl now—who cares? There's nobody with chalk to put a letter on her back. But all that comes out is an epithet. *Shite!* A child walking by with a basket of flowers throws one red rose at her and runs.

The door opens behind her and two girls come out carrying a basket between them. More flowers. What is it with the flowers? But all she has to do is look in any direction to answer her own questions. It's a gray place, this city, gray with grayer buildings. Gray streets, gray people. Not a tree or a blade of grass anywhere. But these flowers aren't real—she can see that as the girls brush past her. They're made by hand. Paper posies on wire stems, twisted together. After all, it's winter, but she wonders if spring will have anything at all to offer. And if it does, it certainly won't be free.

"Greenhorn," one of them says. A mass of black hair sticks out from beneath an improbably wide-brimmed hat. A plaid coat buttoned tight at least two sizes too big hides her thin frame. "Just off the boat, are you? From the war?"

"No. I been livin' at Ellis Island like a friggin' Queen," Maud says, relishing the vulgarity. There's no nun with a ruler here.

"That is no place to be living!" the younger one says in accented English. Polish?

"You got a job?" the older one in the hat asks.

"I'll get one."

"You have to have a job, at least pulling threads at a shop. You can live at a lodging house where you can come and go as long as you keep your shirtwaist on and pay the ten cents a night. This place is for a social club. An industrial school. A library. The health nurses."

Maud's heart stops. Industrial school. Here? "Are there nuns?"

"No nuns. Girls from the college. Do-gooders."

Maud breathes again.

"We have a playground," the younger one adds. "With a swing."

"Who *didn't* show up to get you at Ellis?" the older

one asks.

"My father," Maud admits. She hates to admit it. But she can no longer say he's coming. He didn't. He had plenty of time to and he didn't.

"They do that," the girl in the hat says. "They buy a stool at the Tub of Blood and sit there drinkin' out of a can until they fall over."

The younger girl nods solemnly, but tugs on the basket. "We must go," she says. "We will lose our place at the square."

"Don't I know," the older girl says, but she seems reluctant to leave in the middle of inducting this new arrival into the ways of New York City. "Watch yourself," she adds.

They hurry off. Across the street, a door opens and a man carries a chair down the steps, sets it on the street. Behind him, two more men carry a sofa. Then a bed, all of it stacked in a pile and watched by a boy eating an apple. Last out the door comes a woman in a shawl pleading with him, two small children in tow, but the men push past her, scowling, go back for more. The two children, round-faced little boys, climb onto the sofa and sit, wide-eyed in their new parlor out there in the street with the world streaming by. A woman selling shoelaces displayed on a board set between two ash cans shouts, shakes her fist at the men. They shout back and go on with the business of eviction.

A young woman walks up, her arms full of books. She bends down to get a closer look at Maud. "Are you coming or going?" she asks.

"John Tyrone brought me here," she says.

"I don't believe I know him."

"He said you'd look out for me. Is it true? Because if it isn't, then I'm going."

The woman straightens up again, shifts the books to the other arm to open the door. "Well, then. Let's see how we can help you."

"I'm no orphan," Maud says, standing up, hoisting her suitcase. "And I haven't done anything wrong."

"This isn't an orphanage. Nor is it any kind of juvenile asylum. We'll find you a place to live, at least temporarily. Are you fourteen?"

"Yes," she lies. Being tall always helps. To distract the woman from further questions, she asks one of her own. "Do you live here?" Maud asks, cautiously following her into the parlor, a comfortable room with chairs by a fireplace. Two women sit quietly turning the pages of books.

"I help out with the library. Do you like to read?"

"I do."

"What church do you belong to?"

"I don't have a church." Maud waits for lightning to strike. Even the two women reading nearby don't look up from their books. To her amazement, nobody seems to care.

"Family?"

"I can't find him."

"John Tyrone?"

"No, my father."

"And your mother?"

"She died. Almost a year ago. On the *Sussex*. The ferry attacked by the U-boat. She was on her way to France. To meet someone."

Each time she says it, it gets easier. She will probably have to answer this question many times. But it always stops further questioning.

"Oh, my dear." The woman sets the books down on a table, turns to see who is speaking to her about such a matter. "Miss Farrell, you're a walking miracle," she says. "And nobody's fool."

She climbs a set of stairs, motioning for Maud to follow her. She opens the door onto a small room lined with shelves, a few chairs arranged in an orderly fashion around a table. A braided oval rug covers most of the bare floor. Curtains flank the windows.

"You can come here any time you like. This door stays open. Now, let's find you a place to sleep, at least for the night until we can get you situated."

And once again, there's a room with cots. Once she must have had a cradle but she doesn't remember it. She wonders now whatever happened to it, if it was put out in the street by an angry landlord. Or sold to make her father's passage to America. Or chopped up for firewood by her mother on a bitter cold day such as this. She'd had her own bed in her own room when her mother was still around. Then her father left her with the Sisters of Mercy when he went to America. Privacy is not something she's had long enough to get used to or miss when it's gone.

"Where are the others?" Maud asks, looking at the empty beds.

"Still at work. Some don't get back until nine from the factories. The cash girls at the shops come sooner, especially now that Christmas is past. You'll meet them at breakfast. We'll have a light supper at six. Miss Sarah Fergus is probably preparing the soup as we speak. I'll leave you then, to wash up. The lavatory is right down the hall."

"As we speak," Maud echoes quietly. Things are happening every second here while someone somewhere speaks. At St. Joseph's nothing ever happened, but here, families are put out on the street, girls are sewing after dark. And John Tyrone is on a train going to the West with a ticket paid for by her money, or rather, her father's money, if indeed it was his money to begin with. Is her father slumped on a stool at the Bucket of Blood? In jail? Some other singing girl making him cry? Or he is on that train to work with the freedom this country promised and can still deliver, farther West?

She slides her suitcase under the bed and lies

down. The ceiling is so far away. She counts the little squares of pressed tin. She loses her place, starts over. She hasn't really slept well since she got here. How many nights? She can't remember.

The next thing she knows the room is filled with girls pulling off their dresses and boots, climbing into bed. Maud pretends she's asleep. Surely they'll get in trouble for talking. Have to hold out their hands for the switch. She doesn't want to explain it again—why she's here, why she's not where she thought she should be by now. What happened to her mother in the war.

"A new one," one of the girls says.

She can feel somebody standing near her and then she feels a blanket settling down over her. Something else is set down on the pillow next to her. Warm bread—she can smell it. She waits until the lamps are turned down, until the breathing of every girl deepens, then she takes the piece of bread and tears it with her teeth. A secret communion in a room full of snoring, a murmur of some dream two cots down, an exasperated "Oy!" from across the aisle.

Maud swallows the dissolved bread, tears off another bite. Someone cared that she might wake hungry or cold or both. It's something.

On the street below, she hears a horse's clip-clopping hooves, a cat screeching at another cat. An ash can turning over, rolling, she can tell, off the curb. For now there is this bed, this bit of food, the company of sleeping girls, American working girls whose souls are safe enough out in the world in which they freely come and go. In a day or two or three, she'll be one of them. Pulling threads or making change, twisting paper flowers on a wire stem. Or singing any song she damn well pleases.

If her father's still out there, sooner or later he'll hear her sing "The Parting Glass," not standing in summer on the bar in Gortadoo, but in the streets of

New York in the dead of winter. Will he cry? It's the least he can do.

Ezra
1917

Ezra waits in the freezing rain for Jenny, standing on the corner of 23rd and Broadway. He has no umbrella, just a cap. He searches through the sea of dark coats and black umbrellas for a flash of yellow. He will wait until he's soaked and shivering before he even thinks of giving up.

She was supposed to meet him to watch the last horse-drawn streetcar go by. It was announced in yesterday's paper. They talked about at school. So many things are changing so quickly, too quickly. The Eden Museé went bankrupt a little more than a year ago. The Cooper Siegel store is closing. Ezra used to have to wait for a turn on the bicycle track but just last month he had the track to himself and circled it on a new Schwinn while the orchestra played a rather forlorn version of Yankee Doodle Dandy. He sees the horse-drawn streetcar approaching. A new electric streetcar passes it on parallel tracks going north. In the rain, the event seems somber, funereal.

Jenny might have gone to California already, un-expectedly, with no chance to say goodbye. He pictures her in the sun, coatless, riding a horse by the bright, blue sea.

A man behind Ezra is saying to his paramour (Ezra notes the lack of wedding rings), "I hear Gompers is already talking about taking some of the wax from the Eden to Coney."

"Even Ajeeb?" she says. "I can't imagine the Eden without him."

Ezra pulls his wet cap down on his head, hiding his eyes. This is unimaginable. Ajeeb is what he mostly came to see. He wishes he had known Jenny while the Eden Museé was still open. He would have liked Jenny to see him play chess with the exotic, bearded automaton, even though he never won.

The memory of the last time he went to see Ajeeb is still so vivid. Another day in the rain. He handed over his dime and pushed his way into the vestibule where a gypsy woman in flowing scarves stood next to an ornate birdcage on a pedestal. Inside, a bird, a white dove, sat on a perch above a heap of tiny scrolls. The gypsy said, "For one nickel the bird will choose your fortune." Ezra had a nickel for an egg cream in the café in the Winter Garden. He was curious to know then what his future would be. He *needs* to know now.

Still waiting for Jenny, still in the rain, he re-plays the scene from the thirtieth anniversary of the museum, almost two years ago. The scene unfolds as if in present time. Ezra hands the nickel to the gyp-sy. She drops it into a silk pouch suspended from a cord around her neck. She taps the cage with a small gold wand, and the bird which had been so still as to be made of wax suddenly comes to life. It flutters its cloud-colored wings and grips the perch with its claws, dipping its head down at the fortunes. It pauses, surveying them, then plucks one from the pile, and scoots sideways on the perch toward the gypsy, and waits for her to relieve it of its message. The gypsy retrieves the scroll through a small opening in the cage, a little hinged door, and, taking the scroll from the beak of the bird, deposits a single seed in a shallow cup hanging inside the cage, which the bird immediately devours. She hands the scroll to Ezra with utmost gravity and an almost perceptible bow and immediately turns her attention to the next person in line. Ezra moves on, not wanting to read his fortune here. He walks quickly through the Central Hall, beneath the glass dome, past the Rulers of the World, not pausing to notice the new addition of People Talked About exhibits until he is safely in the Winter Garden with its potted palms, mirrors and wax acrobats suspended on invisible wires from the mezzanine. The Hungarian orchestra is just starting up when Ezra takes a seat along the wall near Ajeeb's dais. Someone has already engaged the automaton in a game of chess. Ajeeb, seated cross-legged with the chess board before him, turns his turbaned head slowly from side to side, surveying the board, weighing his possible opening move. He has a thick beard and the door to his chest is open. Instead of a beating heart, Ajeeb's inner workings reveal gears and levers, whirring.

The challenger in a straw boater watches, wide-eyed, as Ajeeb's gloved hand lifts, hovers over the board, and descends upon a pawn to move it precisely forward to his chosen square.

Ezra looks down at the tiny scroll in his hand. There's a little crease where the bird pinched it with its beak. He opens it slowly, brings it closer to read the hand-written script.

A long journey beckons. Become ready. Be not afraid.

As Ezra remembers this fortune, the pavement beneath his feet seems to shift. For a second Ezra is sure there has been an earthquake or a prehistoric beast awakening, rising up from the Independent Subway tunnel below. The fortune was and is *his*. The bird knew, even back then, that not only would there be a journey, a long one coming, but that Ezra would be afraid. He remembers Ajeeb, his head turning as he stopped, yes, stopped to bestow his piercing gaze, not upon the chessboard but upon Ezra, as if he had heard the fortune read out loud and that he concurred. Ezra opened his mouth to ask him. Ajeeb seemed to be waiting. Try as he might, Ezra couldn't make a sound. And he can't make a sound now as the crowds stream by him. He's an invisible boy in the rain, pulled back by the hands of time.

While Ajeeb is momentarily distracted, Ezra notices something happening that Ajeeb does not. The man in the boater hat changes the position of his bishop. At last, Ajeeb returns his attention to the board, his eyes scanning the squares before him. He lifts his head, looks straight at his challenger and with one sweep of his mechanical arm knocks all the pieces to the floor. The man in the boater hat flees, knocking over a waiter with a tray of soda water. A woman at a nearby table shrieks as she's showered by the fizzing water. Glasses crash to the floor and everyone turns to look. A guard appears, not unlike the automaton policeman in the vestibule that watches over the public. He puts the pieces back on the board, signals to another waiter to clean the broken glass, and presents the wet woman with a coupon for a free ice cream. When the last pawn is in place he says to Ajeeb, "Bet he won't try that again. Drinks on me tonight." Ezra swears he hears Ajeeb answer or at least grunt, but he doesn't see the lips behind the beard move.

Be Not Afraid. He's trying not to be, but he is. The pandemonium in the hall, Ajeeb sweeping the board in anger is the least of it. Startling, yes, maybe an action Ezra himself would have liked to take. A bold gesture. A great big "No!" in response to Lord Carnarvon's letter to his father. Instead, he sits here next to an angry automaton with a fortune plucked out of thin air by a bird telling him to put his fear aside.

It's all coming true now. The last streetcar drawn by a horse approaches. Ezra's coat is soaked. He thinks of Jenny's hand putting her glass of scented chocolate to his lips. But she isn't here. If she isn't gone already, she will be, soon. There's no point in having a friendship. He hates thinking like this. He's been looking forward to becoming optimistic; he wants that so badly. But he himself will be leaving, perhaps before her. If Ezra looks down at his own chest, he fully expects to see a door, an opening into a nest of gears and pulleys. His heart could have already been carried off by an ibis, deposited on the table next to the letter from Lord Carnarvon.

The memory of the Eden Museé is the only shelter he has at the moment. He closes his eyes. He can still hear the Hungarian orchestra tuning up, then resting their instruments on stands. A great sail is unfurled to provide the screen for the motion picture. People in chairs around the tables turn themselves toward the screen as the lights dim. A blade of light strikes the screen and a man trundles down a street, hands in his pockets. He's working in a factory, everyone like automatons assembling machinery at breakneck speed under the watchful eye of an enormous clock. The little man climbs onto the clock with Roman numerals, holding back the hands with his entire body, trying to stop time.

The horse-drawn streetcar is so close now. The horse strains in its harness with the extra load of so many people jumping on for this last ride downtown. The horse passes, its hooves clopping on the street. Then it's gone.

〰〰

When Ezra returns to the hotel apartment, his father is sitting at the table drinking coffee. He's reading the paper, completely absorbed, and doesn't hear Ezra come in, or, if he does, is not finished reading whatever article he's in the middle of. From the frame of the doorway Ezra has a view of his father, as still as a figure in one of Otto's paintings. And how would Otto have painted this portrait? There would be the bearded man bent over the newspaper, part of the outspread page draped over the side of the small table. There would be the ragged crust of rye bread, the stain the coffee cup has made—a brown ring over the printed page. The beard would be as gray as it really is, testament to the fact that the growth on his chin had aged in advance, rushing to add a professorial look while the brown hair remained uniformly boyish in color. His father is fifty-six, he knows. Twenty years older than his mother was when she married him. Now he looks ancient to Ezra. How had he not noticed this before? For the first time it occurs to him that his father had been forty-four when Ezra was born. He was old to begin with. The fathers Ezra used to see at the Eden Museé were youthful, dressed in the current style, while his father adhered to the outdated and set himself apart, not really the result of any effort, but from a long accumulation of academic distraction. And what his father is distracted by does not include or accommodate this ten-year-old being in the shadow of the hallway.

His father always said the Eden Museé was a jumped-up nickelodeon. A travesty of anything seriously academic, a sideshow of mummy's curses and caricatures like Ajeeb—the most offensive example, he always said, of America's idea of an Arab. A mockery of all things Egyptian. He said it had deserved to go bankrupt. He'd come only once to the Eden Museé and Ezra wished he hadn't insisted on bringing him. His father was an avid chess player but only dismissed Ajeeb, said there was a midget inside operating the hands. It was embarrassing. Even infuriating. But to Ezra, Ajeeb only increased in stature that day, and he still feels fiercely protective of him. Especially now. Otto would put Ajeeb in this portrait, sitting opposite Gerald Duval with the final move, a checkmate, clearly evident. Would he also paint Ezra standing in the doorway holding onto his fortune drawn by the bird, "Be not afraid" clearly visible on the single white scroll if one stood close enough to the painting to see?

Gerald Duval looks up from his paper as the clock chimes four.

"Are you going to come in or continue to scrutinize me? There's some ham and cheese and good bread. Help yourself. I'll be going to Brooklyn shortly. But first there's something I want to discuss with you." He indicates the chair opposite. Ezra sits in the seat that just a moment ago was occupied, at least in his imagination, by Ajeeb. He feels small, wishes he at least had a turban which would give him some stature.

His father looks at him briefly, then reaches in his pocket, pulling out Lord Carnarvon's letter. For an awful moment Ezra is sure his steaming of the envelope has been discovered, but his father is only opening the letter, about to read what Ezra already knows is there. But he doesn't read. He summarizes.

"I've been invited on an important expedition. I'll be leaving next week and I've made arrangements with your uncle Michael for you to stay in Staten Island with him until I return. I shall be gone for quite some time."

Next *week?* That wasn't in the letter. That wasn't in the letter at all. And as for Uncle Michael in Staten Island—his father might as well have said he's exiling him to Outer Mongolia with a lunatic. Uncle Michael, who's only his father's step-brother, spends most of his time in the tavern down by the ferry slip. He works on the Pennsylvania Railroad when he's sober. A loud Welsh woman rents him a room in a boarding house.

Ezra is so stunned he can barely open his mouth. What will come out? A refusal? Most likely, his usual compliance, for that is what pleases his father most. He tries so hard not to be any trouble, to take care of himself and all of it's been for naught. He may as well have been a whining baby all along. He could be now.

But if he had once known how to whine and cry it had long ago been eradicated like an errant weed in a strictly-tended garden. He feels something defiant struggling, like a caged animal pacing, desperately searching for an opening to break free.

What would Ajeeb do? Scan the board slowly, notice he has been cheated? Sweep the board in anger. Declare himself.

"I'm staying right here," Ezra says. "Right here," he says again, louder the second time.

His father raises his eyebrows in astonishment. "That is completely out of the question."

Ezra leans forward. "My friends will look after me." He sits back.

"That would not be suitable at all. Besides, I can't afford to keep this apartment while I'm gone."

For the first time Ezra knows this expedition could last a long time. Many months. Years.

"I won't go to Uncle Michael's. I won't."

"Well then, your only alternative is to stay in an orphanage until I return. There's one not far from here at St. Anthony's on Tenth Avenue and twenty-eighth." His father has trumped him once again.

An orphanage. The very word conjures up a harrowing scene, a prison for children. But Uncle Michael's boarding house is not an alternative. He'll never forget the exhibit in the Chamber of Horrors at the Eden—the happy family in the first display, the bottles on the table in the second. The destroyed home in the third. The forlorn children in rags on a doorstep in the fourth. But in an orphanage he would be better cared for, he's sure of it. More than that, he will still be in the neighborhood, just farther west. And his friends can visit him. And after his father is gone Claire du Lac and Senda and Otto can come and get him and take him home to this hotel where he belongs. He wouldn't take up much room.

"I prefer the orphanage." Surely his father only used the orphanage as a threat.

It's his father's turn now to be shocked. "Very well then," he says, a little uncertainly, as if he's not quite sure how to respond to this unexpected obstacle.

For half a second Ezra has won something. He's made what may be the first bold move in his life. But to what end? He's sealed his own fate with a bold and spontaneous statement.

What would Otto's painting show now? A father and son seated opposite, the lighted "E" outside the window throwing red bars of shadow across their faces. But it's not a painting anymore, it's a moving picture now. A pyramid slowly rising, crashing through the middle of the table, impaling the *New York Herald.* Coffee spilling near the edge staining the news of the world brown. And the scale of Egyptian judgment his father once told him about, for the weighing of the heart against the feather of truth at the moment of death—Ezra knows already that his heart is so leaden it will surely tip that scale, forbidding his entrance to the afterlife and its promised treasures.

Claire du Lac paces the floor above him. Did she think she heard something below—Ezra signaling her? Or is the world coming to an end?

"Well, it's settled, then." His father gets up from the table. He puts on his hat and coat and leaves Ezra, slumping now in the chair. He doesn't feel very bold now. The future is unimaginable. The present is frightening. Only the past feels real.

Maud
1917

Clutching her suitcase, Maud passes the girls coming up the stairs of the Settlement House before anybody can stop her. She steps into Henry Street and the sun. On every fire escape, laundry is hung out, taking advantage of the afternoon reprieve from one more cloudy New York winter day.

Men in long black coats with thick white beards go by, talking emphatically in a strange language. The newspapers they hold have letters that look like thick musical notes. She stops a man in a derby hat with a thin mustache reading a newspaper in English.

"Do you know where Elizabeth Street is?"

"Go up to the end of the block," he says. "Turn right until you see Chatham Square under the El. Follow the Bowery until Bayard, then left again, and there's Elizabeth. Can you remember all that?"

"I can."

"Well, you won't get lost then."

And she doesn't, even though all those streets he named are filled to overflowing once she gets past Chatham Square—people with push carts vying for spots on corners and children running, grabbing fruit as they pass, chased by an upraised fist and a curse. She isn't lost at all, threading her way through it. Chinese men in flat hats smoke in doorways. Men and boys with huge loads of cloth on their backs take up what's left of the sidewalk and a man carrying a sewing machine on his shoulder nearly knocks her over. It isn't until she finds Elizabeth Street written in white letters on a deep blue sign that she stops. She waits there, on the corner, the flow of people pushing past her, afraid for the first time this morning, unable to turn the corner. She sets the suitcase down. It's only a matter now of finding the number. And then what? They'd said at Ellis Island he was no longer here. But she has to at least find the actual place the blue envelopes came from, to see the door he walked out of with the last letter in his hand, the one with the steamship ticket, to post to her at the industrial school in Ireland.

She reaches for the suitcase, but before she can get her hand around the handle, someone runs up behind her and grabs it and keeps on running, down the street into an alley between buildings. She runs after him but loses him around the next corner. And now the letters are gone, the actual proof they contained in the return address. And then there's the photograph of the blurred boy with the Indians. The Vanishing American. That, she will miss most of all.

She walks slowly up Elizabeth Street, past a police station. She can't report the theft. How will she explain herself? They would see her as "Likely to Become a Public Charge" and pack her off to the Juvenile Asylum or the Home for the Friendless. Then she might as well still be in Ireland.

She finds 256 in the middle of the block. Climbs the dozen stairs and pushes the heavy door open. In a tiny vestibule with a floor made of black and white hexagon tiles, she searches a row of names on the wall. Cahan, Salak, Bondante, Franzese. More Italian names. No Farrell. She thought he lived in a house of his own. Now she'll have to knock on every door to find him. She'll start at the top.

She walks up the stairway. Gas jets with feeble

flames barely illuminate her way. There isn't even electricity here. Bags of trash spill into the hallways; a powerful stench exudes from a sink. Behind the doors, babies cry, husbands shout, and now there's some other sound behind several doors as if some engine whirrs away within. There's the overpowering smell of burning coal but the hallway's so cold she can see her breath and little else. The wall is covered in oilcloth and pressed tin, a relief map of bumps and ridges eroded by hands such as hers. On the landing of the third floor there are several doors and the gas jets are out in the hallway. She stands in front of the farthest one. She listens. More of that humming, whirring and little else. She knocks.

The door opens wide and a man with a measuring tape around his neck stands there, squinting at her through the smoke that comes from the cigar butt clenched in his teeth.

"No hire."

She doesn't know what to say now that she's here. She looks past him into the room. Sewing machines, six of them, eat up dark fabric pushed beneath the needles. Men work the treadles in stocking feet. There's a stove with a huge iron heating on a griddle, a woman spreading cloth on a padded board draped with felt. Two children sit on the floor pulling threads from finished pieces, their hands blue with dye from the cloth, their faces smudged as if they've been beaten and bruised. All over the floor, a nest of pulled threads, scraps of cloth. Nobody stops working but they all look at her warily. Has she come to replace somebody too slow? Work for less wages?

Pictures hang high up on the walls, not her father's photographs but Old World relatives looking down in grim disapproval. There's a map of Europe with a pin punched in the middle of Poland. She can't imagine her father ever living here.

"My father," she begins.

"Yes, yes?"

"Farrell," she says.

"Yes. He was boarder."

"This wasn't his place?"

"Sleep, only."

"Where is he?"

"I should know? They come, they go. He leave debt. You come to pay? Two dollars would settle. From you, I take one dollar only."

She reaches into her pocket for one of the five dollars John Tyrone left her with.

"No forwarding address?"

"No. But there is letter for him. From Miss Maud Farrell. In Ireland."

"I am Maud Farrell."

"Then I give to you," he says, shrugging.

He steps back. The children pulling threads simply lean in opposite directions to make room for him. They never take their eyes off her. He opens a drawer in a bureau piled with fabric, takes out a blue letter. Her last letter from Ireland.

"Now business is finish," he says, handing her the envelope. "Thank you and good luck."

He closes the door and she's immediately swallowed by the dark hallway. A door opens at the top of a narrow set of stairs and a piece of sky makes a brief appearance before the door closes again. A woman comes down the stairs, a mountain of frozen sheets in her arms.

Maud waits for her to disappear behind the door of her apartment, then she climbs the stairs and pushes open the door to the sky, gasping for air. Clotheslines strung as far as the eye can see give the rooftops the appearance of Bedouin tents flapping in the breeze. Vents and pipes and chimneys stick out like hatpins from the roofs. Several buildings over she sees a young woman with a hat and cloak carrying a black satchel, like a doctor's, lifting her long skirt as she hops from one roof to another. She disappears through a door, down the stairs into the dark hallway of the building below. Another thoroughfare, much less crowded than the one below.

Maud sits on a crate out of the wind. She opens the letter to see what it is that Maud had to say that her father never even opened.

Dear father,

This is the best day of all. My ticket arrived from you and Father Mallory helped me book passage on the Carpathia. I will ride with him from Dingle to Cork. We leave Cobh on December 12 and should reach New York on the 20th, in time for Christmas. Then I shall be an American. I cannot wait. I will not sleep until I get there. I hope you have my piano by now.

Your loving daughter,
Maud

Her writing looks so childish to her. When she wrote it, Maud was so giddy she could hardly hold the pen, her heart a fleshy thing pumping away without a thought. And now that same heart begins to harden like quickly-cooling wax. She lifts the small sheet of paper and lets the wind take it away. A flock of pigeons circle nearby, honing in on a particular roof where a man stands swinging a lure. They follow it round and round, pulled by habit to this person they know will feed them. They settle inside a coop willingly. The man shuts the door firmly.

The Lower East Side spreads out all around her. The sun is straight overhead now, not inclined in any direction. She's not high enough to see the harbor, the rivers that flow into it, or Liberty, either, where this very minute, girls with fathers are probably climbing into the crown and looking back across the water, having their photographs taken.

She's getting nowhere. He should be looking for *her*, not the other way around.

She looks down at the sandpapery rooftop. There's a circle drawn in chalk. She steps inside it. And there, just outside the circle, a green thing lodged against a vent pipe shines every so often in the intermittent sun. She steps outside the circle to pick it up. A cat's eye marble. She holds it up, looks through it until everything goes green—the sky, the buildings, the sheets flapping on the line. There is, for a moment, an entire city inside a globe, like the ones with snow scenes inside that you shake to make it snow whenever it pleases you to do so.

The sun sinks behind the horizon of the West of the country, burning the clouds red, the entire sky reddening now. To the East, the sky is the palest shade of rose. She's on the brink, born five years into the twentieth century, and it fills her, all this immensity around her, not with grief or hope, but a fierce resolve.

Remember this feeling, she says to herself. Do better than just believe it. Know it for sure. She holds the marble between her thumb and forefinger, a lens to summon, from out of all the various pieces, the one, true, unbroken world.

She steps across this roof to the next, to the coop where the pigeons make their home. They're perched, hunched into their feathers against the cold. What if the man swinging the lure died or disappeared? How would they know where to come home?

She finds a place out of the wind behind the stairwell. A few stars poke through the clouds. She sings, softly at first, then a little louder. There's no one to stop her, or to listen to her either. But it's what she came two thousand miles for her father to hear—the sound of herself, her voice a swinging lure.

~~~
~~~

Pier 54, Cunard Line. Another ship from Cobh, groans against the pilings, flustered by gulls, unpacked by shouting stevedores as they heave the trunks from first class onto carts. A sea of heads bobs on deck. Scarves and derbies of third class, the top hats and feathered bonnets of the upper decks. In a few minutes the gangway will be in place, the disembarking begun while the third class waits until last, streaming off the great ship onto the flat, uncovered launches idling just offshore in the Hudson River.

The newsies elbow their way to the front, past the furs and top coats, the rich relatives of the rich arrivals. They jockey for position, pushing aside the flower girls, the train ticket men, the cabbies, the representatives of the German American league.

The gangway falls with a thud and here they come: native New Yorkers returning home from England and France, leaving the war behind. And new arrivals—you can tell—they look up more often than out, tripping on the edge of the gangway as they put one foot into America.

There are far fewer passengers than when she came. Newspapers said the U-boats are firing at will again without provocation.

The newsies start their cries. "Tammany Scandal! Factory Graft! Brooklyn Bridge Suicide!" An average day in the City of New York.

She stays where she is. She's close enough. All she has to do is open her mouth when she chooses to. The free stale roll on the coffee cart she got on the way here is still stuck in her throat. But it's not entirely the stale bread that holds her voice back. It's the newness of it all. Singing in front of strangers, strangers who may be grieving the losses they left behind. Singing on a rooftop is one thing, on a bar as a toddler is another. Before this, it was something she did only for her father and a few of his friends. But that was so long ago. And the kinds of songs he loved—will people in America even want to hear them?

A woman hoisting a parasol approaches with a little boy in tow. Maud starts to sing "Aura Lee" and holds out her hand, palm up. The little boy stops dead in his tracks before her. The mother tries to pull him along but his stubbornness is so great she has to turn around. She looks at Maud now, who's well into the second verse. She stands and listens until nearly the end, then reaches inside her bag—a little red velvet purse with pearls stitched all around the perimeter. She opens the clasp and takes out a coin. She places it in Maud's hand and continues on, the boy turning his head the whole time until he can no longer see this girl who is still singing, but for someone else now.

Maud finishes the song before she opens her hand. A large coin—not a dollar. Fifty cent piece. Silver.

A girl selling posies sidles up to her, looking at the shining coin.

"That's Walking Liberty, walking around without a torch and a crown. I should sing," she says. "But I can't carry a tune." She pushes forward with her basket of fresh chrysanthemums perfect for buttonholes. A winter flower, a real one, not paper.

Maud pockets the coin with the marble. Her first money in America. She adds the numbers in her head. She likes numbers, their indisputable truth. This money could buy her five nights in a lodging house. She'll walk everywhere she needs to go. Let the elevated train rattle along above, or the underground below, without her.

She tries another song. An elderly man in a silk top hat shuffles toward her supporting himself with a gold-tipped cane. He listens, takes out a clean kerchief from his breast pocket, wipes his mouth as she sings "Down from the Salley Gardens." This is how rich men cry. They pay for it.

He gives her a dollar. A whole silver dollar. Now she almost has five again.

Most of the passengers hurry past. Some, from second class, probably, drop a penny into her hand and don't even bother to listen. She's just one more obstacle in the gauntlet to get through.

Soon enough, the ship is empty, at least of first and second class. The taxis have pulled away from the pier, the newsies too, bunching together, arms emptied of papers, pockets full of coins for the theatre or the lodging house savings banks or wagers in sidewalk dice games. But most will go to hawk the evening papers down in the finance district or Times Square hotels.

The third-class passengers look down upon the emptying pier, waiting for passage to Ellis. What can she sing for them? A lullaby? She picks one and sings, her hands down. This one's for free: "The Wind That Blew the Barley." And they listen to this girl who's made it here, this free person in a green hat and ragged coat with a voice that almost carries to where they are, at least to the ones leaning over the rail. They don't need to hear the words. It's the melody from the country they left behind. They know it so well.

When she's done, pennies rain down. She runs to gather them—fourteen in all—fresh from the money changers at steamship offices where the people traded in their heavy coins for copper.

The launch sidles up to the slip, shuddering as the engines reverse.

She doesn't need to stay. She knows what happens next—the numbers pinned to the coats, the filing onto the launch without having set both feet in America.

She can go now. She can walk to West End Avenue and cross over, heading east, money in her pocket, her throat a little sore.

She walks downtown along Broadway. It's the street, like a bending river through this city, that will get her close to where she's going. New electric streetcars roll down the middle on tracks. As she enters the throng, she's part of it now. Nothing green about her except for the hat. And the marble in her pocket. And the coins and dollar bills.

At tenth street she turns east and soon finds herself at a park with a beautiful arch, like something one would see in a European city.

Old men are playing chess on tables built with the black and white squares already set into them. A group of younger men stand behind the players, smoking cigars in silence so as not to disturb the concentration of the players. There's a group of children by a fountain, several mothers or sisters or aunts keeping watch. A policeman on a horse keeps watch over everyone.

A newsboy holds up the evening paper. She stops to ask him where the girls' lodging house is. If anybody would know, it would be a newsie, especially one of the older ones, like him.

"Twelfth, near Second Avenue. Elizabeth Home for Girls."

She can barely mask her surprise. To her, it sometimes seems she's stumbling from one place to another. Elizabeth Street. Now, Elizabeth Home.

When she turns onto 12th Street, she thinks at first that she's in the wrong place. Mothers with babies stream in and out of a building. "Shelter for Homeless Women and Children," a sign says. A county home? A Magdalen Laundry? But no, maybe these girls keep their babies if they want.

Two doors down, she finds Elizabeth Home for Girls. Maybe you graduate from one to the other. It's larger than she thought, but then everything here is either larger or smaller than she imagined. It's a building of brown stone, like Henry Street Settlement House, not a tenement house strung with laundry. A respectable place with a lit foyer. Welcoming.

A heavyset woman with little round black-framed glasses looks up as Maud approaches the desk.

"Yes? How can I help you?"

"I'm looking for lodgings."

"Have you no home?"

"No."

The woman looks her up and down, taking note of the ragged coat, the hat, and especially the shape of her stomach.

"Are you an orphan?"

Maud doesn't know how to answer this. She senses there are criteria here that must be met. Of all the things she's learned about the gloom and doom of this city by seasoned citizens, no one has told her how to get through this. What will make a better story—an orphan, or half an orphan? If she says she's an orphan she might be sent to the orphan asylum where she'll never get out. What does half an orphan gain? A temporary state of reprieve? A marginal destitution that can be aided by such a place as this?

"My father was sent off to work—to the West— my mother died over in France. Because of the war. My father will be sending for me soon." In an instant she's invented a truth for herself that is believable, one *she* can almost believe in.

The woman sighs. "I'm so sorry." It's an old story, apparently. "Can your father not pay for your keep somewhere? The Home for the Friendless?"

"I'm not friendless," Maud says, trying to keep the irritation she feels out of her voice. But she has to think carefully how to answer the question that was asked.

"I don't know where he is."

"I see. Since when?"

She shrugs. She's telling the truth now and her face must show it. The woman looks at her through those little glasses which surely must give her a microscopic view past the flesh into the very bones that still hold her up in the world.

"Are you working? This isn't a charity."

"I don't want charity. I work."

"Where?"

"Sewing. On Elizabeth Street." she says quickly.

"Where on Elizabeth?"

"256."

"For?"

"Mr. Franzese," she says, the only name she can remember from the hallway.

"Do you have working papers? Have you been to the Department of Health?"

"I had papers but they were stolen with my suitcase. I'll be getting new ones."

The woman looks at her, a little bit of softness smoothing the stern assessment. "Well, that happens, unfortunately. And see that you get those papers. It's the law now. Or should be soon enough if there were only enough people to enforce it."

She looks down at a list in front of her. "Name?"

"Maud Farrell."

"Age?"

"Twelve." It will be true, soon enough.

"Legally, you should be fourteen to work, but the law doesn't take into account the reality of many people's situations. Still, it's meant to protect you, not to prohibit."

"I'm not complaining."

"No, I can see that," the woman says, nodding in agreement. "Date of birth?"

"April 6, 1905."

"Religion?"

Now she's really stumped. She doesn't know what to choose here. What's the least controversial?

"None," she says.

The woman writes it down without comment. "We charge ten cents a day for room and board. You can stay, but not indefinitely. We have classes in hygiene and domestic arts. There's a reading room, a small gymnasium for excercise."

"A settlement house. Like Henry Street."

"You were there?"

"For a while."

"Well, you've got some sense then, to go there. Lillian Wald, she's the founder, is a saint in my opinion. Where have you been living since then?"

"Where I can." Suddenly, she's afraid again. The woman is looking at her much more closely now.

"On the streets…?"

"No," Maud says quickly. "A boarding house. But it's too crowded. No privacy, you know."

"Yes," the woman says. "A girl must have her privacy at your age." She looks up at Maud's face, her pen still poised above the paper as if she's trying to determine exactly how much privacy Maud has had, if it's already been invaded, if her work is not sewing at all but servicing some man in a dark hallway.

Maud has some control over her voice but none over her face. She can feel its betrayal, the fear that must surely be written all over it. But if it's guilt the woman's looking for, Maud has none of that. Not here.

"All right then. I'll need one week in advance. I'll give you a receipt."

Maud reaches into her pocket, pulls out the silver dollar she earned singing today.

The woman gives her back a quarter. "That's a nickel short," Maud says.

"Exactly right," the woman says. "I was just seeing if you could tell. And more than that, if you had the cheek to speak up. You'll do all right."

It's not the first time Maud has heard the word "cheek" in relation to herself. How did this word come to mean shrewdness or boldness or whatever, exactly, it means? It seems to be the opposite of what Jesus tried to get people to do—turn the other cheek. This is more like thrusting it deliberately in someone's face, daring them to strike you. This kind of cheek requires a certain amount of outspokenness, but not too much. A certain amount of independence, but not at the expense of virtue.

"We'll give you some clothes since your bag was stolen," she says. "Go see Miss Keane on the second floor. She'll show you to the dormitory. Show her your receipt." She hands over a white slip of paper with her name and date and the word PAID written and circled. "We've a clock on each floor. Supper's at six sharp. Breakfast exactly twelve hours after that. And there's a savings bank—your number will be 16." She hands her a paper circle with the number written on it. "You'd be surprised how much you can save, a little at a time."

Enough for a train ticket to the West? But where or how or when are questions she's glad that nobody's asking her right now. She's a long way from having any good answers.

~~~

Maud gets up today before the matron comes to get the stragglers. Yawning, they stumble into the washroom to stare at themselves in rows of mirrors, a gallery of serving wenches, rumpled with sleep, shaking off dreams they are still half waking from.

"Hey, Colleen," a dark-haired girl says, drying her scrubbed face with a towel, looking into the mirror at Maud and smiling.

"My name's Maud, not Colleen."

"Well, then. And I'm Rose from the Pig Market."

"Pig market?"

"Jewtown. No pigs there. It's a joke. Just chickens. Chickens and knee-pants and suspenders. You name it, we got. Me, I sell papers at City Hall Park."

"I thought only boys did that."

"Do I look like a boy to you?" She throws out her ample bosom. "Some want to touch it. So what? I keep my shirtwaist on. They get a feel, I get a quarter for my trouble. But I got pinched by a copper, sent to the Guardian Society for a good talking to. They preached at me about being a holy vessel and not to tarnish it. I lived through it. I'm back."

"I just sing."

"In the follies?"

"No. Where the ships come in."

"Does it pay?"

"Oh, Rose," a girl on the other side with a crucifix around her neck says. "Leave her be. It's always money with you."

"And I suppose you don't need any, that you're just here visitin' like some royalty. Didn't I see you on your knees at Our Lady of Help shrine recently? You work—making collars, isn't it?"

"But I don't take money for letting men feel my bosom. It's a sin."

"Hah!" Rose snorts. "You will when you're hungry enough. She turns to Maud again. "You make good money, you say?"

"I didn't say. But it's enough."

"Well, it goes either way here. You're either a beauty and perfect or you have an affliction to make good money. You," she says, looking Maud up and down, "could use an affliction."

"Like what?"

"Like burned hands from a fire. Or a crutch. Wait! I have the perfect thing for you."

She rushes back to the dormitory and returns with something in her hand. She passes it to Maud. "An eye patch. My uncle sells them on a cart on Ludlow. I'll help you put it on."

Rose stretches the black elastic band over her head,

settles the patch over her left eye, then moves it to her right. She turns Maud around to look into the mirror.

"There," says Rose. "You'll make a fortune."

What Maud sees is a reflection of Brigid, pagan saint of Ireland, who chose a carbuncle over her eye rather than keep the beauty that would enslave her in marriage. The deformity gave her freedom. Maud looks closer. A pirate is also what she sees. She smiles.

"How much?" Maud asks.

"For you, nothing. Now, you need a good story to go with it. But that's for you to make. Now I have to go to *The World* and get my load for the morning, see what there is to shout about."

"Murder and mayhem," Maud says.

"Scandal's the best. Especially if a gun is involved. A jealous husband. A fed-up wife. See you later, then."

"Later," Maud says, already thinking about her story, how her eye got poked out. Will anybody dare to ask? It'll come to her at the right time, when she needs it. She takes off the patch for now.

Downstairs, she drinks her coffee standing up. Nobody's sitting down for this meal, but milling around the bank, a table with numbered slots cut into the top. She takes her fifty cent piece and deposits it in slot 16. She's not sure yet about the rest, whether or not to put it all in. She'll wait and see.

~~~

When she steps into 12th Street this morning, she's a different girl than the one who came in last night. She's paid her way already from singing. She has new clothes, but not too new. She keeps her old coat—it goes with the story, whatever that will be. She puts the patch on, walks to Third Avenue following the El north, all the way to Grand Central Station, a massive building with statues standing guard.

She turns west, past Fifth Avenue and the public
library, marveling at the lions flanking the steps. Even
without a war, buildings seem to need protecting in
New York.

Times Square spreads out before her with
enormous billboards perched on top of rooftop
scaffolds. Everything is on a larger scale here and the
crowds not so dense. No laundry hanging from fire
escapes. It's a new route and she likes the change. All
along the way people look at her and glance away. As
she stands on 42nd and Sixth Avenue waiting for a
trolley to pass, a man hands her a dime. She looks up at
him with her one eye. He smiles grimly and rushes on.
She didn't even have to open her mouth. Rose was
absolutely right.

She turns north again, up to 54th, then west to the
White Star pier where a ship unloads. She's almost too
late. First class is coming down the gangway. The
newsies are yelling "U-Boats Back in Irish Sea!"

"Can I have a look?" she asks one boy yelling
louder than the others.

"If you can with one eye, but give it right back."

"I mean to pay."

"A penny," he says.

"I thought it was two."

"That's for *them.*"

She hands over the penny and unfolds the paper.
There's an article about a ship called the *Olympic* painted
in zebra stripes to confuse the enemy about how fast
she's going.

"Good story, eh?" the boy says.

She nods, folds the paper back up. She remembers
when the *Lusitania* was sunk off the coast of Ireland
and a hundred and twenty Americans went down with
it. Then the *Arabic* a few months later. The terror of the
torpedoes was so near, the bodies brought to churches
for blessing. But it happened in Irish waters, not here.

Somehow she'd made the crossing in the brief lull between atrocities.

By the time she returns her attention to the ship, second class is coming down the gangway. She steps forward and sings "Killarney," but before she's two lines into it, a heavy coin is pressed into her hand. A woman, weeping, says to her, "I know that song. I just didn't think I'd hear it here."

Maud finishes the song and by the time she's done she has three dollars, two of which will go to the bank, the other for emergencies. Maybe an opera show. The eye patch was a profitable idea.

"Hey, Pirate Jenny," the newsboy who sold her the paper calls out. He leans against an empty baggage cart, lighting up a smoke, or the last half of one. His clothes hang off him like they'd been strung up on a line in a hurricane and torn to tatters by the wind. He smells strongly of fish and turpentine. His face looks battered, literally, now that she looks at him more closely. "How come youse makin' so much money?" he asks her.

"Who are you?"

"Yankee Dan, to you." He spits a fleck of tobacco in her direction. "Didn't I see you at 54 last week? Sure I did. You didn't have no patch on then."

Maud thinks quickly, searching for a story.

"I fell. On a needle. In my sewing job."

"Jeez," he says, wincing. "You Paddies are runnin' Albany now. And the Yids and the Guineas and the Camel Jockeys is takin' all the jobs. What do ya have to say about that, Pirate Jenny? Sheeney Girl."

She looks at his battered face. She can't tell if he's truly bitter or is only throwing around the code names for countries he's probably picked up from the streets.

"Are you an orphan?" Maud asks.

"I wish! Both my parents are sots and have me out here night and day so I can bring home the growler full of beer. That's all they care about. Layin' about and waitin' on me and if I don't bring home enough to quench their thirst I get the belt. My dad had a job but a Guinea took it when he broke his leg workin' on the Manhattan Bridge. Never did heal proper."

"Why don't you run away—live in one of the lodging houses?"

"Don't think I didn't. Twice. They called the coppers and dragged me back. They own me. I'd be better off bound to someone else—at least there'd come a time when I could pay off the debt." He looks her up and down slowly. "Whose thirst are you quenching out here? What else you selling besides a song since you won't be sewing no more?"

"I sing for myself. The money I make is mine."

"If you manage to outrun the do-gooders. Next thing you know they'll be takin' you out to the country with the Fresh Air Fund. And if you're real lucky, they'll take you out West on a train for good and get you a real home with nice folks."

"What train?"

"Any train that's goin.' They pay your ticket and all and take you all the way to California if you want. But they don't take no girls older than twelve."

"Why?"

"Cause they know too much. They're slatterns like you who won't settle for workin' on no farm or keepin' house for lazy wives."

"How do you know so much?"

"I was *on* one of them trains. I told 'em at the Children's Aid I was an orphan and willing to work and they didn't check up. I got all the way to Nebraska. Then my dad figured it out, tracked me down, and sued the Children's Aid. He's not gonna ever let me go. I only hope he drinks himself to death. Soon."

She looks at Yankee Dan—the rakish, greasy-looking cap, the scorn for anyone foreign—not that they put his dad out of work, but that as a result, he's the one has to bring home the money now. A slave to his father's habit. And his mother's as well. Who wouldn't drink themselves into a stupor here? The awful houses with no yard, no trees to speak of, the jobs that come and go and the competition for them putting everyone at each other's throats.

She doesn't have much time since she's nearly twelve. To go to the West. Now there's a way. "Where is this Children's Aid?"

"Twenty-second. East. Why?"

"I might just go."

"Well aren't you just something. You make me sick. Really sick."

"So why are you talking to me?" Maud says, annoyed now.

"I don't know. You might have somethin' I want."

She doesn't like his look, that look of someone with nothing to lose. Lucky is how he sees her. Because her story is in her own hands. Every time he tries to change, his father drags him back. When he looks at her with those gray native eyes she can't tell what they see. Someone he can use? Abuse? Befriend? There's blame in that look. He has to blame somebody. And she's made more money than he has today.

She leaves him there, slouching against the cart. She feels his eyes following her. She walks quickly toward West End Avenue and heads south to 34th. A different route. She takes a streetcar this time. She can afford the five cents this once.

At Eighth Avenue a building the size of the *Carpathia* occupies two city blocks. Pennsylvania Station soars out of the concrete, improbably fragile with all the glass and high arches laced with a thin corset of steel stays. People stream in and out of the doors with valises, some with children in hand. Below the street are the trains. One at least with orphans going to the West. Farther east, on the other side of the street is R.H.

Macy's department store with its windows open like peepshows of plenty, people silhouetted against the windows, gazing in. This part of the city is more what she had in mind. It teems with purpose, a mere twenty blocks above the squalor. God knows what's north of here. Palaces, probably. There is a golden door to the West, but maybe it's down inside a tunnel below the city, past the lost Pneumatic Railway that her father once wrote her about whose single cylindrical car was blown by the wind of enormous fans. It could have taken her wherever she wanted to go. Now she has to go deeper—under the harbor, out the other side. To ride this train you must have no claim upon you, no claim from you to anyone. That's the price of freedom. A one-way ticket to the West of America, all expenses paid by charity.

For now, she is a half-orphan on a crosstown streetcar standing in the rear, leaning over the railing, looking back toward Pennsylvania Station's crystal palace as it fills with electric light. The day is gone. The tracks roll out behind her, glinting silver as the streetlights come on by themselves without having to be lit. A sheet of newspaper lifts from the black street like a white sail turning over and over in the chill wind off the Hudson.

∼∼∼
∼∼∼

"Usher Wanted," a sign says, pasted in the ticket booth of the Thalia Theatre. A man with a waxed mustache sits on a stool adding up a column of numbers. She taps on the window and he looks up, startled. She points at the sign. He frowns. Then he opens a little door in the back of the kiosk, comes around and opens the front door of the theatre, not wide enough to admit her or much of the wind, but open enough to speak through.

"It says Usher Wanted," she reminds him.

He looks at her doubtfully, his eyes lingering on the patch. "I know what it says. You need to have experience."

"I worked at the Grand when the put on *The Jewish King Lear*," she says. "A sellout," she adds. A good story. She's seen the marquee, that's all.

"Well," he says, "if that's the case—but it's only for tonight. The star *vamoosed.* Said she wasn't going to sing in German, because of the war. The understudy isn't so choosey. Good thing it's closing night. This business is killing me."

"Which opera?"

"You know opera, young lady? *Tristan and Isolde.* In English!"

"That's Wagner," she says.

He raises his eyebrows, impressed. He opens the door. "You'll stand at the bottom of the stairway to the balcony. There's a stack of the programs over there. Cheap print job—be careful you don't smudge the ink. Hang your coat in the office." He makes a point of staring at the ragged hem. "But we won't need you until seven-thirty."

"Can I wait here?"

"Why not?" he shrugs. "That way you won't be late. Plenty of places to sit." He goes back to the kiosk and his accounting.

She hangs up her coat and hat on a hook in the office, a little room with an oversized desk piled with past programs, electric bills, all manner of correspondence. A gas burner with a simmering kettle on top. Along the wall, photographs of the opera singers in full costume, their spidery signatures angled upward from the bottom.

She's glad the Lodging House gave her a dress that fits. She opens the double brass doors to the auditorium. It's dark as a cave. She feels her way down the aisle holding onto the seatbacks as she goes. Gradually her eyes become accustomed to the dark and she can make out the rows, the vaulted ceiling with its balconies and boxes. She chooses a seat halfway down, dead center. Every inch of this place is saturated with music, she can feel it. The brocade, the curtains, the cushions, the light fixtures gilded with *arias*.

Her mother had first introduced her to opera. There was a Victrola at the school and she often took Maud to listen to the black records that held so much music on their ridged surfaces. Maud delighted in cranking the handle to make the record spin and had to learn how many times it would take to get all the way through the record. She remembers a few of the names of the operas and only one of their composers, Wagner, only because the neighbor had a dog with the same name. But the memory of that music, of being with her mother, is still etched deeply inside her.

Maud hears footsteps coming from behind the curtains on the wooden stage—just one person. The curtains open and a woman steps from the wings, rubbing her hands together as if the ropes that opened the curtains burned them. Or perhaps she's cold. She calculates the center of the stage and stands there in a deep blue dressing gown, her red hair rippling past her shoulders. She clears her throat, sings a scale, her breath visible, moves a few paces to the right, tries it again.

She's moving, Maud understands now, to the various places where she will stand during the performance, seeing how well her voice carries from each, checking the sound of herself. But to Maud, it's a private preview, a candid moment when the singer does not know she is seen, when the people in the orchestra pit have not yet arrived, unpacking their odd-shaped instruments. It must be Isolde, tuning the instrument of her voice, letting it soar to the *aria's* improbable notes. She stops, starts over again, her breath like smoke in the cold air as if what generates her voice is an essence distilled in the bottom of her lungs.

The music enters Maud's ears and rides through every part of her, filling her until there's not enough room in her to contain this sound any longer. She's heard this very same music with her mother, but never so clearly, sung by a living person right in front of her, not warbled by a poorly-wound Victrola. She doesn't know how she will leave this theatre and do an ordinary thing again. She doesn't know if she can ever rise out of this seat, hand out programs, collect her pay, return to the lodging house and eat boiled meat and drink weak tea, wash her face with brown soap, get into bed between two plain white sheets and even think of sleeping. This song and whatever story it tells gouges out a place inside her. Hearing the music is like being poured full of honey and everything—the city and its hunger, her own hunger, is displaced, now, the song overlaying every other song she's ever heard or tried to sing. She doesn't want it to stop. She's afraid that when it does stop she'll be scooped out entirely and left stranded with nothing to fill herself with except the longing to hear it again.

Isolde is interrupted by a stage hand needing to draw the curtains. She disappears, the heavy curtains close and Maud is left hanging on a note halfway out of the world. She's reduced suddenly to human form, to a small body of a girl in a gray dress and spit-shined black laced boots.

She returns to herself enough to rise up from the seat, push it back into place, walk up the aisle and out through the double doors, into the lobby and the sea of faces outside the second set of doors standing on the sidewalk. She picks up an armful of programs, takes her station by the stairs. Two other girls stand at either side of the now open main doors. And here they come, the audience, taking the offered programs, finding their seats, flooding the hall with their talk and their perfume and their coughing, their buzzing, their *noise*.

The lights go down and finally there's silence. Their ears open and, except for the occasional muffled cough, they listen.

But Maud has heard this in a way they never will. She's read the program, finally, and understands the story—the ill-fated betrothal, the one true love impossible, the indisputable power of the loving cup that binds them together despite their tragic circumstances. Maud heard it all from an understudy Isolde in a bathrobe who had to open her own curtains. She sang in the cold before the furnace warmed the theatre, unaware of the girl in the middle of row M who listened, not with her ear, but with her life.

It was Maud, not Isolde, who drank the potion from the story's cup. She drank it all by herself. Whom shall she love or be driven to love? There is no one who shared this potion with her, and it flows, unimpeded, driven deep by the music through every part of her, even as she walks into the world again, toward the lodging house through frozen streets, with sixty cents for her troubles.

Ezra
1917

Dawn begins in Brooklyn, crosses the East river and spreads slowly across Manhattan. Ezra stands in the first of this light to reach the roof of the Chelsea while the street below lingers in the last gray of the night before. His father is still asleep as Ezra opens the door to Otto's coop. The pigeons stir and coo, turning in tight circles as Ezra's hand reaches in, selecting the darkest one, the one he calls Poe. If pigeons have leaders, Poe is one. He's always first to take flight from the roof, first to return.

Ezra holds the bird to his chest, tucks it inside his coat, and buttons it so only Poe's head pokes out. The pigeon's pulse races ahead of his own. The soft cooing sounds like a kitten's purr—something that emanates from a mysterious source like a second, secret heart.

He reaches in his pocket for the tiny slip collar he'd fashioned out of twine to hold a small metal cylinder. Inside, a tightly wrapped scroll. Not a fortune, but an S.O.S.

My name is Ezra Duval and I am at St. Anthony's Orphanage on 28th Street. If you find this please come for me. There will be a reward.

He ties the message around Poe's neck, unbuttons his jacket and holds the bird in both hands. He raises it up. "Fly, he says, as if it needs to be told. He releases it to the air. Poe flaps his wings furiously, the inner hinges creaking, the white underside flashing in the light that has by now reached the eleventh floor. Daylight brushes against Claire du Lac's window, then ascends slowly like mercury in a thermometer.

Ezra watches Poe wheel, then turn south. The other pigeons scramble to get out of the still-open door of the cage to follow. Ezra moves quickly to close it.

Poe disappears in the few seconds when Ezra turned his attention from the sky to the cage. What will happen to him? Ezra will not be here later to swing the lure. Will Poe land on the windowsill of Jenny Ferguson's apartment? Will she open the window? Or will he simply circle back at dusk and sit atop the coop waiting to be let back in?

Otto will take good care of the birds, he knows. But he can't leave the Chelsea without sending out a signal, to say, at least inside a sealed cylinder, where he can be found. America is in the war now. There's no telling what will happen.

≈

From the balcony of the apartment he watches the newsies scramble for the stacks of papers with news of troop shipments to Europe. The papers are tossed from the back of *The World* truck. An older boy smoking a cigarette divides the newspapers, taking the pennies. The boys trudge to their corners. One disappears below him inside the lobby of the Chelsea and comes out seconds later, his load lightened. Hector, the bellboy, rolls the newspapers, takes them to the doorways of each room and gently sets them down. There will be no paper at his door today.

His father's trunk occupies the middle of the sitting room. At one end, Ezra's small suitcase dots it like an "i."

His father is stirring, clearing his throat of the

phlegm that plagues him this time of year.

Ezra makes the coffee, spreads all the jam he can on slices of bread and still there is some left in the jar. What will happen to it? For a moment he feels anxious and then he knows that Marta, the maid, will probably give it to Hector. He has a fantastic collection of leavings in a large cupboard in the basement. He showed Ezra once, proud of his collection of shaving brushes, books, shoes, brand new postcards, never written on. And once, the jilted mistress of a great Welsh poet left a complete box of Valentine chocolates. Hector said he would keep them all for his mother when she finally came from Cuba. He had almost saved enough of his salary for her passage. Hector will get this jar of marmalade from Ezra's apartment and enjoy it with the fried plantains he makes for breakfast, unless Marta decides to keep it for herself.

"Well, today's the day," his father is saying, as if Ezra hasn't been awake all night dreading it. His father emerges from the bathroom with a dab of shaving cream still on his chin. He always misses a spot, is not in the least bit fastidious about his appearance, only absentminded, already en route and elsewhere. At least today his socks match.

"I'll have Mr. Dupre call a taxi for us when we get downstairs."

A taxi. Such an extravagance. But the trunk cannot be carried otherwise. Once in Egypt it can be hoisted by half a dozen Nubian servants. The trunk is full of books and tools and specimen cases, special solutions for cleaning the bones of the pharaohs. Ezra, on the other hand, owns remarkably little. "The Vanishing American" by Zane Grey. A few items of clothing. A buffalo nickel, which weighs almost nothing at all.

"Don't look so glum. This was *your* big idea, or don't you remember?"

Glum. Is that what he looks like? He tries to smile

but he's sure it must look like a grimace. Everything is changing, too fast.

And then Hector's knocking at the door. He's brought a new boy along to help. Octavio, a cousin from his country. Together they will struggle with the trunk down the hall to the elevator.

Ezra picks up his own suitcase, turns to survey the room once more. Someone else will live here soon, perhaps tomorrow, watching the "E" come to light without knowing what it stands for, not understanding the tapping of Claire du Lac on the floor above.

"Time to go," his father says, snapping his watch.

Ezra follows his father down the hall, his father's coat in his hand. "Your coat!" Ezra calls out, wondering if his father will even need such a garment in Egypt. His father turns, irritated at the reminder, at coats and the necessity for coats, at the hundred things he's no good at remembering.

"Don't know what I'm going to do without you," he says. Ezra is so used to helping his father keep track of things, and he's surprised that this morning, of all mornings, his father has just become aware of it.

His father puts his hand on Ezra's shoulder and squeezes it, briefly. His father is capable of such gestures of affection but they always feel awkward, hurried. Surely there will be something more today.

Ezra is grateful someone else is in the elevator besides Charlotte, the elevator girl. One of the Hungarians, Tomás, clutches his violin. "Oh, I am late and making everything spoil," he says anxiously.

"For what?" Ezra asks.

"I cannot say," Tomás says and makes a motion as if buttoning his lip.

When Charlotte pulls back the elevator cage door at the lobby, everyone is there, waiting. Even his father looks stunned and hurries past them to see Mr. McGarragh, who must have recently changed to the day shift, about a taxicab. Tomás rushes out of the elevator ahead of Ezra and finds his place next to his brother Aleck who's already drawing the bow across the strings. Claire du Lac and Senda, still in their robes, approach the elevator and take Ezra into their embrace. Otto is saying, "I'll save your painting for you when you return" and hands him a leather-bound journal. "For the journey," he says, "so we can read all about it later." Senda, stoic Senda, begins to cry. Her homeland, her country still recedes behind her from her own journey less than a year ago. Claire squeezes her hand continuously and begs her to stop. Hector, having left Octavio to guard the trunk on the sidewalk, hands Ezra a foil-wrapped chocolate. "My mother will not miss it," he says, winking.

His family—that's what this feels like—giving him a grand goodbye. Ezra stands, surrounded, knowing what all children should know, should have known all their lives: the gift of appreciation. They celebrate him as surely as they cheered the dazzling, electrified city from the roof on New Year's together, as they will do on the fourth of July without him. They rose this morning at an ungodly hour after their late-night occupations. For him.

Each detail: Claire's silver rings, Senda's surprising tears, the first notes of the Hungarian rhapsody, Otto's gift of the notebook, the promise of the painting, Hector's chocolate beginning to melt in his hand—even Charlotte, who is usually too busy brooding over boyfriends, has turned her full attention, giving it to him, and Ezra knows that even if his father never returns, he will have these people to come back to and they will all be here, like this, in the lobby waiting for him to walk back through the door.

There is no time for long goodbyes. His father is pulling him and his suitcase through the lobby. The taxi honks impatiently, the meter running already, as the morning thickens with traffic and the cries of the newsies, louder than usual: "America Declares War on Germany." Goodbye, goodbye. To peace. To the age of innocence. Goodbye to the Chelsea Hotel.


~~~
~~~

The Orphanage of St. Anthony occupies a corner of 28th Street near Tenth Avenue. Gargoyles look down at them, glaring from the roof to the sidewalk. Ezra and his father stand on the stoop; a taxi waits to take his father to Pier 54. Gerald Duval does not like goodbyes and has orchestrated this one to be as brief as possible. He explains that his brother will make the weekly payments. "Think of it as a hotel for children," he says. "You'll be well cared for. Many here are not orphans. Orphanage is a misnomer. There are other children here without mothers whose fathers are away on business. Or the war." The matron goes on to say that there's great uncertainty in this day and age.

Ezra doesn't comment. He can't think about the war. He's imagining the gargoyle swooping down, plucking out his father's eyes. Ezra is not a child. Not anymore. That one is still staring at the letter "E" outside the tenth floor window of the Chelsea, still on the roof, setting Poe free. He used to think ten stories up was the top of the world and that he could see so much of that world below, but he didn't see any of this coming. The small person standing next to his father now is ancient already, speaks like an elder. Yes, have a good trip. Keep in touch. His father shakes his hand, gets in the cab. Then he does something extraordinary. He comes back to embrace Ezra. He says nothing but holds him for what feels like a very long time. He finally lets go, gets in the cab, and waves farewell.

Ezra Duval, shaken by this uncustomary affection, crosses the threshold carrying a brand new suitcase.

Inside it, beneath the clothes, is a box with his most prized possession: the buffalo nickel, once given to him by a real Indian Chief. And the leather-bound notebook Otto gave him less than an hour ago. "For the journey," Otto had said. Fragments come back. He goes over each detail, making sure he doesn't forget anything. They were all there—Claire du Lac and Senda and the old ladies pausing in the midst of their tea, turning to see this departure. "*Bon voyage!*" one of them chirped at him and waved her napkin as if he was off to a public school in England. "*Bon courage!*" Claire du Lac said, tears streaming down her face as the door closed behind him.

Ezra might be back before the week is out once his father is safely on the ship and Claire comes for him. In the meantime there is this formality to go through, this checking in to the children's hotel as a little old man, a midget sprung from a chess-playing automaton. But there is no movement now, just this step through the held-open door. When it closes he will begin to wait like the fortune bird in the cage for the signal to pick up the scroll. For the reward of a single seed.

"I'm Miss Eppes," the matron says. "We've been expecting you. Your father was here yesterday filling out the necessary papers."

There is no concierge, no porter waiting to take his valise. There is no elevator. There is an enormous flight of stairs he must ascend behind the crisp, unmoving skirt of Miss Eppes, her shiny black boot heels flashing beneath the hem as each step is achieved. He counts. Fifty-two, like a deck of cards. When he looks up, a gallery of small faces line the railings on both sides of the landing on yet another floor above. Blank, impassive faces, unsurprised.

"Where is my room?" Ezra asks.

The matron turns. "This is hardly a hotel," she says. The gallery of faces erupts in laughter. The

"Hardly Hotel! The Hardly Hotel!" they sing repeatedly in a chant. Ezra's entire being becomes a single bruise. His face must be purple; he feels that beaten. If Claire de Lac were here they wouldn't be laughing for long.

He summons her, at least the image of her, as a shield. The other faces part for him. There are bodies but he sees only faces, not in detail but in blur, ageless, joined into common expression—hilarity—at his ridiculous mistake. Miss Eppes is leading the way through a gauntlet of those faces. There could well be a hundred. Down a long corridor to a room. His room. Their room. A room the size of the Central Hall at the Eden Museé, but instead of a place filled with potted palms and figures of acrobats suspended from the ceiling and Ajeeb sitting upon his velvet cushion Ezra is faced with rows of iron beds, like teeth in a zipper. Identical beds. Identical white sheets. Navy blue blankets folded at the foot of each. Three long, narrow windows, ten feet apart. A frightful orderliness. A shocking lack of color and detail, of life.

"That is your bed, the last one here." She may as well have said, "Here is your coffin. It's ready. You may get in it now."

He sets his suitcase down at the foot of it. He's almost one of them and they know it. His face is becoming the mask of the orphan, the exile. Whatever brief entertainment and distraction he'd offered has already ended. Miss Eppes is saying dinner will be at twelve sharp. She points to a clock. Time is pointed at here. *This is temporary*, Ezra thinks. He says out loud. "Temporary." Jenny's word. His, now.

"*We're* temporary," an older boy says in a mocking tone. "But not you. *You* were surrendered."

Surrendered? He hasn't given up.

Ezra sits down on the bed. At least it's in a corner. The others leave him, file off to wash their hands before dinner. He's not hungry. Besides, he has a roast beef sandwich Otto gave him. A sweet from Hector. How he wishes they were here now bringing bright color, frankincense, perfume, oil paint, turpentine. The string section of the Hungarian Orchestra would banish this gloom by merely tuning. Otto would leave a trace of pigment on everything he touched. The bright yellow of Jenny. The aubergine color of the city night studded with lamplight. The red of Claire du Lac's mouth after eating strawberries. Even the lavender ladies of the lobby—he misses them all.

He draws up his knees, sits on the bed leaning against the wall. His bed is no different than any other. He looks at his corner and the wall, he notices now, has been scratched with initials along the molding by the floor. Someone made notches—four straight, one diagonal. He counts forty-eight. Days or months? They stopped. The person who scratched them was temporary. Or surrendered. Or dead.

How to stay alive? Remember. Remember everything. Grab on to the minute hand and hold back time.

His hand rests upon the leather notebook. He has not opened it and can't bring himself to write anything down; there is entirely too much to say. He takes the buffalo nickel from its cigar box. He has to remember how he got it on the day Chief Wooden Leg came to New York and gave his blessing of the ground-breaking ceremony for the statue of the First American. How he wishes the chief were with him now.

A photograph of that day, never printed in any newspaper, is nevertheless engraved in Ezra's mind, as real as the 1913 buffalo nickel he holds tightly in his hand tonight.

The chief is holding out that nickel to him, buffalo side up, and he is reaching, still reaching, almost close enough to grasp it.

Ezra returns, the memory a swinging lure. He is there again, with the chief, on a smooth-shaven hill on the windward side of Staten Island the day the ground was broken for the statue. It's important to remember each detail, no matter how insignificant, to place himself there once more and fix it firmly so that it will never disappear.

First, the rain. Yes. So much has happened or not happened in the rain. The cold of rain in winter. A small figure carrying a camera on a tripod plants its three spindly legs in mud to capture the scene. The photographer disappears beneath a cape to look through the lens. A boy—Ezra—an eight-year-old then, in an Indian costume, steps in front of the camera, bow and arrow in hand, blocking the view until the photographer emerges from beneath the cape to wave him away.

His father was with him that day. He does not like to remember his father as he was on that day—cold as the weather. Distant, even standing next to him.

The Indian costume is too small; Ezra can feel the constriction of the cloth as if he's wearing it right now. He wishes he had something on his head besides a single feather in a headband. He can still feel the cold of that February day as everyone waited for the ceremony to begin.

President Taft and John Wanamaker arrive. They are both dressed in elegant top hats and coats, shaking hands with the governor, the mayor.

"Your Indians are late," his father, of course it's his father that says it. On time or not, the chiefs of many nations are gathering nearby. They are not the actors in the Hiawatha plays at Wanamaker's Egyptian Hall or pageants at Grand Central, but true survivors of the last of the frontier.

His father takes him by the shoulders, pushes him forward to the edge of the crowd, past the military band just now taking their shiny instruments from velvet-lined cases. The tuba player places the yoke of his great silver horn around his neck. To his right, a newly-planted pole, flogged by its lanyards, waits for Old Glory to be properly raised.

"There's your Indians," his father says, pushing him again toward a group coming up the hill. He stops, stares at the reflection forming in the tuba, a bright circle containing them all: the black-coated men in tall hats above. He turns and there they are, finally, the chiefs. One wears a suit. The others arrive in full regalia, like kings, wearing feather headdresses that require the plumage of half a dozen eagles. One is carried up the hill in a chair. All of the chiefs are smoking. Not peace pipes, but cigarettes; one puffs thoughtfully on a cigar.

The eldest chief stands very tall in full headdress, a large medallion hanging from a leather thong down to the center of his chest. He unwraps something from a red cloth and lifts it up. Smoke rises from the cigarette clenched between his lips and he closes one eye against its gray intrusion.

A man at the podium introduces himself as Dr. Dixon. He explains: "This most sacred buffalo bone was brought today by Chief Wooden Leg, a Northern Cheyenne Indian from Montana. President Taft has a silver shovel in hand; together they will break the ground for this bronze Monument to the North American Indian that will rise one hundred and sixty-five feet in the air from its base."

Ezra stares in awe at the femur of an animal that once thundered across the plains, now held before him in the fog of Staten Island by a man who might well have fought at Little Big Horn.

"Chief Wooden Leg. Now there's a name," his father says. "You'd think he would have enough sense to change it. Maybe he hasn't heard the frontier closed a decade ago."

The chief looks at his father and for a moment

Ezra hopes the chief will say something or at least brandish the bone in warning but he bends instead toward the ground to dig a place next to the gouge made by the president's silver spade.

The photographer has emerged from under his cape, wiping his spectacles, indicating how Chief Wooden Leg should hold the artifact for it to still be in the frame.

The photographer disappears again beneath his cape. The chief raises the buffalo bone from the ground and then extends it outward, toward the crowd of onlookers. Toward a particular onlooker.

Ezra watches it all unfold in memory and an odd shift of perspective envelops him. In some way, *he* is the photographer that was there that day, protected by a cape over the camera. He swivels the tripod to capture this unexpected moment: a venerable chief reaching out to a quite ordinary boy in an Indian costume. At the exact second the shutter opens the boy moves toward the chief, holding out his hand, ruining the photograph. With the long exposure the gray day requires, the boy will be little more than a blur.

Dr. Dixon gestures to the photographer then tells the group to reassemble itself and he places himself squarely in the center. The band, he says, will play "The Indian's Requiem," especially written for the occasion. He instructs the chiefs to raise the flag and it crawls up the pole, stripes wavering, stars hidden as the elegiac music swells around them. A gust of wind straightens the stripes, stretches the field of star-studded blue before it falls slack again.

The president is waiting. Mr. Wanamaker is waiting. The boy who is and was Ezra is still reaching out. Impatient now, Dr. Dixon reaches in his pocket and takes something out, tossing it in the boy's direction. It lands at his feet, a child-sized tomahawk with red and yellow feathers and a Wanamaker Label of

Fidelity firmly affixed to its wooden handle.

"Pick it up," the father says.

But the boy is not looking down at the consolation prize thrown at his feet but up above the chiefs and the buffalo bone, above the flag, limp again, with drizzle. He continues looking upward still to an undefined place above the scene where Dr. Dixon indicates the statue will rise. It will be a native preface to Liberty, hand lifted, two fingers pointing upward in peace, greeting the immigrant ships.

"I said pick it up. What's the matter with you?"

The chief looks at the boy, then at the father. His gaze comes to rest on the tomahawk. His face reveals almost nothing. Perhaps there is a slightly bemused softening of the mouth. He nudges the toy with a moccasin-clad foot and gives it a little kick, not toward the boy, but the father. The tomahawk does not go very far; perhaps the chief kicked it with the wooden leg. The father quickly walks away.

The chief turns his attention to Dr. Dixon and bends to a small table set before him to dip a pen in ink and sign a document, a pledge of his tribe's allegiance to America. The others sign, in turn. Dr. Dixon looks around anxiously. Something is missing.

A man in a hurry runs up the hill with a canvas sack and opens it. He reaches in, picks something out and hands it to Dr. Dixon who announces, "Just in time! A newly-minted coin of the realm honoring the first American." But no one can see what he's talking about until the contents of the sack are distributed. Nickels. A lot of them. A solemn chief in profile. 1913. On the other side, a buffalo. In God We Trust. FIVE CENTS in raised lettering.

The official ceremony at an end, the chiefs shake hands with the president, with Mr. Wanamaker, and then, left to themselves as the dignitaries remove themselves back to the shelter of the fort, the Indians light their cigarettes and talk in low tones to one another, at ease in the rain. Chief Wooden Leg wraps the buffalo bone in the red cloth again. The chief turns his full attention to him now.

The fringe on the boy's Indian costume is crimpled and splayed. He wears no moccasins. Lace-up boots form the pedestal of the small statue he is becoming.

"Are you Hiawatha?" the chief asks.

The other chiefs laugh. They've heard this name so many times.

"No," Ezra says, clearly blushing. "He isn't real." After a moment he adds, "Is he?"

"No," the chief says, his eyes resting on the bow and arrow Ezra clutches in his hand, "but it seems I am now an actual American."

The chief looks at Ezra. His father snaps open an umbrella to cover his head from the weather. He turns and walks farther away from his son.

The chief reaches out, offering his hand.

Ezra looks at the chief's hand, warm and strong around his own, at the surprising wristwatch, emerging from his shirtsleeve, set to a different hour, the true time of the Great Plains.

"Did you get one of those coins?" the chief asks.

"No," Ezra says. "I didn't."

"You can have mine." The chief hands the buffalo nickel to him. "In God We Trust*ed*," he adds.

Nevertheless, he still holds it tightly in his hand.

Ezra closes his eyes. *Be not afraid,* written in the gypsy's hand. To keep those words alive everything else has to disappear—his father, the letter from Lord Carnarvon, the spectre of the war, the home he has just lost. And the long journey in the fortune? It's not his father's journey; he knows that now. It's the enormous distance between himself and the kind of courage he longs for. If he calls out to his future self, will his voice carry that far? Will a braver Ezra answer?

All he has left is the buffalo nickel. The coin might protect him. He trusts no one now.

He walks down the stairs to the dining room, to the long tables with rows of children who pause, spoons hovering over bowls of steaming soup, watching him.

Ezra walks down the aisle, finding his place, the full bowl, the bread waiting for him. When he sits down, it's Claire who takes the spoon, Otto who opens his mouth, Senda who swallows. Ezra the automaton, moved by everyone inside him. This is how he'll be, here among orphans. In his own good company. If there are to be any tears they will be Senda's tears, and if there are things to be written, it will be Otto lifting the pen, pressing it to the page. If he needs courage, the chief will press the nickel into his hand. And what of his father will be with him? That final embrace. He feels it still.

Ezra will surrender these treasures to no one.

Maud
1918

News of the war is shouted by the newsboys:
German U-boats have been sighted in America's waters
for the first time. The war will not be contained in
Europe; it's catching up to her, even here. But it's news
from nearby that comes to Maud from one of the
newsgirls. This one is dressed in gingham wearing a
coonskin cap despite the warmth of the day, standing
by Luchow's restaurant on 14th Street near Herald
Square. In the park across the street cloak workers are
talking about a strike.

"New York Tragedy!" the girl shouts. Maud hands
the girl a penny for the paper. "Two," the girl says,
"this ain't the regular paper. It's a Penny Dreadful." She
hands Maud a booklet. "Shadows and Light – Secrets
of the City." She looks in the table of contents.
"Distraught man searches in Vain!" the third chapter
says.

"Took him to the lunatic asylum on Ward's
Island," the girl announces dramatically, reading over
her shoulder. "There's no comin' back from there.

Nelly Bly put on a disguise and went to Blackwell's for ten days to write a book. She had a hard time convincing them she wasn't crazy when she was ready to come out."

Maud reads. "A man found on the corner of Elizabeth Street and Mott was taken into custody at The Tombs and remanded to the care of the Manhattan Psychiatric Center on Ward's Island. The man claimed to have lost his family and collapsed after searching for them for several days, neighbors reported. The man said he had woken to find himself inside a photograph of Indian Chiefs he had once taken, a photograph from which there was no escape. A head wound seemed to be the cause of his loss of memory and it was presumed he had returned from France after seeing action there. He had French francs in his pocket. He spoke with an Irish accent. He was unable to tell police his name. What is this man's story? The reader well might wonder. This Stranger could be anyone. He could be looking for *you*."

Maud closes the booklet, puts it in her pocket. "Where is this place, this Ward's Island?" she asks the newsgirl, trying to keep her voice steady.

"You look like you seen a ghost."

"I want to know where Ward's Island is. *Please.*"

The girl looks at her sympathetically. "North of Blackwell's. Almost to Harlem. There's a ferry from 106th. My uncle used to be the boatman."

Maud pushes her way through the crowd to get to the El. A knot of girls hold placards: "No More Child Labor!"

"March with us," a girl not much older than Maud says, grabbing her sleeve. Maud pulls away.

"I can't," she says. "Not now."

"Later might be too late," the girl calls after her. And she is too late—for everything.

≋

On the last boat to Blackwell's and Ward's Island Maud sits across from two old women who cling to each other. They talk in a strange language—Slavic, maybe. Or maybe a secret dialect they've made up. A matron in a uniform sits next to them calmly reading a book. On the other side of the ferry, two boys in rags with faces that would frighten a monster—knife scars like second mouths permanently leering—stare at her. One makes kissing noises. A man who looks like some sort of truant officer cuffs him. A pregnant woman, so big she could be close to breaking water right here on the boat reeks of stale beer and vomit. All of these get off at the first stop at Blackwell's, except for the two women across from her. They seem one person. The older one, Maud sees now, is blind, smoking a black clay pipe. The other one must be describing everything to her. Her sister, for surely that's what she must be—clearly disapproves of the smoking for she turns her face away when she speaks. They are like Siamese twins with a single heart between them.

For the first time Maud worries about the eye patch. Does she look like one of these afflicted people about to be put away? She could take it off but it feels, for the moment, like the only protection she has. She's been wearing it most of the time, only taking it off when she sleeps.

When the ferry docks at a small wharf, Maud lets the women get off before her. They match their steps exactly by thrusting their opposite legs out, hip to hip. A single cloak covers their shoulders. "William," the matron calls out, and the one smoking the pipe turns her head. "Tell Franklin to hurry up."

These aren't women at all. They're men. Nothing is as it seems.

On the walkways, people are being wheeled in

chairs, or walking, their bald heads crowned in straw hats. One old man with a beard to his waist stands in front of a just-budding apple tree, looking up. Maud looks up but can see nothing. There is no bird there, no nest where one might return. It's as if he's watching the tree grow, and will wait there until the first leaf emerges from its tight bud. His ear is pressed to the trunk, listening for the sap that will soon rise from hidden roots. He doesn't seem to hear the bird singing from the upper branches.

There is a desk inside an enormous building. There is always a desk with a ledger and a single lamp and a tired woman with a pen, presiding.

"Yes?" she says to Maud. This matron is dressed in a brown and white striped dress studded with two rows of brass buttons. Over that, a white apron, and a wide green belt around her waist from which a dozen keys hang from a ring.

"The man in the pamphlet," Maud says. "The one who can't remember his name."

"Oh, him. They brought him in last week and there were several reporters who came to visit. Shell-shock, it seems. I guess he's famous by now. John Doe."

Maud breathes a sigh of relief. It's not him. "That's not his name."

"That's what *we* call him," the matron says. "Do *you* know who he is?"

"I don't," Maud says, doubtfully.

The woman is looking at her, as if searching for some resemblance. She gives Maud a visitor's pass. "For your sake, child, I hope you don't know him. He's outside, with the cart. He's taken to it. The doctors say he shouldn't have visitors, that there have been too many people from the press agitating him. Under the circumstances..." She pauses, handing Maud a square of paper, "I'll give you a visitor's pass. Through there—there's a sort of promenade by the river. You'll see the cart. It's one of the doctors' inventions for the special cases. It distracts them. And it's a way to get exercise. As I said, he's taken to it. We have to pry the rope out of his hands when it's time to come in. He's hardly let go of it since he's been here, except to eat and sleep and not much of that by the looks of him. Do you want someone to go with you?"

Maud shakes her head. She steps out the east door, putting one foot in front of the other as deliberately as the two men in women's clothing as they stepped from the ferry. She's fighting back a growing urge to run in the opposite direction.

She can make out the shape of a wheeled conveyance, the shape of someone bent forward, pulling it. There's someone sitting inside the cart as well. Closer, the shapes sharpen into people. There's a dark-haired man, a boy, really, in the cart, his eyes vaguely Oriental, his face as round as the moon. He's clapping his hands and laughing as the cart rolls along. He's singing a tuneless tune. As Maud walks alongside, he points to her and says something she can't understand. She walks faster to catch up to the man pulling the rope. The cart wheels, made of wood, creak along the walkway, bumping over the uneven cobblestones. The man is bent like a beast bearing the weight behind him, pulling on a six-foot rope. His head is shaved clean, revealing a stitched gash on his right temple. He's bald as a doorknob. It can't be him. He's not wearing spectacles.

She calls out. He doesn't even break stride or turn his head toward her. She runs to get past him, ahead of him, so that he'll have to stop. And he does stop. The rope does not fall from his hand.

The face before her has two eyes, wide open and blue. Whatever he looks at he seems to see right through. He has a mouth but it does not open. A nose, through which his spent breath leaves him. He simply looks at her, through her, as if she's something in the path he must figure out how to get around.

And then she realizes—the patch. Of course! She's gotten so used to wearing it she doesn't feel it anymore. She takes it off slowly, her eye dazed by the light, and it's through this blurred vision she thinks she recognizes him—two shapes coming into focus as seen through a stereoscope.

He pulls on the rope again, begins to move past her, around her.

"Wait!" she says. Is it him? The boy in the cart has stopped singing now and sits there smiling at her.

"It's *me*. Maud," she says. And it feels strange to say it, to have to tell him. Will he know her voice? She reaches back for the song he loved so much.

Of all the money e'er I had
I spent it in good company.
And all the harm I've ever done
Alas! it was to none but me.
And all I've done for want of wit
To mem'ry now I can't recall
So fill to me the parting glass
Good night and joy be with you all.

His expression does not change. Is he beyond the reach of that song now? Has he forgotten how to cry? She searches his face as if it might be possible to see the source of such devastation. Shell-shock, the matron had said. There must have been a lot of cases for her to be so definite. An explosion so close, so loud, it erased everything he'd ever thought, or dreamed. Every person he loved and lost.

But the boy in the cart listens in rapt attention, his hands clasped together, as if he's heard the most beautiful music in the world.

This can't be her father, this man with the rope looking through her. He can't be. And then he does

something, and this is the thing that will haunt her for
the rest of her life. He drops the rope at her feet. When
he takes a step forward she closes her eyes for the
embrace that's coming. She hears the dried grass bend
and break beneath his boots and feels his hands try to
push her out of the way. She braces herself. She sways,
but does not fall.

She opens her eyes. He is not stopping at the
guardrail but climbing over it, walking into the river up
to his waist.

The boy in the cart is pointing at her. The man in
the river is swimming, or trying to. It's not him, cannot
be her father. Her father can't swim. He turns around,
wild-eyed, and then turns again, going deeper, flailing at
the water. Two attendants climb over the railing to get
him, shouting at her to get back, to make way, to please
leave now. He must not be upset any further.

Maud runs. Runs past the matron in the apron
coming toward her, past the wheelchairs facing the river
in a row. Heads turn to see the commotion. She runs
past the man looking up at the flowering tree, holding
onto it for dear life now.

If she stops she will be taken in hand. She will
become a ward of the state, marked with an indelible
"X" and locked away in a place like this or be sent back
to Ireland by herself. She can't let either of those things
happen. There's nothing left to do but run.

She runs to the ferry which has just cast off. The
rope that held it is pulled and coiled by a man standing
on the stern; the one who had loosed it from the
hawser lights up a smoke.

"Stop!" she calls out. She waves her visitor's pass.

He yells something to the person in the wheelhouse and the ferry comes to a stop. It begins to grind
backwards. The man on the wharf helps her onto the
stern. She heads for the bow as fast as she can.

She does not want to look back at the island as it

grows smaller in the growing dark or watch until it's no more than a dark shape pricked by lighted windows. The ferry churns toward Manhattan, the smoke from its many chimneys rising in silhouette. Behind it, there's a red streak where the sun fell below the world. She can't see Liberty, but she tries to imagine her, there in the harbor, lifting her light. She tries to think about being held aloft by this great lady, armored in the green copper that surrounds her. She only feels her own skin, thin as cloth, holding nothing in, keeping nothing out. She begins to cry and is suddenly so frightened she will not be able to stop. She makes herself stop. She knows only one thing for certain as she steps onto Manhattan Island. She will not sing again.

〰〰〰

She walks all the way downtown, unconscious of the number of streets she crosses. Finally, at 10th Street, she returns to the world where her feet are moving. She can make out the globes of light ringing a dark, oval space. Tompkins Square Park. She's walked by it before, past the benches and trees, the place where a band will play to crowds on summer evenings. She's so grateful it's empty tonight. She sits down on a bench by a tree. An almost violent trembling begins.

A man and a boy approach, then walk by. They don't even look at her. She takes the eye patch out of her pocket, puts it into her lap. She's hardly worth a glance without it. When she looks out again at the park and its trees she's astonished the way her peripheral vision has expanded now that she's looking with both eyes again.

The man and the boy who walked by earlier are leaning against a tree now—at least one of them is. She can't make out their faces from here. The boy is kneeling in front of the man, the man's hands are on the boy's head, moving it back and forth, slowly at first, then the motion becomes almost violent. Then the boy is standing, facing the tree, and they are one person moving together, the man roughly riding the boy into the ground.

The boy stands up, turns around and holds out his hand. The man puts money in the boy's palm, turns and briskly walks away. The boy steps beneath a lamp to count it. Now she can see his face.

Yankee Dan. She'd know that face anywhere. She raises her hand to wave. Seeing motion out of the corner of his eye he approaches her. Looks at her face, then down at her lap, at the patch.

"What are you lookin' at!" he cries. "What did you see?" He grabs the patch. "You're a cheap fake. You trick people into giving you money. You make me sick." He throws the black patch down on the ground.

He slides something out of his back pocket. Below her chin, there's the glint of a knife. He pulls her to the ground. Because he can. Because it was done to him.

He probes her pockets for money. He finds none. There's nothing human about him now.

He grabs her hair and pulls her head back. "You'll pay," he says. He brings the knife to her face. "You can afford it. I'll give you something you won't forget, you Sheeney girl. You'll need that patch now."

She struggles and twists, feels a sharp pain in her left eye, worse than the button hook at Ellis. It hurts worse than anything, this piercing of a part of her that just opened wide to see the world.

He closes the knife with a snap. And then he runs.

Gasping for breath, she lies on the ground, face up to a black, starless sky. She tries to look through the budding branches of the trees as her left eye fills with blood. She searches in her pockets for a handkerchief, finds one and holds it to her face. But she's all cried out. If she had any tears left they would surely sting.

Her money's gone. Her father's gone. And the eye patch. Yankee Dan threw it down beside her. All she can think is if she'd had it on that she would be safe right now.

She sits up. It's Brigid of Ireland she appeals to for strength. Brigid understands the cost. The patch was no protection at all. And the horror is, she will actually need that patch now. She finds it and puts it back in her pocket.

Brigid will not let this happen again.

≈

Tonight, Maud is a different girl going through the door of the lodging house. She hopes they can't smell it on her, the humiliation.

"What happened to your eye?" the night matron asks. That's the wound that gets attention—the one that can be seen, administered to.

"It was an accident. I fell threading a needle…"

"How in the world?" she starts to ask but leaves before Maud can come up with an answer. She goes quickly to find the nurse.

The nurse returns with alcohol and cotton balls and begins swabbing at the lid; it stings terribly. "You're lucky that it didn't go in farther. But you've scratched the cornea for sure. There'll probably be a permanent scar, a small one. I've seen it all, you know. Swallowed pins, yes, but not stuck into the eye. Good God."

She puts down her swabs and bottle of alcohol. "Now, cover your eye. Can you see?"

Maud blinks. "Everything's blurred." Maud retrieves the patch from her pocket and puts it on.

"Where did you get that?" the nurse asks.

"Found it," she says. "Lucky for me." She wants to tell the truth. What happened. Everything. Ellis Island. John Tyrone. Her father. Yankee Dan. The knife. A scratch on the cornea? A lifelong scar? The patch is a badge of a deeper wound. No one will dare lift it now. She wants more than anything not to cry, to not feel the terrible sting of tears. If she cries, if she tells, they'd put her in a Juvenile Asylum for sure. The Female Guardian Society. She did not come to America to have her soul protected; she had come to save her life.

But even as she hardens herself with this philosophy, there's a part of her that wants, more than anything, to whisper what happened, to be comforted somehow. To feel the arms of someone at least trying to soothe her.

She needs the patch now. Not just for the eye. For the rest of her. There is no other protection. There is only the cost of thinking she has any safety at all, that something will save her from brutality when her very existence makes her fair game.

She climbs the stairs to the wash room. Luckily, there's no one there. She stands in front of the mirror and looks; she doesn't recognize herself anymore.

≈

She wakes, one eye open to the world, the other hidden and hurting. She should be on one of those trains this minute heading West, taking her chances somewhere else. But when she thinks of the West, she can't imagine it, no more than she could when she stood at the end of the Dingle peninsula looking toward America. Whatever lay beyond was covered in cloud. She assumed her father would have a life going here that she could simply step into. He had somehow made the decision to fight in the war. How could he not have told her? Did he think the war would be over before she got here? Now it seems that her life as a daughter was so brief—most of it spent waiting to become one.

She goes downstairs, wondering how she slept at

all, down to the nurse's office. A different nurse now. "I heard you had a mishap last night. How are you this morning?"

Maud shakes her head. She honestly doesn't know.

The nurse lifts the patch, swabs the eyelid again. Lifts the lid gently. It's like Ellis all over again. Except she's really afraid now. This injury might be grounds to send her back to Ireland.

"Not too serious. Your sight will be affected, but you won't be blind."

Not too serious! She has no idea.

"What is your trouble?" the nurse says, sitting on the edge of her desk looking at her frankly.

Maud shakes her head. The nurse must know. It's written all over her skin like a headline. She can't pretend any more. But all she can do in front of this woman is to wait for her instructions.

"I'm recommending bed rest, lots of it. You've had a shock. Now get back up stairs."

Shock. Yes. From a silent explosion, echoing still.

Maud doesn't know what else to do. She gets into her bed. Weak sunlight comes through the rippled glass in the window. The others girls are gone to work, bragging about their boyfriends, what picture show they'll go to on Saturday night.

The room is quiet, and with nothing to do but close her eyes, she makes herself think of Ireland. The Ireland she wants to remember. Gortadoo. The cottage on Ferriter's Cove and the constant sound of the sea, where she stayed with her father for a while before he left for America and placed her in the care of the nuns.

Except for the two short months with him, Maud had been raised mostly by women. Her mother, when she thinks of her, seems like a mirage.

Morrigan, the *senachi*, was the first woman of real power Maud had ever met. Older than Ireland and wiser. What Morrigan knew of Brigid surpassed the priests who'd tamed her into a saint.

A neighbor, Annie Kelly, took Maud with her once to celebrate Imbolg, to watch the green man dressed in leaves dance through the fields of Kerry. Spring was not far behind and the green man called it to come. But it was the stories of Brigid around the fire that night that Maud remembers most.

The priest of Dunurlin parish could no doubt see the beach fire from the church but he knew he could no more extinguish those flames than he could summon Mary herself with a bucket of water for the dousing. For it was the women who kept this fire going all by themselves, fed it with branches, fed it with stories. These were women of the ancient faith, not the ones who walked to St. Bridgit's Well in Clare, but the ones who kept the old story of the real Brigid alive.

The women summoned Morrigan O'Bric from Blasket Island. Some called her a witch. But she was a *senachaí*. She lived by herself in a cottage tending a few sheep on the windward side of Blasket where she could always keep watch on the westernmost piece of Ireland, Innishtoosgert, the sleeping giant. As long as he stayed sleeping, did not rise up and go off to the land of snakes in America, Ireland would still be Ireland. Or so it was said.

Children carried candles clockwise around a circle of standing stones. The mist rolled in. Morrigan walked toward a chair that had been set out for her and sat down. One of the girls draped a green shawl over her shoulders.

She began with prayers, singing, all in the old tongue. It didn't matter what the words were. Maud took them in. She finds herself whispering them now.

"Fairest of the Fair," Morrigan intoned, stirring the fire with a stick. "Brigid was promised—such beauty carries a price—but she would have none of it. Her fate, she decided, was not to marry."

Maud remembers the story clearly. A high king of that time got one of his slave girls with child. Brigid was born the most beautiful child in all the land. Her mother was given freedom for this gift to the king. When Brigid was fifteen, she was to marry. But she began to pray to be made hideous. Such a prayer! A carbuncle formed over her eye and a great swelling. No one would have her then. She left with the virgins and widows of the village, went out to start a place of their own in the fields. They tended sheep, but a wolf was killing the sheep at a terrible rate. Brigid made a pact with the wolf, who sat at her side. His hunger was satiated. She hung her cloak on a sunbeam. She protected the crops from storms. She caused the rivers to rise or change direction as needed. She brought plenty to her people.

The fire burned bright, the mist rolled as if the very breath of the Atlantic was coming close to listen, swathing the land in the secrecy required.

And now, Maud feels herself enfolded by this pagan saint. She needs no cross around her neck. The cat's eye marble she found on the roof of her father's apartment building on Elizabeth Street will be her talisman. Green for Imbolg and the season for growing. Green for Ireland. The color green will keep her safe.

≈≈

Dear Miss Farrell,

In answer to your letter, our records indicate that Michael Farrell, as you called him in your letter, previously identified as John Doe, died of a seizure August 19, 1918, according to the coroner's report and was buried in Potter's Field, Wards Island at the expense of the City of New York. If you have any other questions you may direct inquiries to City Hall Department of Records. If you have any wish to recompense the City of New York, then you may contact the Department of Indigent Burials, also at City Hall.

Sincerely,
Thomas Williamson
New York Psychiatric Hospital

≈≈

"I wish to surrender."

"I beg your pardon?"

"I want to surrender myself." Maud looks at Miss Stephenson presiding over her ledger, her keys and accounts. "I want to go to the West. To find myself a new home."

"The Children's Aid doesn't take girls past twelve..."

"I'm not twelve." Funny, she's always wanted to be older. Now, lying about being younger is her ticket out. She's nearly thirteen, and started her monthly, but she won't breathe a word of that. She nearly wept when she saw the first rusty stain on her bed sheet.

There is no more reason to stay in New York. There is only the true West now, farther on, the place behind the golden door. Texas. California. The real America. John Tyrone knew, and now she will go and collect her debt, start over. It's the only thing she can think of to do.

Miss Stephenson looks at Maud skeptically, her gaze lingering frankly on the patch. "They try to take children that will present themselves well. Flaws can be a problem…" She holds a pencil in both hands, her thumbs meeting at the center. "Sometimes, though, a flaw can be an asset, it depends."

"On what?"

"The kindness of strangers."

"You mean pity. It doesn't matter. I want a ticket to Texas."

"They don't sell tickets to specific destinations! This is charity you take your chances!"

Maud can't hide her disappointment. Maybe this isn't such a good idea after all. But to stay here, to be fair game, to always have to look over her shoulder, to have to push her way past the newsies at the docks to find another lodging house and another one after that. It's too much. And there's that man who dropped the rope at her feet. Dropping the gauntlet, a challenge. Go on, girl, go on. One of us has to. If only he could have said it in words, like a blessing.

"Where do I sign up?"

"You don't sign up. Good heavens! We select you on the basis of need!"

"I'm an orphan."

"I thought you said you had a father."

"He died in the war."

"Oh, my dear. I'm terribly sorry. Orphans are the real casualties of this terrible war. There are so many."

Any doubt about being an orphan is gone as the blurred edges of that afternoon on Ward's Island sharpen once more. The truth comes because she needs it now, for it to be forced into bare fact: the conditions of her voluntary surrender.

When he dropped the rope it was that gesture that severed the connection as surely as if he'd cut the name they shared in two. He dropped the only thing he'd desperately held onto when he heard her voice. Whatever security there'd been in that braided hemp frayed with a song that had once made him cry in Ireland. To cry in such a setting in America, an asylum for the insane, to respond to that bit of feeling was to fall off the edge of sanity, if indeed there was any edge of it left. For her, it was like encountering a newly dead person who still had a toehold in the living. All she did was push him with her voice into letting go. She just didn't realize how completely his surrender would be.

"Did you lose that eye? I thought the nurse said it was a scratch on the cornea..."

"I didn't lose it. I know exactly where it is."

"Well. I'll make some inquiries," Miss Stephenson says hesitantly.

"When?"

"Soon."

"I need to know now."

"With that attitude you'll never get chosen."

"I want to be the one to choose."

The patient expression on Miss Stephenson's face turns toward exasperation. The pencil she's been holding in both hands during this entire conversation could break with the weight of the two emotions.

She puts the pencil down, picks up the telephone and holds the small black barbell to her ear. She tells the operator the number, waits.

"Yes, this is Miss Stephenson at Elizabeth Home. I have a girl here to be placed out. Yes, she's eleven." She glances up and looks at Maud who nods in agreement. A necessary lie. "No parents, Miss Stephenson continues. "She has...an affliction. Of the eye." She taps the pencil on the ledger impatiently. "No, not exactly a visible wound." She looks helplessly at Maud.

Maud removes the patch and stares at Miss Stephenson. Light nearly blinds her. The room shifts as her vision adjusts. In that green left eye, slightly off center, is a cloud, a shred of a curtain across the world. It's healed all it's going to and there is this place now, permanent, a veil thrown across clarity. A reminder of what cannot be completely discerned. It is her flaw, yes. The patch is the least of it. That can come and go. It's her vision that's been changed.

"I believe," Miss Stephenson says into the phone, "she will make an excellent candidate for placing out."

〰
〰

On her last morning in New York Maud puts the patch in the pocket of her hemmed and cleaned coat. She pulls her green felt hat low on her head even though the weather's unseasonably warm for September. She walks the ten blocks to the Children's Aid Society. She worries it could be like Ellis all over again, inspections, letters chalked on her back, sent packing back to Ireland.

As she nears the middle of the block there's a group gathered on the steps. A photographer on the sidewalk puts his head under a dark cloth, shielding the lens from the light. The children stand stock still, suitcases in hand. At least forty of them, scrubbed and scared, but they smile on demand.

"One more," the photographer says.

"Wait!" Maud says. She steps into the group of assembled children.

He says to stand perfectly still. She knows what she needs to do.

He counts down from five. At the very last second, she moves, like the boy with the Indian chief in her father's photo: "The Vanishing American."

As soon as Maud is tagged and given a cardboard suitcase, passing muster, so to speak, she puts the patch back on. A young matron, "Mrs. Worthington," her nametag says, herds them up the street to catch the El. They all manage to get on the same crowded car, grabbing onto each other, clutching the suitcases with one hand. Mrs. Worthington shepherds the girls. A Reverend Horton stays with the boys. The other people in the car barely lift their heads from their newspapers and all the news of the war. The Meuse-Argonne offensive has begun.

They make a frantic transfer at 34th to the cross town streetcar and finally they disembark and are counted and recounted. Mrs. Worthington stops in front of Maud.

"What happened to your eye?"

"It's healing. From an injury, not a disease. The nurse said to wear this for a while."

"I'll make a note of it."

Behind her, and them, a great door opens into Pennsylvania Station; people stream out of it like thoughts out of a great mind. The children are ushered in, moving as one now into the vaulted cranium, the sky both continuous and contained inside the leaded glass.

The children around her are stunned, on the verge of tears. But to Maud, it's a grand exit, a cathedral of travel and she, a traveler, at least momentarily blessed. The enormous clocks seem to be the source of time itself, and the throb and tremble of the trains beneath the marble floor are the very heart of the city, all of it inside a vessel of light. No lords and ladies. No titles, here. No cattle chutes like at Ellis. No wards. But soldiers, dressed alike. Lots of soldiers going off to war.

For these few moments before all is sorted out again on the train they are part of the New York morning—people going to work, to school. Magnates and cooks, skivvies and surgeons. Soldiers. And these surrendered children in their midst looking as if they're headed out on a school trip. No one knows they have no specific destination, no ticket with a town at the end.

No ticket by which to return. By the looks on many faces, that mystery is frightening, but to Maud, she feels as if she's standing at a threshold, about to cross over to the rest of her life.

She refuses the conductor's hand. She steps onto the train, pulling herself up by the handle. She takes a seat at the back. She puts her suitcase on her lap. Mrs. Worthington is handing out pencils, telling everyone to write their name on their suitcase.

Maud thinks for only a second. She writes another name on her suitcase. A new name, taken from the street where her father once lived. The name of the home for girls where she surrendered herself. It's an elegant name full of protection, joining the lineage of poets and saints and virgin queens.

Elizabeth is going West.

Ezra
1918

They stand in a long row on the platform at
Pennsylvania Station, so alike in dark little coats.
Blackbirds on a wire, Ezra thinks. All of a feather, but
we do not fly. Each holds a cardboard suitcase with
their name written on the side in ink, and due to the
walk from the streetcar to the station in the early
morning drizzle of this September morning, some of
the names are already blurred, the letters dripping into
illegible graffiti. Ezra sees his own name changing shape
in front of his face and it seems the predictions of the
people at the orphanage are already coming true: they
won't be needing these names, at least the surnames,
much longer.

Ezra takes a handkerchief out of his pocket and
unfolds it carefully. They had been issued one each,
along with a Bible and a new suit of clothes after a bath
last night. He blots the wet cardboard. Ezra Duval.
Smudged, but legible. He folds the handkerchief again.

Inside the suitcase, a shirt, a pair of socks. The
buffalo nickel. A penny box of matches. His notebook.
Tucked between the pages, a thin piece of yellow paper
on which his father's address is written.

Ezra had waited more than a year for his father to
return. On his eleventh birthday, nine months ago now,

he'd looked out the window of the orphanage and seen Claire de Lac in a plumed hat and a Chinese kimono. It seemed she alone remembered him. Evidently, she wasn't allowed in to visit him, and so she stood there, lifting a red-gloved hand when she saw him at the window. She blew him a kiss then she shrugged her shoulders sadly and walked away. He'd never seen her look defeated.

Now, the train rolls heavily, reluctantly, it seems to Ezra, into the station, steam gusting from its dark stack. It looks like a creature breathing in winter air, though it's hot, a sweltering eighty-five degrees. Indian Summer, people are calling it. As if Indians have their own version of a season but must wait for the other one to be over before theirs can begin.

The straight line of children breaks apart even though Reverend Horton and his young assistant, Mrs. Worthington, do their best to keep them together. They've stood long enough; they simply can't be still any more. Too much waiting: for the bath, the Bible, the suit of new clothes and now the train, which is late, to take them to their new homes out West where they've all been told that kind strangers are waiting to take them in.

The train shudders to a complete stop. Conductors swing down from steps between cars like monkeys from trees Ezra had seen on his one trip to the zoo. This image occupies his mind for a moment, keeps it from seizing up with the thought he has been trying not to think: We are leaving. We are leaving and we are never coming back. At least not any time soon.

"They finally found a way to be rid of you lot," Irish Danny said last night. He shoveled coal in the basement at the orphanage. "Very convenient," he'd said to Ezra, who stood near the open furnace door. "Free labor shipping out on the orphan train." Ezra had only come to bring him his dinner on a tray and had ended up having to listen to Danny's diatribe about a Protestant conspiracy to kidnap Catholic children and have them raised as Baptists or Lutherans in some Godforsaken western town. A grand conspiracy in the guise of finding orphans and half-orphans homes. Shipping out. That's what Danny called it. Ezra didn't want to listen, but the whole spectacle of Irish Danny heaving coal into a fiery furnace, shouting out his theories was like getting a peek into purgatory and still being able to ascend the stairs back to the world again.

Reverend Horton had stood at the head of the dining room, the new electric lamps along the wall emitting a steady, benevolent light, and explained to them that the train would stop in towns that had already been selected. People who had been deemed suitable through interviews conducted by local representatives of the Children's Aid Society of New York would be awaiting their arrival, which would be announced in the local newspapers. These people would, he said, be grateful for a chance to choose a child to help them on their farms or in their businesses. "You will all have homes! You will receive an education. You will become a part of a family where hard work and decency prevail!" The Reverend had been so moved by the sight of them all listening, by the sound of a few of the older children crying that he himself was moved to tears. But he'd mistaken the tears of the children for gratitude, as an affirmation of his mission. Later, Ezra heard crying again after lights out and a boy two beds down was on his knees, not praying as Ezra had first assumed when he'd raised up on one elbow to see what he could from the dim light of the streetlamp outside the curtained window. The boy was scratching his initials with a fork into the wooden headboard of his bed like a small ghost rising from a grave to carve its name in the unmarked stone.

Now the train waits, huffing in the station. The

terrible banshee screech of its brakes at last dies down. The line of children break apart again as they move toward the step the conductor has just set beneath the one that is too high for the littlest ones. The cardboard suitcases thud against the step, the contents of some rattling as the children are helped up, one at a time. Even Lars, otherwise known as the bully boy, a tall Norwegian older than the rest, does what he's told though he had swaggered last night down the rows of beds saying nobody was sending him anywhere he didn't want to go, that he had decided already he was going to California—out West—where his new family will give him a horse of his own. Now he charges up the step, refusing the conductor's hand, but Ezra thinks he looks just plain scared like everybody else. When Ezra climbs on and enters the car, he's almost relieved to see Lars pushing another boy out of a seat next to a window he decided he had to have. At least some things don't change.

Ezra deliberately sits in the back of the car on a seat only big enough for one. He isn't an orphan like most of them. He still has a father. And although he wouldn't go so far as to say this whole thing is a mistake, he does still feel it's temporary.

After a year and a half of waiting, Ezra had almost given up the hope that his father would ever return. How long would it take to discover the lost boy king? Ezra had been remanded to The Children's Aid Society and scheduled to be "placed out" on a train. At the end, there had been a piece of paper with his father's mailing address. "Gerald Duval, c/o American Express. Cairo, Egypt" was all it said. At least it was somewhere he could write to.

On the next platform, a train pulls in and soldiers disembark. They must be shipping out. There's a war on—how long has it been off? Ezra wonders. There is urgency to things now, no time, it seems, for detailed explanations of anything. While he lived out inter-minable months in the orphanage, the whole world has become temporary overnight.

Reverend Horton stands at the head of the train and counts heads with one finger. He writes the number down in a ledger. Ezra counts, too. Forty-seven. Like the blackbirds baked in a pie—no, that had been four and twenty. But here they all are, packed tight, steaming in their little black coats with all the windows closed. It's only a matter of time before they will all be cooked.

The train lurches and everyone screams as if it's a roller coaster starting up. Ezra falls against the seat, feels the dizzying pull of the train going backward, watches the platform slide away. Then they're in a tunnel, and the lights in the car flicker as if they aren't strong enough to withstand the dark that presses against the windows. You can hear a pin drop except for the steady thunk, thunk of the wheels slowly picking up speed, followed by an unearthly creaking as the train stretches around a curve. Mrs. Worthington, the matron tries to get everyone to sing a hymn—something about crossing over into Jordan. Those who sing, sing timidly. Ezra doesn't sing at all. He stares out the window at the dim lights spaced far between in the tunnel. As they pass each one he can see a rock wall behind it. Between the lights, when the window goes black again, he can see a startled white face outside the window looking in and it takes a minute to realize that this strange face is his own.

The train slows, then gradually stops. An audible shunting of tracks commences and then they begin to move forward, pulling right. They're under the harbor by now. The walls ooze with water, making the black rock slick as coal. They're going faster and the children sing louder and it seems it might be the singing that moves the train, even though he understands it's powered by steam. He doesn't know what else to do but sing with them. Maybe God is listening. God, he thinks for the first time and not the last, is an orphan, all alone in heaven making up the world, and who is there to praise him except these tiny black specks below rocketing along on a toy train of His own invention?

Ezra's voice has to fight its way out of his throat, cracking as it comes. All that half-hearted singing in the dining hall before dinner—now, he thinks, we sound like we mean it. The train breaks through the tunnel into the glare of morning in New Jersey. Sky. The sun between trees. And, oh, thank God, blue again.

They stop singing abruptly as if shocked at what they take to be their own victory, as if they have, in fact, managed to sing their way right out of Hades. There's the world again, after all. How quickly it looms and recedes, rises and falls, buildings ratcheting by. They slow but sail right through a small station. As Ezra watches, he sees a man on the platform reading a newspaper, looking up as the train passes. "Hindenberg Line Cannot Hold!" the headline says, and the man's face, or half of it, looks above it like the moon. What does the man think when he sees them: a train of children, faces pressed to the windows—glory bound, or headed straight for hell? And what moves this man's arm, Ezra asks himself—how does he know it's what we need—for someone to simply see us and to wave?

≋

A day, a night, another day. Time is marked in increments—so many miles of track and the seconds ticked off by a rhythm that replaces all other sound. Hearts seem to beat to it, songs, if they're sung, are sung to it—a constant metronome that governs their lives. Ezra had intended to keep to himself; any friendships made would be over at the station coming up or the one after that. There's no point in getting used to anything except the idea that everything is about to change.

He writes in his notebook: "Dear Father, the country is bigger than I imagined. Have you ever been to Ohio? Did you know there was a town with my mother's name, Lorain?" He isn't sure if that's the way it's spelled but he thinks his father, when he receives this notebook in the mail, will be amazed at how well he can write by now.

A tall girl comes unsteadily down the aisle, head bent forward and down, like a horse straining against a harness. She tries to balance herself with one hand against the seat backs; in the other she holds her suitcase, not by the handle, but pressed against her like a shield. When she raises her head Ezra is shocked to see she has one eye, a black patch where the other had been, and wonders how this had escaped his attention. He's been trying hard not to miss anything. Her dark red hair hangs long and wavy from beneath a green felt cap. She looks to be about twelve years old, though he wonders if the patch somehow doesn't make her seem older. She falls against the seat across from him.

The girl settles herself in the seat, putting the suitcase beside her. With her one eye she looks at Ezra, sizing him up and dismissing him, he feels, with a single glance. She turns and stares for a time out the window. She seems to soon grow bored with that—it's just green out there, only green—and then she turns her attention to her suitcase. She unfastens it carefully as if she doesn't quite trust the cardboard to withstand the weight of her hands. She searches through what looks to be a folded nightdress. When her hand emerges it holds something Ezra can't quite make out; he doesn't want to be caught staring, but when she opens her hand and takes what lays in her palm between two fingers of her other hand and holds it up to the window he can make it out clearly even from across the aisle. A cat's-eye marble, its almond-shaped center glowing green inside the clear globe. She puts it away again, carefully, and glances up at him once, a half-smile on her face, as if to let him know that she saw him watching every move she made and doesn't mind, has, in fact, counted on his attention and now that she has it, will deliver herself of a few things she has to say.

She leans into the aisle, looks to the front of the car where Mrs. Worthington hands out jam sandwiches and cups of tea.

"I'm the only girl left," she says. "The other one got off back there, but she wasn't hardly more than a baby."

Ezra nods. They're not supposed to be talking. But Mrs. Worthington isn't watching them now.

"They don't want girls. You have to be tiny or ugly to get on this train. Older girls can make their own money, never mind how, but I can tell you they make men pay for kisses. They don't need to go to a farm to wash somebody's clothes for free. I feel sorry for you boys. They'll work you hard. Their own sons are in the war now and there's all these fields for you to plow."

Ezra squirms in his seat. He doesn't want to listen to her any more, but he can't stop, either. These are secrets she's telling and she deliberately chose him to tell them to.

"What happened to your eye?" he whispers. He thought he might as well ask since they're already on such intimate terms.

"I took it out."

He's horrified but he leans a little closer across the aisle. "You took your eye out? On *purpose?*"

"My glass one—I took it out. I threw it away. I put this patch on. I don't want anyone to take me. I'm going where I want to go. Nobody is going to want a pirate for a child."

"Didn't it hurt?" Ezra asks, wincing in advance.

"Not the glass one, the first one, the one that got poked out. I fell on a spindle in a dress factory where I worked. That hurt, though I don't remember exactly how it felt. Anyway," she says, "I can still see with that marble. When I want to."

He has never heard of such a thing but he believes her. When she held it up to the light it seemed not like a marble but like something mysterious which might be able to see into the future or at least into the past.

"Will you take it out again?" he asks.

"When it's dark," she says. "It's for seeing in the dark." Like a queen who's uttered a final proclamation she leans back into the faded red of the once-plush cushion. She closes her one eye. The other, he imagines, stays perpetually awake and open, looking into the black patch as if it's a screen in a picture show. Elizabeth—he sees her name written on her suitcase— Elizabeth simply waits for the cat's eye to open, a gift she obviously does not squander but uses judiciously, or only in emergencies. Maybe, he thinks, she sees into her life, a little at a time, and so far, nothing of what she sees has frightened her.

~~~
~~~

The train stops in Arkansas, in a town near a river. "It could be Ft. Smith. I don't know for sure," Mrs. Worthington says when Ezra asks its name. "It could be Rogers." She seems distraught, unsure of more than her location. She's young. Maybe her husband's in the war and she's afraid he's never coming home.

A small crowd of people are gathered on the platform dressed in black, some holding black umbrellas. They look like people who have gathered for a funeral train like Lincoln's, Ezra thinks, to say goodbye. But they're here to greet and are prepared for rain though the sun is blindingly bright. He sees that the pavement is wet. Maybe you can't trust the sun here for very long. That's something Elizabeth might say, he thinks, and smiles to himself at the complicity he already feels as he follows her down the steps.

The crowd parts slightly to let them all pass. Elizabeth saunters down the platform just behind Mrs. Worthington and the Reverend. Ezra can feel the collective disapproval of her by the people who follow behind. She not only has the patch of a pirate, but her saunter probably seems more like an insolent swagger compared to the slow, sleepy shuffle of the rest.

The Reverend speaks to a man in a dusty top hat who must be the mayor and they head up the street. The children follow, suitcases banging against their shins and the townspeople, umbrellas bobbing, throats clearing, look overcome with emotion.

Ezra, right behind Elizabeth, for some reason thinks of snow. He imagines that he's placing his feet exactly in the prints she leaves behind in soft white powder, though her black laced boots leave hardly a mark in the hard baked dirt.

They file into a hall, a wooden cavern with windows high up. They climb a set of little stairs to a stage at the front. Mrs. Worthington arranges them, pressing them slightly forward or back to her satisfaction. "Now, you must put your best foot forward," she says.

"The best foot—is that the right or the left foot?" Ezra whispers to Elizabeth who lets out huge laugh without filtering it with her hand as most girls are taught to do.

Mrs. Worthington emits a harsh "Shhh!" then says the suitcases should be set down. Shuffling and scraping commence, magnified by the high-ceilinged room. Through all this the townspeople hardly seem to breathe. Nobody knows what to do, how to begin.

Mrs. Worthington decides the children should sing and raises her hands, conducting them through the first ragged verse of "Abide with Me" well into the reluctant chorus before her hands fall to her sides and the singing trails off altogether.

Ezra expects the Reverend to say a prayer, or for the mayor to give some kind of speech, but they seem like they just want to get on with the business at hand. Ezra steals a sideways glance at Elizabeth who has her arms crossed over her chest. If she had a watch this is the moment when she would produce it: flip it open, raise an eyebrow—the one over the patch—at the lateness of the hour, and snap it shut again as if she has somewhere else to be.

He looks down at her suitcase and because he knows that the cat's-eye marble is in there he wonders if it can see through the cardboard. He can almost feel it widening as it sees what it sees: the people stepping forward like a dark wave, mounting the stage, emboldened with purpose. Glasses are put on by those who require them. The inspection of the children is about to begin.

Arms are felt for muscle or the lack thereof, eyes are checked for cauls. A man with hands the size of paddles, the dirt permanently imbedded in the skin pushes a forefinger into Ezra's mouth and prods at his teeth. Ezra, nearly choking on the thrust of it, the dirt and sweat, the unbelievable permission of it, shuts his eyes tight and bites down hard. The man bellows and jerks the hand out of Ezra's mouth, holds up the finger and shakes it at him. "You little dog!" he yells.

Elizabeth laughs, and then, to Ezra's utter astonishment and delight, she actually *barks*, her voice high and clear breaking through all the murmuring, all attention now turned to her as if she is the cause of the commotion instead of its only appropriate response.

Apologies and reprimands from Mrs. Worthington;

the two of them are pulled aside. "I know this is difficult, but you're not helping yourselves!" she cries, then sends them back to the line.

"What are they going to do to us?" Elizabeth says to Ezra, "send us *home?*" and she begins to laugh again.

The inspection resumes, though some are clearly reticent now. One elderly couple walks arm-in-arm onto the stage, leaning in a mutual geometry of support. They approach a small boy who has an obvious limp almost reverently, as if they are on the threshold of a gift and finally, just inches away, worry that they might actually be worthy enough to receive it. It's as if the child is choosing them, not the other way around.

Some paper is signed. The three of them depart, and they make a different geometry now: the shape of three, the child holding the woman's hand, the man holding the child's suitcase as if they are all going home after a long journey they have just taken together.

The kindness of strangers. The Reverend hadn't been completely wrong. Ezra is sure that Elizabeth has been watching the same three. She isn't laughing now, she's just looking and Ezra wonders what exactly she sees for her to grow so quiet.

Another child does not go so willingly, but cries pitifully, and a chain reaction follows. The ones who've been near tears all along let go and a flustered Mrs. Worthington tries her best to restore some sense of composure to the group. She urges them to sing again but nobody does. One child openly wails instead. Mrs. Worthington looks helplessly at Elizabeth who chooses that moment to stare at the floor. She places her hands over her ears and shuts her eyes, not, as Ezra thinks at first, in annoyance, but in an attempt to protect herself. She raises her head up slowly, her ears still covered. She opens her mouth.

Ezra hopes she's going to bark again but what comes out this time is a sound that stops the world.

Her voice rises in the cavernous room, up to where the sun scratches against the windows and dust motes swirl down like flecks of brass descending. Elizabeth's voice keens and soars—soprano—singing an *aria* in another language altogether. An impossible voice from such a girl, but there it is, soaring like some wild bird that has flown in the room and now wants out.

Everybody listens. Nobody wails, nobody even breathes until she stops. The last note of the song spirals upward then straight down and flies, it seems, out the door, back from where it came before it found and inhabited this girl on the bare plank stage of a meeting hall in Arkansas.

"Good Lord," someone says. It's what they all want to say.

A young woman steps forward. She might have a choir in mind. "I would like to take *her*," she says.

Ezra watches Elizabeth's face, a stricken look on someone long accustomed to guarding her own surprise. She looks as if she knows she has just given herself away.

The young woman leans close to listen to Mrs. Worthington. Then Mrs. Worthington whispers something to Elizabeth that Ezra can't hear. But he can tell by Elizabeth's face that she's confused.

"Elizabeth," the woman calls softly. And that does it. The stricken look gives way as an iota of hope fights its way forward. Still, she's divided. Ezra can see it perfectly: a wet streak running down below the patch, her hand swiping at the incriminating evidence. The good eye remains utterly dry.

She picks up her suitcase then sets it down again. She lays it on its side and opens it, kneeling there. She feels for the marble, Ezra knows, and, finding it, holds it out to him. "Keep it," she says. "It can tell you where you're going—if you really want to know." She closes the suitcase. She looks up at him. "But if I'd seen this ahead of time, I never would have gotten off the train."

Ezra takes the marble. Unless it's held up to the light it doesn't look like anything much, a piece of glass you might not even say is green. There isn't enough light left in the room to change it now. "But if you had seen it," he says, "and you didn't get off the train, then no one would have heard you sing, and no one would have called your name."

"I know," Elizabeth says. "But I don't understand it. I don't know what any of this is supposed to mean." She stands up slowly. She's about to leave. He hands her the only thing he has of real value: the buffalo nickel given to him by the chief. She looks at it and in spite of everything, she smiles.

The woman is waiting for her. They walk out of the hall side by side. They do not hold hands. But the woman speaks to her as they walk and Ezra can tell by the way that she turns her head that Elizabeth is trying to listen.

≋

When Ezra gets on the train again, unchosen, and they pull out of the station, dusk has a new color— lavender tinged with rust. He thinks he sees her once more on the edge of town. There are two figures in the road, one smaller and striding ahead, the other, taller, pitched forward to keep from getting too far behind. He can't tell for sure, but he thinks it's just like Elizabeth. Wherever she's going she'll get there ahead of time.

He misses her when he looks at the seat she so briefly occupied. He wonders about how little you have to be around some people to never be able to forget them. They carve themselves right onto your wide open heart, right into your wondering mind. His father— well, blood relation took care of that. With his friends at the Chelsea, it was love. Yes, he could call it that. But with Elizabeth it was her voice—that wild bird darting through the eaves that flew inside him and stayed there and will not let him sleep. It's a sound he will come to associate with moments, and there will be many moments in his life, when he feels both free and lost, the way Eve must have felt moving out of Eden, before she even had a word for home.

〰

"Dear Father," he writes. "We are crossing into Kansas. I have never seen so many stars. We are coming into the West and I believe we will see the Indians soon." He tries to picture his father's face as he writes, but he's having trouble remembering exactly how his features fit together. What expression he might have reading his son's adventures.

Ezra writes by match light. One match to each sentence, approximately. They burn at the rate of his thoughts. Sometimes a sentence takes more than one match. The last one took three.

He presses his face against the window. Out there the sky is truly a dome, nothing from horizon to horizon to interrupt the broad reach of the heavens. He tries to count the stars, but new ones keep appearing and because the train is constantly moving, he can't tell where he began. For the first time he has a sense of the world turning, of living on something round. He thinks there might be fireflies out there though the train moves too fast to see them. "But if there are fireflies," he writes, "you wouldn't be able to tell the sky from the ground. Everything would be shining." That last sentence took practically all his matches. He'll get some tomorrow at the next stop. A penny for a box of twenty—it makes him feel rich to hand over a single coin and get so many of something in return. He hopes

Elizabeth holds on to the Indian nickel. He should have told her how Chief Wooden Leg gave it to him, that it's not just any nickel, that it's something to be treasured, not spent. He hopes it will keep her from harm.

Last night they slept in a town, on palettes on the floor of a schoolhouse and ate a real supper, but tonight they're on the train to make up for a long delay outside Wichita while the tracks were repaired. There's no rhyme or reason to their route. Cars are taken on or let off. In one town, the train was split. They're heading south now, instead of west.

Yesterday, a boy had jumped off when the train stopped to take on water. Reverend Horton isn't taking any chances now. But the Reverend snores away. Ezra can hear him from all the way in the back of the car.

Ezra wants to be awake when everyone else is asleep—it's easier to think and he can go and stand in the place between the cars where he feels the wind. He leans against the gate that closes off the steps. The wind in his face makes him squint. He can smell the prairie grass, sweet and dark with dew. He tries to count the stars—it seems important to try. He loses his place, starts over. At night, alone like this, he imagines himself on a grand adventure whose destination he himself decided in advance. Los Angeles, City of Angels. It sounds exotic, not like the plain names of so many Midwestern towns. He will title his notebook "The Amazing True Adventures of Ezra Duval as Told by Himself." His father will be completely captivated, his full attention finally won. This kind of thinking is always easier in the dark when the others are asleep and the night stretches out around him, beautiful and infinite. There's room for all the longing he feels. In these moments he does not feel lonely, but believes he contains within him a powerful signal that can be heard. He leans out farther, over the gate, opens his mouth and howls the way he thinks a wolf might, the way

Elizabeth surely would; he halfway expects an answer.

He goes back to his seat, opens his notebook again. He can't, for the moment, think of anything to write. Maybe he will draw a picture instead. He decides to draw his father's face in painstaking lines, as true to the details as his skill can manage. Ezra runs out of matches; he burns his fingers on the last two.

He drifts off to sleep close to dawn and when he wakes he opens the book to the page he had labored over for so long. It's a face, but it looks like no one that he knows, or has ever known.

~~~

"Dear Father," he writes. "We have been traveling in Texas for days." He holds the pencil tightly, point pressed to the page, but nothing else will come. Distinguishing features have deserted the land. The prairie has rolled down to nothing now and what grass there was has been bitten down to dirt by cows. He feels cheated that he hasn't seen any buffalo. The only Indians he's seen were hunkered down in the stations back in Oklahoma. Big, spreading women were selling baskets and earthen pots. Some with nothing to sell just waited, watched the children get off, get back on again, herded by a tall, skinny woman in a wilted hat and a short minister who looked too tired to talk to God. Ezra watched the Indians stare at the trains. Orphans on trains—it probably didn't make any sense to them. Wouldn't they wonder about the people who conquered them—so weak they could not keep their own children? Chief Wooden Leg, he's sure, would not have understood.

The train is nearly empty now. Reverend Horton got off in San Antonio due to a cable he'd received calling him back to New York, and Mrs. Worthington was left in charge of two Italian brothers with a limited vocabulary (the older seems to be in charge of verbs) and Lars, the Norwegian bully. Technically, she's still in charge of Ezra too, but she seems to have given up on him. She doesn't speak to him unless she has to but occasionally she still feels compelled to say, usually after a stop where once again he isn't chosen, "You could make more of an effort on your own behalf. No one else can." But he wants to get all the way out West as long as he's going, not get stuck along the way in the middle of nowhere where there won't be anything at all to write about.

He has developed strategies for getting passed over in these small rural towns. In one, he perfected a nervous tic, in another, a fit of coughing. He hasn't had to bite anybody again, but he's prepared to, if necessary.

Since he can't think of anything to describe in words he might try to draw a landscape. But this part of Texas isn't giving him much to go on. All he comes up with is a single flat horizon line embellished by a solitary cloud.

"What's in your book there?" Lars, the bully sprawls his Nordic lank over the seat in front of him. There aren't enough boys left to bother, and evidently the Italian brothers aren't worth his time, or maybe between them they've come up with a convincing comeback. So he's finally ventured back to Ezra's private domain.

Ezra sits there as Lars towers over him, acutely aware of the embarrassing fact that his feet don't quite reach the floor.

"It's a story," Ezra answers after a long moment of trying to ignore him, a moment in which Lars only leans closer to peer at the notebook.

"What kind of story?"

"For my father." He feels a strange thrill at saying these words. It's been so long. "For my father," he says again, louder.

"Your father is alive?" Lars asks. "Then why are you on this train—did he send you away?"

"No! He's working to get enough money. Then he'll come."

Lars raises his pale eyebrows. His eyes are small and hard and not a very nice blue. No wonder he doesn't get picked, Ezra thinks.

"That sounds like a story you made up," Lars says.

"It is *not*. It's the *truth*."

"What are you, five years old?"

"I'm *nearly twelve*."

"Eleven. You're not old enough to know the truth. You only believe what people tell you. I'm sixteen and I know the truth. I was a mistake. I was a mistake but I was not to blame. But you, you're living in a fiction."

"I have proof," Ezra says heatedly, not exactly sure what *living* in a fiction would be like but almost certain he doesn't want to find out. "I have the address where he is." He practically tears his way through the pages to get to the slip of yellow paper. It's not where he put it. He searches frantically, a page at a time. He upends the book and shakes it; he gets down on his knees and searches the floor under the seat, around, in front of it. Nothing. Nothing.

Lars gets down on the floor to look but doesn't put much effort into it. "What did it say?" he asks. "I'll bet you have it memorized. *I* would have. You don't need the piece of paper."

Ezra sits back on his heels. His hands are gray with soot from the floor. "It said Gerald Duval, see-slash-oh... American Express..."

"What?"

Ezra writes it with his finger in the soot on the floor. "c/o." He can only imagine the ridicule when he says "Cairo, Egypt." Before he can get another word out Lars interrupts him.

"Don't you know anything? 'In care of' is not an

address. It's not even a place."

"But he works there! They know who works for them there!"

"You really believe this?" Lars asks this question almost gently, the meanness gone out of his face and his eyes for a moment are on the blue side of gray. "He's probably in the war by now anyway. Everyone is going. I will, soon."

Ezra pulls himself back onto the seat. Of all the thoughts he's had lately, this is one he has tried so hard to keep at bay. Until now. His father is close to the war. And it's spreading. He'd heard the conductor saying just last night that there might be a battle in Palestine. The idea of that war, the World War, and his father fighting in it and all that could happen or not happen because of it is too big; counting stars is less overwhelming.

He pulls his knees up so his feet won't dangle. He reaches his arms around his knees, one hand holding the other. "*I am not an orphan*," he says, more to himself than to Lars.

"But you might as well be," Lars says. He stands up, but unsteadily. The train rockets across a long trestle bridge. A brown river surges far below. Lars makes his way slowly to the front of the car, looking back over his shoulder more than once along the way as if he thinks Ezra might run up and grab him from behind. Ezra puts his feet back down. He looks out the window. An enormous cloud of birds passes in front of the sun, darkening it, as if doubt has just crossed the mind of God. Ezra places the book on his lap and stares at it. What's in it, after all, but a bunch of words and a couple of sketches that don't add up to much of anything? There's nothing to believe in now.

There was something about Elizabeth's song that sealed her fate. For the first time since he got on the train, he's afraid he'll never get off, that he'll be shunted from town to town, state to state forever until even America disappears and he'll be on the straight and endless horizon, a ruler laid out to the end of his life, day after endless day without division.

He takes Elizabeth's marble out of his pocket where he's kept it safe and holds it up to the window. He brings his eye up to it and looks. The world bends down, out of its infinite width and breadth and is, for a moment, contained inside a green corona. Quite suddenly, everything, the dust and soot on the seat cushion, the yellow light that falls equally on the dark heads of the Italian brothers, the hills that rise from the ground again, the water tower in the distance that means a town, a horse that has to be coaxed, pulled forward by a girl, to step out of its traces near a barn just outside of this town, even a man folding a newspaper just as the train comes into the station— Marathon the wooden sign behind him says—all of these things are so vivid and fragile he's afraid if he doesn't write them down they will vanish forever.

He does not see the future anywhere inside Elizabeth's green eye. He can't clearly see the man who folds the newspaper, how he will become his next father within an hour, how he, Ezra Duval, will let himself be chosen. He can't predict how later, much later, the man will say he chose him because of the notebook, that he had not come to the station for any child that afternoon. But he had seen him on the platform, writing, and was moved in ways he never would have imagined, by a child who came from nothing and found so much to say.

Elizabeth
1918

Elizabeth Farrell enters the Ozark woods holding the hand of Liberty Watson. Liberty asks her to sing, but she cannot open her mouth. It's all she can do to breathe in this humid, Arkansas air.

Liberty Watson seems to know every inch of these woods. She leads Elizabeth through a forest tangled with ropey vines, across creeks, up steep hills and down into deep, rocky valleys. Elizabeth studies her. Liberty looks as if she could be about twenty or so, about Mrs. Worthington's age, but she could be younger. She's not a Mrs. as far as she can tell; she wears no wedding ring.

How is it that the Statue of Liberty has such a namesake, this woman in a patched skirt and frayed shirtwaist with these work-rough hands? How is it that she is following a woman lighting a lantern to see by? The lantern swings back and forth on a wire handle, squeaking with every step.

Mrs. Worthington pushed Elizabeth to a decision she wasn't really ready to make. Seeing her hesitation, she had whispered to Elizabeth, "I dare you to accept this good woman's offer."

Now, entering a shelter cave with Liberty leading she feels very confused but also protected in a way she has never felt, at least in the presence of another human being. Liberty seemed to know without asking that she needed to rest and found this place for her to sleep. She lets go of Elizabeth's hand to make her a bed of leaves; she sits down and keeps watch over her while Elizabeth sleeps. She doesn't waste her breath with talking. And Elizabeth doesn't try to make conversation. To be an orphan is to have no needs or preferences; she's expected to be grateful. She almost is.

The rhythm of the wheels on the tracks will not let go of Elizabeth. Her body feels like it's moving when it's not. Dream and memory have no border. Days of smoke, soot. The thirsty train stopped for water every eight to ten miles. At some stops, there was nothing to look at but the water tank and its pipe; at others, there was a tiny community, a family living in an abandoned boxcar pulled onto a siding. In one, there was a child in diapers holding a half-eaten, brown apple in one hand, a puppy on a string in the other. This little boy stared, open-mouthed, at the strange cargo of children who looked back, soot-faced from the open windows. One older boy threw a stone.

A mother in the midst of washing raised her head then looked back to her task. A man swung the water pipe to the engine, exchanged some words with the fireman and the engineer. The engine literally sighed as water cooled it. The pipe swung away from the train, dripping, and they were off again, slowly, as if they were terribly heavy, as if the engine could barely shoulder the load it dragged behind.

~~~
~~~

Elizabeth wakes. A rough hand shakes her. At first she has no idea where she is. A strange woman leans over her. And then she remembers. She remembers the train. The boy, writing. Herself, singing. The marble exchanged for a nickel. Being chosen by this woman, here. Liberty.

What does she want with Elizabeth? Right now, she only seems to want her to wake up and get walking.

In the light of day the woods are golden, russet, deep scarlet in places. The dark canopy of trees is so dense the sunlight seems squeezed through a sieve of leaves. Clear creeks crisscross their path. They head south, then east along what Liberty says is War Eagle Creek. To Elizabeth, they are walking straight into the American wilderness, into a place even the Indians must have missed. Liberty says the train depot is fourteen miles from her home.

Liberty tells her the names of trees and flowers and birds along the way. "Bo-dark. Goldenrod. Raincrow." A mockingbird sings a completely different repertoire from the birds of Ireland.

It isn't until they reach a cabin in a glade that Liberty lets go of her hand.

The cabin is made of wood logs. At one end of the long porch there's a single bed. Liberty sets the suitcase on top of it.

Elizabeth can't think of much of anything except her stomach growling, and Liberty must have heard it too "I'll fix you a plate," she says.

The mattress sags when she sits down; the springs sing a rusty refrain, as if glad for human weight again. There's a window at the head of the bed and she stands up to look through it into the cabin. It's just a single room with a curtain dividing it. Newspapers, magazine covers, and seed catalogs paper the walls. There's a table in the middle. Against one wall, a stove. Liberty stands in front it, frying something in a cast iron pan.

Elizabeth gets down from the bed on the porch and goes inside. Above the table, there's a map of the

United States. She comes closer. Where is Arkansas? It takes her some time to find it; she'd assumed she was farther West and is dismayed to find she's only in the middle of the country, and barely that. A state surrounded by other states. America is so enormous it took days to get here from New York, and that was on a train. Walking would take years. The fourteen miles to this cabin took two entire days.

"Daddy's in the war now."

Elizabeth doesn't want to tell Liberty her own father came back but never returned. Maybe there's still hope, for her.

"He used to follow the harvest this time of year. Maybe when he comes back, you can sing in the brush arbor on Sundays. He'd like that. My brother used to sing." Liberty slides the plate onto the table. Steam rises from some kind of stew.

Elizabeth doesn't detect an ounce of doubt in Liberty's voice about her father coming back from the war. But when she mentioned her brother, her voice changed, grew softer, less certain.

"My mother left with a railroad man from Pettigrew. Said he would set her up at a Harvey Hotel out West where she could make good wages. That was some years back. She left my little brother with me so I could take care of him. He was only seven. She sent money. For a while."

"Where's he now?"

Liberty looks at Elizabeth. Her eyes fill but no tears fall. "I found Lucas in a shelter cave. Last spring. He was curled up, the way animals do when they know it's their time. I was in town. To get the doctor. He'd been sick. I really thought he would be all right 'til I got back. I really did."

Elizabeth sits back in the chair, the spoon poised over the bowl. She can't imagine a boy crawling into a cave, dying alone. He must have been very sick. How long had he been there by himself?

"I looked everywhere. Everywhere before I found him. It was his secret place. He never told where it was. He had the influenza. I didn't know then how bad it could get, how fast. Maybe some wounded soldier brought it back, someone he met walking home through the woods."

Elizabeth can't imagine having to search for him, finding him. After how long? She looks at this young woman who found the body of her brother, this sister who knew she shouldn't have left him alone.

"Doctor said it was a miracle I didn't get it, too. There were times I wished I had."

≋

It doesn't seem possible that winter is just around the corner. In Ireland, the wren boys would soon be about, knocking up the doors, singing with their blackened faces, their feathered hats and dark capes, asking for treats, threatening mischief if the treats are not forthcoming. But it hurts to think of that here. Something she once took delight in, as a child. She's no child. She can't remember what it was like to be one.

A shrill whine from the trees fills Elizabeth's ears as night comes on. She's washing the dishes in a tub, handing them to Liberty to dry.

"Katydids," Liberty says. "Calling back the sun. They hate to see it go." She hands Elizabeth a bucket of scraps to toss out, mostly cornmeal full of bugs. "I've saved all I can. Somethin' out there is gonna eat really good tonight."

Elizabeth tosses the scraps in a decaying pile near the garden in the side yard, then lies on her bed, this strange bed that rustles with every move she makes. She feels inside the mattress to see what it's stuffed with. Something thick and papery. She pulls. A dried husk of some kind. No wonder.

The night is full of sounds—the creek and the katydid song is more like a ringing in her ears. A descending note breaks through it all, lonelier by far than a train. A night bird whose name she doesn't know yet? Maybe it's the ghost of Lucas, still waiting to be found in time.

She sits up in bed, the mattress rustling. The dark is fuzzy, the trees indistinct. Birdsong cuts through the wall of ceaseless sound and they stop, all at once, to listen to something else moving in their midst.

An animal the size of a large cat with a bushy tail waddles across the side yard straight for the pile of peelings and scraps. It's wearing a mask, or appears to be. It picks through the scraps then waddles back the way it came, stops at a stump and places something on it. Another creature approaches from where it has been watching, takes the offering. Only when it has finished eating does the first one return to the compost pile to eat. There's a hierarchy, even here.

Elizabeth steps off the porch and the animals scatter. Her bare feet are tender on the many stones imbedded on the path. She stops at the rock ledge surrounding the well. The katydids stop, parting the air around her. She listens hard for Lucas. "Hello?" she calls softly. An owl, somewhere, answers.

〰

In the days that follow, the leaves turn, curl like claws and drift to the ground. Elizabeth watches Liberty's every move, fascinated by this woman on her own in the woods. Since Liberty's father is in the war this is Liberty's world now, a rhythm that almost lulls her, keeps her here a little longer.

"Beans came late this year. Drought one year, flood the next. Next year might not be any. If we're lucky we'll have enough left over to go sell along with a little corn at War Eagle—that's the nearest town with a mill. A grist mill." Liberty sighs when she sees Elizabeth trying to keep track of all this. "You don't know much do you? Nothing practical anyhow. I need your help with turning the leather britches on the roof. I'll go first. You come on up behind me."

Liberty's speech mystifies her. At times she applies the rules of grammar, at others, rules are thrown to the wind. Leather britches. The nouns she uses sometimes make no sense at all.

She climbs up the ladder and Elizabeth gets a good look at the holes in Liberty's shoes, at the ragged muslin that passes for a petticoat. Insect bites cover her legs, mostly on the back of her knees. Elizabeth has a lot of those. They drive her crazy at night and scratching only makes them worse.

The roof has been draped in a patched sheet and spread out upon it, just like she said, are the leather britches. Green beans wrinkling in the sun. Liberty starts turning them over, motions to Elizabeth to do the same.

From the roof, the top of the woods looks like a rolling green sea turning gold. Up here, there's a lot of sky and she finds when she climbs back down the ladder that she's descending into a shaded world in which it would be so easy to lose her bearings.

She could simply walk away; there's nothing holding her. Nothing except the world where a woman presides, a woman who has no particular stake in saving her soul, at least not yet, who has more everyday concerns. Who needs her help with beans for the winter. A woman she can learn something from.

High above them, she can hear a chorus of cries, irregular but steady.

"Geese," Liberty says. "See how they go? It may be hot some days, but they know."

"Where are they going?"

"South. Texas, maybe."

"How far is Texas?"

"Depends on which part. It's as big as a country, all by itself, at least that's what Daddy says. Parts of it have no trees a'tall. Just wheat, everywhere you look. A lot of the men around here go for the harvest. Like the geese, they go south. Their wives and daughters stay. If we had any sense, we'd fly. Some years we nearly starve to death here. Last year we didn't have a hog to scald and hang in the smoke house. We live off what we grow. With daddy gone and no one to hunt, it's been a mean year. We've hit it rough."

"And now you've got another mouth to feed."

"I need somebody to talk to! People don't go out much, since the influenza. They say people from across the ocean don't get it 'cause they got used to it a long time ago. I figured an Irish orphan from a train would be happy to keep me company. You're worth your weight in gold."

It has never occurred to her that she might have cost something. "What did you pay for me?"

"You were free, girl. They just give you away."

Elizabeth doesn't know if that's better or not. Free. She still is, or will be, one day.

They climb down the ladder, Liberty first. Now it's Liberty's turn to get a look up her skirts. "You're chigger-bit bad, girl. I'll make up some tobacco juice to put on 'em. And you need to look out for snakes. Copperheads in particular. You get bit by one of them even a granny woman with a mad-stone won't draw out the poison."

New York City, Elizabeth thinks, with all its sinister streets was easier to navigate than these woods. Leather britches, scalded hogs, chiggers. And granny women with mad-stones. She's not going to ask about them. She doesn't want to know.

One day, Liberty will have to find someone else to talk to. The war could go on a long time; Elizabeth may not stay here until it ends and Liberty's father comes back. She'll wait for the right time. Like the geese, she'll know when it's time to go. But there are things Liberty has to teach her first. That's why she's here. To learn how to survive in the woods. Then she'll start walking to Texas. Follow the geese to the place where the trees make way for the wheat and the sky. How long will she stay in Arkansas? Another hour? A year? One way or another, she hopes she'll get out alive.

〰〰

Liberty wakes her on a night when the moon is full, shaking her out of sleep. It's the creaking of the bed springs that wakes her, the rustling of the husks. She was rolling on the Atlantic until she heard her name. Even that took a while to respond to. It's still hard to get used to being called Elizabeth.

"Get dressed," Liberty says. "I'm going to need your help tonight."

Elizabeth pulls on her boots while Liberty moves about the porch gathering up a burlap sack and a stick about the length of a broom handle with a knob on the end. She hands both of these to Elizabeth then lights a lantern. She steps off the porch into the woods, the light flashing against the trunks of trees.

"Where are we going?" Elizabeth says, using the stick to steady herself as they climb the steep hill behind the house.

"Shhhh. You'll wake them," Liberty says.

Are there faeries here in these Arkansas woods? It doesn't seem likely. The Ozarks have their own spirits, not delicate, but gnarled, she imagines. Tap-root creatures with hair like something from the edge of a marsh—dry, rustling stalks, eyes like burning coals, hearts like wheels of grist mills, grinding.

Elizabeth follows the swinging light, finding it hard to keep up with Liberty's long strides. They pass the arbor made of brush Liberty mentioned, its empty benches just waiting for a congregation to convene. But no one is here; only moonlight illuminates the grain in the benches.

Near the top of the hill the trees give way to a small clearing and on the edge of that, bushes and brambles hunch like crones. Liberty holds the lamp before her, lifting it slowly, peering into the brush. She motions for Elizabeth to come closer, then holds out her hand for her to stop. She reaches for the stick Elizabeth's been using to climb the hill. She hands Elizabeth the lantern, indicating that she wants her to hold it up close to the bush. Elizabeth holds the light. She hears nothing. There's nothing to see. No. Wait. Eyes. Dozens of them, opening, staring. Red in the light. Waiting.

Before Elizabeth can suck in her breath Liberty swings the stick straight into the bush knocking whatever's in there out. Again and again she swings the stick, hard. Frantic rustling follows, sharp cries. The bush erupts but not before Liberty has knocked a dozen to the ground.

"Bring that tow sack over here," she says, no longer whispering. "Pick 'em up and get 'em in there quick."

Their bodies are warm, soft. Red breasts, gray wings. Birds she's heard singing in the mornings.

"Why?" Elizabeth asks, lifting them gingerly.

Liberty laughs. "To eat, girl. To eat. What do you think you've been putting in your mouth ever since you been here?"

Elizabeth shudders. Chickens are one thing. Quail another. But songbirds? It's unthinkable.

"How…"

"The light blinds 'em. Confuses 'em."

"No, I mean how do you eat them?"

"Same way you eat anything else. You put it in your mouth and chew it up."

"Aren't they supposed to go south?

"Some do, some don't. These didn't. There is no other meat right now but robins. Daddy comes back, maybe there'll be deer if we're lucky. Squirrel and rabbit at least. I won't touch a gun. I don't lay traps. Lucas hated all that. And he never would help with the robins. No way."

"Isn't there a butcher shop somewhere—in War Eagle?"

"A butcher shop! In War Eagle! Now, that would be something. You'd have to go all the way to Rogers. It would also take money. Which I haven't got."

The sack is not heavy; it's easy to carry all the way back down the hill. Liberty draws a full bucket from the well and lugs it into the house. From a tin on a shelf above the stove she takes a fistful of something, stirs it into the water. She takes the sack from Elizabeth, pours the birds in carefully. Water barely splashes over the side of the pot.

"You salt 'em overnight," Liberty says. "Easier to clean tomorrow. "Get some sleep now, Lizzie. You did good. Soon you'll be swinging the stick and I'll be holding the light."

It takes a long time to fall asleep. She can't stop seeing those eyes, those red, opening eyes. Can't stop hearing that soft sound their bodies make, hitting the ground. Why were they so close to the ground to begin with? Shouldn't they be in nests, high up in the trees, safe? Robins. An American bird in a country not that far from being wild. How long before the robins understood the light coming up the hill was not the moon? Knew what it would mean to look into its eye?

~~~

She wakes later than usual. Breakfast is on the table, the birds plucked smooth, cooked brown in a cast iron skillet. They're drowning in gravy.

"I made some biscuits to go with," Liberty says. "Saved you some."

When Liberty says grace, the usual one about asking God to bless the food, Elizabeth says a silent one to the birds, asking their pardon. She closes her eyes as she cuts the bird with a knife. Brings a piece on a fork into her mouth. Chews. Swallows, somehow.

"Just thought you should know what you're eating, how it's come by," Liberty says. "To have some part in bringing it to the table. If you ever get lost in the woods, you won't starve. You don't need a gun to survive, you know."

Elizabeth knows this is the kind of knowledge that can save her. This is why she's here, what she came to learn. Something Brigid was probably born knowing. In New York it was hard to imagine this America; some said it was already gone, but this, here, is the America she'd read about in the books of Twain and Long-fellow. A place where money and class mattered not a wit. Where knowing how to keep yourself alive in the woods is something well worth knowing. She's proud to be learning these things. And here, the war seems very far away.

~~~

The nights are cool now, but some days are still sweltering. To Elizabeth, it's just plain hot; no wonder robins don't go south. Today she follows a long ridge-line past the robin's roost, having to go farther and farther to search for greens. On the other side of the hill, as she's descending, she finds a shelter cave like the one she and Liberty spent the night in on their long walk back from the train. Right now, this cave seems like a place where she might crawl into. But is it the same one where Lucas died? The air coming from this cave is cool on her face as she enters, a welcome gift; she's flushed from walking in the heat.

She smells the charred scent of an old fire; she finds a circle of stones around ash. There's a quilt, not far from the mouth of the cave spread over a bed of leaves and farther in, a table of some kind, or at least a plank over top of two logs. There's something at the far end resting upon it. She finds a lantern on a stool and feels for matches that might be near. There are. She strikes one against the plank and in the flare of the burning match sees what's resting on the table. A piece of wood about a foot in length, carved crudely into the shape of a boat. Or, it could be a cradle. The match nearly burns her fingers. She drops it and it glows red, then goes out by her foot. She strikes another and lights the lamp, holding it above the boat. Inside, there are wooden figures. Animals. Their shapes aren't distinct but they are clearly four-legged, and there's two of each.

Did Lucas see it coming—the Great War? His father going off to fight? It must have seemed like the end of the world to him, someone who hated killing of any kind. She backs out of the cave. If Lucas' ghost returns he'll know somebody was here. She probably has a scent, like any other creature.

The next morning she wakes to find a feather on her pillow.

Ezra
1918

Elizabeth, he writes. Ezra does not know her last name. How will he ever find her again? The clarity of his memory begins to blur the more he tries to bring her to mind. He wonders if he has imagined her. Did she actually sing or does he only hope she did? But no, he has the cat's-eye marble in his pocket. He no longer has the Indian nickel.

He turns the wick of the oil lamp on the table beside the bed lower until the flame falters. One more turn and it's out. She said the cat's-eye was for seeing in the dark. He needs it now. He holds the marble up to his eye. The window is all he sees. Four panes of glass and a nearly-half moon beyond. A star, only one, Venus, maybe, the light of all others overwhelmed. Through the lens of the marble the window seems a door he might step through and disappear. He wishes it were so. He does not want to be in this room any longer. He does not want to be in Texas another hour. He's made a mistake. A terrible mistake. The man who took him from the train is a complete stranger, and so this town, with its paltry collection of buildings beneath an enormous sky, feels like his fate, his punishment. And what, exactly is his crime? Failure of nerve. He should have gotten off the train in Arkansas. He should never have let Elizabeth out of his sight.

He sits in the dark, simply holding the marble in his hand. He hears a strange moaning sound outside. A chorus of moaning. He goes to the window. Lifts the sash. A vast sea of something moves in the moonlight near the depot. He opens the window and leans out. Cows. Lots of them, herded by men on horseback into a large pen. The cows sound terrified as they're lashed through the gate, roiling into the pen, nearly running each other over. The bawling of the calves obliterates all other sound as they try to find their mothers. Ezra has never heard such a sound. It doesn't stop, even when the cowboys close the gate, tie up their horses and walk across the railroad tracks to the saloon next door. Earlier, Ezra had been horrified to see a bear chained outside that saloon, guzzling beer that men poured into his once-ferocious mouth.

Ezra can hear their laughter, the rattle of the bear's chain. He sees a square of light as they open the door. Human noise disappears, leaving only the loneliness of the cattle. And the dreams of the drunken bear. There will be no train until morning. This is not the West he hoped for. Maybe even Texas isn't West enough any more.

What had the stranger said to him? First, he'd said his name. Mrs. Worthington must have told him. Or he'd read it on the suitcase. Samuel McPherson introduced himself and said he was an aging bachelor. That he threw himself into his work—an Editor at Large, he said—and had just come from a colloquium in San Antonio. He was on his way to Terlingua, where the train did not completely go. All of this meant nothing to Ezra. He might have nodded politely; he hoped he had at least done that, but he didn't offer anything about himself in the way of conversation. Ezra had decided, at the moment he surrendered, that it would be conditional. He will not speak again.

And now, in Texas, with the cattle crying, over-whelming the music in the saloon that only escapes like steam when the door opens and closes, Ezra hears another sound, below him. Samuel, the stranger, pacing the floor.

When Ezra turns from the window he sees a square of light on the floor near the bed. A heating grate of some sort. He walks to it, careful to make no noise. He gets down onto the floor, peers into the latticed vent. The sound of the stranger walking grows louder and now he can see the top of the man's head of thinning hair coming into view, pausing, turning, then disappearing as he walks to the other side of the room.

In a few seconds, he's back again, though he pauses a little longer before he turns. The next time he simply stops. Does not turn. Just stands there. Ezra moves very slightly, feels something fall from his hand. The marble drops onto the grate then falls through it altogether, glancing off the man's shoulder and onto the floor where it rolls, hits the floor molding, then ricochets a few feet before it stops. The man looks down at the marble, regarding it, stoops to pick it up.

Slowly, very slowly, the stranger looks up until his face is centered in the frame of the grate. Ezra doesn't breathe. Can the stranger see him or does he only hear something above him? The face intersected by the metal grid is not unkind, only puzzled.

Please, Ezra thinks, don't say my name again. Don't say anything to me. Pretend I'm not even here.

Samuel McPherson reaches in his vest pocket and pulls out a handkerchief. He puts it on the table and sets the marble on top of it. Elizabeth's eye cradled in cotton. He passes once again beneath the heating grate without looking up. A door opens. A door closes.

The eye of the marble remains open, waiting. For the second surrender, which is the more difficult. The letting go of the story about his father. Lars had been right about that. "*In care of* is not an address!" No, Ezra's father will not be coming after his son on a speeding train. He abhorred trains. He is, at the same moment Ezra is looking through a heating grate in Texas, somewhere in Egypt, deciphering hieroglyphs on an obelisk, perhaps in Luxor, searching for clues to the burial site of Tutankhamen in the Valley of the Kings.

How would Elizabeth have seen it? Hieroglyphics carved in stone about a boy king dead for thousands of years more compelling to a father than a son who painstakingly struggled to scratch his own story in a notebook with a pen. She wouldn't approve at all. But then, she didn't know. To her, Ezra was probably just another orphan on a train. He'd given her his most prized possession. He'd forgotten to tell her his name.

≈≈

In the morning, the bear is gone, the chain slack around the post. Had it escaped? Or did someone turn it loose? Ezra prefers to think of it running in the mountains, heading for home.

He stands with his suitcase next to Samuel on the boardwalk in front of the hotel, waiting as mules are brought into harness "by Mexican buckaroos with the indispensable help of a bell mare," Samuel explains. Four of these animals are about to haul the canopied wagon that serves as the mail stage. They are the only passengers: an old man and a child. The other cargo: a trunk, a typewriter, a small suitcase. A canvas sack of mail for the village of Terlingua.

The driver talks to his mules in such a way that curse and praise could be distinguished by varying inflection in the pronunciation of the word *pendejos*. Technically, this is Texas, Ezra knows, but by going farther south, they're inching toward the bottom edge of America, a country barely held in place by a river.

Have they crossed all the way into Mexico when he wasn't looking?

As if sensing Ezra's anxiety, Samuel shows him exactly where they are and where they're going on a map spread across his knees. His finger traces the bow in the Rio Grande that cinches Texas eastward before it plunges south toward Laredo. There are no towns to speak of in the part of the map they're going. The word *Desplobado* is printed across it. Ezra points to it. "It means unpopulated," Samuel says.

If Ezra were still speaking he would ask, "Where in the world are you taking me?" because it doesn't look like the world, at least not the inhabited one he left behind. Outside the window of the stage everything looks prehistoric, unfinished, passed over, and empty beyond imagining. And Samuel, frowning at the map wouldn't be able to answer anyway. He may have a map, but he tells Ezra he hasn't been here before, either. The only comforting thought is that Samuel might be just as inexperienced here as he is.

Grassland surrenders soon enough to bare bones, ground without soil, rivers devoid of water. This virtually unpopulated landscape has been barely altered by man. Leaves of plants thrust like daggers; bouquets of thorny sticks scrape the air. The mountains long ago shrugged off any but the most defiant vegetation from their chiseled flanks and look on imperiously from all sides as this tiny mule train inches along.

"We are at the mercy of mules," Samuel says, "on our journey to the south. A paradoxical conveyance considering they freight the raw materials that go to making the detonators for bombs. The same bombs that will bring down the civilized capitals of Europe. That being said, this may be one of the last mule-drawn stages in the area. The combustion engine may be able to haul the mail to and fro, but not the cinnabar; the loads are far too heavy." Samuel clasps and unclasps his long-fingered hands, as if he needs to do something in the absence of a two-way conversation. But taking in these facts requires nothing of Ezra. He simply listens.

The cloud of dust stirred up by the mules hangs like a thin curtain, softening the sharp line of mountains to the west as they climb toward a gap in the hills. Del Norte Gap. Samuel points to it on his map.

"Nobody in New York or Chicago has the first idea about this area. It's the overlooked frontier."

The frontier. His father said it was closed. Gone. Ezra gets his notebook out of his pocket. Finds a pen and writes:

Why?

Samuel watches the word form, the question mark accompanying it that includes him, that invites response. He takes off his glasses. Wipes them. Puts them back on again. For once, words escape him. "That is what we are here to find out," he finally says.

Are there Indians?

"Not many Comanche any more. But Pancho Villa is a notorious son of Mexico."

Is he a bandit?

"Perhaps Villa wants to remind us that taking Texas came with a price."

Ezra considers this, writes a response.

He's too late. Then adds. *Isn't he?*

"The publication of the Zimmerman telegram was the last straw. People worried that the Germans will finance Mexico's recapture of Texas. We wouldn't be in the war otherwise."

Then it must belong to them.

Samuel looks at the boy as if his city upbringing shows on the very features of his face, that he may know a great deal about New York but nothing at all about the rest of the country. "I'm risking everything on a story about a different kind of bandit. An American bandit. An old style robber baron that turned a desert hamlet into a veritable boom town. He's making a fortune. The twist to the story is that the mineral from which he wrests his considerable fortune is hacked from the earth by Mexicans he doesn't trust and then carried to market by mules he has no choice but to depend on. And it's all to profit from the war."

Ezra closes the notebook. He doesn't know what else to write to someone who composes such eloquence out loud. There's a great deal to think about. To look at. To be distracted by. To keep the cresting wave of despair from breaking over him. And so it's a relief to simply listen, to be mesmerized by Samuel's verbosity. His oratorical style fascinates him; it's like listening to one of the lecturers at the Eden Museé. To speak in turn would be a betrayal of the promise he made to himself. He will be an observer with a voice inside a pen. He will not be able to blurt out something he wishes he could take back. Like what he said to his father, "Well, I'll just go to an orphanage, then." Writing urges him to consider everything he says. If he makes a mistake, he'll cross it out, begin again.

In a strange way, since everything else is strange, he just might be in the right place for now. Ezra realizes he's at least lucky. Other boys were picked for their muscles, their full set of teeth. Lars, the bully, is probably pulling a plow right now. And may soon have to go to war. So it's a relief not to speak. Why hadn't he thought of it before? Every word he writes down for this man is gold. His first, simple word *Why* was so powerful Samuel had to take off his spectacles and wipe his eyes before he could even begin to answer.

Distant rumbling. No clouds, no storm brewing in a blue, unbridled sky. Two mules pass from the opposite direction. Two more. Two more. Another six, pulling a wagon stacked with heavy lead flasks. The smell of sweat from the animals is so strong, the sound of their breathing a great effort. Ezra leans out of the Terlingua stage almost close enough to touch the flank of the first mule to pass them. A bell mare. The bell around her neck seems to hypnotize the other mules and they follow her wherever she goes. He looks at the man driving the mules who sits, not on the wagon seat, but in a saddle, on the last, left-hand mule. In one hand he holds a long, braided leather whip. With his free hand he touches his hand to his wide-brimmed hat as they pass. Behind that mule train, there's a second one.

"Quicksilver. The mercury cooked from cinnabar. That's what's in those leaden casks. Those freighters are carrying it to the railhead. It takes them ten days to two weeks to complete their journey; you and I will arrive at our destination tomorrow." Samuel shakes his head in wonder. He makes a quick calculation. "Those Studebaker wagons carry three to four tons each. So there goes about six thousand dollars' worth, give or take. At least a hundred flasks in each wagon," Samuel says. "Could you make a note of that?"

Ezra writes: *September 27, 1918. 200+ flasks. 24 mules. 2 wagons. The driver of the first wagon had a picture of the Virgin on the wagon seat above him.*

"I missed that part," Samuel says, reading over his shoulder. "Good eye."

Samuel has quite a lot to say on this long, tedious journey. About how he heard, to his great dismay, at the Columbian World Exposition in Chicago in 1893 that the frontier had been officially closed. Ezra is not happy to hear this corroboration of what his father once told him.

Samuel said he had searched for the last vestiges of that once limitless frontier and had discovered that this robber baron from the Gilded Age, Howard Perry, had finagled land in a remote part of Texas. From his

Chicago office with the help of an Austin lawyer, he had the land resurveyed, putting any local mining operations and claims to an end. He regularly ran advertisements in Chicago papers for engineers and foremen—that's how Samuel heard about him in the first place.

Ezra listens closely. It's a good story. As good as anything Zane Grey might have written. What Lars might call "a fiction." But Samuel writes for a newspaper. He has to be sure of his facts.

After a long hour of the rutted road, the sun comes into Samuel's side of the wagon. They're both speechless now, the heat stifling, the air helplessly still. Ezra's thinking about the war. This one. The last one. The next one. And the small truce that was struck today. Terms of his second surrender: also conditional. As long as he can hold this man's attention, he has a chance of survival.

~~~

The sun finally drops below the blind of the mountains but leaves the last bit of light undecided on color. Gold, bronze, garnet. The sky tries them all on, takes them off and settles, finally on crimson. Red as the cinnabar before it's squeezed to silver. The evening star asserts itself as soon as the red bleeds out. A coolness descends. The mules slow down, the iron wheels stop grinding. A profound silence older than the dark floods in. Ezra can feel the mountains' exhalation of the day's accumulated heat. He can barely see Samuel's face. His eyes are closed. It's too dark to write. There's so much nothing all around them, they must both be dead by now.

Ezra's hand floats in front of him, a blunt, gray star. He touches his fingers to Samuel's wrist.

Samuel moves. He opens his eyes. Ezra slowly

withdraws his hand.

A lantern hovers in the dark then grows larger as it comes near.

Words in Spanish. "*Señores. La casa de la viaje.*"

"We'll stay the night here," Samuel says to Ezra. "We're halfway."

Mules step out of their traces; the chains ring a dull chime. Leather reins slap the ground as they fall. The animals, carrying only the weight of themselves now, walk a short distance to water, their shapes disappearing into darkness beyond the reach of the lantern light. But they can still be heard, sucking noisily from a trough. The moon sets, leaving a smear of orange in the west.

Ezra crawls out of the wagon, steadied by the man with the lantern. His body, unbending, is still rocking, his muscles taut and tired from bracing and balancing over ten hours of rock and rut.

He is led inside a large tent with a wooden floor, guided to a palette onto which he immediately collapses. He falls asleep only to be awakened by his bladder that he was too tired to empty before he lay down. Or is it the coyotes that wake him? Or the escaped bear roaring once again? He stumbles outside into a sky so riddled with light that even with no moon at all he needs no lantern. The Hudson Fulton electric exhibition had been a pale imitation at best. The stars that belong only to Texas press close and stare as if this is the first human they've encountered relieving himself in their presence. Some of them, as he watches, throw themselves, streaking, out of the sky leaving green exclamations behind. Whatever he might write in the notebook is insignificant in comparison. He finds a stick of wood near the tent and scrapes the letter "E" as large as himself upon the rock-hard ground.

He's never felt so far from everything, from everyone he's ever known.

≋

Another day of hooves, sweat and dust. The grinding of the wheels is internal now. They've exchanged mules and stages for the rest of the journey and pass not a single house or barn in this broad basin where Samuel says leviathans once roared and roamed here, multiplied and lost their way. This is a West that Zane Grey couldn't even have dreamed up.

By late afternoon they cross a creek and ascend a long, slow grade that levels out in a cluster of buildings. One building predominates, crowned with tall smokestacks. "That's a furnace," Samuel says. "One of several places where they cook the ore down. They fire it, then condense it into the liquid mercury we saw in all those flasks. You can smell it from here."

That furnace could be the source of heat for all of Texas. The pervasive sulfur smell makes Ezra think of an anteroom to Hell where sinners endlessly toil. That's how Ezra will describe it when he's good and ready to write it down.

But there's life here. Wagons come and go bringing ore, taking away an essence. Mexican freighters load and unload. Women and even children carry water in buckets on their heads in the last of the daylight.

To the east lanterns drift among low rock buildings like fireflies in the dusk. As they come closer, Ezra can make out elderly women carrying the lanterns, escorting young girls in their dresses of blue and yellow and pink. They head toward a red, tin-roofed building bursting with light and music. A dance. Even here.

Crowning the hill above the mine there's a mansion of sorts, all its windows dark. Stylized Spanish porticoes grace a very unremarkable two-story cement box. "That's where God lives," Samuel says, following Ezra's gaze. "Howard Perry's hardly ever here. But nothing happens without his official say-so. Except the Saturday night dance."

Near the hotel a long, low building with a porch running its length swarms with lines of people. They go in empty-handed, come out with sacks. All of this activity can be seen from Howard Perry's mansion. But the mansion is dark. God isn't at home tonight.

In front of a small stacked stone building, three men tied to iron stakes scoop beans from battered tin plates and look up as the stage passes. The mules stop in front of the Chisos Hotel, a two-story building made of wood and tin, also with a long porch. Their new home, for now.

"Pay attention to everything," Samuel says. "Describe what you see."

Can Samuel not see? He can. And Ezra can talk. But this is the bargain they have struck. As scribe, Ezra will need two notebooks, one to be seen like a copybook at school, one a diary, for his father. There's a great deal to be written. Mrs. Worthington had said to send letters back, that they want to know how he's doing. He can do that. One day, he'll send the notebook. It's the only way his father will be able to find him when he returns from Egypt. His father will have to search a little, start at the orphanage, discover that he was sent to Children's Aid, find out that he was sent away on a train and that Samuel McPherson, Editor at Large, took him to Terlingua, Texas to become an assistant reporter. His father will have to make an effort. At last, Ezra will be worth searching for, leaving a tell-tale trail of words behind him to make sure he can be found.

Ezra walks into the dim entryway of the Chisos Hotel. The bare wooden floors amplify every step, no matter how cautiously taken.

He looks around the lobby, if you can call it that. A high desk near the door has only eight keys hung on nails. No bellhop. Definitely no elevator. It's so different from the Chelsea, no balconies, just a long, wide porch overhang that shields some of the small dining room from the relentless sun. What would Claire du Lac make of this place? Senda would surely cry.

Samuel gets the key to their room from a woman who appears when he rings the bell. They climb creaking stairs to the second floor to find room number eight at the end of the hall.

Ezra puts his suitcase down. He sits on the bed, not sure what to do next. Samuel sets the typewriter on the crude table that will serve as a desk and places a folder full of paper next to it along with several fountain pens and a bottle of blue-black ink.

Samuel sits down on the opposite bed. "I'm sure this is all very strange to you. It is to me, as well. But I'm glad you're here."

Ezra only nods. What would he say if he took the time to answer on paper? Could he even begin to say where he's come from and why? But maybe Samuel knows. He spent a long time talking to Mrs. Worthington at the depot before the train left. He looked sad about whatever she'd told him. He hopes Samuel doesn't ask him a lot of questions. He really doesn't have any answers. One day, his father might appear, ready to take him back to New York. But if he showed up at this very door tomorrow, Ezra wouldn't know what to say to him, either. All he can do for the time being is watch and wait. Something he knows very well how to do.

QUICKSILVER COURIER–October 15, 1918
by Samuel McPherson, Editor at Large

Arriving on the Terlingua Stage a fortnight ago with my young protégé Ezra Duval I find Howard Perry's mining operations in a state of enviable production. From his manse on the hill he can survey his kingdom. E. Duval likens this kingdom to a hive on the moon, an apt analogy considering the terrain of lunar demeanor and proportion. Three shifts keep the mine producing around the clock. This honey squeezed from rock requires the Scott furnace to be going at all times. Indeed, it must not cool. A constant stream of mule-drawn wagons brings the raw ore down from the mine. My able assistant recorded the tally for the week: seven hundred and forty flasks at $300 per flask one can quickly ascertain the enormity of profits to be made in this unlikely cul-de-sac in Texas. The war in Europe has created an unprecedented boon in quicksilver, though that war may be very close to being over. My assistant points out the wonder a soldier might feel knowing that the bomb he sends flying is detonated by a material hacked out of bare mountains by Mexicans and hauled to market by their mules. Thus the nineteenth century and the twentieth remain irrevocably entwined.

November 15, 1918

Dear Children's Aid Society,

You asked me to write. It took a long time to get here. The train was the easy part, believe me.

Four days ago when the war ended everyone shot guns in the air. It almost seemed like another war was starting.

I am in a place called Terlingua. It is in Texas, but just barely. I live in a hotel (I have always lived in a hotel). This one is called The Chisos, after the mountains. It means ghosts, but I haven't seen any. It only has eight rooms. We're in number eight.

There is no elevator and when I look out the window I see mountains instead of skyscrapers. In place of the trolleys on 23rd St. there are mules who only understand the Spanish language. I am helping to write a column called "The Quicksilver Courier" for Samuel McPherson, Editor at Large, for a newspaper in Chicago.

Have you heard from my father? Please tell him I am well. Tell him I am having my own adventure.

I remain, very truly yours,
Ezra Duval (still)

Elizabeth
1919

Every time Elizabeth thought she'd leave, like the geese, she only stood and watched them go. Yesterday, on the first of February, there had been snow. It was more decoration than accumulation, lasted less than a week. The ice that followed is another thing. It casts a kind of spell, a clear sheath over everything, living or dead. Everything shines in the light of both the sun and moon, shattering like crystal when the wind blows. Her heart hibernates, draws down the shade. Life goes on indoors, slower all the time.

The Armistice had been signed back in November. They wouldn't have known if it hadn't been for a soldier Elizabeth came across tramping through the woods. He was on his way home to Clifty and was amazed she knew nothing about the war being over. He told Elizabeth it was high time she had a radio. But she and Liberty have no electricity. Or telephone. And so Liberty still waits for her father to return.

So much has become familiar that was once strange: not just the names of things that Liberty taught her, but the deep song of the woods that she hears so clearly now. If she were blind she would know her way by sound alone, ice breaking in a bucket, a deer snorting when startled, the sound a rain-crow makes just before rain. But even with a patch over one eye she is not blind and she pays close attention to the differences between medicinal and poisonous plants, which animals go to ground, which take to trees. She's nothing but eyes and ears now. Elizabeth is waiting, too.

And still, Liberty's father does not return. By March, Liberty has no choice but to go off the mountain. She takes Elizabeth with her to the post office in Larue. The postmistress, a new one, Liberty tells her, might have something for her, a letter from France. She'd written her father about Lucas. But there's no letter. Elizabeth isn't surprised, not really. She knows how this story goes. Fathers disappear. And when you do find them you wish you hadn't; the face they turn to you is a face you can spend your life trying to forget. Wars may be declared to be over, but they never end.

~~~

Liberty places an order for seeds from a catalog and puts a dollar in change in an envelope. When the seeds come, she tells Elizabeth they'll be taking them to sell them near War Eagle and that with the war over, people will be thinking of spring. They'll go up and down the roads of Benton County knocking on doors, or, rather, Elizabeth will while Liberty watches from the road. Elizabeth remembers the raccoons the first night on the cabin porch, the lookout getting fed by the scout and that's how she'll be now, bringing money back.

A week later the seeds arrive and regular visits to the world at large begin. The first house, more than two hours walk from the cabin, belongs, Liberty says, to Leroy Brawley, who'd fought at Fayetteville with Ben

McCullough and the Texas Infantry. He was at the War Eagle mill when they had to burn it down to keep the Yankees from getting it. He survived that, then lost his leg to a Yankee bullet lodged deep against the bone. "He still gets a soldier's pension. He has money," Liberty says. "You go up there and knock on that door and tell him you got tomato seeds—Arkansas Travelers. Also Blue Lake Beans. He's nearly seventy, but he's not completely mean."

Elizabeth climbs two tilting steps to a sagging porch stacked with yellowed newspapers. The top one says in bold letters, "Kaiser Wavering?" Elizabeth looks at the date. Five months ago. "The Hindenberg Line cannot hold if the Western Front continues to push back the German army." A lot has happened. Alliances formed and broken, armistices signed while she sat by the stove in Arkansas. Is there still an Ireland? She's fallen through the cracks somehow and if it wasn't for Liberty needing provisions, they'd still be up there waiting for her father, cut off from the rest of the real world where real history is being made.

She knocks on the screen door, and it nearly comes off the hinge even though she's barely tapped it. She listens. A thumping sound emanates from deep within the house. Several dogs begin to bay. Leroy Brawley emerges from the back, swinging on his crutches, knocking the dogs out of the way with them. A long, white beard falls onto his chest over the brass buttons he's left unbuttoned on a tattered gray coat. His left pants leg is pinned up, swaying slightly as he comes to a stop on the other side of the screen door. The hounds flop down on the floor around him.

"You must be the orphan," he says, "from the train. You're still here?"

How does he know? "I'm selling seeds," she says, avoiding the question. "Arkansas Lake. Blue Travelers. Those kind of seeds."

"Now that would be something to see," he says. "An agricultural wonder. Blue tomatoes. Beans that won't stay put on the poles." He looks over Elizabeth's head to where Liberty stands, waiting on the road.

"The other orphan up and left, went back to New York," he tells her.

"What other one?"

"The other orphan. Family in Combs got her over in Berryville."

Other orphans? Other trains? They must be the children whose fathers died in the war, whose mothers cannot keep them.

Why did Liberty really bring her here? Maybe her mother sent for her, has a job for her at a Harvey House and the only reason Liberty got Elizabeth from the train is so there'll be someone left to take care of her father, if and when he comes back. She doesn't know what to think now.

"Do you want some seeds or not?" she finally says.

"Well, Missy. I can see you've got a schedule to keep. The world's going to end any minute, if it hasn't already. But I'll take two of those Arkansas Blues." He hands her two nickels. "Keep the change."

"There isn't any," she says.

"Inflation! Everything goes up except my pension. War ain't worth it, young lady. It doesn't end anything. And the wounded walk around forever, looking for missing parts." He looks up, beyond her, at Liberty again. "Some of us," he says, shaking his head, "have lost more than we can admit."

Elizabeth takes the two nickels to Liberty. They're not like the nickel the boy on the train gave her, the one with the Indian and the buffalo. She put that one in a box under the bed this morning so it wouldn't get mixed up with seed money and get spent by accident.

Liberty's impatient to get to the next house. "Two more of those nickels and we can buy some coffee, flour, maybe, if we're lucky. So far, we're lucky, but it's too soon to tell. "*You're* good luck," Liberty says.

Elizabeth doesn't feel lucky. She walks down the rutted road, thinking of the other orphan who went back to New York. To find what's left of her family. The dirt road is flanked on both sides by dried weeds. "Yarrow," Liberty says. She's used to anticipating Elizabeth's questions and beats her to it this time. But now Elizabeth wonders if all Liberty's teachings are for a definite purpose. She's not being taught, she's being trained. Now, out in the world of newspapers and news and other people with their superstitions and attitudes, she feels exposed. Liberty looks shabby, harried. Guilty. And she herself is no more than the orphan girl from the train, talked about all over Benton County. Up until now she's been a rumor, evidently. Now she's actual.

"Do you think your father's coming back?"

Liberty answers with her own question. "Since we're talking about family, I didn't want to pry, but who are *your* people? You never did say."

Anything would be better than describing the truth, the scene at the asylum at Ward's Island, that half human being pulling a cart while an idiot laughed and sang and flicked him with a switch. She doesn't feel like making up another story. Or telling the true one about her mother. Let Liberty make her own conclusions.

Liberty waits. Without impatience, she says, "Well, keep your secrets, if you can. I don't seem to be able to keep mine."

A wagon piled high with logs drawn by a team of trotting horses comes around a curve. The man holding the reins tips his hat as he passes and Liberty and Elizabeth walk into a tunnel of dust.

"Here's the next house. Miss Bowen's. She used to be the Postmistress."

Elizabeth goes up to the door. This porch isn't sagging, it's swept. Elizabeth knocks and sees a hand push aside the curtain covering the glass pane. The knob turns and the door opens.

"I don't need any seeds."

She looks beyond Elizabeth to Liberty standing in the road. "I thought Liberty would have lit out by now, gone and become a Harvey Girl like her mama, what with the war and all the rest, now that Lucas is out of the way."

"What do you mean Harvey Girl? Are they dancers in a show?"

"A Harvey Girl works for Mr. Harvey in one of his Harvey House hotels or restaurants along the railroad. They're high dollar places, cloth napkins and all. If I was younger I wouldn't think twice about joining up. It's like the army except for women and you don't have to shoot anybody. You might think about it; since you know a lot about trains already."

Elizabeth can't help but feel that Liberty has a plan, a plan for escape. Miss Bowen seems to think so and postmistresses are supposed to know everything. This seed money could be Liberty's ticket out leaving her orphan girl to tend to her father. A stand-in, not only for Liberty, but a substitute for Lucas as well. Maybe she did get rid of him, or didn't go to get help on purpose.

Everything's changing now that they've come down from the mountain. She's been asleep for too long. She needs to be more careful. Pay closer attention. Make plans to leave before Liberty does, starting now.

〜

Liberty's father returns on an ordinary spring day, gray and gaunt, a shadow walking up the hill through blooming redbud. Elizabeth is surprised to see him in the flesh. To her way of thinking, he had either died in the war or had stayed in France. Or left his memory there at the bottom of a trench.

He's not in uniform, as she expected. He's not exactly old, but aged, his dark hat molded to his head, his black clothes shiny with hard travel.

Liberty turns from the stove, actually drops the pan she's just washed and dried onto the floor. She doesn't bother to pick it up, just stands there waiting, as if she's not completely sure it's him or what she should do if it is. Maybe she hadn't planned on being here when he got back.

He cuts his eyes at Elizabeth when she moves in the corner where she's writing out the accounts of the seeds they sold.

"Where did she come from?" Those are his first words. Not "hello," not "how are you, daughter?" Not "It's so good to be home." His home has been invaded while he was gone.

"She came from New York. An orphan, on a train," she says hesitantly, as if she didn't expect his first words to be a question that had nothing to do with a father coming home from the war. She rises from the chair but remains behind the table. Her father doesn't take a single step toward her. Finally, she crosses the room and kisses him on the cheek.

"Daughter," he says. As if he just remembered who she is.

Elizabeth waits for him to say something more. Surely he must have a lot to say.

"I'll eat something if you have it, if not, then I'll just sleep. I'm dead tired."

"I'd like to know about France," Elizabeth says.

"I don't want to talk about France."

"I'll bet people there don't have to eat robins," Elizabeth persists.

"Elizabeth's been helping me up at the roost," Liberty says, pouring coffee into a chipped mug. "Now you're back, we can have venison again."

"One more mouth to feed. Not a problem if you're useful. We can use a useful girl."

"She can sing. When she wants to," Liberty says.

"That'll make Lucas happy. Where is he—out traipsing around the woods, as usual?"

Elizabeth looks at Liberty, at the sudden stiffness in her stance. She drops her hands to her sides. "I wrote you about Lucas."

"Since when can you write? I didn't get any letter. Where is he?"

Liberty looks helplessly at Elizabeth then back at her father. "Daddy, Lucas died. About a month after you left."

Elizabeth watches his face closely, the muscles working underneath, struggling against the shock of this news. He sets the coffee down.

"He had the influenza," Liberty says. "I couldn't find the doctor. When I did he said he couldn't have done anything anyway."

Elizabeth watches her tell this story, leaving out the part about the cave. If death of a child has any reason, then it has to be illness or accident. Not because his sister left him by himself, not because she couldn't find him when she returned.

Elizabeth slips away. She doesn't want to hear Doyle Watson's next words. He looked like he was barely able to contain himself. She can hear their voices, strident, rising and falling. Shouting. Crying. She can't go back there tonight.

An owl glides from a treetop past her, so close she can hear the air strained through the thick feathers of its outstretched wings. It finds another perch and begins a plaintive call. After a time, she thinks she hears an answer, though it's coming from so far away it's hard to tell. She follows its call all the way to the shelter cave, the only place she can think of where she can stay warm for the night.

The mouth of the cave reveals itself, a black mouth open in the dark. She bends to enter through it, feels her way to the table—she remembers there was a table with a lantern. Some matches. Somewhere. She lights the lantern. Sits down on the quilt, hugs her knees to keep warm.

Doyle Watson's frame fills the mouth of the cave. Liberty must have told him where it was. Or, he followed Elizabeth. He looks around, peering into the dark places beyond the lantern's light as if he expects to find Lucas, alive after all, only hiding.

Now he's walking toward her. She stands up. He stops in front of her. "For God's sake! I didn't know! I didn't know I'd never see him again!" His eyes beseech her. "I need to know if *you* can see him," he says.

She feels a cold heat run through her, a freezing heat that holds her in place.

He reaches out, touching the patch over her eye. He lifts it slowly. She lets him see the cloudy scar. He's leaning so close she can feel his breath upon her face as she keeps herself from blinking, looking past him, like she did with the inspector at Ellis. She has never felt more exposed. Not in the showers at Ellis, in the bath beneath the watchful eyes of the nuns lest she touch herself in the wrong way. But this is not about touching. It's about being seen as if her clouded eye affords a view of everything inside her, open now to this father grieving for his son.

The thin layer of hope she's held onto begins shrinking, cracking, peeling away. Everything she thought she knew is now in question, what she has come to think of as solid and real about Liberty and herself, the very nature of shelter. It's so temporary. Now this man looks at her, into her. Through her.

"I want to know if you can *see* him. Talk to him. If that's why you come here. To his cave."

He looks like he's going to cry. "Sing to Lucas," he

says. "Please. Liberty said you could."

She feels herself falling though her body doesn't move. She didn't know she was afraid. Hadn't she managed until now? She can't sing. She can't even open her mouth to say she can't. The animal in her body, like a muzzled thing unleashed, trembles. So this is fear, not that he will harm her, but that she has no idea what to do with the kind of sorrow he's letting her see. He might completely break down and weep and that she simply can't bear.

"*Please*," he says again.

Should she run?

There's nothing she can do to help him. Or anyone. She runs.

Elizabeth nearly knocks Liberty down on the path to the cabin. Liberty grabs her by the shoulders. "Did he hurt you?" she says.

Elizabeth shakes her head. He didn't hurt her. It's worse than that. Physical violation is one thing, but what he did—pleading with her, as if she could bring Lucas back with a song—scared her half to death.

Liberty reaches for Elizabeth's hand. "I want you to take this." She presses something into it. Elizabeth opens her hand. A single coin—her Indian nickel from the box under the bed. She must have known it was important. Liberty also hands her a few dollar bills. The seed money. Not for Liberty's escape, but for her own.

Elizabeth puts it in her pocket, looks up at Liberty for some explanation.

"It would kill him if I left. I don't need more guilt following me down the road. I'd never get far enough away. Now go, Lizzie. Please go."

Liberty walks past her toward the cave. Elizabeth wants to run after her; she's been following her for almost two years. This woman can somehow stay by her father, even when he's badly broken. That's what daughters do.

Ezra
1919

Ezra and Samuel are treated as total strangers in Terlingua no matter how long they've been here; everyone seems to regard them with suspicion. When Samuel telephones his editor in Chicago, the store manager listens in on his conversations. The woman who gave Samuel the key to their room the night they arrived turns out to be the cook, and when she brings their food to the table in the dusty dining room, she studies their faces, searching for some resemblance that, any day now, will reveal itself. Or for an ulterior motive that could jeopardize the continuing operation of the Chisos Mining Company.

"They probably think we're spying, that we're trying to start up our own mine. Perry's known for his paranoia and strict secrecy," Samuel confides. With the war over, the need for quicksilver is fading.

Ezra doesn't know about mines and mining. He does learn the names of plants and birds and other desert animals from a book Samuel purchased for him at the Trading Company. *Ocotillo. Lechugilla, Candellia.* These come from the plant section. Cactus. They're bare now but in the spring, from the illustration and description in the book, they will have vibrant flowers. The birds are strange to him; there's not a pigeon anywhere, but the white-winged doves must be their cousins. And there are curious birds that hop about and sometimes fly right through the window, if it's open, or perch on the sill looking in, if it's closed. He finds them in the book. Cactus wrens. There's a lot to learn in Terlingua, Texas.

The few white adults mostly keep to themselves on the west side. Ezra is drawn to the families of the miners; after all, they make up the great majority of the population here, and carry on much of their lives outdoors. If he didn't have things to write down he'd be lost. Just watching the families together, herding goats, gathering herbs, hanging out laundry, singing, dancing, drinking, fighting, loving, in general, leaves him feeling like a homunculus that tries to bring back news to Samuel about what the living still do.

When Ezra begins to attend the school, housed, to his shock, in a tent, he starts to learn a lot more than spelling and arithmetic. He quickly learns a new language, at least by listening. If and when he starts to speak again, it will be in this language. The teacher, Miss Gaynor, doesn't seem to know what to do with a child who doesn't talk. She does, however, give him high marks on his written assignments.

Speaking Spanish is forbidden in school, but he picks it up at recess and lunch in the sun-baked yard. There are two different camps, one playing mumblety-peg, the other something highly competitive with marbles. He lingers with the latter, learns slang, at first. *Cabron.* Goats are more than livelihood; they make good insults as well.

Inside the tent classroom there is conversation but once outside the makeshift door a protocol everyone agrees to takes hold. Mexican girls go to the south and east side of town to tend their goats, or carry water, or sew their dresses for the *baile*. In baseball there is regular intermingling of the races, at least among the boys. Only at the dances do races of both genders mix but the girls are heavily supervised by a gauntlet of wary, watchful grandmothers.

Ezra leaves the school by himself, walking past the stacked rock houses of the miners, watching mothers greeting their children with excited cries and questions about what they learned that day. At night, after a silent supper with Samuel in the hotel, he haunts the streets, looking in windows at people eating supper together. Lingers before the scene of children being put to bed. Some of them are sung to. He walks back to the hotel alone, caught in a bind of his own making. He can't communicate with anybody but Samuel, and with him, only in writing. Samuel gives him a lot of freedom, for which he's grateful, but sometimes he feels quite at loose ends. Samuel's often busy, writing. Translating the notes Ezra brings to him.

Ezra begins to take an interest in the ubiquitous goats that graze the hillsides. These desert goats scavenge with impunity, eating at least some of the tin cans strewn on the hillsides behind the houses, devouring all fruit and vegetable peelings.

Today, a boy and a girl herd the goats together near the crest of a hill east of town. Ezra watches them from a respectful distance. If they notice him, they ignore him. They've seen each other at school. The boy, Enrique, is leaning over one of the kids, trussing its four feet together. He then slips the creature over its mother's head where it hangs like a yoke. The mother accepts this burden. There are four others bunched in a group in the small shade of a greasewood bush, waiting their turn.

Enrique releases the first nanny. His sister, Consuela, picks up a stalk cut from an *agave* plant and begins to walk toward the goats with their upside-down offspring. Slowly, they move down the hill to a crude corral made of *ocotillo* sticks bristling with thorns. Ezra knows it's *ocotillo* because he stopped to look at the spindly plant once on one of his early morning walks with his guide book. He had been surprised to see leaves sprouting from what he thought were dead sticks. It seemed they only had to have their roots a few inches deep and they could keep growing, even when cut off from the original plant.

The nannies navigate the rocky terrain, their kids swaying slightly as they walk, transporting them to the corral after their risky birth in the open. Ezra follows a few feet behind. He would have asked questions, if he were speaking, but they have been answered just by watching and he marvels at the economy of the nannies carrying their own kids instead of having to be hauled one by one by the boy and his sister to safety.

Inside the corral, the kids are lifted off the necks of their mothers that shake their heads vigorously, no doubt amazed at the sudden lightness they feel. Now the girl goes inside a small lean-to and carries a young dog, barely more than a puppy, back to the corral. She glances at Ezra, who watches everything. Her brother pulls one of the nannies to the ground and holds it there while the girl puts the puppy to suckle. It does so, happily, and although the nanny lifts its head to look she seems reconciled to feeding this changeling.

Ezra moves closer to the corral.

Consuela looks at her older brother—they look very much alike, now that Ezra sees them together.

As if Ezra had asked what they're doing, Enrique turns to him and answers, "It is so the goats will know the dog and follow. It is no longer just a *pero*. It is not really a *cabron*. But it will think like one."

He wishes he could already speak fluently to them in their tongue, walk with them and the goats and the new dog who will soon understand the nature of the animals he watches over. To even be here on "their side" is not the norm. He does not know what they are thinking, if they even give him a thought at all. Maybe Consuela only feels sorry for him. He wishes she, in particular, did give him a thought. That she and her brother might want to know him and will one day invite him into their home.

Consuela approaches Ezra, surprising him. "*Donde es su madre?*" she asks.

He looks down.

"*Muerto?*" she says.

He nods.

She crosses herself. "*Lo siento,*" she says as if he is someone to be pitied here. "Most people have mothers. Fathers die in the mines, yes, the wars, but *las madres* should be forever."

She calls the goats by name as if they are part of her family, too. Estrella and Mocho are the only two names Ezra catches. Enrique says something to Consuela Ezra doesn't understand and then he leaves, perhaps for a baseball game behind the school.

The puppy, Loco, knows many things innately. But in this terrain, Ezra must learn everything from scratch, by acute observation. He must take notes. First and foremost, he must be respectful. Consuela's grandmother, her *abuela*, he guesses, must be the old woman who right now gathers herbs in the hills nearby; she keeps a close eye on him, observing his every move. Maybe she's taking notes, too. Consuela's uncle, he remembers Enrique saying once in school, is mucking ore, underground. But Ezra does not know anything about their parents. Perhaps they are *muerto*, too.

Clouds have been building all day. A burgeoning citadel of indigo forms an anvil filled with rain. Lightning frets inside the cloud, undecided, until a bolt is chosen to be sent down to the ground. A volley of thunder follows.

The goats panic as cherry-sized hail pelts them and Loco whirls around the unraveling herd. Consuela runs on the precarious hill of loose stones and *lechugilla* never losing her footing in bare feet while Ezra hobbles awkwardly in leather-soled, slippery boots. He falls behind and his feet slide on scree, pitching him forward. He catches himself with his hands, grabbing instinctively at anything that can break his fall. His left hand closes hard around a stalk of *ocotillo* that punctures his palm in several places. Consuela doesn't hear his cry of pain. She has to get the terrified goats through the gate with the help of a dog new at this task. But the goats have suckled this whirling, barking dervish and soon surrender to its authority. All get through the gate except for one kid skittering back and forth in the rubble of rocks. Consuela tries to grab it. In its panic the kid wriggles free, bolts back up the hill. Ezra waves his now-bleeding hand to turn the kid around but it shoots past him. Then Consuela is running past him, shouting as he turns to follow her up the hill. A tawny shape streaking sure as an arrow toward the kid, with hardly a pause in stride, grabs it between its jaws and disappears over the crest of the hill. Consuela stops, cries out something—Ezra can't hear the words. Then she's turning and looking at him and his bloody hand. At his useless, wordless mouth.

Lo siento is not even close to conveying what he feels. Her distress is crushing and he sees clearly that she is not a little girl upset by a lost pet but a person charged with the care of her family's livelihood. Because he could not help her she has just failed; others will suffer because of it. Even if he could speak, there is nothing Ezra can say that will change anything. There is too much to say, always. When he was still speaking, he could change nothing at all with words.

The grandmother lumbers up the hill, shouting at

Consuela, at the sky. Ezra reaches into his pocket for a silver dollar he earned in the store stacking shelves this morning, her uncle's wages as a miner for an entire day. He hands it to Consuela and runs.

≋

Supper at the hotel that night is utterly inedible. Samuel saws at his steak, glancing up every once in a while at Ezra. "I want you to be careful," Samuel says. "There's been some trouble with the soldiers. They're restless, with little to do here except to guard the mines. There was a knife fight last night. An argument over *sotol*, I'm afraid."

Ezra nods. He knows about the fight. He knows what *sotol* is, but more importantly, what it does to people who drink it. He takes a bite of mashed potatoes, stiff and cold, but puts the fork down, not wanting any more.

"What's wrong?" Samuel asks, pushing his chair back from the table so he can cross his long legs.

Ezra shrugs again. Even he knows that must look childish, sullen.

"Let us retire to the veranda, then," Samuel says, "to look at the extraordinary light on these mountains. It's good for the soul."

They take their seats in wooden chairs on the hotel porch. Samuel lights a cigar and sighs deeply as he exhales. He looks out on the mountains, at the rose-colored light deepening to crimson. "I learned today that *Chisos* means ghosts," he says. "I'm sure you know that already; you're way ahead of me in Spanish. I'm sure they must be Comanche ghosts. They used to rule this area, stealing cattle and horses, running them to Mexico. Used to be a lot of grass for grazing here. Cottonwood trees. There were a lot of things, evidently, before the mine."

Ezra hasn't thought much about Indians being here. It gives him a new respect for the place, and he wonders about the warrior ghosts riding the rough ridges of the mountains named after them.

"If there's anything you want to ask me, go ahead. I've got a few secrets, too, you know. Some are even tell-able even if they aren't printable."

Ezra writes, "How long will we be staying here?"

Samuel holds the notebook Ezra passes him in the path of the light coming from the hotel in the window behind them. "That's not a secret, but I don't have an answer. At least not yet. I'm rather enjoying being off the map, so to speak. When people like Howard Perry think they can't be seen, they do all kinds of things. Like build empires. Believe it or not, you are witnessing the afterglow of the Gilded Age."

Ezra has no comment about the Gilded Age. He's only interested in right now. And tomorrow.

Samuel smokes a while in silence. "I suppose that's all a bit out of your *milieu,*" he says. "Indians are probably a lot more interesting."

"Did you ever know any Indians?" Ezra writes.

Samuel smokes thoughtfully. "Once, a Comanche managed to steal my Uncle Frank's prize stallion." He pauses, looks at Ezra to see if he's interested. Ezra gestures with his hand for Samuel to continue.

"Uncle Frank took out after him, following the tracks in his Model T to the Canadian River—that's in the Panhandle of Texas, not Canada. It wasn't very deep or wide, there'd been a drought. But the Model T couldn't cross it. On the other side, the Comanche watched him. He was on horseback and holding the stallion by a rope. The way my uncle told it, they both looked at each other across the river for a long time. Maybe the Comanche knew Uncle Frank didn't have a gun, that he would have fired it by that time. Uncle Frank finally turned the engine off. He got out. He hollered that he wanted his horse back. The Comanche laughed. Uncle Frank held up the key to the Ford and then threw it hard across the water. The Comanche looked down at it but didn't get off his horse. After awhile, he dropped the rope tied to the stallion. He still didn't get down for the key. Then he just wheeled his horse and rode off. Uncle Frank always said he looked like he needn't bother with the Ford that couldn't even make it across a shallow river. But maybe the Indian was impressed with the offer, that my uncle cared that much for the horse, less about the car. All I remember is Uncle Frank driving home, the stallion trotting along beside him as he held the rope. When he got through the ranch gate, he let go of the rope and the horse raced ahead. Uncle Frank gunned the T but the horse still beat him back to the house."

Ezra smiles. "I like your story," he writes. "My father didn't have any. Horses or stories." Somehow he has to mention his father, include him. As a swap, of sorts. Something tangible on the edge of a secret. But the idea of his father chasing a Comanche is so far-fetched it's almost laughable. He's not ready to laugh.

"I read an interesting article today in the paper," Samuel says. "An Indian by the name of Chief Wooden Leg was buried at Little Big Horn. Imagine that. The article said he had been to New York in 1913 for a ceremony, a ground-breaking for a statue of the First American. But the article said the statue was never built. No money, evidently."

Ezra sits forward in his chair. How can this be? He wants to tell Samuel he met Chief Wooden Leg on the day of the ceremony. It's a story he could tell. But he can't. There's too much of his father in the memory.

I met him once, is all Ezra can write.

Later, he opens the notebook he has kept for his father, his field notes. The names of plants, birds. Descriptions of the landscape. Tonight, he wants to write

something about Chief Wooden Leg, an experience
they had once shared, that he had remembered so
vividly his first night in the orphanage.

Dear Father, he begins at the top of a new page.
Nothing else comes to mind.

〰️

Soldados. Ezra writes the heading in his reporter's
notebook and sits down to watch them on the porch of
the Chisos Store. At breakfast, he heard grumblings
about the presence of soldiers, how they stirred up
trouble because they had nothing better to do. Samuel
had said that though most of the regiment had been
ordered back to Alpine two years ago, this handful still
remains and curse their luck at becoming Howard
Perry's private army to guard the mine. They had
wanted to be overseas in a real war, but now that was
over; they'd missed their chance.

There had been a knife fight, Samuel had admitted
last night at supper in the hotel, an argument about the
price of *sotol.* Whatever price was paid, the soldiers are
drinking it now. Five of them.

A tank wagon drawn by mules toils up the hill
from Cigar Springs to deliver water to the storage tanks
next to the store. Mexican water. Water for the Anglos
is delivered to their door. The girls, the young women
are lined up before it arrives; poles across their
shoulders hang with two lard pails waiting to be filled.
Smaller girls have a single bucket balanced on their
heads. This was one of the first things Ezra learned
here, that water may flow freely in the ground but its
distribution turns it into a political commodity.

He looks for Consuela in the line for water, but
does not see her today.

The girls walk past the soldiers, followed by wolf
whistles and plaintive, mocking calls, "Hey, señorita.

Señorita Lookee!"

The men coming from the mines, brothers and fathers of these girls, talk in low tones. *"Pinché gringos,"* one says, raising his voice.

Pinché gringos. Ezra writes it down.

"He's insulting us. Aren't you insulting us?" A soldier rests his hand on his rifle.

"How would you know?" one of the others says, leaning back on a wooden porch support.

"I sure as hell know the word *gringo* by now. And I doubt *pinché* is a compliment. God, I'm bored. I never thought I'd miss Alpine," he grumbles, draining the last of the *sotol,* dropping the bottle off the porch. It hits the hard dirt but doesn't break; it only rolls several feet before it comes to rest, stopped by a rock. They all look at it in silence. Someone finally opens another bottle.

The girls stare straight ahead, form a line. Each holds a small square of cardboard imprinted with a number that they hand to the man who distributes the water. As the buckets fill, wooden sticks nailed into the shape of X's rise to the top. "A simple way to keep the water from spilling," Ezra notes after he witnesses pails without them losing water. One by one, the girls, weighed down with water, make their way to their houses on a hillside east of the store.

He sees Consuela, finally, but at a distance, herding her goats along the mesa. *Mocho*, despite his limp, is out front. Ezra's starting to be able to tell one from the other, to learn more of their names. The goats seem to talk to one another as they pick their way through the broken stones, nibbling on bits of bunch grass.

There's nothing more to write about these soldiers. They're just getting *boracho*. As quickly as possible. He knows the word for drunk.

Ezra decides to join Consuela, if she will allow him. After his last effort to help her in the hail he's almost afraid to approach her.

The soldier who knows what *gringo* means jumps off the porch and nearly falls. Several of the girls in the water line laugh out loud. He swears something unintelligible and walks unsteadily past Ezra, raising his rifle with difficulty as he goes. He stops twenty paces beyond Ezra, braces his legs, takes aim at the silhouetted goats on the top of the mesa. A shot rings out, echoing off the hillside. *Mocho*, at the front of the herd, goes down. Ezra steps forward and then stops, too shocked to go any farther.

The soldier fires again. Another goat falls. A cheer from the porch. Others aim and fire. The rest of the goats start running over the rocky terrain. Consuela, screaming now, runs after them. One by one the goats go down. Fifteen in all.

"Pinché cabritos!" the soldier calls out. "That's the word for goat, isn't it?" he says to one of the other soldiers on the porch.

Consula stops running.

The soldiers lower their rifles, grinning. The one who shot first looks at Ezra. "Write *that* down," the soldier says.

Ezra picks up the empty *sotol* bottle and throws it as hard as he can. The bottle flies then falls and shatters. Shards fly, and one, no bigger than a tooth, falls on the soldier's boot. He looks down at it. Looks back at Ezra, surprised.

The other soldiers aren't laughing now. The last girl drawing water puts the pail down. Consuela comes closer, clenching something in her hand.

The manager comes out of the store, a group of men with packages close behind him. He looks alarmed, as if he's expecting to see people bleeding on the ground but finds instead the mute boy, pummeling a soldier with his fists.

Samuel comes down the steps and hears Ezra shouting in Spanish. *"Boracho. Pinché Boracho."* Consuela, heading for the soldier with a rock in her hand, stops in her tracks, looks at Ezra incredulously, as if she cannot decide whether he has tricked everyone with his silence or she is witness to a miracle. She backs away.

Samuel moves toward Ezra who is spent with shouting. He collapses on the ground. Samuel gets down on his knees in the dirt and tries to hold him. Ezra struggles at first then gives up. He shudders in Samuel's arms.

Consuela leaves them, climbs back up the hill alone. Over Samuel's shoulder Ezra can see her as she goes from carcass to carcass. He can hear the last goat bleating frantically. She goes to it, bends down, lifts a rock with both hands, brings it, with all her weight, down once. Again. Again, until the crying stops.

QUICKSILVER COURIER – May 13, 1919
By Samuel McPherson

When men and drink and people of color
mix, trouble brews on the border. Especially
when the ones with guns are outsiders. Howard
Perry's soldiers, brought in to protect his
interests from the raids of bandits and *rev-
olutionistas*, have turned out to be a liability.
Yesterday my assistant in the field reported that
fifteen goats herded by a thirteen-year-old
Mexican girl were summarily and needlessly
shot by intoxicated soldiers. The girl's uncle is
demanding reparations from the U.S. Army but
high command in Alpine refuses to pay the
$2.50 per goat requested. It is rumored that
even this remnant of the regiment will be
recalled to Alpine at the beginning of the New
Year. Not soon enough for some. There have
been many incidents here, though this the most
brazen by far. Howard Perry sent no comment
from his yacht off the coast of Florida.

E. Duval has also been silent on the
subject until recently. Now, a few words speak
volumes. I close this column with an astute
observation from my assistant: "*Cabrito* tops the
menu at the Chisos Hotel today. Yesterday," he
said, "they all had names."

Elizabeth
1919

Elizabeth sits down by the river to rest. She's come a long way alone in the dark. Where has she gotten herself to now?

But she barely has time to catch her breath before she sees a shape in the water that startles her. A muskrat, a beaver? It's snagged on a branch from a tree that had fallen in the water and try as it might, cannot free itself. She takes off her boots, wades in, teeters on the slippery, rocky bottom, arms out for balance. It's shallow enough to navigate while hiking up her dress, holding the blue fabric with one hand. She knows what it is by its color and shape before she's close enough to actually see it. The boat with the animals that Lucas made. A final gesture from Liberty? Or her father? She untangles it, pushes it free and it spins in an eddy before it moves downstream.

She takes off the eye patch and drops it into the water. It too, floats downstream. All she has left is the Indian nickel in her pocket, a few dollars to tide her over, this name she invented for herself to carry her further into this country—four syllables instead of two. Liberty had called her Lizzie, sometimes. Now she's Elizabeth again.

She's following the river, tracing its curves and brief straightaways. There are paths for part of the way.

Sometimes she has to push through brambles and vines. But she cannot lose sight of the river. She knows it eventually goes through the town where she got off the train. A train is what she needs once more.

By late afternoon she's hungry and exhausted. She hasn't seen a soul or even a dwelling of any kind. She thinks about killing robins. Starting a fire. She knows how to do these things now. But it's different, being on her own.

Voices filter through the foliage. She makes her way toward them and as she gets closer, she wonders if she isn't having a vision. She's trying to take in the tableau coming into view: curved boats on the water. Women walking in pastel-colored dresses holding matching parasols. Children in bathing costumes emerging from a catacomb of bathhouses beneath a grand hotel with a three-story tower at one end. Stone bridges arching gracefully across the water near a large tent with rows of people seated on benches. A gray-bearded, elderly man is speaking to the people sitting before him. She cannot hear what he's saying, but by his posture he appears intent on pressing matters of utmost importance upon his audience. He's gesticulating, holding his hand high to indicate something that will one day stand there, perhaps. Or something that may thrust from the earth. Everyone looks up to where he's pointing. Whatever he's talking about is vivid enough to hold their attention on some invisible point far above their heads.

She wonders if she has, in fact, died. The whole place seems other-worldly, a vision of paradise; the bearded man could be God Himself lecturing to the newly arrived. But he's an ordinary man, his arms too long for his sleeves. His talk finished, he walks from the rows of benches toward a building where many people are also headed. Someone stops him on the path, gesturing, talking excitedly.

Parasols are folded, children taken by the hand. The sign over the door says "Oklahoma Row Hotel." The guests must not be wealthy or finicky people. She can see from their attire that they are not like first class passengers at all, nor are they third class. Just ordinary people with extra time and a little money.

Elizabeth approaches the hotel entrance and becomes immediately aware of her shabbiness. She does not belong here, even as a maid. But no one pays the least bit of attention to her. One woman in a straw hat says to a man who might be her husband, or brother, "That Mr. Harvey is quite the visionary. But he's been talking about building the pyramid for quite some time. I was here several years ago. He was talking about it *then*."

Elizabeth doesn't know what in the world this woman is talking about, but the name Harvey is the one thing she understands. The Harvey Hotel. Was this where Liberty's mother ended up? If so, she certainly didn't get very far.

The bearded man who was lecturing, Mr. Harvey, evidently, veers from the main path. Elizabeth follows, and rounding the corner, sees him just ahead, stopping at some sort of outbuilding. He opens a door with a key and disappears inside. He nearly runs into her on his way out with a typewriter the size of an anvil balanced in his arms.

"I'm sorry!" they each say, though he says it slightly ahead of her.

"What is it you require?" he asks, a little flustered when she makes no move to continue down the path.

"I want to work for you." She says it before she's had time to think, and so there's a boldness in her voice she doesn't quite yet feel.

"Are you—a typist?" he stammers, eyeing her uncertainly.

"No, but I can learn. Until then, I can clean rooms.

Believe me, I know how."

"Oh," he says, sounding the tiniest bit disappointed, as if this serendipitous collision should have brought him the very person he was looking for.

"I can learn to type. In my spare time."

He looks confused now, as if he had not even thought about looking for a typist. He says the typewriter is a particularly fine specimen for the pyramid, a perfect example of civilization's inventions, this one from the Remington Company before they diminished its size for the traveling person.

"I don't do the hiring," he tells her. You'll have to see Miss Faubush. Say I sent you, whoever you are."

"My name is Elizabeth Farrell."

"I'll try to remember that but I can't promise. Now please, let me get on with my obligations." He hurries on, ducks into a doorway. He's forgotten to close the door of the outbuilding. She takes a quick look inside. A unicycle leans against one wall, a plow against the other. At the back, a great jumble of things or parts of things. She closes the door to keep it all safe—her first task for Mr. Harvey.

Miss Faubush raises her eyebrows when Elizabeth tells her Mr. Harvey sent her. She looks Elizabeth up and down, her gaze repeatedly drawn to the left eye, at the small cloud partially covering the green iris. "You'll do for cleaning rooms. Not for serving in the dining area. Wouldn't seem right."

Girls in aprons scrub potatoes furiously during this induction. They steal glances at the new girl who barged in here with Mr. Harvey's blessing. One cuts her thumb because of her misplaced attention and promptly pops it in her mouth.

"I'll get you a uniform. Will you be staying with us in the dormitory or has Mr. Harvey reserved a suite for you?" Miss Faubush says.

The girl who cut her thumb takes it out of her

mouth and giggles.

"The dormitory will be fine," Elizabeth says.

Once again, she is the object of scrutiny. She's introduced to the other girls—Betty and Bonnie from Springdale, Linda from Gravette and the rest from Cave Springs. They all give her wide berth.

"Where are you from?" the one called Bonnie asks, once she's got her giggling under control.

"Ireland," she says. "New York," she adds, as if they might think better of her. But they pull back. Either way, she's foreign.

"But I'm working to go out to the West, to work in Mr. Harvey's other hotels."

They look at each other as if this is news to them.

After a week of watching her, they whisper a running commentary, loud enough for her to hear.

"She's strange." Bonnie gives her opinion in the kitchen this morning over coffee while Linda butters toast. Elizabeth is already in the dining room setting up the silverware for dinner and can easily overhear them.

"Mr. Harvey doesn't have any other hotels out west. At least this Mr. Harvey doesn't. She acts so smart, how can she not know?" Bertha blows on her coffee, then looks over her shoulder to make sure Elizabeth is within ear shot.

Bonnie sticks up for Elizabeth, at least a little. "At least she doesn't lord it over us, put on airs."

"You just wait," Linda says, wiping the counter clean of toast crumbs with a damp cloth.

Elizabeth ignores them, finishes the place settings for dinner. After they've gone, she eats by herself in the kitchen. Dicey Jett, the cook, lets her eat later than the other girls. This morning Dicey puts a cup of coffee with cream in front of Elizabeth. "Are you sure this isn't keeping you awake? The other girls say you're up at all hours reading, that you wander around at night."

Elizabeth drinks her coffee without comment. She can clearly hear Dadie Brawley from Cave Springs in the dining room saying she's convinced Elizabeth "must be sweet on Mr. Harvey, that they meet on the sly down by the lagoon to spark. What does she do with him—sit on his knee?" They all have a good laugh over that one.

Bertha goes on to say that Elizabeth has no interest in boys, but then if she is really in love with Mr. Harvey that might explain everything.

Dicey Jett leans through the serving window. "You girls are wasting good time with gossip. Now get back to work."

Today, even the proper Miss Faubush crosses over into the lower echelon of gossip, speculating that Mr. Harvey suffers from neurasthenia, a nervous condition that renders him anxious and sensitive, even eccentric. Although Elizabeth doesn't quite understand the word, she knows it puts him in a most questionable and distinct category.

Elizabeth does her own sleuthing while cleaning rooms and finds no whiskey in Mr. Harvey's suite. She's heard Dicey say that his wife lives elsewhere. Elizabeth finds no photographs of her on his dresser. She's also heard his son was killed in an automobile that had stalled on the train tracks not far from here. Yet, there are no pictures of his son anywhere.

Mr. Harvey's great obsession seems to be time— the lack of it. He believes only in children, the last hope of civilization, though he doesn't do as well talking *to* them as *about* them. The children who hear his lectures—and these Elizabeth always attends—grow restless with his admonitions about the importance of sunlight and clean air. They say they want to be playing in it, not hearing about it. They want to ride in the gondola, listen to the musicians in the dining hall, not to be captive to an old man that drones on about good habits and disciplined minds. Only Elizabeth stays to the end of his talks, taking copious notes. It isn't what he says so much that holds her attention. He's actually quite a tedious speaker. To her, Mr. Harvey is two different people—by day he's a sort of dreary professor. By night, he feverishly wanders about like a lost soul. And he always comes back to the storeroom of the things he plans on putting in the pyramid. When the lights in Oklahoma Row are extinguished for the night he returns to the base of the pyramid. This is a man, she thinks, who has never cried. He does not get in his cups and sing, overcome with nostalgia on holidays. He broods about impending doom.

He is a man so unlike her father she wonders if they can be the same gender. Mr. Harvey has a vision and needs someone else to see it. He must feel it—this audience of one who can see what no one else will—the pyramid rising, complete, from its foundation containing within its vault the best this world has to offer to the next one.

Elizabeth is certain her presence here is necessary. Mr. Harvey has a great deal on his mind. He seems lost at times and relieved to see her. He is absent-minded, but then his mind is occupied by very important matters. The future is fast approaching. And if the end of civilization truly is at hand, evidenced by the recent World War, then is there any point in going any further West? The safest place could be here, helping him. For the time being, she only changes his sheets and towels, keeping to his periphery.

〰
〰

Elizabeth follows Mr. Harvey out the door one autumn night, expecting him to go to the storehouse, retrieve another artifact for the future. But he walks slowly past the storeroom and its treasures, head down, hands clasped behind his back. When the time is right, she will press him for action. Tonight, she can tell already, is not the night.

He walks toward the amphitheater, still under construction, but veers on a path through the woods, coming to a stop in front of a large domed box made of cement. She stays back, submerged in the blue shadows of trees that shelter it. A twig snaps beneath her feet. She holds her breath.

"I know you're here," he says without turning around. "You're always here but I can't see you. I try to talk to you but I don't think you can hear me. You have no idea how lonely I've been. How much I long for your company."

Elizabeth's heart, the beating fist it has become, opens its hand. She had no idea, no idea.

She steps forward tentatively, to stop this loneliness while she can.

"Son," he says. "Son."

Elizabeth freezes. Steps back once, twice. He does not turn around. For all her silent attentiveness she is not here, her physical certainty less substantial than the ghost he beseeches. And he is a confused and confusing man. Mortal. Subject to grief. His vision of the future does nothing to abate the past. His son's ghost still holds him hostage. No wonder he doesn't build the pyramid. He doesn't have time.

She does not wait but leaves as quickly as she can. So what if he hears? He will think it is his son, running away from him.

Dicey looks up from her work as Elizabeth comes into the kitchen. She takes her coffee but doesn't sit down. She stands next to Dicey, watching her separate eggs in a bowl the size of a chamber pot, cracking the shells hard against the crockery.

Elizabeth wants to talk. But her loneliness has hardened around her like the wax seal of a mason jar. What is she doing here? Nothing is clear anymore.

Dicey keeps her eyes on the froth the egg whites are creating as they slowly rise higher in the bowl. "So now, Miss Elizabeth. What's on your mind?"

"I don't know. I'm not sure what I'm doing here."

"Don't you have family?"

"I didn't run away, if that's what you mean."

"That's not what I asked."

"My parents are dead." It's the first time she's ever said this, at least out loud. Different than saying she's an orphan.

The egg Dicey's breaking now slips down the outside of the bowl. Elizabeth watches it slide onto the marble countertop, the yolk quivering. Inside the bowl, a dozen others ooze like frog spawn in the shallows. Dicey lifts the heavy bowl, setting its edge below the counter and sweeps the rogue egg into it. Whisk in hand, she pauses for a moment as if it's almost a shame to beat them. With only a few strokes they lose their separateness. They're quickly beaten together into a common yellow soup.

"I haven't forgotten my parents," Elizabeth says, "if that's what you think." The voice of a child escapes her. A trapped bird finding a tiny opening, too small to fly through.

"Why would I think you've forgotten them?" Dicey asks carefully.

"Because sometimes I do. I try not to, but I do." She leans against the counter, her hands gripping the edge as if it's the only thing holding her up.

"Are you lonely?" Dicey asks. She doesn't look at Elizabeth when she asks this, as if she knows that such a direct question, coupled with a steady gaze, might upset her.

"Not at the moment. I'm here with you," Elizabeth says, setting her cup down. Without another word, she leaves the kitchen with the feigned confidence of someone who understands the necessity of being the first to leave.

≈

She knows it's time to tell Mr. Harvey to hurry. There's less time than he thinks until the end of the world. It's breathing right down his neck. And hers. The pyramid will have to be built. *Soon.*

Elizabeth can almost see it rising from these Ozark Mountains. Just like he said it would. There's a door at the top of the pyramid and inscribed upon a metal plate his own words, *When this can be read go below and you will find records of the cause and death of a former civilization.*

He has said in his lectures that the pyramid would need three doors, one below the other. He said he didn't know how far the pyramid would be covered up by a war or by just the Ozarks falling down on their own. He called it a caution "against the unpredictability of geology and the rampant greed of willful progress gone riot," a lot of words to say to mean he didn't trust the weather or people as far as he could throw them.

Everyone at Monte Ne gets ready for the fireworks, the dance, the fiddle and flagpole-climbing contests. The pyramid is nothing more than gray lines scribbled on paper, the base it will sit on only a slab of Portland cement, its radio transmitter not here but only on order from the Philco Company. It should be sending out the signal he promises will join all nations in peace and good will. That's the kind of freedom Elizabeth wants to celebrate. Not just America's.

She knows he's trying. She's seen him carrying

many things to put in the shed near the place where he wants to build an amphitheatre. He puts all the things the pyramid will one day hold that say something about humankind—who we were. What we made. How we were so busy we forgot to finish what we started.

She goes there now to make sure nothing has disappeared. And yes, here it still is, all together: A grandfather clock. A Singer sewing machine. A Victrola. A collection of marbles in a glass box. A dictionary. A cash register. A bathtub. A banjo. A zither. A printing press. A model of a flying machine. An hour-glass. A brand-new suit on a hanger. A woman's fancy hat in a round box. A hammer. An egg beater. An Appaloosa rocking horse with a actual leather saddle and a real tail and mane.

She wants to put a letter *inside* the pyramid, so that the first person from the future who reads it will know that Mr. Harvey was a man of vision, ahead of his time, and that Elizabeth Farrell, too, was here. But there's not enough time right now, even for that. She has to get back to work.

When she walks into the great ballroom of the hotel to polish the floor, Mr. Harvey is standing by the window looking out at the lake, his hands clasped behind his back. He almost looks like a prisoner in cuffs. But he unclasps his hands, turns and catches her watching. He points out the window. "Come here, young lady, and tell me what you see." She puts the polishing rag and the bucket on the floor and comes to him. She looks out the window that she had just washed the day before. She had done a good job— that's what she sees at first. Then, when she looks beyond the glass, it's like looking at a painting and she sees Monte Ne the way she saw it when she first came here, over a year ago now. There are boats upon the lagoon, and the gondola brought all the way from Venice floats like a black swan through the arches of a stone bridge. There are women holding pink parasols, walking along the banks with children who laugh and splash in the clear water, getting their mothers' dresses wet. There are men in rowboats, their coats draped over the seats, their white shirts rolled at the sleeves, their suspenders looking like harnesses making big X's across their backs as they row. She knows Mr. Harvey didn't ask her to describe these things. It's more like he's asking her to say what's missing. So she says, "That's all very nice. But the pyramid, Mr. Harvey. I don't see the pyramid anywhere."

He looks completely taken aback. He turns and looks right at her as if she's more than just the hired help, as if she's whispered from the future to remind him. Since she has his attention she says, "I'd hurry if I were you."

She goes back to her polishing. She concentrates on the piece of the floor in front of her, the grain in the wood rising from the dirt of the last dance a week ago. Mr. Harvey leaves the window and hurries out the door.

She moves across the floor on her hands and knees, erasing the footprints Mr. Harvey left behind. He's been experimenting with cement again and he's always a little gray with the dust of it. He's one of those men who need a great deal of cleaning up after. He has extraordinarily big feet for not such a very tall man. There must have been a loose nail in his left boot because there are tiny half moon marks like a baby's fingernail everywhere he's been.

She gives up trying to polish by hand. She takes her shoes off and ties a rag to each foot. She stands up, hikes up her skirts and slides, her left foot erasing his, then the right. He has a very long stride.

Out of the corner of her eye she sees him pass by the door. Has he been watching? He stops, backs up, stands still in the doorway. He holds an electric fan in his arms. She's admired it often, how heavy it is sitting

RIDERS ON THE ORPHAN TRAIN

on the pedestal in the lobby, moving its head back and forth. But it makes her sad, too. People don't trust the mountain breezes to be enough any more. It's a shame. That's what they once came here for.

In Mr. Harvey's arms the black blades turn a little as if he's been running; its cord dangles from the base like a long tail, as if it pulled its power directly from him. Is it her imagination, or does he bow? He looks like an ambassador from the past presenting a gift, a machine to move the air, whirl it into wind. He trips on the cord as he steps away, and then he practically runs.

She can't explain it. She's had no feeling like it before. Elizabeth feels, in this moment, almost like a woman. Not a girl anymore. A young woman with a certain power of her own, to quicken a man, or turn him to stone.

She runs after him, calling out, "Wait, Mr. Harvey! It's me!" But it isn't any more. He's running away, the cord flying behind him, down the stairs, across the bridge, out of sight. It's the future he's running from as well as the past. The future of her.

≋

Tonight, people come from Springdale, Rogers and Fayetteville to see the fireworks, to dance to the band, the Black Diamond Boys, from Bentonville. She watches it all from the wings crowded with the kitchen staff. She laughs along with everyone to see the fat man from Cave Springs trying to shinny up the greased flagpole to get the five-dollar bill taped on top. He slips back two feet for every foot up. A boy who plays the fiddle catches her eye. His name is Kelly Stilley, from Harrison. And if the world is going to end, then she isn't going to waste any more time; Elizabeth is going to fall in love while there's still time.

She listens to him play his songs for the contest,

the required "Arkansas Traveler" wild and fast as if the devil's chasing him but he's far ahead and not a bit out of breath. Then he plays his own composition. He files the strings so sweet with a bow he holds light as a willow switch and the white rosin powder falls on his shoulder soft as snow.

Mr. Harvey sits in the audience of men judging the contest. They don't allow women even if they do have the vote now because it's too much of a distraction or maybe they just want to smoke and drink to their heart's content, at least for a little while.

She has an idea as Kelly takes his bow that she could be the one to bring the blue ribbon to him. He's going to win. He's that good. Then he will see her.

And he does win. She's ready. She grabs the ribbon from the master of ceremonies before he even knows what's happening and gets herself onto the stage.

Kelly hardly looks at her. He takes the ribbon and goes. She feels the barest brush of his hand. Then it's just Elizabeth looking out into that great room filled with blue smoke curling from cigars and the tiny lights on the tables flickering through the long-stemmed glasses filled to the brim with bubbling champagne. She can't help but think of the *Lusitania* or the *Sussex*, how those people were sailing along celebrating the journey and there was a U-boat with their name on it, waiting. Only this time she and Mr. Harvey know what's out there somewhere, waiting in the dark, and it doesn't have a name.

She can just make him out at the first table, lifting his glass to his lips. There's a lot of silence. A lot of waiting. She turns to the audience, to Mr. Harvey in particular. A few point at her, laughing, as if she's there by mistake, or one of the clowns has stumbled by accident onto the stage. But she isn't laughing.

Glasses stop clinking and even the serving staff stand still. Mr. Harvey himself leans forward, his arms on the white tablecloth, his hands folded like a preacher or the president. He's listening. Listening to *her.* To what *she* has to say.

"What's she doing up there?" someone finally says, loud from the back of the room.

So she goes ahead and says it. What she's been meaning to say all along. "The future, Mr. Harvey," she says. "It's right here in front of you."

Everyone looks at Mr. Harvey. He rises up slowly from his chair—she can hear it scrape on the floor as he pushes it back. A glass of champagne like half of an hourglass tips over, spilling toward the edge. Elizabeth hears it dripping on his shoes. He doesn't even look down at the mess he's made. Tomorrow she'll probably have to clean it up.

He looks right at her. He takes the glass that fell over. Light catches it as he raises it up, a beautiful piece of etched crystal, to her. There isn't anything left in it except a drop, but he drinks it anyway. And then a few people begin to applaud, not sure if they should. The band starts to play a waltz.

The doors open and a great wave of women come in who've been waiting to find their husbands and dance. Mr. Harvey leaves the room, taking the glass with him. He wipes his forehead with a napkin, nearly knocking over a waiter as he bolts out the door.

Elizabeth hurries off the stage and follows him. Mr. Harvey walks down to the water. A singing party on the gondola drifts at the far end of the lagoon. He stands there, looking out upon the water, then at the mausoleum beneath the trees where his son is buried, where he's left a place for himself next to him. She stands near him. They both look toward the place where the pyramid should be. All he's managed to complete is a retaining wall to keep the water back. Surely he can see the rest of it—he's drawn it so often. She can see it, and she knows there won't be nearly enough room in it to hold very much of the truth of their civilization, at least not for very long.

He finally sets the glass down on a stone bench. He bends to pick up something from the shore. He pulls his arm back, then lets fly. She hears the stone skip—counts three. She finds a stone of her own and throws it. Five.

Above them the sky breaks open and fireworks spray red, white, and blue across the black sky as if streaks of heaven are showing through from the other side. It's beautiful—the bright explosions, the waltzes coming from the open windows of the hotel, the laughter of the people dancing who think they still have all the time in the world.

To the people of the future, this is how we must look, she thinks: a plain man in a black-tailed coat stands on the edge of the water and a young woman lifts up her skirts, wading in. There's nothing they have to bring to the future. The warm wind coming off the water will be miracle enough.

The truth is, maybe the pyramid will never be built. To have thought of it may suffice. But she can feel it already—a gust of regret, blowing through her hair.

Ezra
1920

Even though Ezra has been speaking for quite some time, it's Consuela who's not speaking now, at least not to him. He turns all his attention to being Samuel's eyes and ears.

Even though there is no war effort to supply, the mine doesn't slow down much. After all, other wars could well be brewing.

If Samuel asks him anything about his past, he becomes silent again. Not in the old way of total silence—he simply leaves the room. But he misses the way that Samuel used to watch him, writing, waiting patiently to read whatever he had written. Now, what he writes is for publication, to be read by total strangers. And ever since he started to speak, he hasn't written in his notebook to his father again.

The world of facts protects him. Ezra learns that the peso-dollar exchange is in Howard Perry's favor, that the reason the smelters are running double shifts is due to the discovery of the new high-grade ore. A geologist was run out of town last week after asking to enter the mine. New pipes arrive by wagon—plumbing for the Anglos—along with a Ford and a Studebaker for sale, parked in front of the store with $400 written on the windshields. For Samuel, all of this adds up to the portrait of a nineteenth-century self-styled robber baron he came here to write about. Ezra supplies the sensory minutiae. The sweat of the mules that bring in the wood to feed the rotary furnace. The daily ritual of mothers and children bringing tortillas and beans to their husbands and fathers on the road by the mine. The way that wax from the *candellia* cactus is dripped onto the straw hats a week before summer rain begins. The dresses of the Mexican girls bloom like bouquets of bright flowers as they sit close together on the wooden bench in the tin-roofed hall. The boys peer through the windows, picking their partners in advance, and, when the door opens, they rush in to claim them.

Samuel, with Ezra's help, synthesizes everything and the monthly column is sent back to the *Chicago Tribune*. Do the people who read it there have any inkling? Does Terlingua still matter now that there's no need for bombs? Evidently it does to Howard Perry, the absentee landlord of everyone. His manager asks Samuel to leave, something which Samuel tells Ezra he has no intention of doing.

But for all of Ezra's watchfulness, some things elude him. With the help of a dictionary he learns many Spanish words, but nuances are hard to comprehend. He learns from Enrique that he and Consuela are *huerphanos* and have only their grandmother and uncle to care for them. Their parents had been killed in Ojinaga by *federales* in the revolution. The rest of the family came to Terlingua for refuge. Here, they also found help. Enrique learned from his Uncle Eduardo only recently that it was Samuel McPherson who paid for a new herd of goats for his family, that he wished for it to be an anonymous gift. The manager of the store, though in Perry's employ, adds extra goods to Eduardo's weekly groceries for his family. Ezra learns that he pays for it out of his own pocket. These acts of philanthropy are made in secrecy, which is, after all, the unwritten code of a mining town that owes its existence to the prosperity of war.

On the rare occasions when Howard Perry does come to Terlingua to visit his mine, he inhabits his mansion for less than a week. He's small and seemingly lonely for such a powerful man, his face hidden by a fancy Stetson hat. No one comes with him or to visit him even though his mansion's nine bedrooms are ready with sheets that Señora Leon from the hotel hung out wet and washed the week before. Like sails on a Spanish galleon they flap, snap taut, slackening in the wind off the Solitario. The Chisos hold their breath the whole time Perry is here, hoarding their evening, rose-colored light for those who need it most until he departs and the fumes of gasoline, the wake of alkaline dust linger in the air long after he has gone. There's something ominous in the air, but in spite of Ezra's descriptive skills, he finds he can't describe it. Ezra sees him only from a distance on his annual visit.

There's time, all the time in the world for a real friendship to develop between Ezra and Enrique. Enrique invites Ezra to explore a closed mine shaft west of town. For the first time since he got here Ezra begins to feel like a living, breathing person, a participant instead of an observer. Best of all, he actually has a friend to explore with.

They walk together after sunset toward a once prosperous mine a mile from town. Enrique lights torches for them both at the entrance to the shaft. They walk through the narrow corridors that burrow into the heart of the gutted mountain and just when Ezra feels like he might faint from claustrophobia he emerges into a vaulted room so enormous their torches can't illuminate it more than a few feet around them.

Enrique plants their torches in a rock cairn near the center of the cavern. He reaches in his pocket and hands Ezra a smoke after he lights it from one of the torches. It's not any kind of cigarette Ezra has ever seen. It's rolled into paper as thin as the wings of a moth. The walls of the room come closer, as if they're curious to see these boys who carry no picks or shovels, boys who don't curse but laugh and speak in a mixture of two languages.

"Those two sisters, the ones who never dance, who sit on the benches at the *baile?*" Enrique says. Ezra nods, though he doesn't really know. "They were born stuck together, and so the *curandero* came from Boquillas to cut them apart with a knife!"

"I'll bet one *chica* got the heart, the other one got the brain," Ezra whispers.

The torches burn low and the fate of the eviscerated sisters is lost in the darkness beyond the reach of torch light. They smoke in silence for a while.

Now, the torches are almost out. They'll need to leave soon. They certainly don't want to be in this mine shaft without light.

Enrique is talking now about an animal Ezra's never seen, even in the Bronx Zoo. A *chupacabra.*

Ezra listens for something only he may be able to hear clearly.

"What does it *do,*" Ezra asks, "that makes it so awful and terrible?"

"It can devour a goat in one sucking breath. Imagine what it could do to you!"

Ezra's imagination doesn't need much prompting to set it running wild. Something looms, darker than anything the torches can push away. Ezra feels the heated breath of the *chupacabra* on the back of his neck.

But Ezra knows the heated breath he feels is more than that of a legendary animal. It could be the force of darkness itself that has followed him here even into this labyrinth. Danger crouches right behind him and his new friend.

The torches go out as if something blew them out. Ezra tries to find the narrow corridor, feeling his way through the dark. It's so dark it makes even a moonless night seem gray. He feels his way along, palms against the rough walls, stumbling on the uneven path beneath his feet until he emerges into the blinding light of the Milky Way. Enrique is not far behind him.

When they can talk again they agree the *chupacabra* must be too large to squeeze through the narrow vein of the tunnel, and that it has to remain in the cave at the center. Perhaps it was swallowed by the mountain when young, and feeds on the unfortunate *mineros* or *exploradores* and has grown too large to ever leave. But finally, Ezra has to ask, "I know we didn't *see* it. But I *felt* it. Did you feel it, too?"

"Yes," Enrique says. "Sometimes, Consuela does. My *abuela* says only orphans can really feel it—the breath of the dead."

Orphans. *Huerphanos.* In any language, it's the last word a child should know, let alone be.

Ezra stops walking. The phrase, used only once on the train, becomes part of conversation again. But he's not like Enrique. "I'm not an orphan," he says. He can barely see his friend's face.

Enrique doesn't have to say anything. His silence enfolds Ezra's declaration the way deep water absorbs a stone leaving only ripples where it disappeared long after it was thrown.

≋

No one knows how death finally comes to Terlingua. In the air? Carried by a stranger from a city to the north? Everyone thought they had escaped it, were too far removed in their isolation. Soldiers had brought it back from the war to the rest of the country—the influenza had come and gone in most places—but no one here had been anywhere near a war.

A white man who freighted dry goods from Alpine died and his body was smuggled out of Terlingua in a truck by Perry's manager. Soon enough, it spread, a sickness so indiscriminate even the *curandero* died within a week of falling ill. Even the ultimate tonic made from the earth-baked flesh of a *paisano* bird could not clear the fluid from the healer's lungs, and a new grave is added this very morning, pick axes breaking into ground for something other than cinnabar. A procession from the church leads to the cemetery, a pattern that will repeat itself almost daily.

Ezra watches the exhausted doctor making house calls, the carpenters who now cannot keep up with the building of caskets. The graveyard grows stones and wooden crosses at the edges; a great many candles will be required for *Dia de los Muertos* even though most are buried quickly in mass graves.

He overhears people saying there is a curse but they cannot discover its meaning. Some say it is punishment for mining the cinnabar for the war across the water, even though the war is over. Retribution takes time. To Ezra, the source of sickness comes from what he felt that night in the cave. There may be peace, but danger is never far away.

♒

Samuel lies on sweat-soaked sheets, putting up a brave fight. The doctor arrives, does what he can, which is precious little. He gives Samuel something for a cough, a fever. He quickly leaves. Ezra sits by the bedside and leans close to look at this familiar face drained now of all color. He puts his hand on Samuel's forehead to check the fever. Hot. Still. He leaves his hand there, part of his weight resting in balance as he leans farther forward in the chair. A breeze sirs the curtain. Samuel opens his eyes, closes them.

"I'll be right back," Ezra says. "I'm going to find some help." He rises from the chair but Samuel says nothing, doesn't even acknowledge that he heard.

Once outside the hotel Ezra runs to the east side of town to Enrique's to ask his *abuela* for a poultice of herbs. He's seen her at her work when he helped to carry a man bitten by a rattlesnake to her house. The man stayed for three days until he was cured and walked home on his own. Or so Enrique said.

Ezra finds her pouring water from a lard pail into a clay jar.

"*Señora,*" he says, out of breath.

She sets the jar down, straightens slowly and turns to face him.

"*Pues?*" she says, eyeing him with her customary suspicion. "*Que quieres?*"

"*Mí...*" what is Samuel? Not father. "*Abuelo,*" he says, which, he realizes, is how Samuel probably looks to everyone. "*Es muy malo. Infermo.*"

She nods. Waits. Her face softens slightly.

"*Ayuda, Señora. Por favor. Ayuda.*"

She studies him. It's because of her that Consuela now herds the goats farther from town. No doubt she can see he is not so bold now. He is frightened. He has seen death looking through his own window.

She enters the house, does not invite him in. He hears pounding, scraping, silence. A long silence. He resists the urge to knock on the door.

She emerges, a thick piece of dark cloth in her hands. She hands it to him. For a second he's confused. He thought she would come with him. She pats her forehead with her palm indicating where he should place the poultice. "*Tres horas.*" She turns her palm over, waiting.

A half-dollar is all he has in his pocket. He gives it to her and her hand closes over the coin. *"Rece a Dios,"* she says, crossing herself.

As instructed, he places the poultice on Samuel's forehead. It's just a small pillow, but pungent with a power he has to believe in. She told him to pray. He doesn't know any prayers. He doesn't believe in them anyway. In his experience, they've never worked. All he can do is to wait. And hope.

Sometime near dawn Samuel stirs but does not open his eyes. He murmurs something unintelligible, speaking in the unaccented syllables of unconsciousness then grows quiet again.

After two years with this man Ezra knows so little about him. It's as if they've both arrived here as fugitives with secret histories. Their names are not disguised, only their identities. As far as Samuel knows, Ezra is an orphan with the countenance of an orphan: watchful, a heart divided between then and now. Ezra had once overheard a conversation Perry's manager had had with Perry on the town's only telephone at the store, his voice carried north a great distance by the barbed wire that served as the line to Alpine. The sound quality was so poor that people always seemed to have to shout to be heard. One had only to sit on the porch to listen in, to imagine the other side of the conversation. Ezra hadn't been paying much attention until he heard the words "that reporter and his sidekick" and something about "...stirring up the public. Nobody reads the *Tribune* down here. And up there—who cares what people earn? The way I hear it, McPherson has his own ghosts to run from."

Well, they know less about Samuel than he does. Samuel isn't running away. He chose to come here. But he would not choose to die here, be buried on the rocky mesa with the miners. Who would need to be notified? Who and where are his next of kin? Ezra has never asked Samuel any of these questions. He takes this man at face value and in exchange offers none of his own shameful story—left in an orphanage. Some things should be left unsaid.

He looks around the room, finds Samuel's wallet on the bureau. Maybe there's a clue about his family in there. He searches through the long, slender billfold that has held many train tickets in its time. Behind a sheaf of receipts he finds a picture of two small boys on an enormous horse, the reins held by a man in a cowboy hat. On the back, a date: 1872. Samuel could be one of the boys, but which? They look nearly identical. Will Samuel die before he can ask him about this photograph and the story behind it? He knows more about the town of Terlingua than he does about Samuel McPherson. He thought they had all the time in the world ahead of them.

Ezra sleeps in the chair, wakes with a start in complete darkness. Has it been more than three hours? Is he late to turn the poultice over? He can't see his hand but he reaches out, brushes against Samuel's chin, his stubbled cheek. He finds the poultice, warm to the touch. He turns it over, as instructed.

He waits. Not for God or *La Virgen* but a *milagro* shaped by human hands. Hope, that he's forgotten what to do with until now, urges him to say something like a prayer.

He lights a lamp. " "Please, he whispers. *"Por favor. Por favor."*

If Samuel dies—here, in this moment—then what? He feels precariously close to being at the complete mercy of death's arbitrary decisions. He can't watch. He can't *not* watch. He is a sentry again, with a much more serious task: the necessity of keeping death outside the door. But it's there, in the hallway. And it wants to come in.

Ezra opens his notebook. *Dear father,* he writes, but

gets no further. He hasn't written those words in so long. Whom is he writing to now? He shifts in the chair and the pen slides from its place in the crease of the notebook. It rolls noisily across the floor and then disappears beneath the bed.

Ezra gets on the floor and crawls on his hands and knees to retrieve it. Light from the lamp does not reach beneath the bed. He hopes he won't come across a scorpion before he finds the pen. He has to slide onto his belly to reach and then he's completely under the bed, face down to the floor, the pen at last in his hand. Above him, face up, lies the man whose obituary Ezra will have to write on his own.

Ezra turns over on his back now and lies there, feeling like a child, though his length matches that of the bed above him. He's fourteen years old. It is silent here, completely so, like the silence at the bottom of a well, the sounds of the world extinguished. What will become of him? Will he die, too, under this very bed?

Come back. Come back. He whispers over and over in a chant. His ears ring with the silence that answers. He feels the heated breath he felt in the cave. Death is very near and coming closer. *If you can't come back, then please take me with you.*

The embers of panic begin to flare into wildfire, the instinct to shout, to run an unbearable urgency. Something else in him fights against this heat and a cold paralysis creeps through his veins. An antidote is summoned, ice to freeze the fire in its tracks. The heat finally succumbs.

The springs above him squeak. Or does he imagine it? His own pulse pounds loud enough to be a knocking at the door.

"Ezra?" Barely a whisper.

Does he dare answer the ghost's question?

"Ezra, are you there?"

The heat of hope floods through him now,

thawing the ice. But he feels suddenly ashamed. Found out. As if he's been hiding all along.

He slides out from under the bed on the rough wooden floor, dust coming with him.

He stands up, returns to his true size.

He looks at Samuel, the living breathing Samuel who died. Who didn't die. Who came back. Whose brief death brought something else to life. A wish he'd put away because it only had to do with his mother and his father. Reunion. Return.

"I thought you'd gone..." Ezra says.

"I heard you. I came back."

"Did you go far?"

"Very far."

Ezra doesn't know what else to say. They're not all the way back yet, wherever they were.

Ezra looks around the room, desperate for some reassuring detail. He sees his own notebook. Next to the notebook, a blue glass pitcher.

"Would you like some water?" Ezra asks. "You must be very thirsty after your long journey."

"Yes. I'd like that."

The notebook lies open on the chair. He closes it. Ezra lifts the pitcher. It's heavy. He holds the glass steady, pours it full. Now the hard part. He sits on the edge of the bed, slides his hand behind Samuel's head to lift it from the pillow. He holds the glass so the rim rests on his lower lip. Tilts the glass, just so.

Samuel closes his eyes, draws the water inside him. A simple thing, the easing of thirst. He drinks all that Ezra gives him.

QUICKSILVER COURIER-
December 24, 1920
by S. McPherson

The smelter cools for one night a year. On this eve the miners are walking home, their paths lit by *luminarias*, candles set in paper sacks weighted by sand. They create a warm glow from an unstuttering flame sheltered from wind. A path to heaven? No. Toward home.

Here, in these crude houses there is much to celebrate tonight. Prosperity in all its forms. Peace, the greatest gift of all.

E. Duval asks me to wait at the window. And so I do. At precisely seven o'clock, he tells me, there will be something to see. Something he has helped to make. I wait, pen in hand, writing this as it happens. Until then, I watch the children line up to receive their bags of candy from the manager of the store.

Oh!

An electric star as tall as Ezra Duval himself burns back the dark. This star has been carefully situated on the roof of the Chisos Mining Company store for all of Terlingua to see. Tungsten, not cinnabar, is the element of the hour. The miracle of light. This is what he wanted me to see. That man can do more than just extinguish; he can, if he chooses, illuminate.

The mules wander freely on the mesa without harness or halter. Empty wagons line the road. There is a great deal of singing, all over town. All over the world.

Feliz Navidad from Terlingua. And to all a good night.

Elizabeth
1922

Elizabeth runs alongside the slowly moving train. She grabs iron like Kelly tells her to. "Jump!" he cries and she does, her waist hitting the bottom edge of the open boxcar door, the top half of her falling in. Kelly grabs her other hand, tries to brace himself, one foot against the edge of the door, desperately pulling, terrified that they'll pass a switch and that the pole will break her legs off before he can get her all the way in. He said he'd seen that happen down in Mobile, when the foot of a twelve-year-old kid was taken clean off. He'd been dangling his legs, sitting in the open boxcar door, kicking his feet high for the hell of it.

Kelly pulls her, his leg braced harder against the door and he drags her in as the train picks up speed outside Rogers. He releases her hands and she rolls over, face up, stray strands spilling out of the cap he'd given her to hide the length of her hair.

The boxcar shudders, groans, and creaks as if it's breaking in two as they slide into a curve. The emptiness of the car with only herself and Kelly in it now fills with the sound of the grinding of the wheels and a terrible thump at regular intervals like a heart going wild.

"Just our luck. Flat wheel," he says. "We'll have to move when we can. It'll drive us crazy."

She's leaving, finally, leaving Arkansas. She'd waited so long for the pyramid to be built. It looked like it never would be built, no matter how long she waited. Almost three years had passed, enough time for Kelly to return to play two more fiddle contests. This time, she wasn't going to let him leave without her.

She sits cross-legged near the open door as the Ozarks stream by. A field of fireflies like the lights of a distant town hovers in the humid atmosphere above the tall grass. In a second, they're gone, as if extinguished by the wind from the train. The arc of sound as they approach a crossing bell sounds not unlike the change in pitch of the engine whistle as it nears the end of its measured gasp. Everything descends, recedes, then disappears as they pass.

As the train slows to a stop near Springdale they jump out, grab the ladder and find another open car, this one with its wheels evenly honed.

After Fayetteville the train picks up considerable speed. Kelly leans back, stretching out his long legs in front of him. "Soon, a boxcar like this will be full," he says. "Men going off to the wheat harvest in Texas, Kansas."

She wonders if Doyle Watson will be among them. "How long," she asks, "have you been riding?" She has to get very close to him so he can hear her.

"Three summers, following the wheat. There's always something needing to be picked. Winter's hard everywhere. You freeze. You wait for it to be over."

The noise of the train makes conversation almost impossible. They have to shout, no matter how close to each other's ears they are. Anyone listening would think they were arguing.

"What do people in Ireland do?" he asks.

"Pray."

"Does it help?"

"It didn't help the potatoes."

The sound of the wheels suddenly changes, drops in tone, and Kelly crawls forward until his head hangs out the door. He lies down, motions for her to do the same. The world falls away and she's looking down into a chasm, the silver thread of a moonlit river like spilled mercury sliding far below. Her sense of depth is distorted but for several long minutes the train in all its unbearable weight seems suspended on the lattice of a trestle bridge, its heaviness no more than that of a caterpillar pulling itself along a slender branch. Just as she begins to fully feel it, the weightlessness around her closes down abruptly and the train hurtles through a tunnel of trees on solid ground again.

Kelly rolls to his side and pulls her to him, holds her, and they rock together as the world opens and closes below them each time they cross the White River. She tries to kiss him, thinking this is what should happen next but he turns his face, this boy who amazed her with his fiddle playing back in Monte Ne. He doesn't even own one. He borrowed from other people. Now he has nothing but the clothes on his back and those probably cast off by someone else. And he acts like he's not about to have a sweetheart, that it would be the end of traveling light.

What at first felt like a gentle rocking from the motion of the train now begins to feel like she's being shaken, admonished. You should have known, should have known. You're not anything he wants to put his hands on for long.

If he wants to, she has no idea how far she will go. Whenever her time for love comes, she hopes it won't be in a bed, in a stationary house. Everyone should have a train to rock them through their first time, a long whistle at every crossing to shelter whatever human sounds might come. She'd heard all about it, first from the older girls at the Magdalen laundry in Ireland. There they were paying for it for the rest of their lives, paraded through town on the walk to church as examples of what happens to harlots. The girls in Monte Ne planned their weddings whether they had boyfriends or not.

Trains have so far taken her from places she's finished with or places that were finished with her, toward places where something is still possible. In Ireland, a train took her from the brides of Christ who could not save her, in New York from the age of reform and her father, and now from the man in Monte Ne who took too long to believe in her belief. All of them extinguish like the lights of Arkansas towns. Before her now lies deeper, unbroken country. She's in motion, and when she's in motion she feels most alive, and, oddly, most alone.

Beside her, there's a boy, moving on to the next place to work, to borrow a fiddle if there is one, to go with a girl for a little while if she's willing. No promises, no declarations. Just this fleeting intimacy, curled like children, both now half asleep, roughly rocked toward Oklahoma.

∿

At the next division point they climb down hunting a hotshot freight heading west. A Negro tramp jumping out of the boxcar behind them points one out. "I'm catching out for Louisiana. Shrimping," he says. "Had enough berries to last me a lifetime."

A man with a stick walks the boxcars. "Railroad bull," Kelly whispers He has that heavy-footed swagger of a dog bred for bite. They crawl under the train until they hear the bull pass. They look for an open boxcar but this train's hauling coal and the two boxcars they come to behind the tender are locked.

"We'll have to ride the blinds," Kelly says. "How long can you stand?"

"How long can I stand what?"

"On your feet?"

"As long as I have to."

They balance, facing each other where the two boxcars are coupled together. They hook their arms through the steel ladders behind their backs, holding tight as the train lurches forward.

Hours pass, the two of them in a strange, swaying dance, not touching. They pass through Oklahoma City with the sun high overhead. The heavy doors of the locked boxcars they've been riding between slide open. Sacks of something are taken out, others thrown in. They jump off, scurry into a sand shed to wait for the train to take off again.

After Oklahoma City everything changes. The trees surrender altogether to the high plains and when they veer south along the Canadian River to Pampas, Texas, the air feels different, not so heavy, holding the heat in a different, more tenacious way as the cooling ground seems to draw it back down. The train stretches out in the Texas Panhandle, longer now, added to along the way for the long haul. No more undulating hills. When she leans out, looking back she can see clear to the end of the train. And the beginning. This is a country so vast the train is no bigger than a hyphen creeping across it, trying to keep two words together at a time.

~~~

At a hobo camp outside Amarillo a man from Missouri brings out a fiddle that he won in a card game back in Dodge City. He doesn't know how to play it yet. He says maybe he'll give it to his brother in Clovis,

New Mexico to clear a debt. Maybe he'll keep it. Kelly tunes it up while two older hoboes send a young boy into town for turnips, to sweep the floor of a grocery, preferably, and take his payment in food. He'll return to feed them all, just like the raccoons in Liberty's yard. She hasn't thought of Liberty in quite a while. Is she still there, taking care of her father? Or has she lit out, too, for the wider world, her own wages?

Kelly puts the bow to the fiddle and the rough camp near a low trestle bridge transforms by firelight to the Ireland of Imbold when the Roma camped outside of town. And now, Elizabeth, hearing the music so close, wants to sing but knows she still cannot. She'd opened her mouth once at the depot in Arkansas and look what happened. These men here, leaving their homes if they even had them to begin with, listen to music between trains, temporarily grounded and melancholy, longing for the weightlessness and freedom of a fast freight. She knows that freedom lasts as long as one can fly. It lasts until you have to jump off, tumble into one of these camps where a boy from Arkansas might play a fiddle like he was born to it and it will make you want to cry. Which she dares not do. This is not Ireland. There is not enough whiskey and history to make it so.

"There's work for me," Kelly says to her. "In Friona, a little south and west of here. I'll stay on through the harvest."

She looks at him across the fire dulled by daylight coming on. The oldest tramp who calls himself Cincinnati Sam pours boiling coffee from the can it came from into two other cans, hard to hold without handles. The others have already gone, caught a freight toward Lubbock late last night.

Elizabeth pulls her sleeves over her hands to hold the hot coffee. She looks at Kelly again, waiting for an invitation at the same time she knows there won't be one. It's hardly worth the trouble to learn names. And names can be changed. Places are more permanent. So Cincinnati Sam could lose that little tail of his given name and still have an identity. A place in Ohio everybody has heard of. If she were to pick a place for her name what would she choose? A place she's from or wants to be?

Kelly had called her his sister around the fire. So had John Tyrone, at Ellis Island. She's always some-body's sister, needing a brother, it seems, to gain entrance to the rest of the world. No wonder Brigid took her eye out in Ireland. To be a woman, especially out here, is to be fair game. Trousers and a cap help. She wishes she'd kept the eye patch.

Cincinnati Sam says to Kelly, "What about your sister—isn't she going with you?"

"She's got a job at a Harvey House in Belen."

"Oh, well then," Cincinnati says. "That deserves a spoon of sugar. For the road to Belen."

She looks at Kelly. Sugar, indeed. She'd barely mentioned the idea of Harvey Houses to him. And now it's goodbye again, hunting freights in the Amarillo yards, Cincinnati steering them toward the Southern Pacific split in Clovis. Toward Belen, wherever that is. A convenient way to get rid of her.

Elizabeth will ride on top this time; all the boxcars are closed. Kelly takes off his belt, loops it through the top rung of the ladder and buckles it to a loop on her trousers. "In case you fall asleep," he says. He kisses her goodbye on the cheek and goes running after his own freight just pulling south, an open boxcar waiting for him to climb in.

It takes forever for her train to pull out, the couplings crashing as they find their places. Cars are added on endlessly. Finally, they go, heading due west.

The glow in the sky that was Amarillo fades quickly and stars burn through the darker side of blue.

The entire Milky Way builds a bridge between this world and the one left behind. And that home is so small, so temporary, to a country of exiles like she is, always on the move. Just passing through.

She's grateful for Kelly's belt even though she felt like a child buckled into a carnival ride when he first tied her to the train. Without it she would toss and roll into the last edge of Texas. She could end up in a place like her father, without memory, holding on to the broken belt, one last thread linking her to the frayed fabric of the world.

But she does not roll off. She rides. The spine of the train is straight, an arrow flying west, the engine with its three eyes hurtling through the fragrant, pungent dark of New Mexico.

She checks to make sure the Indian nickel is still in her pocket. For luck. She has a feeling that it's working.

〜〜〜

Dawn floods this place without the diffusion of humidity. Elizabeth sits up, unbuckles Kelly's belt as the train slides slowly toward an X. North, south, east west. Everything converges here. She climbs down the ladder to bare ground. No brush to dive into. No place to relieve the terrible ache in her bladder. She squats between two cars and lets go onto the tracks, surprised at the hiss of steam from the cold rails.

Two men, railroad bulls, walk away from her train toward a large two-story building with a Spanish-style tiled roof and portico. "Harvey House," a sign proclaims. Another: "Belen."

She stands up, turns around. Clay houses, buildings that look like they've pushed up out of the ground stretch out into streets and the streets reach toward the brown, jagged mountains both east and west that bookend the valley town. She turns back to the Harvey

House, heads toward it. Indians, they must be, seated on blankets in front of the station are selling pots, baskets, rings with blue stones as bright as the sky is turning out to be. Shy children run barefoot. They look at her cautiously.

She goes to the door and stops. Through the windows she can make out a horseshoe-shaped counter. A dozen people sit on stools, served by girls in black and white uniforms. Like nuns, she thinks, without the wimples. They wear big white bows in their hair, instead. They move with efficiency and precision, some filling cups, some setting down plates or taking them away in a choreographed swirl as intricate as blackbirds on the wing, wheeling and turning, inches apart without colliding. She watches, fascinated. So *this* is a Harvey House. She's heard there are many along the Santa Fe line. A place of speed and attention to detail. These girls write nothing down. No one ever has to ask for a refill.

A woman, older than the girls serving the customers, looks up, her field of attention extending beyond the counter to include the entryway, the pane of glass framing a face. A face hastily arranging itself, her fingers combing tangled hair.

The woman leaves her station behind the counter, walks quickly to the door to open it. She stands in the doorway, her eyes traveling away from Elizabeth's face to the trousers and boots. "You're the girl from Arkansas?" she says doubtfully.

"How did you know?" Elizabeth asks.

"Well, Miss Darcy Green, we've been expecting you. You're late. Why are you dressed in such a disheveled fashion?"

Evidently, her new identity has been waiting for her arrival. Elizabeth's mind races back to New York, the stolen suitcase a useful alibi. "My luggage was taken while I slept. A conductor gave me these clothes."

"How terrible! We'll get you a uniform from another girl until I can order you a new one from Kansas City. We say we like to start with a blank slate but this is—extreme."

She searches Elizabeth's face as if waiting for a smile at her small joke. Elizabeth gives her none. As if taking offence, she goes on, her words rushed now, racing ahead of the next train to arrive. "Belen can't be choosey. Girls go on to grander places in the Harvey chain. They get their training here and then go on to La Fonda, El Tovar. You, however, look grateful to be anywhere. But they shouldn't have sent you by herself. I guess that was all they could do in a pinch. Well, we'll get you situated. The rooms are on the second floor. Rest a bit."

Something in Elizabeth's face must have given her pause. She takes another deep breath and when she continues, her voice is slower, softer. "I'll need you back here at eleven sharp. Two trains come through, twenty minutes apart. You'll cut your teeth in the thick of a frenzy."

~~~

"Darcy Green" puts on a uniform of a proper Harvey girl: black stockings, black dress, white apron covering everything girl about her and a big white bow for her unruly hair to remind everybody she is one. With this disguise she crosses the threshold from the kitchen to the dining room and lunch counter, grateful to be assigned the counter where the trainmen eat. The dining room with linens and glassware and china would be too much right now. She'd break the glassware just by looking at it after her journey, blasted by wind and covered in soot across the Great Plains. Now she is being instructed in minutiae by Irene Laslo on the secret code of cups and saucers: right side up, coffee.

RIDERS ON THE ORPHAN TRAIN

Turned over, tea. Glass on the left, milk. The girl taking the customer's order leaves the signal for the beverage girl without having to say a word.

"Darcy," Irene says.

"I like to be called Elizabeth. My middle name."

Irene raises her eyebrows. "Darcy sounds friend-lier. More accessible." She looks Elizabeth right in the eye as if noting its flaw. "I'm going to tell you something about the Harvey Houses. Fred Harvey has a reputation to uphold, the excellence of the food only part of it. These girls from Arkansas and Missouri, Kansas and Nebraska escape from a lifelong sentence behind a cook stove. Little mules. At least here they're raised to the stature of respectable working girls with spending money and time off. Many of them will go home to those kitchens after they've sent every penny they earned here to pay for their father's whiskey if he's that kind of man. Or for his bread, if he's the other kind. Come fall, the girls flood in here to keep their families alive for the winter. Spring, they thin out.

"When they get home they can't quit straining their ears for the sound of trains, the two whistle blasts meaning two miles out, get ready. They sit in a three-legged cane chair and cry. I know. I did so, once. Don't let it happen to you."

≈

Two whistle blasts. Elizabeth is caught up in the synchronized stampede, hastily shown how to make coffee and how often by a girl from Childress. Dot, her name, if you can call it that. "Extra scoop. They like it strong. Expect it strong. If they complain, they get their way. Don't get uppity about it. And don't get sweet on a train man. Irene will put you on the next train out with him. Cowboys are OK to dance with. Just don't marry one."

"Anything else?" Elizabeth says. Everyone who talks to her gives her a list of things she's supposed to somehow remember. Maybe that's all part of the training. They're testing her memory. But she has questions. "What about Indians?"

"What about them?"

"I see," Elizabeth says. No explanation needed.

Another girl introduces herself as Evie. She pulls coffee from the shining urn that looms like an altar behind the counter. She sets a pot aside, fills another. "Indians, she says quietly, "are off limits. The boys. But you can buy all you want from their mothers and sisters and grandmothers out there. Pueblo and Navajo, mostly. A few Zuni. I got a really nice bracelet last week." Elizabeth looks at her wrist. "No jewelry allowed with the uniform. It doesn't look right anyhow, even if they did let you wear it."

The train pulls in, chuffing slowly to a stop. A swarm of passengers climbs out of it, then enter the hive of the Harvey House, guided to their seats by Irene if they want the dining room. Their orders are already cooking, telegraphed in when the train left Los Lunas. The rest take their own seats at the counter, sending out a cacophony of orders. Elizabeth watches the cups, the code, and begins to fill them and try to keep them filled without running into the other girls who are zooming in and out of the kitchen. For the first time she appreciates the economy of the Catholic church, the single cup of communion for an entire kneeling row waiting their turn. These people are definitely not in church. They talk. About the weather in Chicago. The score in St. Louis. The price of beef in Ft. Worth. Copper in Bisbee. Wheat in Dodge City. Corn in Des Moines and Ames.

"This coffee's cold." A tall man in a boater pushed back on his head frowns.

"I just poured it," Elizabeth says.

Evie nudges her. Elizabeth brings him a new cup with coffee she pulls straight out of the urn's spigot. She waits while he takes a sip, too much of one, she can tell, for the temperature. He sets the cup down. Nods at her curtly. Unfolds a newspaper.

Full plates with slices of roast beef, honey-glazed carrots and asparagus come sailing out of the kitchen in hands well-accustomed to their weight. She threads her way through the girls, glad to be on the front lines instead of in back of the swinging door like she was at Monte Ne, chopping, washing endlessly. Out here at the counter there are the customers with their quirks and preferences. Their unexpected kindness and rudeness. The power of the tip to say exactly what they think of you.

"This coffee's cold again," the man says.

Elizabeth looks at his untouched cup.

"You have to drink it when I pour it. It won't stay hot while you read the stock report."

"Nevertheless," he says.

Elizabeth wants to argue. It's a waste of perfectly good coffee. Of her time. Evie hovers. "It's his nickel," she whispers. "Don't let Irene hear you sass."

Elizabeth takes the cup. Replaces the saucer this time, too. Darcy Green wouldn't put up with this for a New York minute. She probably turned around halfway here after a stop at a different Harvey House and saw what she was in for.

The man lowers the screen of the newspaper and looks at her. "Well?"

"Just who do you think you are?" she says.

His smile loses a little of its warmth. She can see straight through his blue eyes, his brain shuffling through facts and figures. "I'm John Nielson. Your customer. I'm on my way to take a position as a foreman at the Shannon Copper mine in Arizona."

Elizabeth sets the pot of coffee on the counter,

ignoring protocol even further. She wants to ask him about the owner of that mine, obviously Irish, from the name. A successful Irishman.

Irene is heading toward them, exasperated. Two whistle blasts interrupt her forward progress. All the girls freeze in the midst of taking empty plates away. The other train is early. Irene looks stunned, her careful synchronization gone awry, the world colliding in five minutes' time.

The train in the station blasts its whistle calling its flock and the passengers fumble for their wallets and handbags, their unnecessary umbrellas. They pay their bills of fare and beat a hasty retreat out the door just as the other train starts to slide in from the south.

John Nielson lays down a quarter for his meal. He lifts the cup of cold coffee, sets it aside and puts a turquoise ring on the saucer.

Evie stares at Elizabeth's gratuity in the brief lull before the next wave of hungry passengers arrives. "I'll have to start insulting people myself," she says. "Nice going, girl."

Elizabeth puts the ring on. It's so small it only fits her little finger. The ring of an Indian child, probably sold for pawn.

The minute hand of the clock creeps toward ten o'clock p.m. Curfew. Conversation comes to a close about plans for a picture show, a dance on Friday where they can practice the Charleston. These girls act like they're at college, Elizabeth thinks, but has no idea what college is like. She'd educated herself with Liberty's Sears Roebuck Catalog and the small library at Monte Ne. But these girls aren't studying. They're folding dollar bills, putting them in letters home. Across the Midwest, their mothers must be waiting patiently at mailboxes for the tithes of their daughters.

Aline from Bloomington, Indiana, is tethered to her grandmother who would blanch if she saw Aline putting on lipstick, rouge, every night "in case I meet the man of my dreams *in* my dreams." She has to wash it off every morning before work. Dorothy from Red Cloud, Nebraska, is reading "My Antonia" for the third time this month. "I saw Willa Cather when she came back to do a play at the opera house. She didn't look like her pictures. Big as a house." Lizzie Tapp from Rappahannock, Virginia, scowls at the camera when a photographer comes from Albuquerque to take a group picture. She can imitate the calls of all the birds in the Blue Ridge Mountains. Somebody said she's part Indian and had changed her name from Tappahonso. She doesn't admit to it. She doesn't deny it, either. Sue Ellen from West Plains, Missouri, complains about the heat and goes to bed in a wet nightgown. She wears a ring she says is an engagement though it looks like something from a dime store. And it doesn't fit. She says she's lost weight since she got here. The ring is held to her finger by a wad of wax pressed inside the setting. She takes it off every time she washes her hands, places it carefully on the edge of the sink. Louise from Allentown, Pennsylvania, says she's going to college. Last week she said she would study Home Economics, as her mother wishes. This week she elects Anthropology after overhearing a professor from Princeton in the dining room talk about the secrets of the Lost Tribe of the Anasazi hidden in the cliffs of this very part of the southwest, just waiting to be discovered. "Egypt," he'd proclaimed at the table, "has nothing on America. You'll see. Too much of a fuss is being made about King Tut."

Evie from Carrizozo, New Mexico leans her back against her pillow propped against the iron bedstead. She watches Elizabeth who's standing barefoot on the bed with a rolled-up newspaper ready to swat a sizeable insect scuttling along the molding.

"It's not a scorpion," Evie says. She's the sole native of these parts, and should know, even from across the room. "It's a vinegaroon."

"Still," Elizabeth says, astounded daily by the things that crawl, that thrust from the ground, bristling with thorns. Their outlandish names. She'll have to start all over on flora and fauna. She collapses, cross-legged on the bed, dropping the newspaper on the floor. "I'm going to have to trust you on this."

Evie shrugs. "You might as well."

Elizabeth checks on the progress of the non-scorpion. When she looks back at Evie, she's still watching her.

"What are you looking at?"

"I'm still trying to figure you out."

"Don't waste your time," Elizabeth says, adjusting the turquoise ring on her finger. If anything, she's gained weight here on leftover turtle soup, potatoes Anna, asparagus in Hollandaise.

"How long will it take? Is it that difficult to get to know you?"

Elizabeth brings her eyes back to Evie. Of all the girls here, she's glad to have her as her roommate. Aline would annoy her with her array of cosmetics kept in a locked box under the bed. Lizzie would hypnotize her with her birdsong. She prefers to hear it from down the hall. Evie is interested in Indians. In animals. She already took Elizabeth walking with her one day toward Los Lunas, teaching her the plants, the lizards. Her father is a botanist. A person who goes on field expeditions, a butterfly net at the ready while his daughter collects plants for him to press. Evie doesn't talk about her mother much except to say she reads a great deal and paints for her pleasure. As far as Elizabeth is concerned, Evie is the only normal person she's ever known: two living parents, each having their own profession. Very modern. Elizabeth likes her stories about their horses and a lone burro named Charlie and a dog she calls Cooper who has great respect for cats and doesn't chase them. Something out of a story book, her life. Eminently readable.

"Don't you miss your home? Elizabeth asks, trying to divert Evie's attention away from figuring her out. The birds singing from Lizzie Tapp's room echo down the hall.

"Sure I do. But it'll be there when I go back."

Elizabeth looks at Evie curiously. This statement comes from someone with experience at continuity. Her mother isn't going to run off with a Protestant. Or be drowned in the English Channel. Her father won't be sent to an asylum. Evie isn't going to get on a train and give herself away. Evie's soul isn't in need of saving. It's intact. She comes and goes. She doesn't have to make up stories or change her name She trusts that what she knows is no mirage, that a mirror will hold her true reflection, no matter how long she looks.

"I can't figure *you* out," Elizabeth says.

"I'm not a mystery. Not like you."

"What is it you see, since you've spent so much time looking?"

"You look like somebody who's all inside out. Your face is turned away even when you're looking straight at me. Like you dropped something inside a well you built yourself but don't remember any longer how deep it is."

Elizabeth can almost see this face, her mouth open slightly in amazement. Is it all there—every story, every place, every mistake? She wants to turn her face fully to her friend. But whose face—Maud's? Elizabeth's? Darcy Green's?

"I'm listening," Evie says, "if you want to talk."

Irene calls, "Lights out!"

Without taking her eyes away from Evie, Elizabeth reaches up behind her for the light switch, feels for it. Evie's eyes guide her to the right, not very far. Her fingers close upon it and she pulls. The light goes out in a snap.

"Goodnight, Evie," she whispers.

The last of Lizzie Tapp's song flies past curfew and even at Irene's warning knock, continues on for a few notes before it stops, roosting for the night.

"Evie, are you still there?"

"Still here."

"I'm glad you are. Goodnight."

"Sweet dreams. Goodnight."

Ezra
1922

KING TUT FOUND!
Treasures Abound in Boy King's Tomb.
11th Hour Discovery.
Tutankhamen Takes Revenge.

Ezra stands bolt upright from a leaning position against a porch post on the Terlingua store. He scans the article quickly. It's a week old. He finds the name Lord Carnarvon, the financier of Carter's expedition. A name he'll never forget, written in elegant penmanship on the letter that changed his life. Below the headline is a photo of Carter, a blurred group behind him, none of the faces distinguishable and when he holds the paper closer the faces dissolve to gray dots without form or familiar feature.

He reads further, dreading what he may find. The Egyptians are calling it "The Mummy's Curse." Carter himself inexplicably died in his hotel room in Cairo.

And there, in ten point typeface is his father's name. *Duval Carries On With the Expedition.*

ALISON MOORE

He puts the paper down, and with unsteady hands, folds it. Samuel is waiting for him right now in the dining room at the hotel. He's not ready. What will he say to him?

The broad, normally gray flank of the west-facing Chisos Mountains catches the last of the sun and holds on until it blushes. Watching this transfer of light, the sun's last glance east is a ritual he has kept. This time he can't keep his eyes on the mountains in the distance. He keeps returning to the blurred photograph, looking for an image of his father and finds it, finally. His hat is pulled so low over his eyes he's almost unrecognizable, his once-gray beard completely white.

Right now, his father's journey to Egypt feels too bizarre to be really true, a story an orphan might make up. There were times, many times in the last four years, when a certain light on the Chisos, or the way the moon lifted above them made him aware that his father might be gazing at something similar on the other side of the world. And every time the heat pressed down and took the last ounce of moisture in his breath away he thought, "My father is also wiping the sweat from his eyes." There were mornings when he shook his boots for scorpions that he could see his father, left boot first, as was his custom, performing the familiar, pre-cautionary ritual of one who dwells in the arid places of the world.

The heated breath he felt that night in the abandoned mine with Enrique—was that the warning? Had his father ever had any intention of returning? *You might as well be an orphan,* Lars, the bully had said on the train. Death is not necessarily what makes you so.

Now, with the sun down, the Chisos unremarkable and dreary gray, a chill settles in quickly and he feels the full force of suspended grief descending. Someone should have contacted him, told him. Ezra's left a trail a mile wide all the way from St. Anthony's Orphanage to

the Children's Aid Society to here. All he's left with are
unanswerable questions. He will not send the notebook
to his father, ever. "In care of" is not a place and never
has been.

≋

Ezra sits in a chair but does not pull it to the table.
He stares out the window though there's nothing to
see. The light is gone, but it's not dark enough for the
window to hold his reflection.

"Ezra, is something wrong?"

"No."

"I see. Well, I have something to discuss."

Ezra closes his eyes. What Samuel just said is an
echo of what his father said to him when he told him
he would be leaving. He won't be left a second time.

"You might be wondering why we're still here. I
told you we came to do a story…"

"It just takes time," Ezra says. "It might take a long
time. We have to finish what we came to do. Don't we?
Isn't that right?"

"A most egalitarian response followed by a
rhetorical question." Samuel leans back in his chair
enough to make it creak, a clear indication that he must
have been on the edge of it before. "Like any empire,
Terlingua cannot last. But yes, I feel I must play this
out, to the *denoumént*, if not the actual end. Have you
seen the papers? King Tut, found at last! The great
mystery revealed. With a price."

Does Samuel know about his father? His face
gives nothing away. "The closest I've been to Egypt is
Pyramid Lake, Nevada, where I own some property. A
far cry from the Middle East. We must carry on here,
even if this story here is miniscule by comparison to
what's happening elsewhere."

"Samuel, I want to be here," Ezra says.

Samuel nods emphatically. "It seems to suit you. You're brown as an Indian. You ride Hector's mule like a Comanche."

"They had horses," Ezra says.

"And so shall you. I've spoken with Hector…"

"You don't have to do that."

If Samuel knows about his father staying on in Egypt, then is this offer some kind of consolation? Their dinners arrive, served by a young boy, new to the hotel. *"Tortillas?"* he asks. He doesn't know their preferences, doesn't know that Ezra always asks for *maiz,* while Samuel prefers *harina.*

"Will you allow me to give this gift? By my calculations, you should be… sixteen? Ezra, this is something I very much want to do."

Ezra shifts in his chair. In many ways, the silence he started this journey with was easier. But when he does talk, Samuel listens. More than listens. He responds. With his father, there had been only brief, necessary exchanges, and his father had a way of contradicting or criticizing whatever Ezra offered and so closed down any further conversation that might have brought them closer. Thinking of his father is painful. Anything they used to do or might have done differently is done. Gone. Samuel is here and now, waiting for his response.

If he were still the child who cried out at the slaughter of the goats that day, he could do so again and be held in Samuel's arms. But Ezra is a young man and this is what men do—wipe their eyes, release the grip of their tightly clasped hands in order to do so.

~~~

Ezra's horse, a pinto named Rio, is led into town by Hector Valenzuela from his ranch across Terlingua Creek. Samuel watches from the hotel porch while

Hector shows Ezra how to saddle and bridle him. The mules Ezra has ridden with Enrique had neither, only a rope halter tied loosely around their muzzles. Rio has the patience of a saint while Ezra masters these tasks and stands perfectly still while he climbs on.

"Bravo!" Samuel says. He has commissioned a photographer for the event, a reporter for the Alpine *Avalanche* in town to document changing fortunes of the Chisos Mine. Samuel looks delighted to see Ezra on Rio and wants to mark the occasion. Ezra thinks that if his father were here he would be proud. Or would he? Samuel is proud for him.

"*El Vaquero!*" Hector says.

Ezra nudges Rio forward. Rio responds to the slightest pressure of Ezra's heels. He's exquisitely sensitive to any signals coming through the reins. And Ezra can feel signals coming back.

Hector mounts one of his mules bareback and rides with Ezra, telling him how to put Rio through his paces and soon Ezra's on his own galloping beyond the stiff-legged trot of the mule.

He sees Enrique and Consuela tending the goats near Cigar Springs in the hills north of town. They see him. He wants Consuela to notice him, how well he rides already. But he cannot stop now, has to gallop past them. The speed, the freedom is intoxicating.

Ezra looks ahead to Hen Egg Mountain, Agua Fria beyond. He has his bearings, at least in terms of landmarks. He has a horse that will carry him willingly in any direction he wants to go. But he's alone. His friends are on foot, far behind.

He could go and keep on going. North. Further West. He goes at a gallop for hours until Rio can gallop no more. He drops the reins. He lets the horse decide.

Rio turns toward town and walks as if he knows his rider needs time.

Home, Ezra thinks, is not a fixed location. It's the

place where someone is waiting for you to return.

Is Samuel waiting? It's late. Very late. The half moon is straight up and waning. Samuel will have gone to bed long ago.

Rio walks steadily south. When they reach town, the lights are off for the night. But Ezra sees something glint, moonlight on a pair of spectacles.

Samuel is sitting on the porch. Slowly, he rises from the chair. He's standing now. He's coming toward Ezra, arms thrown wide in welcome.

〰

Ezra's world expands far beyond the town of Terlingua, and Howard Perry's kingdom. He's followed Terlingua Creek all the way down to the Rio Grande to Santa Elena Canyon. The towering cliffs carved by eons of erosion are more impressive than anything made of concrete and steel thrust into the air from New York's narrow island pedestal.

Once he saw what he supposes were bandits fording cattle across the river to Boquillas. He's promised Samuel he won't cross the river but he has, more than once, ridden into the river and felt the thrill of Rio's hooves leaving the earth, surrendering to water. He's ridden a swimming horse in what he calculates to be the true boundary between the two countries, a place in the middle, flowing freely.

He spends his first night completely alone in the mountains near the Chisos basin. He builds a campfire that barely makes a dent in the dark. If there are bandits here, they pay him no mind. He has no cattle to steal and if they have their eye on Rio, Ezra has a bow and arrow that he made himself and he's spent many an hour practicing. He's come a long way from that day in a frayed Indian suit at Ft. Wadsworth. He wishes Chief Wooden Leg were here, riding into his camp to greet him. And he can't help it. He wishes his father could see him now.

If his father could read a story about this boy he would surely envy his freedom, admire the life he leads. Perhaps his father can see all the way to this campfire on the rim of Texas where his son is becoming a man without him.

≋

Howard Perry arrives on a gray day in July. The news has preceded him: he's here to close the mine temporarily. The *avisadores* have been flashing the news, mirror to mirror in the mountains long before the black touring car arrives.

This time, the shiny touring car is barnacled with mud. This time the powerful automobile does not arrive under its own power but has to be hauled up the hill by four of Hector Valenzuela's mules. It had rained all afternoon, a heavy, pounding monsoon and the otherwise rock-hard bentonite clay had been transformed into the consistency of lard. It is almost dark when the mules finally make it to Terlingua.

By the time Perry rides past the store everyone is already waiting, lining the road to his mansion. He sits behind the wheel, appearing to be steering. His gray hat is pulled low over his eyes as he passes the hotel on his way up the hill. No triumphant entrance this time. Flooding in the mine at the 800-foot level has necessitated a shut-down. Temporarily. But no one knows for how long. The war is over, after all. In the meantime, the Chisos Store will have to make up for the mine's losses. Even though the miners won't be paid, some have scrip they've saved from before that can still be used at the store. Profits will wane but not disappear.

Samuel stands next to Ezra in the crowd that lines

both sides of the road. The headlights of the
Studebaker turn on defiantly but illuminate little more
than the rumps of the toiling mules before it. No one
speaks even after Howard Perry passes. They continue
to watch his procession all the way up to the mansion,
tail lights like two red eyes glaring back. Finally the
lights of the car extinguish, and after a moment the
lights of the mansion go on.

Hector comes back down with the wagon and the
team. Everyone is still waiting at the bottom of the hill.
Hector lifts his hat and waves. Somehow, the safe
arrival of their benefactor, even if he's here to close the
mine until the water recedes, is reason enough to
celebrate. To Ezra, the fact that Perry had to be
transported by mule is unprecedented and noteworthy.
As if hearing Ezra's thoughts, Samuel says out loud.
"The emperor truly has no clothes."

Bottles of *sotol* are passed around. Two guitars and
an accordion arrive and an impromptu dance begins,
not in the accustomed place inside the dance hall on the
east side but behind the store, an area which can clearly
be seen from Perry's mansion. Ezra wonders if he's
standing on his veranda, watching from afar.

Young women who had waited and had hung
back on the edge of town flow into the crowd. For a
moment, on a steamy night in summer, everyone
dances together in spite of the mud. Samuel bows to
Señora Ortiz, one of the cooks at the hotel, and holds
out his hand. Ezra dances with Hattie Green, the new
schoolteacher who only arrived last week from Odessa.
She's winded after a single waltz and Ezra searches for
another partner.

Consuela is no longer a flat-chested, barefoot
shepherdess but a young woman in a yellow dress, the
color so much like Jenny's coat in Otto's painting it
takes awhile before Ezra understands who is standing
before him tonight. She is wearing shoes, new shoes.

White. He stares at them. When he looks up again her face says she will not wait all night for him to ask her to dance with him. Her grandmother is not yet here.

Ezra lifts his arms out to her. She bends to take off her shoes, sets them on the porch of the store to save them from the mud.

His hand covers her waist as he supports her. At first, she's awkward in his arms. For them both, it's difficult to be fluid, braced as they are to keep the requisite foot apart from each other as they spin, very, very slowly in mud.

Besides the yellow of Jenny's coat, there's something of Elizabeth in Consuela's hair, not the color but the length of it. He tries to return his full attention to Consuela. She smells faintly of wood smoke, but something from the past pulls him again and he catches the almond and cinnamon chocolate Senda used to make at the Chelsea. It was Senda who first taught him to dance on the roof of the Chelsea Hotel. His thoughts are moving faster than his feet.

The grandmothers have gotten wind of what's going on now and have formed a phalanx to make sure nothing inappropriate happens. The couples move slowly through the turns of a waltz, here for no other reason than to dance. When the music stops, the girls let go of their partners, but Consuela stays in Ezra's arms after the song ends. The two of them stand there, imperceptibly swaying in the mud. Will she speak? He waits. He pulls back to look at her. She smiles very slightly but says nothing. Finally, she turns and walks to her grandmother who has been moving closer ever since the music stopped, ready to take her home.

The mud begins to dry. People drift away. The accordion player plays a final *cumbia* and Hector, the driver who started dancing alone, finishes alone fueled by enough *sotol* to be the last man standing, or swaying. Finally, even the accordion player snaps the leather straps to the folded bellows and goes home.

Hector climbs back in his wagon and continues where he was going all along, back to the smelter before he'd been dispatched to rescue Señor Perry's stranded Studebaker.

Ezra stands alone, looking at the trampled place in the mud where he danced with Consuela. He looks up to the dark windows of the mansion on the hill and wonders if Howard Perry, at first light, will see the aftermath of that dance from his porch. At first, he would see his own tire tracks scoring the road. Then he could not fail to notice a rough jumble of footprints, wet clay baking to nearly white where his people danced and laughed. In spite of the closing of the mine. From up there, lonely on the hill, it might look like the effort of a giant's only child who tried to draw the surface of the moon.

Ezra's viewpoint comes back to earth, to the porch, empty now, except for Consuela's shoes. Did she leave them so he could return them to her? He picks them up. They weigh practically nothing. Slippers a ballerina might have left behind.

He walks to the east side of town to her house where already the lights are going out. By the time he gets there, her *abuela,* as if anticipating his presence, extinguishes the lamp.

He sets her shoes on her doorstep, the toes pointing not toward the house, but away, ready for her to step into them.

As he walks away he hears the door open but by the time he turns around, the shoes are disappearing; he sees them in Consuela's hand just before the door closes again.

〰〰

Ezra rides east today. He gallops across the mesa

to find Consuela. They have taken many walks in secret ever since the dance, beyond the sight line of her grandmother, away from the scrutiny and gossip of town. Today he'll surprise her; they'll ride. Together, they'll talk again about her plans to go to college to study law. He doesn't know about college, what he would study if he went. But he'll wait for her, if she goes away. Surely she'll come back.

She doesn't turn around when she hears the horse but hurries down the path. He quickly overtakes her and she whirls around, a rock in her hand.

"You scared me!" she cries.

"I didn't come to chase you. I came to give you a ride on the horse."

"I've never been on a horse. We have no money for horses."

"Then it's time."

"Both of us? At the same time? You would do that with me?"

"Why not?"

"There is only room for one."

"Not if you put that rock down."

"For the sake of the horse, I put the rock down."

She finds a ledge of shale to climb on and with Ezra's help, slides in front of him.

He hands her the reins. He rests his hands on his thighs, nudges Rio into an easy ramble. He moves his hands to her waist, very carefully, one at a time.

The rolling motion of the horse, the rhythmic way they both move in response to it makes his blood pound. She does not pull away. He wants to kiss the back of her neck—it's right there. He can't help it. He kisses her.

She drops the reins and Rio immediately stops. Slowly, she turns, nearly falling off the horse. Ezra holds onto her waist, lifting her up and after a precarious moment when she's standing on Rio's

withers she turns slowly around, balancing like a
barefoot circus rider. She leans over, rests her hands on
Ezra's shoulders and lowers herself, resting her thighs
on his, her legs dangling as she adjusts her cotton dress.

All they've done until now is hold hands and
dance. He's not sure who gets to whose lips first but
their mouths fit together, their teeth knocking as Rio
shifts beneath them.

"This is as far as we go together," she says. "You,
Ezra, will go on."

"I'm not going anywhere. But if I do, you'll come
with me."

"You have been here—how long? Six years? You
study everyone and everything. How little you know
about us. About me. You come and go. You ride because it pleases you. I have my family and they depend
on me."

She gets off the horse and walks away. How little
he knows. Like Elizabeth, Consuela sees what he can't,
that there's a great deal between what he observes and
what he thinks he understands.

April 11, 1923

Dear Ezra,
How happy we were to receive news from you after all this time! All of us at the Chelsea have wondered and worried about your well-being. St. Anthony's has been very close-mouthed about you, only saying that you have been "placed out" but now that you are of age, you are no longer their concern.
We can see by your splendid photograph on the horse that you are well. Claire du Lac says she always knew you'd become a handsome young man and if her age were otherwise, she would have you on her arm for the ball. She has never gotten over the fact that the orphanage would not release you to her custody. She went many times. She says she hopes you can forgive her. She says she is sure you are in love by now.
Other news: Senda has gone back to Cuba for a family funeral. Claire takes her meals from room service until Senda's return. Otto had an exhibition of his paintings with the Ashcan group at a gallery on Bleecker Street and sold many paintings. He says to tell you that his painting with your paramour is not for sale at any price and hangs in the lobby. We shall put your photograph on the wall next to it where we can see you, often.

We all hope for your continued happiness in the West,
Yours truly,
Robert McGarragh, Manager (at last!)

Elizabeth
1925

The burros Evie borrowed from the brakeman's brother pick their way along a narrow switchback trail. Unlike the other girls who head for the picture show on their day off, Evie and Elizabeth go east toward the ruins in the hills outside of town.

The burros thread their way through prickly pear; the yellow nodules that once held the fruit have turned hard and wrinkled now.

"*Nopal,*" Evie says. "If my father were here he could tell you exactly what kind."

"Did your father teach you the names?"

"He only talks about the proper ones, in Latin. I learned the Spanish ones. I like them better. They seem like the true names, to me."

"Do you like your name?" Elizabeth asks.

"I do. I always have. But it was Eve when I started out. I grew into Evie. Doesn't anybody ever call you Lizzie?"

"Not for long. I like a lot of syllables."

"Did your father pick your name or your mother?"

"I did."

"So you came into the world proclaiming yourself, did you?"

"Shouldn't everyone?"

The burros' small steps are sure among the rocks.

Elizabeth relaxes into the short stride, turns back to look at Belen, the long straight line of a train approaching from the south, its red and yellow and black cars like the bands of a coral snake Evie had shown her in a guidebook sold at the station newsstand. It's nice to think of somebody else having to scurry around filling and refilling bottomless cups of Fred Harvey's special brew today for the ten trains that will stop at the depot. It's nice to be here, carried higher through the country on the back of a sure-footed animal that knows its way.

Here in the Southwest, Elizabeth begins to see the makings of the world, the raw materials, the un-completed experiments, the spectacular extravagance of color and form. The sun and moon are brighter, more at home here. Ireland is demure, pastel in comparison. Worn down except for the raw edge of the Cliffs of Moher. New York had its ridgeline of steel but here, at last, are mountains. Great paperweights set down on a steadfast surface. No foothills to soften the effect. There is no getting around them, at least not easily. Belen, she learns, owes its existence to the engineers who created the cut-off that opened up east-west traffic. Before that, the steep grade of Raton Pass on the other side of the state required the Santa Fe line to drop sand below the engine for friction on the climb up; brakes wore out going down. Still, Belen's a small town, a token of civilization on the verge of the wild, its buildings upstaged by the mountains on either side of the long valley cut by the Rio Grande.

Something about the long view, the mountains to the east forming a backdrop to the long valley running north and south, gives her a sense of the wide band of time stretching out and herself a grain of sand upon it. This is the proper scale of things. Geology may take eons but her own life speeds up.

The life behind her, almost twenty years of it, is

only a tiny facet, added each year in the midst of April.
And before that, long before that, this place had no
name and was unclaimed. America had no states drawn
within it. "The Great American Desert" was the only
title for all of it on the maps of 1850 she'd seen in the
old encyclopedia at Monte Ne. That's what drew her
here. The desert. More than the Egypt she once tried to
walk into in her father's lantern show. This is a part of
America that isn't used up, like New York, where land
is still cheap enough that someone like her might be
able to buy a little piece of it one day.

The Anasazi that Louise always talked about had
dug their homes in the sides of cliffs, set themselves
apart from what moved above and below. But one day
they disappeared, leaving only the empty stone hives to
say they'd been there at all. And long, long before that,
a sea filled the trough between the mountains, and fish
left their feathery bones imprinted into rock. Whales or
something even larger broke the surface for air. All of it
is still constantly shifting, changing, disappearing, and
rearranging.

Brigid must be here. She probably quit Ireland like
everybody else, packed up her wolves and rainbows and
moved to these mountains. Along with Santa Teresa of
Cabora about whom she's just read, a saint now
included in the virgin witches and banished women of
Christendom. Well, she's one of them. Unsaved. Un-
repentant. Itinerant. A secret country inside herself to
which she alone belongs.

"My mother," Elizabeth says and stops, surprised
to have said it, to admit she once had one, "would have
liked it here. Ireland didn't suit her. She went to
England. With her lover. Then she tried to go by ferry
to France."

Evie listens, waiting for her to go on.

Elizabeth tells Evie that her mother was a
wanderer and would have liked to go farther than

England or France. Maggie Farrell would have been drawn to mysteries at the extremes of east or west. She admitted to Evie that she was, in a way, grateful that her mother had died *en route*, that it would pain her to think of her mother getting only as far as Folkestone, haunted constantly by the voice of the ferries calling out as they headed toward France. She took her chances. Booked passage. And became a casualty of the war to end all wars.

"Why do you think your mother would have liked it here?"

"I can only guess. She left Ireland. She might have felt stifled. She would have appreciated the sky, how much of it there is. How much air there is to breathe."

"She'd be surprised by you—how far you've come on your own," Evie says.

Elizabeth says nothing.

"She might even appreciate these burros. I'll bet she liked to ride."

"Why would she like to do that?" Elizabeth says, wondering how Evie knows.

"Because you do. Because she's like you."

"Isn't it usually the other way around?"

"No. She takes after you."

Elizabeth wants this story they're weaving together to be true; her own imagination regarding her mother isn't big enough. With Evie, her mother becomes someone almost knowable. A girl, like them, before she was a mother and a lover and a leaver of daughter and husband. A girl who would take off her hat, like her daughter, and lift her face to the sky.

"Do you still have a sweetheart," Evie asks, "where you came from?"

"I'm not ever going to get married," Elizabeth announces vehemently.

"I didn't ask you that."

"Queen Elizabeth didn't need a husband."

"So you'll be Queen Elizabeth of New Mexico, riding a burro instead of an Irish stallion. A robe of coyote fur. A crown of copper. A raven for a falcon."

Elizabeth laughs out loud, an awkward laugh. She's out of practice. But she likes Evie's flights of fancy.

"I'll be getting married to a boy from back home," Evie says. "Harlan and I went to school together. He's in medical school now. I'll keep on working here until he graduates. Then he'll set up a practice in Carrizozo. We'll live on his father's ranch."

"Don't you want to travel beyond your home town. See the country? At least another state?"

"Ten sections of land seem like plenty to explore. When my time in Belen is up I'll hang up my apron."

"And put on another one?"

"No, more likely a pair of chaps and shiny spurs. I'll have at least three children."

"How can you know that?"

"Some things you just know. This trail here, for instance. Has been here forever. A trade route for the Pueblo Indians swapping corn for buffalo with the Plains Indians."

The steady progress of the burro beneath her carries her over the trail where people traveled to trade what they grew with the people who hunted. Evie knows all about it and now Elizabeth knows something about it, too. There are not many Indians, now. They had their likeness preserved on nickels. Like the one she has, still.

"There's Abó," Evie says, pointing to an adobe citadel ahead. Nearby are the remnants of a Catholic church from when the Spaniards came through. Elizabeth thinks it's just like the Church to appropriate a sacred site, to supplant all the old stories with the one story they claim to be true.

They leave the burros to graze and Evie takes Elizabeth by the hand to show her the circle of the *kiva*.

In this sacred place the people sat and wondered and looked up, waiting through seasons for the return of the brightest stars to tell them when to plant or marry or be born or die. Evie lets go of her hand and climbs down into the *kiva*, leaving Elizabeth on the rim.

Elizabeth feels rootless, severed. She has no family behind her. No husband or children in her future. She could have chosen otherwise. She still can, though in Ireland she'd already be an old maid.

The broken stones of Abó are hot beneath her hands as she sits down on the rim of the *kiva*. Ten feet below, Evie turns slowly inside the circle, arms out, a clock marking eons instead of hours. Evie, sister for a day, a month, at most, a few years.

A stray strand of long brown hair, one Evie has not pinned beneath the hat comes loose, starts to wind around her. She has already counted her children, has probably picked out their names and will know their faces as they form inside her. Elizabeth is only a loose thread that will have to be cut. She can already feel the pain it will inflict. Here, well beforehand, she will begin to get used to it so that when the day comes to leave— she must leave before Evie, or at least at the same time, the pain will be minor. The cut will be like the sting of a bee, sharp but not fatal.

Right now, Evie's scarf is flying. Elizabeth jumps down off the rim into the *kiva* with her. She reaches, misses, catches the scarf on the next go around but instead of stopping Evie as she intended, she feels the pull, lets herself go with it, finds an orbit and keeps it. She holds onto one end, Evie the other. Turning and returning. Verse and chorus. The first wind of the world was no doubt born this way, is turning and returning still.

≈≈

Elizabeth checks the water glass for spots, sets it down north of the knife. Inspecting the silver surface for smudges, she polishes the coffee urn with a clean, white cloth. Rituals. It's what keeps her sanity intact a little longer. Evie's gone home for a week to help her parents make arrangements for her wedding in October. Elizabeth can't imagine staying in this place without her.

The 8:05 train bound for Los Angeles pulls in for a scheduled stop. Only a few passengers disembark, head straight for the dining room. A soldier with a cane comes limping through the door and sits down at the counter before her. It's been a very long time since she's seen a soldier come through these doors. She wonders why this one is still in uniform.

"Breakfast for you?" she asks. "There's time."

He nods slowly, as if he isn't sure. About breakfast, or time. She draws a pot of coffee from the urn. He lifts his cup to be filled.

"Where you from?" he asks, as if her foreignness is obvious, as if everyone's from somewhere else. As if she is the one who just got off the train.

"Everywhere," she says. "Here, for now."

"But originally," he insists, as if he needs to place her accent.

"The West of Ireland," she admits. "Your turn now. What about you?"

"I'm from just one place. Solano Beach, California. *California*," he says again, pronouncing each syllable of his state as if he hasn't said it in a long time, as if he needs to say it right. "Since you're only here for now, where to next?" he asks.

"Down the line," she says. "Farther West." She will not be lulled much longer by Belen. Farther West, surely she can still find what she's looking for—it's what all the railroad brochures still promise. You can

276

leave the gray, soot-filled East, the endless, treeless plains and even if the gold in the hills is gone, the sun still belongs to California.

He nods as if he knows this isn't West enough. His own dark eyes are still focused on some distant point. "All I thought about over there was getting back home. Buying a car. Driving along the coast highway. Not just in any car—one called a Moon. Made in St. Louis. Imagine! Now, the real thrill is walking without falling. This new leg is hard to get used to. I still feel the old one."

The steam in his coffee billows, thins, a brief atmosphere absorbed quickly in dry desert air. He stirs, his long fingers holding the spoon lightly. His hands, Elizabeth thinks, might have made music before they ever held a weapon.

"My girlfriend—my fiancée," he frowns, as if the word, like the artificial leg, takes getting used to, "said she'll love me no matter what." He puts the spoon down. "But she hasn't seen me yet. Like this. What do *you* think?"

Elizabeth shrugs. "It's hard to say."

And it is. It's hard to predict anything. Of that, she's sure, as sure as she is that every mile traveled is marked upon her twenty-year-old face—a complete cartography in the flesh—she doesn't have to say anything about her life at all.

"You're the first person I've talked to. Since the hospital. Most folks won't look at me. They're afraid. And grateful—a terrible combination," he admits.

"Grateful for what?" She retrieves a plate of bacon and eggs from the window to the kitchen, slides it in his direction.

"That I went to the Argonne, not them, that I was taken prisoner there. They don't even have a clue what country it's in. They have no idea." He breaks the yolks with the tines of his fork.

"France," she says. Once, it was not so far away.

He seems pleased that she knows. He almost smiles. She smiles, happy to have something to share, if only knowledge of a country across the sea. But she suspects it's more than knowledge of distant geography they have in common.

He pushes his plate away, egg yolks hardening like spilled paint. "Miss—can I ask a favor? Those Indians out front who sell jewelry—could you help me pick something out? For my girl. Meredith."

Why is he asking her? Doesn't he know what Meredith would like? Does he really believe a girl with such an elegant name is still waiting after all this time? That a ring will fix everything?

The cafe is empty. Irene and the others are working back in the kitchen. It's a slow morning. She might as well help him. She won't be missed. She steps from behind the counter, away from the altar of the urn, her station, into the wide-open room. A full person now, not just a torso. But still hidden—long legs behind the long, black skirt. Feet laced tight in shoes.

The soldier drops his cane. As she bends to pick it up, she knows that at this very moment, her head bowed, he would be able to see the pale, exposed part in her thick, mahogany-colored hair, the combs that barely hold it all in place. If he's looking.

She glances up as she hands him the cane, watches shame and something else flood his face. The dark eyes are fully focused on her now. "Won't you tell me your name?" he asks, as if she's already refused a previous request. As if he really needs to know.

Loneliness is something a person their age has no business knowing. She feels a bright needle threading through her, stitching together something torn and tender. He's put his finger on that place because he has it, too. And she feels an urgency now, in this tentative bond born of happenstance. Two people with twenty minutes between trains. Something could happen. But nothing will if she doesn't speak up, and soon.

"My name is Maud," she declares. A single, secret syllable, without any flourish. She hasn't given her real name to anyone in years, and she brings it back now because he asks. She wonders if he knows it's the same name as an Irish revolutionary who made the great poet, Yeats, cry.

"My name's Carter," he offers, though she didn't ask him.

But she does say, point blank, "What took you so long?" Seeing his confusion, she quickly adds, "Everybody else came home ages ago."

"Just trying to come back. All the way back."

Like you, he might say next. He might.

He holds the door open. They walk through it together into the blinding sunlight, beneath the blue, unbroken bowl full of sky. Hopeful travelers. Moving toward, not just along.

The Navajo women watch them approach, whisper excitedly to each other. She's often spoken to Mai and her mother, Tiba. They've come east and south from Farmington on lands the government decrees is theirs. Their men work on section crews, their livelihoods dependent now on the iron horse that changed their lands forever. Every time they see her they always ask her where her husband is. How many children will she have? What will be their names? In spite of everything they still see the future in any child's eyes. Today they look as if their wish for her is about to come true.

Carter leans on his cane, surveys the bright turquoise spread on ocher blankets, pointing, finally, to a ring with a deep sunset-colored stone.

"Spiny oyster shell," she tells him. "This used to be the sea." It's something she appreciates about this place—a vastness, wet or dry. It takes eons to change from one to the opposite other, the shells of former creatures fragile, but enduring. They have all the time in the world. Not just minutes. She hands the ring to him.

"Try it on?" He places it on her ring finger. Studies it, holding her hand. "Yes. This is the one."

She stares at his hand holding her own, reckless with longing, appalled that she no longer seems to have any control over herself—she who has only one friend here in the dormitory of girls, all much younger than she is now, except for Evie. They have families, fiancées. They call her The Iron Maiden behind her back, and she's heard them often enough to wonder if they might be right.

For all of two minutes she's engaged to this soldier. Spoken for. Until he lets go of her hand.

She pulls at the ring but heat has swollen her finger enough to try to keep it. She has to twist it off to give it back to him.

Mai and Tiba look confused now. They confer in vehement whispers. Their faces grow solemn, wary, Mai holds up five fingers and Tiba holds up hers as well, doubling the price.

He pays what they ask without complaint, puts the ring in his breast pocket. "Funny. I don't remember if she wore jewelry. I never looked that closely at Meredith's hands. I just tried to hold them."

The rising vibration of the impatient engine shakes the ground in warning. The other passengers board the train. He hesitates.

There's still time. They could continue on to California. Drive the car, the Moon, to the ocean while it's still an ocean. Go as far as they can go, as West as they can. She'll spread a Navajo blanket on the sand and together they'll watch the sun give the last of its gold to the waves breaking against the blue border, the last of the West of America. She'll rest her hand at the place where the prosthetic joins what's left of the leg he was born with. She'll leave her hand there until both flesh and wood grow equally warm, until the phantom limb, wakened by touch, remembers.

The whistle blasts, startling them both. The train shudders, inching forward. Carter lurches after it, swings himself awkwardly up the two steep steps, refusing the conductor's hand. The whistle blasts again. If he said goodbye, she didn't hear it.

The train is moving faster now. She walks alongside, her hair coming loose from the combs. She stops just short of a run.

She will not run after him. Or anyone. The dream dissipates like the smoke from the engine, dark at the stack, pale gray as it blows further behind. But it was her dream, forged in the heart of the Iron Maiden, loose now in the wider world.

She sees him once more, leaning over the railing of the caboose—he's made his way through all the cars. He looks back as long as he can, arm raised in greeting and goodbye. The train pulls him forward, toward California. To a place where he may still be welcome, a place he once called home.

She turns, walks past Mai and Tiba who look at her now with eyes long-accustomed to broken promises, but vindicated, too, as if some justice has been served by extracting a high price from this soldier who took the ring away with him.

She could try to explain to them but they wouldn't believe her. They know what they saw—the giving. The taking away.

When Elizabeth returns to clean the counter she finds a Walking Liberty half-dollar. Twice the price of the plate he slipped it under. It's been quite a while since she's seen one. She puts it into her pocket.

Later, after supper, when the girls divide the tips to send back to Kansas and Arkansas, she will not declare it. She will declare nothing at all.

He gave it to *her.* An amulet of sterling for her own

journey west—a silver woman holding a sheaf of wheat, walking boldly toward the sun.

Ezra
1928

A newcomer to Terlingua causes a stir, not just in his charismatic demeanor or his already legendary drinking but in his fraternization with the Mexican miners. Samuel shares more than one drink with him and remarks to Ezra that it's odd to be the one interviewed, for a change. Mr. Brown has many questions about the goings-on of the Chisos mine. He's read Samuel's column in the *Chicago Tribune* and admires his outspokenness. He's finally come to see the place for himself.

Ezra has watched Brown in action at the Lajitas store, listened in on his questions to the miners. Mr. Brown is not just a curious visitor. He has many technical questions he asks the miners in Spanish: the quality and quantity of the ore they're finding, but most importantly, the specific location of the latest findings. He is part owner of the Rainbow Mine, adjacent to the Chisos Mine, and by the conversations, Ezra quickly figures out that what Mr. Brown is after is information regarding underground trespass, that Perry has mined ore that does not legally belong to him.

The miner most helpful to Brown is Consuela's uncle, Eduardo. Ezra recognizes him, is, in fact, greeted with a handshake by him when he rides Rio to Lajitas after the *avisadores* flash the news that a new shipment of *sotol* is coming across the river. It's always a celebration at the trading post.

By the time Ezra gets there the *sotol* is flowing. Mr. Brown is talking, laughing, even singing in Spanish when a man with a guitar strikes up a soulful version of Brown's request: *"La Paloma."*

Eduardo and Brown have much to say to one another and Brown even puts his hand on Eduardo's shoulder at the end of the evening and shakes his hand most emphatically. Eduardo tips his hat to Ezra when he leaves.

〰️

A week later, Ezra sees Eduardo coming out of the mine manager's office. He throws something with as much force as he can into the dirt and walks quickly toward his house.

Ezra finds what he threw: his *ficha*, his labor token with his number: 8. For years he has taken it from its place on the pegboard each morning, presented it at night for his pay. Now it lies in the dirt near the water tank. He must have been fired. Or, more unthinkable, he quit.

Ezra goes to find Consuela waiting for him in their usual meeting place on the far side of Bee Mountain.

He tries to take her in his arms but she pushes him away. "We're being taken back to San Carlos. *Taken,*" she says. "They don't trust us to leave on our own."

"They can't do that," Ezra says.

"Perry can. He's *La Ley*, or haven't you heard? This is his private country."

"Can't Eduardo appeal?"

"That is not the kind of law they have here. This is Terlingua. He says go, we go."

284

RIDERS ON THE ORPHAN TRAIN

"Then I'll come with you."

"What are you going to do in San Carlos? Herd goats? My *abuela* will never allow it." She looks at him defiantly. "*I* will not allow it now."

"Why?"

"You were there."

"Where?"

"At Lajitas. Eduardo said so. Also, your *abuelo* Mr. Samuel has been seen drinking with Mr. Brown at the hotel. And even though I try to believe it was one of Perry's spies who must have told him, my family does not understand. I cannot make them understand because *I* do not understand."

"We can meet..."

"*You* don't understand, do you? You stay on your side. From now on."

≈

He sees Consuela for the last time on the shoals of the Rio Grande at Lajitas, ready to cross the river. Her family is already on the other side, waiting for her. He leads Rio by a rope. He hands the rope to her.

Her kiss, when she gives it, is a different kind of kiss, tender at first, in the way that he knows her to be, then insistent, her tongue pushing against his teeth as if they are a gate, now closed. Her tongue speaks without speaking but he hears her clearly. *Go.*

Rio, confused, tries to follow him until Consuela gets on and urges him into the water. He watches them both plunge through the water until Rio's hooves leave America and he swims his rider into Mexico, where she'd begun her life without Ezra and now would continue to do so.

Giving her Rio is not enough, but the horse is all he has of value. Even though he did not pass on any information to Perry's manager, the fact that he visited

Consuela often, that he is friends with Enrique, that he saw Eduardo in Lajitas talking with Brown and that Eduardo had greeted him publicly; it all implicated Ezra. Even here, there are eyes. What actually happened is beside the point. As far as Perry's spies know, secrets were passed from one side of town to the other, with Ezra as the likely messenger. How naïve he's been, imagining his comings and goings to be his own. He had implicated her, marked her as someone who could not be trusted to stay on her side until she was literally pushed back across the border.

Before he even kissed her for the first time he had explored shelter caves, Comanche trails across the Mesa de Anguila. He swam naked in the *tinajas* after summer rains. All of these things return to him now and these fragments, along with the enormity of the mountains and their tumultuous storms, can barely be contained inside the small space of his memory. He already knows from experience that things eventually lose their vividness. Claire du Lac's singing, for instance: not only the words, but even the melody is long gone. Or was that Senda's voice he heard? At this moment, he cannot imagine ever forgetting Conseula's last kiss, as if it burns with the words she could not say out loud.

QUICKSILVER COURIER –
November 17, 1928
by S. McPherson

Ezra Duval and I will leave Terlingua soon in quite a different manner than when we arrived ten years ago.

From here, in transit, any new enterprise will seem tame compared to Howard Perry's empire. For the record, he has asked us to leave. That we do so now without protest is because there is little left to say. Gone are the rich rewards of the war years; he made well over a million dollars in 1918. These days, production is a fraction of that and he resorts to theft for profit.

I will give E. Duval the last word: "Innocent people are always in the way of greed. Readers may remember an incident involving the slaughter of goats by drunken soldiers in 1919. That shepherdess, Consuela Obregón and her entire family have just been deported. For telling the truth. Let it be known here and now that there is definitive proof that Perry's Chisos Mining Company has penetrated the neighboring Rainbow Mine's ore and that the law will prevail. But the red mineral in question has stained the hands and hearts of the Obregon family forever. They have been resettled across the border, to a town from which they once fled in fear for their lives. They may be close to the border, but justice for them is very far away."

∿∿∿

Leaving Terlingua is harder than Ezra ever would have imagined. With each mile north he feels swallowed into an alien country. He wishes he were on a mule train, leaving the way he came. He would have time, with the plodding steps of the mules, to slowly let it all go. The truck that now serves as a stage, though much faster, seems to labor, gaining speed slowly as if it's taking the desert with it, dragging it behind.

What will be required of him elsewhere? He'd more than entertained the thought of staying behind. In the end, Consuela reminded him about his obligation to Samuel. "How can you leave someone who died and returned to you? He is your *family*." He was ashamed that it was she who had to point out this undeniable truth to him. Samuel once saved his life; Ezra may have inadvertently saved his during the epidemic, but Samuel's vulnerability now is under his guardianship, and rightfully so. Ezra imagines they will both be fragile, like antiquities, long protected, disintegrating in the vigorous air of the modern world.

Elizabeth
1928

Elizabeth and Evie sit together, customers at last waiting for their respective trains out of Belen. There are far fewer trains now; people seem to be buying automobiles. Soon enough, roads will put passenger trains out of business.

Woodrow Washington, the engineer from the ATSF train from Los Angeles, takes his usual seat at the counter. Before the war he worked as a brakeman. In the war he got training, drove trucks. Now he goes back and forth between Kansas and California supporting a wife and two children in Albuquerque. He goes home every other weekend.

"What are you hauling today? Elizabeth asks.

"Copper from Arizona, mostly."

"Seems like copper is all I hear about from Arizona."

"Big money in copper. I dropped off parts for a smelter in Lordsburg. They're living it up in Clifton. Phelps Dodge bought up everything—the Metcalf, the Longfellow, the Shannon Mine. "

"I heard about that mine when I first came here," she comments. "It's either an Irish family name, or somebody honoring the old sod."

"You're probably right. Man by the name of

Tyrone owns it," I hear.

Elizabeth nearly drops her cup. "*John* Tyrone?"

"I believe that was his name. He met my train to help transfer his shipment to the spur line. Yes. His name was written on the freight manifest."

She sets the pot down. "You have no idea how important that information is to me."

"Kin of yours?"

"In a manner of speaking."

"I guess the Irish have to stick together, out here."

"Especially here," she says. "Particularly now."

Evie gets up to say goodbye to Irene, working in the dining room.

"With a face like that," Elizabeth says to Woodrow, "you must be still a week away from going home."

"No." He sets the spoon down but doesn't take his eyes off the cup. "It's not that. It's not that simple. I killed a man. Two days ago. It was broad daylight and he was standing by the tracks as I was heading out of the yard. He looked right at me—I was leaning out the side of the engine. I waved, you know, like I do. He waves back and when I was ten feet away he falls on the tracks.

"I know it's part of the job, hittin' things. Cows, hoboes, dragging brand new automobiles with a drunk at the wheel. But that man...Why me? Why my train? I've had the shakes since Barstow."

"Do you know who he was?"

"I don't know a name. Don't want one. But you read about these men, the ones who came back and can't get all the way home. Shell-shock, they call it now. My granddaddy in the Civil War called it soldier's heart." He shakes his head in dismay.

Elizabeth looks at the clock on the wall, watches the call boy get ready to ring the gong for the crew change. In these last few seconds where nothing more can be said, she tries to imagine the man stepping in front of the train. What were his final thoughts in the last few seconds before he took that step? In the last second when it was too late, did he change his mind?

Evie comes back to the counter and sets a small package with a California postmark in front of Elizabeth. No return address. Addressed to: "Maud. Harvey House. Belen, New Mexico." It made the rounds, but nobody claimed it.

"Is this *you*?" Evie asks. "*Maud?*"

"It used to be." She opens the brown wrapping paper. Inside, there's a smaller package. Wrapped in cotton, the ring she helped the soldier, Carter buy. For Meredith. He included no letter.

"You look like you've seen a ghost," Evie says.

Elizabeth's hands are shaking as she puts the ring on. "There was a soldier here. About a month ago. He was afraid his sweetheart wouldn't be able to accept him with an artificial leg. I helped him pick out this ring. From Mai and Tiba. They thought he was buying it for *me*." She's afraid it may have been Carter that stepped in front of the train, and that sending this ring was the last thing he did before taking his life. A bad omen for the beginning of her new journey. Very bad.

"What kind of girl waits through the war for her soldier to come home, waits another three years for him to make it all the way back, greets him at the door and then turns away? I don't get it." Evie looks at the ring as if it might hold an answer.

"She must have been frightened," Elizabeth says.

"Then she was the wrong girl."

"Maybe she saw that something else was broken. Something she couldn't fix and she knew she would never be able to make him happy."

The ring is heavy on her finger. Will she grow used to it, not even notice it's there after a while, like the sound of trains in the night that used to wake her? Last night, she slept right through the rumble and roar. Now, trains have a new meaning—they are a way to leave the world, not just travel through it.

"I understand her," Elizabeth says. "Evie I left him. I came all the way to America. I'd waited for years to be with him."

Evie listens as if she knew all along that Elizabeth was in love. Had been all along. She claimed she wasn't, but here it is, the true story at the eleventh hour.

"He didn't recognize me. Maybe I'd changed. But my voice—I sang the song that used to make him cry and it had absolutely no effect on him. It was as if I wasn't there."

"He hasn't forgotten you, obviously," Evie says, reaching out to Elizabeth to hold her hand.

Elizabeth stares at Evie, realizing she doesn't know what she's talking about. How could she? "You don't understand, Evie. Everything and everybody in your life is right where you left them."

There's no time to explain anything. Evie embraces Elizabeth until the last moment, and then she lets her go. Evie's train leaves first, Elizabeth's right after, their trains neck and neck on separate tracks until Evie's turns east, toward the desert hills that have always been her home.

November 26, 1928

Hotel Hidalgo
Lordsburg, New Mexico

Dear Mrs. Worthington,

*I hope this letter finds you well, that it in fact finds you at
all. I don't imagine you are still with the Children's Aid Society
but then I can't imagine you doing anything else. I still see you,
lining us up on the stage at the opera house in Rogers, Arkansas.
I now know the name of the town, though you didn't when I
asked you at the time. You accompanied forty-seven of us in
September of 1918, to find new homes in the west.*

*Although I did not stay in Arkansas I have, in a manner
of speaking, continued my journey by train, as far as Belen, New
Mexico where until recently, I worked at the Harvey House there.
I had intended to go to California, but here in Lordsburg, I was
able to confirm some information I recently came by. In a few
days, I will board yet another train, the Arizona and New
Mexico line, to Clifton, Arizona, to collect a debt from an
Irishman I once loaned my life savings to in New York.*

*I am writing not just to tell you the ordinary details of my
life or to inquire about yours. I am writing to ask you to assist me
with your memory in answering some questions. The answers are
very important to me. I know this may seem an unusual request
but I want to know if you remember what happened on that
train, if you in fact remember me at all.*

*There is a great blur between what I believe happened and
what actually occurred.*

*I'm having trouble with the details. I remember a boy—I
never knew his name. I'm wondering if you can tell me. I believe
you pulled us out of the line for some misbehavior. After that, I
have no reliable memory. You may wonder why this is important
to me after all this time, but I need to know exactly what
happened that day before I can move forward with any certainty.
In my present circumstances, en route to a new destination, I*

believe I may have given the boy something I can no longer do without. You see, even with this declaration to you, I have a habit of giving too much away.

In hopes of your assistance, I remain
Sincerely,
Maud Elizabeth Farrell

October 30, 1928

Dear Miss Farrell,

*Your letter reached me at the Children's Aid Society where
I am now employed as a secretary. I am surprised you remember
me and I hope that your memory was not too deeply inscribed by
any insensitivity on my part. I do not have to think very hard to
remember you. In fact, I have never forgotten you, at least not for
very long.*

*What happened that day has haunted me for some time.
Indeed, it made me question my calling to be a matron on such a
train, to shepherd my charges in the progressive philanthropy of
relocation. That day I saw its darker face: the face of <u>dis</u>location.
One child crying was all it took and others joined in, a Greek
chorus of woeful souls, as it were, collectively voicing their distress.
You stepped forward to soothe them, I now believe, by singing.
But you sang something so strange it may have had the opposite
effect. It was no lullaby. It may have been in German, which
surprised me; you were obviously of Irish descent. But the children
stopped crying, not because they heard something familiar but
because it was altogether strange. I find it stranger still that you
do not remember. One hears, in this day and age, and the
popularity of séances bears this out, that those who have departed
still have a great deal to say. But do the dead sing, one might
ask? And if so, Miss Farrell, if I may be so bold, who, exactly
was singing through you that day? For myself, I was not soothed
but frightened by the voice that broke through that melee in
Arkansas. I have done a great deal of spiritual inquiry since and
I concluded God sent a message to me through you. I have also
greatly questioned my whispered challenge to you that day to accept
a home, sight unseen, to leave in the company of a complete
stranger I could tell had come from poor circumstances. Yet she
was enthralled by your voice. I took that as a sign. And so I
strongly advised you to accept her offer of a home.*

*After that journey, I never boarded another train to take
children West. The last train to take such a journey may be as*

soon as next year. Now, I wonder if I misinterpreted, if I have, in fact, always put to poor use whatever talents I once may have had.

Perhaps I have turned unwittingly from my true calling. I was only briefly married, widowed, like so many, by the war. Hence, my work in shepherding children on the trains. I continue to work at the Children's Aid, but now I tend to correspondence, hence, my answer to your letter. And here you are again, a persistent echo reminding me of what must have felt like an agony of confusion in your young life.

I do remember the boy you mentioned. Alas, I do not recall his name. There have been so many! I do remember he spent all his waking hours writing; I have wondered more than once what he had to say.

In my first year as a secretary I found the 1910 census of the "Placing Out" done by Children's Aid. 110,000 children! By now it may have doubled. In any event, I only know, not from records, but from memory that the boy you mentioned got off the train in Texas. I could provide you with his last name if records were accessible, but we seem to have misplaced correspondence between 1910 and now. I have searched in vain; there is much to rectify and creation of some sort of archives is imperative.

I wish I could be of further help to you in locating whatever you gave him that you feel you must now recover. The search itself deserves attention, whether or not the sought-for object is ever found. Sometimes there is something else well worth having in its stead.

I wish you God speed in this, and all endeavoring.

Warmest Regards,
Ethel Worthington

Ezra
1929

The sharp smell of creosote, the grinding friction of the wheels assault his senses as this enormous train comes to a stop before him. It's been a long time since he's heard the hiss of expelled steam, the calling of the brakeman, the creak of leather handles bearing the weight of luggage lifted up the step.

The smell of dust-filled plush and smoke combine into the unmistakable scent of departure. How many times on that trip from New York had he gotten on and off? At each stop the company of children he'd started out with lessened.

Elizabeth. She's very much here, leaning back in that seat across the aisle, regarding him with one eye, sizing him up in a single, knowing glance. The frozen boy, no matter what he tries to say, barely says a word. He may be leaving a written record of facts behind, but nobody who matters will read it. Not his father, not Elizabeth, not Consuela, now, reading only the weekly paper from Ojinaga, not Chicago, in Spanish.

He turns his face to the window. He has to have the window. He watches the town of Alpine slowly disappear as the train picks up speed and the emptiness at the edge of town dissolves in a blur of blue and brown and green.

What happened to your eye? He once asked Elizabeth that very question.

I took it out.

All he can do is close both of his against all the incoherent emptiness until Samuel, somewhere still in the world, shakes him and says, "Ezra, wake up. Ezra, we're here."

〰︎
〰︎

Slaton. Still Texas. Only a stop for supper. Samuel is keen to dine at the Harvey House but from the minute he steps off the train Ezra is ill at ease. For one thing, it's cold. Really cold. There's a smell of snow though it hasn't fallen yet. He wraps his coat close around him and goes through the door of the depot. There is no dining room here, just a large horseshoe-shaped counter tended by starched girls, sexless as nuns. No singing from the kitchen, shouts from the street, no braying of mules. Everything is murmur here.

And there are no tortillas. Here, they serve rolls, insubstantial pillows of wheat that require butter to make them edible. Salt and pepper make for very insufficient spice.

Ezra picks at his food, staring at the unnatural shine of glazed carrots, the fish swimming in a viscous sauce of lemon.

Samuel studies him. "Quite a shock, isn't it? I'm glad I don't have to navigate this alone."

Once more, Samuel is trying to make conversation. Ezra's not going to disappear into silence as he once did. But he can't talk right now.

"You've hardly said a word since we left Alpine. I've been worried you might have stopped speaking again, that it's what you do when you move from one place to another—leave your voice behind you. I don't think I can go through that again."

"It catches up with me, sooner or later."

"Ezra, you don't have to be here."

"I want to stay with you. To follow the next story, wherever it goes. But so far, I don't see much worthwhile to write about."

"There's always something to write about. There definitely will be something to write about in Dalhart. Wheat is the next boom. But in the meantime, have you noticed, for example, that the silverware here is exactly, and I mean exactly one inch from the edge of the counter? The water glass is set at true north of the butter knife."

Ezra looks at the place setting next to him. "Now *that's* frightening."

"Then you're a relic already. This is the future of travel. Dependability. Consistency that is rigorously maintained from Topeka to Santa Fe. It's a comfort to many who might not have ventured out of the safety of their homes otherwise."

"Then they should stay at home." Ezra searches the counter for something out of place. All is in order. The waitress doesn't have a single hair coming loose from her pins, not even the tiniest stain on her white apron. Her movements are practiced and efficient. It's Ezra who is in disarray.

〰〰

In Dalhart, in the Texas Panhandle, Ezra becomes anonymous as soon as he steps off the train into the throng. It's disorienting, this activity stretching out in all directions. Fancy hotels. Cafes. Automobiles. Women shop in a variety of shops, not just a company store. Ezra feels himself swept along in all of this motion.

There is so much he doesn't know, couldn't have

known from their outpost in Terlingua. America has been busy. Very busy. Samuel sends him to the library with lots of paper and well-sharpened #2 pencils to find out who, what, where, how, and why.

This part of the country, he soon finds out, has multiplied, expanded, pushed its edges, both horizontally and vertically. The dark cave of the Mission Theatre in Dalhart is the smallest place he can find where things move at the speed of life, calibrated properly in the projector. Outside, the film runs on and on at high speed.

Dalhart, born from the crossroads of two railroads bringing immigrant homesteaders to town, now sees itself on the cutting edge of prosperity. He and Samuel were received by white-gloved doormen as welcome guests when they took up "extended residence" in the DeSoto Hotel, one of many businesses owned by a local impresario on Denrock Street. Today, from the second story window Ezra watches the street below. The street fills as the trains arrive—Rock Island Line or Ft. Worth and Denver. No mule trains here. The Felton Opera House fills up and later lets out. Denrock Street empties only in the last hour before dawn when the streetlights wane; people, it seems, will do anything to keep from going home.

He goes to picture shows in the darkened theatre to see "Nanook of the North." The struggle in the Arctic. Igloos. He'd seen an exhibit at the Eden Museé once, an igloo melting in the basement in an unseasonably warm winter.

He goes to see Nanook a second time and feels he almost knows this indigenous fisherman: a man rising with the sun, going to sleep when it dips below the horizon. Planting nothing. Drilling for nothing. Living on solid ice. Caring for his dogs and they, for him. Eating what he catches and using every last scrap down to the rawhide strips for harnessing the dogs to the sled. Nanook knows who he is, where he is and how to keep on living there. Nanook would be horrified in Dalhart. Ezra would take him to the picture show to remind him where he came from, where he must go back to as soon as possible now that he's seen what he's seen and knows what he knows. Too much. It's too much. Why is everyone living as if there's not enough of anything and no time left to keep it?

He wishes he were back in Terlingua. With Consuela. Maybe she's riding the old Comanche trail where they used to walk together. Or fishing in the Rio Grande at the other end of Santa Elena Canyon, a place so primal it seemed, the first time he discovered it that the sun itself must have slipped down that very gorge to be born.

DALHART DISPATCH
August 10, 1929
S. McPherson & E. Duval

We are surrounded by wheat, waist-high, as far as the eye can see. The tractors run all night, their headlights moving across the fields, back and forth, like someone who has lost something and cannot rest until it's found, until the last acre is turned over.

"Every man a landlord!" "Rain follows the plow!" We shall see what promises Nature decides to deliver.

〰〰

When Ezra steps into the foyer of Dalhart's sanitarium to have a look he cannot help but be curious about the wonders and horrors on display. A human heart floats in formaldehyde. The left hemisphere of a brain has turned the color and density of over-cooked cauliflower. A tight-fisted fetus floats in a jar, one eye open wide, the other mysteriously sealed. Ezra stands in front of this altar of autopsy, transfixed, imagining these parts inside his own, unopened body, working without a thought or even awareness of the relation of one part to another. The fetus disturbs him most of all, the terrible softness of its flesh, the umbilical cord still attached. Protruding from a convex navel, the cord dangles like a frayed, severed rope. Only one eye is open. It was shocked, perhaps, by the sawing of the cord while the other eye still gazed inward, prolonging the safety of maternal darkness as long as possible.

It's hard to imagine himself like this, not yet a full-born, breathing baby but floating in a fluid-filled jar like a clapper inside the bell of his mother as she walked through the world. And what was it like to be born, the vessel broken, sinking? She was gone by the time he took his first breath without her.

All he's ever known of his mother was a photograph his father kept in a drawer. She's standing in front of a lighthouse, her dark hair blowing in the strong wind from the sea. His father had told him when he asked, that it was taken at Montauk Point, the end of Long Island, on their honeymoon. After that brief conversation, the picture disappeared and Ezra never found it again, though he looked everywhere.

The human heart that floats heavily in the jar here looks nothing like a heart. How in the world did the popular shape come to be printed on playing cards and Valentines? Before anyone ever saw an actual heart they must have thought of love in that beautiful symmetry. The organ is an oddity, a lump, an oversized tuber blindly sprouting roots in all directions.

He wonders why there isn't a penis on display. There probably is one, in the basement. Shriveled and forlorn. To look at anything separated from the whole is to render it ridiculous. And the people these parts came from—where are they now—buried deep, ashamed of their insides on display for all to see?

He tries to turn his attention to the living, to anyone's story but his own.

Elizabeth
1929

The whistle shrieks, reverberating in the slot canyon. A ragged ribbon of a mud-red river winds alongside the tracks. Elizabeth watches the other passengers. There are others on this train, two men in suits, half a dozen women who have stuffed the overhead racks with purchases from Lordsburg, none of them looking out the window; they've obviously made this trip many times before. To Elizabeth, it's brand new, so different to be closed in by a narrow canyon after the broad Estancia Valley in which Belen barely made a dent. And because of this more tangible topography and the serendipity of learning of John Tyrone's whereabouts she feels that the idea of collecting her debt, with interest, seems not only plausible but destined.

She tries to imagine what he'll look like, what expression will come to his face when she confronts him. Delight? Dismay? But what if this is another John Tyrone? Anything is possible. The name itself has given her a destination. Beyond that, she has no plan at all. But then, she never did think very far ahead.

Talk of mining dominates the journey. Phelps Dodge has become the latest monopoly. Copper is king in Arizona. The men read the stock reports. Who would have thought such vast mineral wealth was underneath The Great American Desert? Land people once hurried to get through on their way to the timbered hills of California is well worth having. Owning. Evidently even the desert can be wilderness for only so long.

She notes the dresses of the other women on the train. Even in this rugged outpost hemlines have gone up. For so long hers has had to remain nine inches from the floor, regulation strictly enforced from Harvey House headquarters in Kansas City. She sees no reason to change that now. Hair got shorter and clever caps replaced wide brimmed hats. She feels like a relic in her long, navy skirt, her white shirtwaist. A wide leather belt with a silver buckle divides the dark from the light. And now that she's not serving customers she lets her hair hang long and loose about her shoulders, lighter than it used to be from so much time in the sun, a burnished copper color overlaying the dark mahogany. On her head she wears absolutely no hat at all.

The train comes out of the canyon and crosses the narrow river on the right. A large white house surrounded by green grass, of all things, humbles other structures, including the court house. Smaller houses spread upward toward the hills followed by shacks barnacled to cliffs. The train, all two cars of it, stops at the depot below the business district to the north with its back literally to the wall of rock in the still continuing canyon.

As the train slows to a stop, she can see horses in the street. A mule-drawn wagon loaded with ice. An automobile or two. She gets off, walks into the small depot where the women are met by husbands or fathers who bear the bundles of merchandise homeward. She follows the men in suits, walking up the canyon to the hotel, passing a Chinese restaurant and an Italian grocery along the way.

The lobby of the hotel, she can see upon entering,

serves as the social club of this town. The women cluster in chairs around a low table away from the bar in back. Prohibition never seemed to matter much in the West.

It's after six now. She thought John Tyrone might be here, though she has no reason to think this other than the fact that her arrival might have been a prescient thought that pulled him from whatever he was doing to greet her. She still dreams like an orphan. But he'd shown up more than once in her life with no warning. Now she's the one coming out of the blue.

At the back of the bar a curtain hangs over a doorway through which men come and go; smoke billows outward with every parting.

From what she'd read in the books left behind by passengers at the Harvey House she's expecting a card game, pistols drawn, a bartender getting ready to duck. A buxom madam leaning on the piano while a man half her size in a vest and bowler hat plays something tinkley and just a little out of tune.

There's no piano here. No madam surveying the lobby. Only the men from the train sitting down at a table, a group of others in work clothes at the bar sipping what probably isn't undiluted ginger ale. The bartender looks at Elizabeth skeptically. The workers just stare.

"Lose somebody?"

"As a matter of fact, I have. Yes. A long time ago. I'm looking for John Tyrone."

"What's he done now?"

"I'm his sister."

The bartender leans forward, studying her features. "Didn't know he had one. I don't know where John Tyrone is tonight. Up in Morenci, probably."

"He still does payroll himself. Doesn't trust the new owners to do it right," a man at the end of the bar says. "I could take you up there. When I'm done here."

"I'll wait in the lobby. I've waited this long. Take your time."

"Miss, since you're Irish and all, can I buy you a drink?"

"I didn't get a chance to start before Prohibition."

"I never stopped." He takes a flask from his pocket, pours a hefty dose into the ginger ale. Lifts his glass to her.

She leaves the bar to sit in one of the upholstered chairs near the window in the lobby. Dark comes early to the canyon, everything west blocked by a wall of rock. By the time it's completely dark, her chauffeur walks with feigned steadiness out of the bar, and signals her to follow him outside.

He's older than she realized. Gray hair curls from beneath a dun colored hat. He ceremoniously opens the door of a truck, leans in to brush off the seat with his coat sleeve, stands up too quickly and bumps his head on the doorframe.

"Do you know how to drive?" he asks.

"Hardly."

"Well you might need to learn tonight."

Should she wait for morning so he can sober up? No. She's so close. She knows where he is now, keeping accounts up the mountain. By morning he could be gone, word out about his Irish sister in hot pursuit.

The man pulls his hat on tighter though there is no wind to speak of. He starts up the truck, backs up to turn around, all without mishap. The sound of the truck's engine echoes off the canyon walls, completely out of proportion to its three pistons stuttering uphill. The fourth finally kicks in as they pass a bridge.

"Eleven years ago a wall of water come down through here and tore up the town. They're not calling for rain tonight, though, you'll be glad to know. But can you swim, Miss….I didn't get your name."

"Today it's Elizabeth," she says.

"I'm sure there's a story to go with that remark. Half the people who wind up here are running from something or somebody."

"What about the other half?"

"They look the other way."

The truck careens around switchback turns, back and forth, higher all the time. The lights of Clifton appear and disappear as if they're going on and off, a child playing with the switch. At a certain altitude they out-climb the moon which struggles to clear the jagged mountains.

"Pretty," he says, meaning the moon, she thinks, until his hand rests heavily on her thigh.

"What do you think you're doing?"

He takes his hand back. "I had to at least try."

"Try it again and you'll see what happens when I really lose my patience."

"Well, aren't you something? Irish have done nothing but cause trouble here, let me tell you."

"What kind of trouble?" Elizabeth's keeping her eye on his hand.

"More than trouble. An uproar. More than twenty years ago, a priest sent for a Mercy Train of Irish orphans in New York and gave 'em away. To *Mexicans!* People around here have never gotten over it."

She turns to him, incredulous.

"Well, I guess I've got your attention now, Miss Elizabeth. You never saw such a commotion. Puts the flood to shame. We rode out in the middle of the night and got those kids back. I wanted one but I didn't have a wife. They were little bits, those Sheeny kids, to cause so much trouble. And the thing is, in New York those kids were nothin' to nobody. By the time they got here you'd think they was made out of gold."

"You've had far too much to drink."

"I haven't had near enough! Those kids were *sent* for and the nuns in New York didn't think to ask who they was goin' to."

"*Sent* for?"

"If you ask me they were trying to get more Catholics in here to tip the vote. Or those nuns in New York were trying to get rid of bastards they'd had with their priests. You think the good Methodist ladies in the Social Club were gonna let those kids go to Catholic Greasers? Hell no, they needed saving and the husbands were glad to get their guns and bust in the doors of a few who'd caused trouble with strikes. And that got stirred up after a union organizer from Chicago come down here by the name of O'Brien. Now do you see what I'm talking about with the Irish? What goes around comes around. And now here *you* are. What are you up to, anyway?"

She doesn't dignify his impertinence with an answer. She's thinking about Catholics sending out their own so they could guarantee their souls in the heathen West. It figures. If she had been on a different train she might have ended up here, a golden Irish girl rounded up in the night by riled-up Anglos on their own mission of mercy.

"I'm collecting a debt," she finally says.

"Well, get in line. Your brother, now he's a piece of work. Blows in here from Ft. Worth with cash and big ideas. Started a mine. Got rich. Just sold to Phelps Dodge. Got richer. Hopefully he hasn't spent it all up yet so you can get your share."

The truck finally clears the top of the canyon and although she's no longer tossed back and forth from switchback turns she's still reeling. How much of what he says is true?

The truck stops abruptly when he yanks on the handbrake in front of a long, low building. A single light burns at one end. She gets out of the truck and the world falls away from where she stands. Clifton looks to be no more than a shiny trinket tossed to the bottom. At last, the top of the moon clears the eastern mountain and its light spills slowly down the canyon opposite as it keeps rising.

John Tyrone and the twenty dollars seem beside the point now. How many children on trains— hundreds? Thousands? Ethel Worthington had hinted in her letter that the figure she calculated, 110,000, might have doubled.

Her chauffeur knocks on the door of the building and it opens. A trapezoid of light falls outward as if pushed from behind. One man goes immediately to the truck and gets in and her chauffeur, unsteady on his feet, seems glad to get back in the truck and sit down in the passenger seat. In a moment, they're gone, the headlights sweeping back and forth on the long way down to the town of Clifton.

She stands in the dark, waiting. She hears the braying of mules from deep in the canyon, as if they'd fallen in somehow.

"Mary?" a voice calls out.

"Maude," she says. "I *was* your sister. For a single afternoon. On Ellis Island. Or don't you remember?"

"Oh, sweet Jesus," he says and steps out of the small island of light into the dark with her.

"What?" he says, and stops, as if he can't find the next word. "What in the world are you doing here?"

"I found you, by chance. From now on I'll have a lot more respect for gambling, for the concept of sheer luck. I don't expect you to understand this. I barely do. But on the road between the bottom of that canyon and this place here I heard something completely by accident that throws everything into question. From someone who had a bone to pick with Ireland. But he gave me something else instead."

"Please, come inside."

"I prefer it out here. I'm not ready to look at you yet, for everything I remember to be different. You're the only link I have to all that, back there. I'm here *because* of you. And I have hardly thought of Ireland until I had to listen to that driver's story about Irish orphans rounded up by vigilantes in the night. Until I heard your voice just now.

"I'm not who I thought I was. John, I'm not unique at all. I'm one of *them*. And I didn't even know it until now. I lied to almost everyone along the way. You're the last person I told the truth to."

"What are you talking about?" His voices changes in tone, from curious and concerned to cautious.

"America. It isn't free. Or fair. There's all these extra people in the way that get put somewhere. Tucked away in places like this. Doing them all a big American favor. Why, we should be grateful! We had so much less before!"

"I don't have a lot to complain about, myself. I've gotten my share, and then some."

"Spoken like a true American."

"Did you come here to give me a lecture? I don't believe I noticed anyone putting up a Chautauqua tent."

"You're missing the point."

"I'm still waiting for you to make one. Look, I skipped out on you. I intended to pay it back." His face darkens. "That debt has haunted me ever since."

"I'm sorry."

"For *what?*"

"I thought I was coming here to collect a debt. I've moved too many times since the Settlement House where you left me—you wouldn't have been able to find me even if you were looking. But on the way up that mountain I realized I'm here to make amends. To a countryman. For standing there, silent, pretending not to know you when they marked you at Ellis Island with an X."

"What exactly do you think you could have done? You were a child. You didn't owe me anything. You hardly knew me. We met on a ship. Two people out of thousands. By chance."

"Yes. It's all about chance, isn't it? The one I didn't take. For Ireland. For the only family I had left."

"But you're here now."

"Yes. Finally."

"Now what?"

"I honestly don't know. This is all too much to think about."

"Think small. For just a little while. Have dinner with me. That's a start...."

She hesitates, the gears of her mind stripping as she tries to throttle down. His face, even in the absence of much light is tense with concern. This invitation is something she can accept. "Chinese," she says. "I saw a Chinese restaurant. I've not had that."

"That we can do something about."

~~~

Red lanterns and dragons. Gold writing on shiny banners. It all feels very exotic in this outpost of eastern Arizona. It's not the steak dinner in a grand hotel he said he'd dreamed about as they waited to disembark on Ellis. They order *moo goo gai pan* and *wonton* instead.

Several cups of oolong later, she says, "You're not as dashing as you seemed back then."

"And you're not a child."

"I never was a child."

"Maybe not. But you are definitely a young woman now wearing the clothes that were in fashion when you were the age of a child. I see you are making a statement about shunning current fashion. Bully for you. It's commendable. There's something turn of the century about you. A time when things were still innocent, or at least seemed to be. As for me, I've only managed to blend in."

She notes his accent. More American now. Ten years will sneak into one's speech, blurring country of origin. Any good actor can do that. John Tyrone did not know her when she wore a patch so there's no need to talk about her eye. But he unconsciously gravitates to it. Most people look at the right eye when they're talking to you. He's drawn to it as if something of her history is held back behind it. An eye she doesn't use to look at but to see through. It's probably unsettling him.

"You've been staring at my eye the whole time. It's an old injury; I've never lost the scar, even though it's smaller than it used to be. I know I'm not pretty, at least in a conventional way. I have no wedding ring. Just Navajo jewelry. I'm just married to myself."

"I married a doctor's daughter," he says, "We eloped. In Wichita Falls. Had to high-tail it out of there because her father, a proper Englishman, was going to have it annulled. We ran away to Albuquerque. She stayed there while I set up shop out here."

"Your wife? Is she here now?"

"Actually, she's in Tucson for the weekend, shopping. She's a proper lady. Eloping was the last subversive act she committed. Now she holds high teas at the Morenci Club. Her daddy would approve. By the way, did you find your Da'?"

She shakes her head. She leaves her father completely out of this conversation. The train will leave in the morning; she'll have her money. She'll be on her way somewhere. Where? He'll stay here and get back to his business and his wife.

She's disappointed. It's been lurking at the edges and now, the evening almost over she gives some of it free rein. "I thought you would turn out to be more than married and mercenary. Back then, I thought you seemed heroic, tragic and self-centered, with an artistic flair. Now you're an entrepreneur with your hat on straight, your beautiful red scarf replaced by a tie."

He smiles, ready with a comeback. "Weren't you going to be an opera singer?"

"No..."

"Yes, yes you were. You said so with great conviction. I admired you for it."

It stings, that reminder. That brash little girl who still had a father waiting who'd bought a piano to celebrate her arrival. And what is she now? Not daughter. Not wife. Not mother. Or war widow with honor. And if he's an adventurer turned investor then she's a singing girl who traded her voice for wages and bed and board.

"I'm afraid I've left my opera house elsewhere."

"I happen to have an extra."

"What do you mean, extra?"

"I bought it. Or, rather, it was thrown in to sweeten a deal for a piece of undeveloped property I bought on Chase Creek. It's not really an opera house. It's a cinema, a picture show. Or was. Not exactly up to standard, needs a bit of work. The Alcazar."

"Then you should give it to me."

"It's not worth much but it's worth considerably more than twenty dollars!"

"Considerable interest has accrued..." She leans forward, elbows on the table.

He leans back. "Maybe I'm getting off easy. For being haunted all these years by a debt of twenty dollars to a child."

"Then you should rectify it tenfold." She takes her elbows off the table and places her hands in her lap beneath the table so she can fidget in private.

He signals the owner for the check and it arrives on a red lacquered tray with two curled shells sealed like a secret with a tiny white paper tongue sticking out.

"Pick one," he says. "I'll let the gods decide."

She chooses the one farthest away from her. John Tyrone takes the other, snaps it open before she does and reads out loud, *"Magic time is created when unconventional person comes."* How true!"

Elizabeth picks up the hard crescent, breaks it. Takes out her fortune. It's upside down. She turns it around. *"True gold fears no fire."*

"That could mean a lot of things," he says.

She looks at him long enough to make him uncomfortable. He simply looks back at her this time. He doesn't seem to have an ulterior motive. "This is a copper mine," she says.

"Yes, but the real gold could be in the Alcazar. Or, the place could be a wreck," he says. "I've only seen it from the outside."

"You're not backing out, are you?"

"And be haunted the rest of the way to the grave? Not on your life."

It's the reference to the Irish orphans—Black Irish in New York who turned gold when they came West— that she's thinking of. *True gold fears no fire.* Those children were flesh and blood. They must have been very afraid.

≈

Alcazar. She likes the name. The irony of it. Her treasure palace. Of all places, here.

He fumbles with a ring of keys, trying several before he finds the one that belongs to the lock on the door of the theatre. Inside, they both feel for light switches on opposite walls. Finding them, they push the buttons. Nothing. He strikes a match which stays lit long enough to find a utility closet. Another match locates a lantern. The third match tries to light it and goes out. He turns up the wick. The fourth and final match flares, holds steady, transferring its brief fire to the lamp that shields it under glass.

They enter the theatre through an arched doorway

flanked by carved columns. He lifts the lantern as high as he can but she only sees the bottom of things illuminated, fading upward into darkness. Through the arch into the theatre itself, space opens above their heads; she can feel it. The walls have been painted with Moorish scenes: camels, palm trees. A proscenium laboriously inlaid with deep blue mosaic forms graceful arches across the stage. The entire motif is someone's idea of Egypt.

He moves to the back with the light. From there, adorning a small balcony, a train of camels moves from left to right. On the back wall above the balcony she can see a tiny window for the projector. Dark. Closed. Though any second now she expects it to open, for light to flare and hit the screen and project upon it the very place she once walked into when all of Egypt drew her in. If that small girl in Ireland could stop, turn around, shielding her eyes from the cone of light, what might she say or sing for her audience of one? What would make *this* man cry?

She climbs the little set of stairs onto the stage, crosses to the center and stops. "Now," she hears Mrs. Worthington say, "You must put your best foot forward." She plants them both firmly, side by side, almost feeling that other, nameless boy beside her.

John Tyrone holds the lamp steady but it sputters and goes out. Or did he know this is what she needs? The closeness of that darkened theatre in New York where she sat and listened and learned. Then there was that stage in Arkansas where she sang, not to make someone cry, but to make them stop. She shifts her weight. The floorboards creak.

The young man she pretended not to know at Ellis, whom she hardly knows even now, is waiting. She opens her mouth. Absolutely nothing comes out. Not "The Wind that Blows the Barley," not the national anthem or a German tragedy. Just an art song called

"Linden Lea." She hums the melody out loud. She sings the words in her head.

I have trod the upward and downward slope
I have endured and done in days before
I have longed for all, and bid farewell to hope
And I have lived and loved, and closed the door.

She can't see a thing now but she saw just enough when the lamp was lit to feel the arch above her, the balcony beyond. Just below her, she can hear him breathing. The edge of the stage is inches away. She steps forward, feels with the toe of her boot until she finds it.

"Catch me," she whispers, and leans forward. She steps into air.

One hand finds her waist, the other her hip and he holds her, suspended for several seconds until he slowly lowers his arms and her feet find the floor. She does not pull away when she feels his breath close to her ear. She cannot see him or he her.

She touches his face, searching for evidence of her old power to summon a grown man's tears. There are none. But there is this man's mouth, moving closer to her own.

So this is a kiss, this eager devouring of another, where the teeth must be reminded to be gentle, the heart advised to do something more than beat. For a full five minutes she lets herself be that hungry.

He will go back to his wife. She will keep this: a blind, stolen kiss in the Alcazar that will soon belong to her. To seal the bargain. Nothing less. Nothing more.

She pulls away first. Without discussing how to make an exit they feel their way along the aisle, the uniform seats as measured as the graves of soldiers. Ten rows to the door. Twelve. A half dozen steps more and they're out on the sidewalk, a narrow ledge above the deeply cut street. Water should come roaring down the street right now and carry us away, she thinks. We wouldn't drown but would let everyone think we did. Where would they go? South, across the border. Where we could start all over.

"So it's settled then," he says.

"Everything's unsettled, to be honest."

"I mean the Alcazar."

"Yes. The Alcazar. If the offer still stands."

"It stands. Do you need a room?"

"I have one. At the hotel."

"Well then. I'll get you the deed and a key as soon as I can."

"John."

"Yes."

His face—is it expectant or worried? She wishes it were harder for him to part with the Alcazar. "I don't want this if there are any strings attached. Give it freely or not at all."

"Property is not so hard to part with. Especially if it can set things right. Good night, dear Maud."

"It's Elizabeth. Didn't I tell you my new name?"

"It suits you. Hold onto this one."

≈

An upright piano arrives in a wagon drawn by mules from Morenci. It's trussed like a baking hen and hoisted by four Mexican workers onto the sidewalk and over the step where it can finally be rolled on its tiny brass wheels into the Alcazar.

And here it is, coming down the aisle, the piano her father promised her. Only this one is from John Tyrone, preceded by a note left at the hotel desk: "Your fortune for today—expect a piano. P.S. I am relocating temporarily to Tucson for business. I'm afraid I shall not see you for quite some time. Meanwhile, I trust you to restore this place to its former splendor and to add some surprising elements." Enclosed in the envelope was a copper-plated key to the door of the Alcazar.

The instrument rumbles and the unused wheels shriek all the way to the stage where it's lifted again, this time accompanied by curses. They think she doesn't understand but she learned well from the cook, Cesar, in Belen. A piano described in the anatomical terms of the reproductive organs of a goat, however, is surprising. Or maybe it's each other they're cursing as they wrangle the unwieldy instrument upward.

She climbs the stairs to the stage when they've settled the piano on level ground. She bends to the keys; no bench or stool came with it. The piano is shockingly out of tune. But she plays the song, "Linden Lea" that her father loved so well that she hummed last week for John Tyrone. She had learned to play by ear at the Magdalen Laundry—one of her special privileges after her mother died—but was reprimanded for playing what the nuns called "pub songs." No one can scold her now.

The men who carried the piano stand behind the instrument and listen. "*Que linda,*" one says.

"*Que trieste,*" says the other.

"*Tienes un canción?*" she asks. They shift, uncomfortably, turn to the oldest, though he can't be more than forty. She thinks she hears the word "accordion." He looks at the keys, the long, straight road of them. He studies the keys in the middle, stretches his fingers into a chord. With one hand he plays a melody.

"*El Relój,*" one says to her.

It's a word she recognizes. She makes a ticking sound with her tongue.

They all sing the words, about time passing, not enough time to love.

"*Qué linda y trieste,*" she says. "*Tiene un guitar?*"

"Ignacio Torres," the man who played the piano says. They all nod in agreement.

"*Aquí*," she says, pointing to the stage. "Ignacio Torres *aquí. Mañana?*"

She's forgotten the word for bring, but it's enough, this lace of language. So many empty spaces, but it holds.

"*Sábado.*"

"*Sí, Sábado.*"

They look at each other uncertainly as if speaking to her might be dangerous. It's not done. Somehow, singing is different. But their wives will think they've found *una casa chica. Chica blanca,* at that.

"*Con permiso de su esposo,*" the oldest man says to her.

"*No esposo. Con permiso de mí,*" she says.

She's only been here a week and she's already caused a stir. Dinner with a married man. *I shall not see you for quite some time.* Maybe his wife insisted on relocating when she found out he'd given Elizabeth the Alcazar. Now she's making music with Mexican *mineros.* Everyone probably thinks she's a *puta.* Except these three here. These are not bawdy songs they've shared. They're ballads. In any language, the words of longing for love.

Ezra
1930

Cowboys. Somehow, there are still cowboys in Texas. Samuel's latest assignment: Ezra will interview at least one.

They wear hats and chaps and spurs and ride into town on horses. They arrive at a full gallop and the half-wild horses roll their eyes and dance sideways as they're tied to hitching posts. They must have come in from the last remnant of what was once the XIT Ranch, flush with cash in the old days, when there was an excess of grass and beef was high. Now that land is being plowed up, tractors rolling into town on trains, an agricultural artillery. Nowadays you can't give a mule away. He's overheard many of these things, but he has to see for himself.

Ezra positions himself at the tie-up in front of the pool hall. The doors are wide open and ready, the colored balls corralled in wooden triangles.

Ezra wants to choose the oldest cowboy and it's hard to tell age except by the creases on faces, the sun's deep signature, like the rings of trees. One man of the three looks melded with the saddle, his particular weight and shape sinking into the leather. And the horse may not have been ridden by anyone else, ever. Horses, he knows, accommodate to their owner's voice, weight, particular way of holding the reins. He misses Rio, hopes he has adapted to Consuela, and that she is, at least when she rides Rio, free from harm.

The cowboy swings down off the horse, simply drops the reins over the horse's head so that they touch the ground.

"Aren't you going to tie it up?" Ezra asks.

"It's tied. Who are you?"

"I'm Ezra Duval and I'm a reporter. I'd like to ask you some questions."

"For the *Texan?*"

"No. It's for the Chicago *Tribune.*"

The cowboy stands in front of Ezra now. The horse made him appear taller while he was on it. He's coated with dust from head to foot, his blue eyes startling in contrast. The whites of his eyes are reddened with the constant friction of airborne grit and dust. Ezra flips open his notepad, pulls his pencil from behind his ear.

"What in the world does anyone in Chicago want with me? What is it they still don't understand? They need to be thinking about getting people back to work."

Ezra didn't expect that he would be the one answering questions. "What would you like to tell the people in Chicago, Mister...?"

The man studies him, evidently not ready to give out his name to a stranger, especially one about to write it down. Finally, he says, "Wainwright," and pauses. "B.W." he adds. "You're not from Chicago."

"No. I've been living down near the border for the last ten years. In the Big Bend."

"Now that's country that won't get plowed."

"Down there they dig."

B.W. nods thoughtfully. "You've got a point," he says. "People just can't leave the ground alone. I don't see how any good's going to come from any of it in the long run. A few people will get rich; most won't. Some will starve just trying to make enough to get by."

"What do you think is going to happen here?"

"I *know* what's going to happen. Sitting Bull saw it coming, said the land would get its revenge, that death would come from the sky."

"I'm not sure what you're talking about," Ezra says, embarrassed that the interview has gotten away from him.

"I'm talking about making things right," B.W. says, hands clenched now. When he opens them again he does not seem surprised at all to see those cracked palms bleeding. "Indians think if things are brought back to their proper place that it will rain. I wish I believed that. I don't have a lick of hope left in me."

Ezra is writing all of this down. The rack of balls breaks with a crack from inside the pool hall. B.W. Wainwright watches Ezra's hand moving across the page, interested in the translation taking place as if nobody had ever asked him what he thought about anything let alone write it down to put into print. For a moment, he almost relaxes.

"Some say the dust is buffalo bones," he tells Ezra voluntarily. "A stampede of ghosts."

"What do *you* think?"

"I've got too much sense to try to live my life by a story. The Bible included. The truth is, we went too far, too fast. And the only thing stopping us is the weather. I'm not fool enough to think everything would be fine if we'd kept the cattle. We'd already brought in too many of *them*. It's a kind of thinking that can only come from money, the notion of making not just enough but a whole lot extra. People like me are *done*. It's all about suitcase farmers with shined shoes and a ticket for the next train out."

"You have a lot to say, after all," Ezra says, looking up from the notebook.

"If you were looking for a typical cowboy I'm not

it. I'll go get Joe Danko in there if you want that. He'll tell you all about the stars and the coyotes when he's had a few. He might even sing you a song. I'll bet you were weaned on all that, down in the Bend."

"I read Zane Grey as a kid," Ezra confesses.

"Zane Grey would have a heart attack if he knew what's really going on."

"You've obviously been thinking a lot about this."

"There's not a whole lot else to do, son. Time and opinions—I'm a rich man. Maybe I should start writing it all down, like you. I'd have enough to make me a magazine."

"Anything else to the people back east?"

"Yeah. Quit dreaming America up. Start living in it. You can tell 'em that."

He watches Ezra write the last quote down. "What in hell is a nice kid like you doing in Dalhart? You're a half inch from Hell, you have to know that by now. Come to think of it, *that's* what the railroads should put in their fancy brochures."

"I'll be sure to put that in. I think my editor will appreciate it."

"I heard about him."

"What did you hear?"

"Is this part of the interview? I heard that he knows this place well. Too well. He couldn't get away fast enough. I doubt he recognizes it any more. I'd like to buy him a drink. He probably needs one. I know I do. Now, if you'll excuse me, I'll go inside that pool hall. I've got some catching up to do."

Letters to the Editor

To the Editor,
I want to comment on E. Duval's column about B.W. Wainwright. Finally, the voice of the American West. What's left of it. The man is a prophet. Would that our senators had ridden that many miles before they sat down to govern the rest of us.
　　Name Withheld
　　Evanston, Illinois

Dear Editor,
I take offense at B.W.'s indictment of our great country. If he doesn't like what's going on why doesn't he go to Mexico? The American West needs optimists now, not blowhards. Only six inches to Hell. Bunk!
　　Franklin Watkins
　　Public Relations Manager
　　Rock Island Railroad
　　Chicago

Dear Editor,
While BW is a colorful character and the dialog believable, I think he's fictional.
　　Wesley Hayes
　　Gary, Indiana

≈
≈

Ezra turns to numbers—he's always been good at numbers. He starts with wheat: Twenty dollars a bushel fell to forty cents. Twenty-five inches of rain per year to less than half an inch. Even the price of oil has fallen and it costs more to bring it up than it's worth. What was once two dollars and fifty cents is now just ten cents a barrel. There are several tons of surplus wheat and great piles of the grain rot by the depot while thousands in the country go hungry, live in cardboard shacks called Hoovervilles. In Dalhart, some people are living in abandoned railroad cars. Half an inch from Hell. The cowboy was right.

In Terlingua he'd enjoyed being Samuel's eyes and ears. Because Samuel's long recovery from influenza is still incomplete and he shows signs of permanent loss in his vision and hearing, Ezra is becoming indispensable. In addition to physical deficits, Samuel, although of sharp mind, is becoming increasingly dulled with despair. He's lost all his savings in a failed bank in Chicago. He has nothing left but a few savings bonds and a hundred and sixty acres in the desert of Nevada he took in lieu of a bad debt owed him before the Great War.

Samuel's despair is contagious. Now Ezra literally must see what Samuel cannot look at, hear what he cannot bear to hear. What does he really know about Samuel? What's he running from? It's as if the man's life began the day he found Ezra. What if Ezra's train had been late? The first moment would have been missed and so, too, everything after. The hinges of history, not the doors themselves, are, in their necessary but minor role, crucial. Another day at the orphanage and he never would have met Elizabeth. He wouldn't have the marble with him now.

He wishes it could help him here.

≋

Tonight, something wakes Ezra besides the absence of wind. Almost like a hand on his shoulder. But there is no one, no hand reaching toward him. Dreading the wind has become his first thought on waking. Most days are filled with that obsessive scouring; there's no such thing as a breeze anymore. Tonight it's as still as a September night in Terlingua broken only occasionally by coyote commentary or the subtler scratchings and scurryings of nocturnal insects and animals. The wind's white noise always drowns out everything else; tonight its absence pulls him right out of bed.

Samuel continues sleeping even after Ezra knocks over a cup on the table while searching for his cigarettes. He's taken up smoking lately and likes it, the deep breathing in defiance of the dust that now coats everything around him.

He steps outside in the warm stillness and the stars reassert their old sharp edges instead of being dulled into flat sequins by the constant shroud of dust. Tonight the sky is so deeply black it's velvet and a shooting star tears a seam in the thick fabric for an instant before it's stitched tight again.

What if this is the last night like this? He feels an inward sinking, counterweight to the uplift of the night sky. A sense of urgency floods his mind, not to run but to walk deliberately, slowly down Denrock Street to see everything one last time before the wind comes back and finishes everything off. He's been reading H.G. Wells; it's hard not to think this way.

He pauses in front of the opera house that he's never set foot in, the ice plant, the old sanitarium, the abandoned railroad cars outside the switchyard—the interchangeable pieces of a Panhandle town. He stands looking at the dull paint of a once-shining railroad car, sanded relentlessly so that the words Rock Island Line, formerly gold, are barely legible, a sign painter's rough sketch waiting for the definition of the brush. He doesn't remember what line he was on that other time, more than a decade ago. It could have been this one, this very car, though he doubts it. But it wouldn't surprise him, either. Nothing is improbable any more except rain.

He grabs the iron handle and swings onto the steps. Something scuttles inside: a pack rat? His hand rests against the seat closest to him. There's enough light from the switch tower to see by. But he feels it first—plush nibbled down to lichen. He walks slowly to the back of the car, touching the seats to the right and left for balance as a conductor would do, though this train hasn't moved in years. People have automobiles now; he will, soon. He's been saving, not in a bank, but in a safer place, in a tin box beneath the mattress. He's not in any hurry. Where would he go? Samuel needs him more than ever now.

He stops at the last seat, sits down to take the place where he once sat, frightened, hurtling through an endless tunnel that could squeeze shut at any time. His face was reflected in the window: no one he recognized. He had been that changed already, not five minutes into the journey. A ghost sat in the seat until she came.

She sat down in that seat across from him. She was rummaging around in that cardboard suitcase as if she had many important things inside, producing at last a marble into whose small green sphere he fell headfirst. What would explain, then or now, why it was and still is the most intimate and vivid moment in his life? In the silence before she spoke she drew him out of vast confusion into a small but believable world in which he in some way still feels himself suspended.

The marble is here, inside his pocket and he wonders: if he takes it out now and holds it up will he see that child, like the fetus in the jar in the sanatorium, not mute and severed but safe and very much alive? She gave him the marble as if she knew he needed it, that he couldn't see what was right in front of his face without it. In that moment when he met her, everything was possible. And maybe it's not Elizabeth so much that he longs for. It's who he was when he was with her. He misses that Ezra most of all.

If he had seen this ahead of time, would he have done any differently? Not gone with Samuel and discovered that he had a lot to say and that there was someone who very much listened, is listening still?

He would not be sitting here, in an abandoned railroad car in Dalhart, Texas, thinking of her so clearly on this windless night. The only thing he knows for certain in this changing landscape is that it was Elizabeth who woke him to bring him here. Her purpose is clear: it is so he would not, could not forget her, no matter where he is when he turns out the light.

Elizabeth
1930

A group of well-dressed women, their powdered brows damp with unladylike sweat, looks up as Elizabeth enters the Greenlee Cafe. A ceiling fan pushes hot air around in circles, cooling no one.

"Good-day," she says, and nods in their direction.

They whisper. One of them says "Good-day" in response, as if delegated.

They return to their business, making lists, it would seem, on pads of yellow paper. A few words escape the murmurs stirred toward her by an ambivalent fan. "Library Hall. Bazaar." A committee planning for next year's Christmas charity, no doubt.

The youngest in the group steals a glance from time to time at Elizabeth, and once, when Elizabeth turns and smiles at her, she looks immediately away. Elizabeth isn't used to this—being shunned by women. The nuns never let her out of their sight. The Settlement House in New York was more than welcoming and the Elizabeth Home for Girls made sure she knew she could count on food and shelter and company. In Monte Ne, the cook took her in. In Belen, the other Harvey Girls tried to include her in their picture show and dance outings at first, but it was to Evie alone she aligned herself, exploring the cactus-studded hills and Indian ruins together. She would have thought these women here would welcome her, put her to work on their committee, but they seem more inclined to keep her in the outfield. From the moment she set foot in this town without a wedding ring she was regarded as if she were an invader.

She orders coffee, black, and scrambled eggs with toast. She picks up *The Copper Era* newspaper the customer before her left on the table.

WEST STILL LARGELY UNAFFECTED
BY EASTERN BANKING CONCERNS

Below the headline, a list of those eastern banks that are experiencing an unusual amount of withdrawals of deposits.

She finds her name in the public notices on page two. And there it is, bigger news here than eastern financial malaise: the legal transfer of property to one Elizabeth Maud Farrell from John Tyrone, papers filed at the Greenlee County courthouse. Finally.

No wonder people are whispering. You'd think it was an announcement of an engagement rather than a business deal.

When she stood on the corner of Elizabeth Street with her suitcase and five dollars to her name, she couldn't have predicted she'd be reading about herself as a property owner. If John Tyrone had paid her back in New York she'd only have twenty dollars. Now she has a building. And some responsibility to that building in deciding its purpose. She's the sole proprietor, with no one to have to explain anything to. Especially not these women at the table twenty feet away, not adding her name to anything requiring invitations. No matter what, no one can take the Alcazar away from her.

≈≈
≈≈

Elizabeth spends her working hours at the Alcazar and she sleeps at the Clifton Hotel. Her window looks out on the eerie lava glow cast onto the hills after a pour. The smelter stacks look like a ship run aground, smoking day and night, spreading a constant mist of soot on everything.

She labors with the music and gives herself to it as she's done to nothing and no one else. Even in its variability there is constancy. Her skills increase. Feeling comes slowly back to her in the shelter of the Alcazar. It's a cool cave with an open door. All week no one comes in. No man with a guitar or accordion. Definitely no John Tyrone.

He's still in Tucson. Cooling his heels, some say. Letting the dust settle as well as the soot. Nothing's settling, no matter how long he stays away.

In the stilted houses clinging to the hills, the Mexican people talk about her, too. She hears them whisper as she walks. They don't know that she understands at least some of what they say.

"Josephina," some say. *La chisa de Josephina,* others say, crossing themselves. Someone else says, *No chisa. La huerphanaa regreso.'* Not a ghost. The lost orphan, at last returned.

A shape fills the bright doorway. That's all Elizabeth sees from the stage, a shape blocking most of the light behind her. *"Bienvenidos,"* she says. The shape doesn't move or speak at all in answer.

She waits. She cannot see the people behind the shape, waiting also to see what will happen next. The shape claps its hands, as someone would do upon entering a cave to flush the bats from the corners. Or spirits of the dead. Or old movie stars, their ghosts lurking behind the screen that once gave them life. In no hurry the shape moves forward and the displaced light begins to fill the doorway once again. The shape descends into the dark middle of the room, emerging into the lantern-lit orchestra pit.

The shape is still forming. An older woman, slightly stooped, materializes. She stops at the edge, a dark blue shawl draped over her head, the top half of her body. The rest of her is white, a dress that stops just above the floor above her sandaled feet. She's taking note of the length of Elizabeth's skirt.

"*Bienvenidos*," Elizabeth says again from the stage.

This time the shape responds, or at least the shawl is pushed back from the woman's face, falling around her substantial shoulders.

"OK," the woman says. "I heard you the first time."

"I didn't realize…"

"That you can speak a little Spanish or that I can understand and speak a lot of English?" She takes a seat in the front row, completely filling it. "I am Filomena Torres, the midwife, but I am called *La Vieja* by everyone. I have been here a very long time. I have delivered most of the children in this town. I have come to see what you are doing here. I hear you have asked for my son, Ignacio, to come here with a guitar. His wife has asked me to come to find out why."

"Tell her I am hoping to make an orchestra."

"For what purpose?"

"To make music."

"Where will you make this music?"

"Well, here."

La Vieja shakes her head. "*Cuidado.* You know this word? You should."

"Why should I be careful?" Uncomfortable with speaking from the stage Elizabeth sits down on the edge of it but now, but instead of feeling imperious, her legs dangle like a child's and *La Vieja* openly stares at her untied boot laces.

"Where do you come from?"

"I was born in Ireland. But I came to New York before I came here."

La Vieja leans forward. "So you *have* come back."

"I've come home. That's how it seems to me. I can't explain it…"

La Vieja studies Elizabeth's face. Her hands. She approaches the stage, reaches up to touch Elizabeth's hair. She nods. Then she takes one of Elizabeth's booted feet in her hands and ties the laces. Then the other.

"I will tell the people you have come home."

~~~

The next day a young man stands in the doorway of the Alcazar, a silhouette, a black cut-out in the bright rectangle of sunlight. How long has he been there, watching her? Elizabeth has been so intent on trying to play this tuneless piano she didn't notice. Through the open door she can see a mule loaded with newspapers waiting patiently in the street.

"Come in," she says.

The figure moves forward, hesitates, comes closer and keeps coming, emerging in detail: white cotton shirt and pants. Bare feet. Ten, maybe twelve years old.

"The piano is very bad," he says.

"You're absolutely right about that."

"My father knows how to fix it."

"Who is your father?"

"Ignacio Torrés."

"I have yet to meet him. Who are you?"

"Tito Torres."

"I'm Elizabeth."

"I know. *Mi abuela* told me."

"Do you think your father would come to tune it?"

"I don't know." He looks at the piano, not her. He's either more interested in the piano or unsure of looking at her head-on.

"Are you interested in the piano—would you like to learn?"

He steals a glance at her as if to ascertain her sincerity. "I don't have a piano."

"You could learn to play this one. In exchange—for your father giving it back it's voice."

"I don't know…" he says.

"Well, when you find out, you let me know."

He goes straight from the theatre, probably, Elizabeth thinks, to tell his friends he's been face to face with her. Either way, whatever Tito says will be breathless and heard by many. The Paul Revere of Clifton, astride a burro.

At the Alcazar, she has a piano. No audience. She never thought she'd become such a pariah. Only yesterday she'd heard in the hotel lobby as a visiting bishop from Tucson paid a call to his parish priest that Teresa of Cabora, who was technically a saint buried in this town, had been brought down by a common rogue. A saint and a healer with a golden reputation had been tarnished in a single night. Kindred spirit, marked by a dangerous kiss.

One kiss could easily lead to ruin. Everyone here assumes she is an adulteress. And where does that title begin? Or end? She will have to be careful. John Tyrone had told her to keep the name Elizabeth. It's her *good* name she'll have to hold on to.

≈

They come on different days, different times. The women arrive first, with their children, then Ignacio Torres, at long last, comes into the theatre with his guitar. He's been working at the mines in Bisbee for quite some time. He looks to be about Elizabeth's age. And he's already a father. It's hard to tell ages here. The men who work in the mines look older than they probably are.

Tito carries the guitar for his father. The children sit quietly at first, their gazes drawn upward to the starry ceiling. Some lie down to look up at it. Others stand in front of the line of camels on the wall.

Tito hands the guitar to Ignacio. Tito says his father must know a hundred songs, but will play only one for Elizabeth now.

His hands upon the instrument bring tones from its strings she's never heard before. Rich and dark, with an intensity earned by an older man. A father. She watches his face and Ignacio returns her gaze briefly. Despite the brevity, she feels it like a heat upon her face as if his hands have brought something forth without even touching her.

A woman starts shouting at her son. While everyone was distracted with music a child drew a burro at the end of the line of camels with a piece of charcoal.

Elizabeth goes over to her, touches his shoulder and says, *"Un buen idea!"* She makes a point of thanking the now confused child that is trying to hand her the piece of charcoal. She goes over to his drawing and begins to draw a bird. She hands him back the piece of charcoal and urges him to continue. His mother searches for the right expression, trying several on before she settles on cautious relief.

"La pájara," the boy says, pointing to the bird, then at Elizabeth. She wonders what kind of bird she just drew on the wall.

"What does it mean besides bird?"

"Not just any bird. A clever bird," Ignacio says.

She turns around, faces this musician who has, from the moment he walked in here, looked at her in a way no one has before. *"La pájara,"* he says to Elizabeth, and bows.

Silence from the others. It is not exactly

uncomfortable. The silence of surprise, filled with wondering. It could quickly turn to whispers.

"La huerphana," *La Vieja* says. She takes Elizabeth by the hand and leads her up the aisle. She's followed closely by Tito and Ignacio. Everyone else falls in. Several people begin to play their instruments. Those who don't play, clap their hands for percussion. Outside, a surprised man with a trumpet watches this procession, the music coming to him, not the other way around, and he lifts the instrument and joins in the music in motion heading up the narrow street of Chase Creek.

The street itself is muddy from a storm nobody heard inside the Alcazar. They form a narrow column moving up the sidewalk. Other people come out of the Chinese grocery and run to catch up. As they pass the Sacred Heart Catholic Church, the priest comes to the door, frowning, but does not join the procession. Further up the street, the women of the Clifton Social Club adjourn their meeting. They cluster on the sidewalk and quickly notice the crowd coming toward them. A pregnant woman in the middle of the clutch is jostled to the front and without conferring, the rest form a solid wall behind her on the narrow sidewalk.

Elizabeth and her company come to a halt. The music stops in mid-measure. The ladies do not appear to be in any mood to let them pass.

The young woman scrutinizes Elizabeth, the wide belt—a man's, encircling the small waist. Heavy silver beads around her neck, her hair loose and wild, like a Mexican girl, as if she's nothing more than a half breed whore with a mariachi band.

Elizabeth feels John Tyrone's Alcazar kiss, faded until now, arise, unbidden, to her lips like a tell-tale red flower blooming from her mouth. This must be Elaine Tyrone. She's heard the name whispered more than once at the Greenlee Café, that she is with child. So what is she doing in Clifton if not to size up the woman she perceives as a threat?

Elaine is not looking only at Elizabeth's mouth. She's looking quizzically at her rival. Elizabeth can almost hear her thoughts about the unbecoming color of her skin heedlessly exposed to sun. The disarray of her red, unpinned hair. The company she keeps. Hardly a threat. She's no more than a bell mare that the Mexicans to follow up the street.

Neither Elaine nor her companions move an inch. Then Elaine does something that confuses everybody. She beckons to Elizabeth and then steps aside to make room for her and only her; the other women behind Elaine look at each other for guidance. They make room as well.

Elizabeth steps forward, enters the narrow gauntlet of Clifton-Morenci society and it immediately closes behind her. They will not make way for the Mexicans; they have culled Elizabeth from their herd and surround her. Elizabeth turns, looks back at *La Vieja*, at Ignacio pushing past her. And then she sees the surprising number of people stretching all the way back to the Alcazar.

La Vieja is old enough to remember the strike of 1903. In Elizabeth's visits to the library to read old newspapers she learned, at least from the newspaper's point of view how the town was "invaded" by two thousand Mexican *mineros* marching with guns until the Arizona Rangers showed up to confront them. Before anyone could fire the first shot, the river crested and a torrent of water swept through the street. Fifty people drowned. The strike died and, as punishment, wages went to hourly instead of daily after the working day was changed from ten to eight hours. Today, the storm has already passed and the river takes no one away.

Elaine and her entourage are not old stock here, having arrived during the war boom in copper.

Elizabeth, sensing their lack of solidarity, their confusion over Elaine's decision to bring her into the fold for no clear reason, pushes forward. The woman closest to her, feeling the shove, pushes back. Elizabeth loses her balance and due to the narrowness of the sidewalk, has to step off it to keep from falling. Her boots sink in mud. She stands there alone, searching for the right words to hurl back at them. She could say plenty in Spanish and they wouldn't have a clue.

Ignacio steps from the sidewalk into the mud with her. *La Vieja* follows much more slowly, helped off the high curb by Tito. They all step down and, once in the street, come forward, the long line flowing forward to fill the width of the thoroughfare. *La Vieja* takes Elizabeth's right arm, Ignacio the left, and they continue on, past the stares of the women and the sheriff, now arriving on the scene. He looks as if he's expecting a riot. But it's women and children, mostly. Except for a few from the night shift, the rest of the men are at work. There are no weapons, only musical instruments. They are not marching to the mine shouting slogans and holding signs. At the moment, they are completely quiet. They turn east, approach the bridge across the river, and when they reach the middle, they stop.

The river, swollen by the rain but not enough to spill over the banks, rushes, red and muddy, beneath the bridge. "La Llorona," *La Vieja* says, indicating the river, "is crying again. I thought she had stopped." She lets go of Elizabeth's arm. Ignacio holds on until *La Vieja* reaches forward to take his arm away.

Elizabeth doesn't know anything about *La Llorona* other than the fact that she must be a woman with good reason to cry. The red, swollen river rushes below the bridge. How terrible it would be to drown.

The women of Clifton-Morenci, a unified front led by Elaine Tyrone, have boarded the Morenci stage, which bears them up the mountain with a good deal of diesel exhaust from the Packard's tailpipes and a single, long blast of the horn well past the bridge, an afterthought of Elaine's, perhaps. An epithet that's not worth repeating.

᠌᠌᠌᠌

On a Saturday, an ordinary Saturday, John Tyrone walks through the door of the Alcazar.

Elizabeth, behind the curtain on the stage watches. She heard he was back. She's been waiting. What can they possibly have to say to each other now? Whatever spark had been ignited once has long since burned out.

No one else, least of all his pregnant wife, knows that he sits now in the third row of seats by himself. He leans back, looks up at the painting on the ceiling that he and Elizabeth could not see that first night they entered with only the light of a lantern to see by. Silver stars set in azure reveal their splendor, veiling the hand-hammered tin. He looks a long time, as if some pattern will reveal itself. She steps out from behind the curtain. He looks at her, begins to come forward. He hesitates. She holds out her hand from the stage. He takes a step back. He turns around, and without a word, he leaves. It's all she can do not to call him back.

Elizabeth makes herself concentrate on music. On any given day, music can be heard emanating from the Alcazar. A blend of guitar, mandolin, fiddle, piano. Lately, an accordion. Ignacio comes every evening after work, bringing some new musical instrument and its attending musician with him. She leaves the door open in case anybody needs to verify that it's music being made and nothing else. In case John Tyrone wants to come back in.

Instrument by instrument they come; gradually a small orchestra forms. They are learning Irish lullabies.

She is learning *corridos de los mineros*. Ignacio sings the history of Clifton in song. The flood that took the lives of many. The strike that took so many more.

Today, Ignacio has brought her a drink made of chocolate and milk and cinnamon. The scent of cinnamon permeates the air as if he's grated it himself and his clothes are dusted with the powder. He has also brought a piano key. He turns his full attention to the piano and sets to work exploring its interior, listening to its notes one at a time, shaking his head at the neglect as if the piano has absorbed more than temperature extremes over the years. In each hesitation between notes a sadness rings as if the piano is shamed by its demise, like an aging woman exposing her body to a young lover. Ignacio reaches inside, puts his ear to that body and listens.

Elizabeth watches him work, fascinated.

She climbs a ladder while he's working and begins painting a gallery of faces on the wall. An attentive audience comprised of several races emerges: Indian, Mexican, Spanish, American, Negro, Chinese, Geronimo, Coronado, the rest less luminary. At the center where she touches her brush at the moment is the face of a small, green-eyed girl, her mouth open. A bird on her shoulder.

Elizabeth's been spending a lot of time at the library and has found photographs of the town and its former inhabitants. Teresa de Cabora is standing, her hand on the shoulder of her father, sitting on a chair next to her.

"*Viva Santa Teresita*," Ignacio says.

"What do you know about her?" she asks. "I'm becoming very curious."

"She healed the sick. Men called out her name in battle during the *revolución*. They had a photo of her over their hearts." He gazes at the wall. "You have invited her here."

"I mean no disrespect..."

"No. It is a *retalbo*. You honor her."

"This isn't a church."

"No. Only in a painting could those people be standing together."

"We're not in the painting," she says.

"Perhaps we should be," he says. He looks at her. He's close enough, finally, to see the small cloud in her eye. He looks and she lets him look. He doesn't ask. She doesn't say.

He holds the guitar to his chest and plays. Just music, no words. The audience on the wall listens, perhaps surprised to find themselves all together. Someone stops in the doorway to listen, blocking the light from the street.

When the song ends Ignacio looks at Elizabeth as if he is afraid. Of her, or for her. Afraid for himself, coming alone today? His face is in shadow but still she sees the unmistakable gaze of desire.

He starts walking toward the door but stops halfway up the aisle. The person in the doorway is gone. Was it John Tyrone? Light fills the doorway again and backlights this man with a guitar leaving her alone to explain to her witnesses on the wall.

≈

The gallery of faces on the wall grows, its population increasing every time she turns her back. She leaves the paints out all the time now and while she's practicing the piano; someone—a child or the grandmother of a child—will pick up a brush. It has become a shared project, constantly evolving. Flowers appear, candles are lit when she's not looking, replaced before they go out. Cinnamon and chocolate are left as gifts, offerings at this constantly quickly-growing altar. She knows Ignacio leaves them for her but she has not seen him in quite some time.

It's an effort to put the brush down, to stand back, to look. Really look. She doesn't recognize herself anymore. Who she was. Who she's trying to be now. Who the people think she is, or, more importantly, what they expect from her.

The story has formed around her, cohering to mythical proportions. *La Pájara*. She is *the* lost orphan, returned. The one who flew away.

She's always been in control of her own story; she's losing that control now.

∿∿

La Vieja brings Tito every week for piano lessons. If *La Vieja* knew the real story she wouldn't entrust her grandson to her. Elizabeth is no saint, not like *Teresita*. Tito says his mother is in Mexico now, that when she returns, she will give birth to his new sister or brother so the child will be an American. Meanwhile, she attends aging relatives in Sonora. This is what families do for each other.

Elizabeth keeps working on the mural. Tomorrow is Sunday. She will not see *La Vieja* or anyone from the Torres family. Or anyone else. They will all be with their families, going to mass. All of them will be sharing a meal while she will make music for her silent audience. She'll light the candles herself, not for their immortal souls, but for them to see by. And it's fitting, she thinks, that she receives no applause. Nor jeering or derision. She has their full attention. Tonight, with the new additions, they seem to want hers.

"Welcome! *Bienvenidos!* I dedicate this performance to all of you." She plays an Irish lullaby, married in its rhythm to Mexico.

Someone comes up behind her. She doesn't turn around. She feels as if she's inside the painting instead of looking at it.

She has waited such a long time. She doesn't dare move or speak.

She doesn't turn around. Tries to read him, the current of energy that surrounds him that he's now passing on to her. The people on the wall look on impassively. She spreads her fingers across the keys, plays a tentative chord, her foot pressing down on the pedal so that the chord continues to ring—a minor seventh—long after she lifts her hands and places them on her lap.

She listens with her body now. He says nothing. He's listening, too.

For a moment she's afraid. All she can remember is Yankee Dan bending over her. The feeling is never far away, the shame of being vulnerable to trespass. If she is hurt or killed the Anglos will say she had it coming, that she brought it on herself.

She feels the calluses on his fingers from the pressure of the strings of the guitar. Ignacio's hands. Not John Tyrone's.

She looks at the people in the painting. They can clearly see the man behind her. No one on the wall looks the least bit alarmed.

The faces see what she cannot: Ignacio's hands hover just above her shoulders and he holds them there, just inches away, as if torn between wanting to touch her and not daring to.

"*La Pájara,* he whispers over and over. She can still hear him saying it long after he leaves.

Ezra
1932

Terlingua's barrenness was a given—it was a desert to begin with. But here in the Southern Plains Ezra feels like he's witnessing an acceleration of an eon into less than a decade. To see such a desert where there shouldn't be one, a new desert-in-the-making, rapidly wears a person down.

His own life is changing, too fast. The long continuity of his time in Terlingua began to fragment the moment he stepped off the train in Dalhart. He doesn't plan to stay long, not if he can help it. He has no interest at all in making friends; he would have to leave them soon. And as for love, he is far from being able to forget Consuela. Or Elizabeth.

But Samuel is aging rapidly, as if the erosion of the land is working upon him as well. All Ezra can do is help him, literally take his arm as they walk. Read the paper to him at night.

Samuel knows the keys on the traveling typewriter by heart so he doesn't need to clearly see them. Even so, Ezra is usually the one typing.

In Terlingua, they reported on the rise of fortune; here, they chronicle the demise of this once-prosperous railroad town.

DISPATCH FROM DALHART
January 2, 1932
by S. McPherson

Duster is not a word that can apply to the black blizzards of Texas. The end of the world rolled toward us from Amarillo "as if all the slaughtered buffalo had returned to stampede the naked ground that had once sustained them." Another apt analogy from E. Duval. No photograph can render it. Once, this dirt stayed put. Now, the solid ground of Texas has just departed for Arkansas.

I lived not far from here before the plow. No, those were not ancient times but a mere six decades ago. My family's ranch on Rita Blanca Creek was home to cattle that fed on grass so thick and rooted and fertilized with the blood and bones of buffalo that it withstood any climactic calamity. Now, I see the bald ground, Samson shorn of strength. People of Chicago, you cannot imagine what is happening down here. Children lost in dust storms die twenty feet from home! Animals are buried alive from the inside with a stomach-full of indigestible dirt. Black that rained from the sky and shattered windows is now piled in huge drifts throughout the town, bulwarks against nothing.

A certain editor here would have you believe that the people will be forged by this test, that there is a competition that is winnable by will. E. Duval says we may have already lost. I am not ready to agree, even though yesterday I could not see my hand in front of my face. Like the aforementioned child, we wander blindly, collapse in front of the disappearing place we once called home.

≋

When the *Tribune* comes with Samuel's most recent column Ezra reads it incredulously. Here's something of this man's history in print that he never knew. He'd always imagined him to be from Chicago. Rita Blanca Creek, just southwest of here on the map, is a blank part of Texas without a town. To picture Samuel riding the range as a boy requires some extensive revision of what he thought he knew. It explains why, increasingly, he does not go out. It's not just because of his lungs, as he claims; it's his heart. To see the before and after, to know as so many of these sodbusters who took a free train ride on the Rock Island Line are just beginning to understand—it was so easy to squander. The land has been forsaken in half a generation's time.

It's as if a pact to leave the past alone has been broken. Not that he and Samuel had ever had a formal agreement. Ezra's early silence set the tone and now there's a tear in the veil, that thin protection, as if secrets, too, have been penetrated by dust.

It was one thing to provide an anecdote—he had told Samuel about his trips to the Eden Musée, about Ajeeb and the Chamber of Horrors. Samuel had recounted his adventures at the Chicago Exposition of 1893, about the White City at its center, the unforgettable debut of the Ferris Wheel that carried over two thousand people more than two hundred and fifty feet in the air. In these things they found a commonality. He and Samuel have always been objective onlookers, or tried to be. Now there is something specific and personal: a horse. A home. Samuel's horse once had a name and now it has to be known before Samuel dies and takes that story with him when he goes.

Ezra finds Samuel at his desk and he stands for a time at the edge of it, tracing his finger across the dusty surface. Samuel, bent over a book, watches Ezra finger painting in the periphery without lifting his eyes. He reaches for a glass of bourbon to the right of the book, takes a sip, something he's been doing more frequently of late. He puts the glass down.

"I didn't know you had a horse," Ezra says, carefully framing the statement as one of mere curiosity, not confrontation.

"I did," Samuel says. He still doesn't look up from the book, but gazes at it as if through a window. He turns a page. Another. He takes another sip of whiskey. Between the last sip and this one, a thin film of dust has settled on the amber liquid. "Star. That was her name."

Star. What can he trade for Star? The story of the pigeon, the one called Poe? He wishes Poe were here right now, at the window with a note for Samuel saying, "Please. I want to know." Not just the name, but the color of the horse, its gait, where they rode and what they saw when they got there. He remembers the photo he found in Samuel's wallet back in Terlingua the night he thought he died. There were two boys, twins, on that horse. Samuel mentions no other name besides Star.

"I'd like you to write your own column next week. We need more than my point of view now," Samuel says wearily.

Even if the weather can't be changed, the subject can. Animals of other lifetimes recede to afterthought. Samuel hardly seems capable of having once been a boy who rode through grass that must have reached Star's withers. So long ago. And Ezra once had a bird called Poe. What had he written on that last day at the Chelsea? He can't even remember now. Some kind of plea for "help." A caption for an interrupted life. "I was here. At least for a while."

Now, his own column, at last. His name a byline, his point of view personal. Whole paragraphs, not just sentences between the lines. A larger canvas of facts to hide behind.

ALISON MOORE

AS I SEE IT – January 14, 1932
E. Duval

Every other week I will be reporting in the
Dalhart Dispatch column formerly written by
Samuel McPherson to bring you expanded
views of things as they develop here.

The only gold in California now comes
from the sun and that disappears below the
horizon every evening. A steady stream of thin-
tired jalopies filled with tired people goes by
this town. They may be driving but still they
trudge, an exodus of people more shell-shocked
then those returning from the Great War, the
very ground beneath them blowing away. It's as
if America is dissolving before our eyes.

How can this be? One expects the Statue
of Liberty to relocate, to stand at the western
edge of the country, her back to the Pacific and
hold out her hand to halt the tide coming right
at her.

Meanwhile, our representatives in Washington look the other way.

Pieces of crumpled tin and cardboard
comprise makeshift houses on the edge of
town. One family from Missouri lives in their
car that broke down outside the city limits.
They pushed it here. Sold the tires. The Ford
rests permanently on its stumps, doors closed,
windows rolled against the dust that is coming
to be a common thing.

A boy of maybe six years old said to me,
"Mister, when I grow up I'll fix this car. Then
we'll drive away."

≈

"Don't let that editor, McCarty, at *The Daily Texas* get wind of that," Samuel says when he finishes reading Ezra's copy. For once he doesn't pick up his editing pencil.

"He blames it on Kansas now."

"*Kansas?*"

"He says that our dusters are spin-offs of *their* storms. He's good. He's really good. And he calls himself a newspaperman," Ezra says with disdain.

"It's an editorial, Ezra. *The Daily Texan* is his newspaper. And hope sells."

"What happened to the truth?"

"That depends on who you talk to. If this were happening in your home town, would you want to wake up every morning and read the news that says you're done for?"

"I might."

"If you had a son or daughter, what would you want him to believe?"

What a question! How can he even imagine it? "I didn't volunteer for any of this. I didn't want to leave Terlingua. I certainly didn't plan on leaving New York."

"Then what's keeping you here, Ezra?"

This question hangs interminably like the dust itself in midair.

"The possibility that one day it might still rain. To write *that* story."

AS I SEE IT - February 9, 1932
E. Duval

New York received part of Oklahoma recently in the form of a cloud that settled not only over the metropolis but on the decks of ships miles out to sea. Roosevelt's agenda has new urgency. The CCC arrived yesterday, setting up tents, writing letters home.

I asked one man what he was writing. He answered by reading it:

Dear Mother,

It's worse than I thought. Picture the tailings at Frackville. Now spread that throughout the town. It's trying to be spring here...

He said that's as far as he got. That he was still looking around for something growing to describe to his mother. She loved gardens. He gave up.

Levon Raley from Stone County, Arkansas said between long draws on a Lucky Strike, "I thought we had it bad. We were eating dandelions back home. They don't even have dandelions here." He wasn't writing that to anyone.

You think these men exaggerate? Come and see for yourselves. I happen to know there's plenty of room at the DeSoto Hotel.

≋

Elephants in Dalhart is something even Samuel comes out to see after two weeks of seclusion in the hotel. Dust pneumonia on top of his already-scarred lungs had to be treated with sulfur and laudanum and has left him in such an altered state that he emerges, blinking, into the sunlight like a mole. A parade comes down Denrock Street from the depot. The gray hills on legs lumber toward the south edge of town where the tents are already rising out of the red dust an Oklahoma storm had delivered yesterday. Behind those gray hills, a small but colorful parade musters.

Ezra watches it all, grateful for this bizarre diversion. He describes the approaching procession out loud to Samuel whose distance vision is becoming very poor these days.

"There's a woman waving from the first elephant," he says, knowing, as he says it, how preposterous it sounds. "They're two blocks away now. Everyone in Dalhart lines the street." The circus might arrive in the nick of time, its presence nothing short of miraculous, he thinks but does not say. If not rain, then they'll settle for magic. Ten cents a ride.

The sun burns through the haze trying to get a better look. The crowd surges as the first elephant comes out of the distant mirage at the end of the street. It's not a gray hill, after all, but a great beast with eyes, fantastic ears whose edges ripple when they move, whose trunk lifts on a signal from the rider to give a deafening salutation. The roar divides the children watching into those who step toward it, squealing in delight and those who turn and hide behind their mothers' skirts. One child runs pell mell into the hotel. He wants his father to protect him and says so before he stops, breaks down and wails, tugging on a man who will not tolerate sissies and says so.

Samuel says, "Is there, by chance, a giraffe?"

"I don't think so," Ezra says. At least not yet."

"Be sure to let me know."

"You should be able to see *that* coming from a long way off."

"I'm afraid I can't."

"What do you mean you can't?"

"I cannot even bring your face into sharp focus."

"You're looking right at me," Ezra says, alarmed.

"There's a kind of smudge where your face should be. But I see Miss Delphine Anisette standing to your left. I see her quite clearly."

Ezra looks over his shoulder. Miss Delphine, the faux-French girl at the "house" is decked out in a flagrant pink dress, a reminder of color, a distant memory of the kind of spring that used to conjure flowers in profligate hues.

"Monsieur McPherson," she says, nodding hello. And it's strange to see her here, fully clothed, wearing a white cloche hat and gloves, of all things. She wears lipstick on the same lips that could bring men to the threshold of oblivion in two minutes flat, or so it is said in the bars.

She looks right at home in this parade and seems now like one who has just stepped out of it into the crowd. But it's Samuel, picking her out, knowing her voice, her name, and she, his, that worries Ezra. What does she do to *him?* And Samuel saying he can't see Ezra's face—does he still have one? What must it look like now?

Clowns come tumbling down the street with red hair and redder mouths, lurid as they race back and forth in a chaos of imported color. To Ezra, they're frenzied, not funny at all. A man in a turban with piercing eyes looks neither left nor right. He begins to turn his gaze slightly, taking in the crowd without moving his head. For a moment, Ezra smiles.

A woman in a white tutu astride a black horse loses her smile—Ezra sees it slide from her face. He looks around. And then he knows. The circus is looking at *them*, at Dalhart. *We're* the ones on display, our faces only smudges now, the once-prosperous town especially shrouded today with dust and despair. They've taken to hiring people with explosives shot into the air to make the rain surrender. It won't. Only dust rains down.

The drifts on the courthouse steps swirl in rust-colored eddies as a gust rolls down the street.

And then the parade is past, pushed by the wind to the fairground. The crowd of onlookers has been pitied by a second-rate prairie circus sent to this outpost like a wayward priest sent to Idaho.

"Is that all there is?" Samuel says.

"There's no giraffe," Ezra reports, still in a daze.

"But I saw one yesterday—did I tell you? In the hotel! Most delightful! But what I want to know is why those Confederate soldiers are bringing up the rear of this circus parade. Veterans should be up front."

Is it the laudanum? Senility? Samuel, who has been so present in his life, is receding into another dimension, one populated with giraffes and rebel soldiers, the boy he took from the train only a blur now. Ezra feels more than featureless. Maybe he should dip into Samuel's laudanum. It might bring some relief.

"Are you quite sure there isn't a giraffe?"

"I'm quite sure."

Samuel hangs his head. "Pity," he says. "Your vision used to be so very clear."

AS I SEE IT – March 3, 1932
E. Duval

A young woman stood in the middle of Denrock Street, hair flying in the wind. She did not move out of the way of traffic and it bypassed her like water around a stone in the river. "The wind!" she cried, pulling on her hair as if it was the only thing left to hold onto, turning in one direction, then the other, a vane railing against its fate. A doctor driving by stopped and spoke to her, asked her if she needed help. She looked at him as if he were insane and started to laugh. "*Help?*" she cried hysterically, then repeated the word, "wind" countless times. He finally persuaded her to get into the car and he drove her to the Loretto Hospital run by the Sisters of Charity.

Shortly afterwards, it became common knowledge though it was not in the *Daily Texan* that a woman had been committed to the asylum in Wichita Falls, her children now wards of the state. No written record. She didn't, evidently, hunker down hard enough, as they say around here.

Her name, for the record, was Lydia.

≈≈

Words leave Samuel as steadily as soil leaves the earth. An odd turnabout—now Samuel is the silent one and Ezra has learned to stop asking.

Samuel is not writing his questions and comments in a notebook. The typewriter has been given a vacation. He is, however, trying to read with the aid of a magnifying glass, Whitman's poems and the complete works of Aristotle, Chekov, and Nelson Algren. He practically lives in the library, open only on Saturdays now; the librarian, Mrs. Ayres, gives him the key.

Ezra watches cars roll down Denrock Street dragging chains beneath the chassis as a ground against the powerful force of static in the dry air. He's used to it now but the first time he saw it, it looked as if the car had broken free and the driver had jumped in to steer it back to jail.

A newsreel has been showing Dalhart at its worst—Denrock Street the day after a duster, heaps of dust plowed into drifts as if the town were barricading itself against an invading, human army. Meanwhile, the population is dwindling.

"I'm starting to see McCarty's point," Samuel says. "The Last Man's Club he wants to start—to try to get people to stay here—well, it makes a kind of sense to me now. Maybe all that's left for me is to refuse to go any further. I'm getting old, Ezra. I may be ready to make a deal."

"With whom?"

"The devil. Since he's now the one in charge."

"Then I'm revising my opinion. Of you."

"I'm starting to miss that time when you didn't talk at all."

Ezra looks at Samuel's face, a face whose constancy he's counted on. Now he looks worn down and when Ezra thinks back to that long silent ride to Terlingua with this man who respected his need for silence, he wonders if Samuel knew, first hand, the speechlessness that comes from a final door closing. That time, that sense of coming into uncharted country, witnessing a mining town in prosperity is hard to recall. Now everything is murky, rubbed raw. The Lone Star State tarnishes right before his eyes.

Ezra walks to the town's most notorious address. He'd passed by many times, watched the men come and go. Watched those girls on their day off riding down Denrock in their madam's pink Cadillac. In high times people came for lust. Now it's for relief, almost medicinal, like a whiskey prescription for insomnia.

It's the woman, Lydia Jenks, who went mad from the wind that Ezra thinks of when Delphine Annisette at 126 House takes him upstairs. He asked for her, specifically. How strange, the very presence of perfume, a defiance against the dust that clogs everybody's noses. He feels himself grow quickly hard in a total stranger's hand, harder still in the almost unbearable softness of her mouth. He takes her hair in his hands trying not to pull, a purely animal instinct, the climax on the thin edge between fight and flight.

He hears weeping in the next room. A man's voice. This is where they come to cry, something else they cannot do with their wives. Certainly not in front of their children. Home is a lonely place to be.

Elizabeth
1932

Tito comes to the Alcazar on the morning of the fourth of July to tell Elizabeth he's going to be a brother. His mother has returned from Mexico; when she left it was a secret, but now it shows. He can't wait for the baby to be born. But he's also a little sad today. An accident in the mine claimed the life of a miner this morning. A cousin.

Elizabeth sits down in the front row after he leaves. Of all of the thoughts she's had about Ignacio, the idea of him being a father again was not one of them. And now the death of a relative. The family will be together. Mourning the loss of one person, celebrating the imminent arrival of another.

For the Anglos, it's a holiday. Everyone from Clifton has gone up to Morenci to get ready for the fireworks. In Little Mexico and Shannon Hill, the workers and their families celebrate with a feast. No one is alone tonight except Elizabeth Farrell.

She puts a record on a Victrola that Ignacio brought to her after finding it broken in a trash bin. But all it needed was a replacement of its needle with a cactus thorn—a much faster and less expensive fix than ordering a needle from RCA in El Paso.

Caruso tonight. Appropos since Amerigo Vespucci started the great wheel of America rolling, at least in lending his name.

Her fortune: not long life or success. No journey in any direction in sight.

She isn't alone for long.

John Tyrone comes in without greeting her and sits down in the first aisle. "I came to see how you are. How you've been." His voice is serious. Nervous.

"You know exactly how I am. There aren't any secrets in this town." She's surprised he's here. Is Elaine gone?

"I wanted to bring a new fortune for you but Hop Ying's is closed. I could make one up for you." John Tyrone closes his eyes, holds his hands up in the air. "Someone has been thinking of you. Often. Too often. Who can it be?"

He lowers his hands to his sides. "Elaine lost the baby. The second one. That Mexican midwife came to help but the doctor sent her away. Now Elaine's in Tucson with her sister. I don't know when or if she's coming back."

"I'm so sorry. I didn't know…"

Elizabeth doesn't know what to say. If he's come here to talk, then she can listen. But he's not talking. He's pacing in front of the gallery of faces, looking at everyone closely.

Finally, he turns abruptly to her and says, "Drive up the canyon with me, Elizabeth. We'll be able to stop halfway up and see the fireworks in both directions. Independence Day, yes? That's something even the Irish can celebrate. Even in Arizona. Listen, Elizabeth. No one will see us. I'm beyond caring what they'll think if they do."

"They've already thought it anyway," she says. "I'd hate to disappoint them. Wouldn't you?"

〰
〰

The mine does not stop for any holiday or celebration, Mexican or American, and as John Tyrone drives Elizabeth toward Morenci, the gondola cars on the ore train, as always, dump the magma down the side of the mountain. It's so hot the hillside burns blood red. They're close to it, enough to feel the heat. Above Morenci now, fireworks scratch at the sky with red, white and blue, upstaging the stars, the delicate paring of a new moon. Elizabeth feels she's watching a ghostly gray afterimage of smoke, the birth of the world, the first world, elemental and mineral, volatile and consequential and that she and John Tyrone are its first and only inhabitants.

He stops halfway up the hill on a turnout. He turns the engine off. The distant popping of the fireworks, the roar of the San Francisco River below, swollen with this afternoon's monsoon rain, are but a whisper from here. On Shannon Hill, mules are braying, frightened by the explosions. Lightning comes fitfully from the southeast, conversing in pulses with the fireworks. An argument of light. A debate of desire. The continuation of a kiss. Isn't this why they're here? Or is something else at stake?

She does what she didn't do at Ellis Island. She declares herself first, pulling him to her. He is her countryman in this strange country, this dark place in between towns, knowing what his American wife will never know: what it is to be a stranger no matter how long you've lived here. They taste a trace of Ireland again, in each other. Two mouths move urgently with the unspoken agreement: *You know. You know. Or you once did.* How much have they both forgotten?

The heat of the smelter radiates upward as if the copper lusts for the fire that brings its essence to the surface. But when John Tyrone touches her she thinks of Ignacio, what his hands would feel like instead.

The thought hits her like a blow. This is as close as she'll ever come to the man she makes music with, in the heat of her imagination.

What if this is the last time she ever sees John Tyrone? Maybe it should be.

What if she never sees Ignacio again?

She is her mother's daughter, about to commit adultery. She is Eve's descendant, except Elizabeth's sin surely must be the greater. She's torn between two men, one even more inaccessible than the other. The more reckless one is here now, to stake his invisible claim upon her.

Feeling reckless herself, she will allow him. All three of them have a tenuous place in this town.

It should not be gentle, she thinks. It should hurt, more than a little, this great taboo.

And it does. He is both rough and tender, as if he can't decide which speaks for his truer nature.

Did he sense her thoughts about Ignacio's hands?

Did he see her from the doorway of the Alcazar when Ignacio came to see her?

If so, is this, at long last, her punishment? There is nothing else to do but to get through it and be free.

She struggles, not to get away, but to get closer.

To what?

She cannot say, but she knows that John Tyrone is in the way of it, some greater thing that might still be able to truly hold her.

What she would reach for if she could is far above her, like color blooming in darkness, un-harnessed electricity revealing the briefest portion of the root structure that holds the entire sky together. And she, herself, beneath this canopy is infinitesimal.

To anyone looking down, do they make, together, even for a moment, their own kind of light?

What on earth does it mean?

Does it even matter?

From the concrete bridge over the San Francisco River, Elizabeth can see the swelling has finally subsided from river to creek again. She watches the Anglo boys disobeying their mothers, no doubt, fashioning a raft from crates, pieces of wood stranded at the high water mark. On the west bank Mexican boys do the same. She sees Tito among them. The girls on both sides look on. Where are the older girls? The rich, white ones have gone to the beach in California for the summer, the not-so-rich at the Morenci Club drinking iced tea and playing bridge. With school out, the divisions return and children who sat side by side in classrooms now stake exclusive territories on opposite sides of the river. Today they're racing to see who's seaworthy enough to get into the water first.

The Mexican boys, more adept in working with used materials, push their ungainly craft into the water where it wobbles in the shallows. Everyone piles on. One boy plants a Mexican flag on the stern. She recognizes one or two of the five who make it on. She smiles at the curses of two who remain, marooned in the water. They dive in and swim behind, holding on. Cheers from the girls now that the boys are launched. They scramble down to the bank where they stand barefoot, timidly holding their skirts above their knees.

On the other side, a flurry of catcalls, a tilting American flag. Then the Anglos are in the water shouting "Greasers" as their craft pitches two of them off. Their girls laugh at first then think better of it. Loyalty is imperative. They come as far as they dare in their sandals. With great effort the boys gain on the Mexican Navy, hurling rocks from an arsenal they've cached in a barrel on their raft. They usually reserve this ammunition for the mules of their enemies. A salvo of mule droppings returns fire.

Elizabeth applauds their ingenuity. "*Perfecto!*" she

shouts more than once. The Mexican girls—none of whom she recognizes—look up at her as their Navy approaches. The rafts disappear beneath the bridge. Curses amplify. The girls look at one another, then back at her and their expressions stop her cold. They look embarrassed. There's no other word for it. They duck beneath the bridge on the narrow strip of dry land. Children don't like adults around, especially when those children are disobeying and having fun doing it. But there's something else, too. Their faces hold a warning, as if *she* is the child caught in defiance of order.

Elizabeth did not realize until this moment that she has crossed a line as she runs to the other side of the bridge to see who comes out the winner. And although it's victory today for Mexico, one boy at the back of the raft is hit in the forehead with a rock to exact a price for that honor. It's as if a transformation took place underneath the very bridge she stands upon. The children were simply children going in and when they came out the other side they had taken on the grievances of their ancestors.

The Anglo girls, seeing their armada defeated, stand awkwardly in their jumpers and hats and sandals as their flagship is dragged ashore. The Mexican boys sail on downstream toward the depot where the evening train from Lordsburg is just pulling in. The sheriff, who had evidently been in the depot waiting, comes running out, shouting at the boys. He fires his gun into the air. They jump in the water and together swim their boat back to shore.

Elizabeth watches it all from the bridge—a diorama in a canyon, the boys' raft no bigger than a matchbox, the miniature sheriff, the boys in the water no larger than flecks. The boy on the back who was hit must have let go of the raft. He flounders in the water and the sheriff, about to deliver a public humiliation to the crew, becomes distracted by the boy. He clearly cannot swim. Everyone shouts as the boy goes under. The sheriff yanks off his boots and dives in.

Elizabeth is off the bridge now, running down the road behind the girls. They're screaming. The sheriff surfaces, gasping for breath, dives again. Bewildered passengers step off the train, walk across the road to stand on the bank of the river. The other boys are yelling now, helpless at the water's edge as the sheriff surfaces again. This time the boy is wedged under his arm as he swims with difficulty with the other arm toward shore.

Elizabeth arrives, winded from running, and bends forward, hands on her knees trying to catch her breath. She raises her head enough to see the sheriff pull the motionless boy out of the water. All the shouting and screaming stops.

The sheriff's body hides the boy from her view as he bends over him, pushing down, over and over. From where she crouches, it looks strangely, obscenely slow after all the frantic headlong rush to save him. The sheriff sits back on his heels then loses his balance, catching himself with his left hand. His shirt is torn, the star of authority gone. Everyone is motionless and silent except for the train as the engine slides on the wheel of the roundhouse and turns as slowly as the second hand on a clock. The boy does not breathe again. He looks up at the sky; on his right temple, a small, red wound, a silver star held tightly in his hand.

The girls are sobbing now and holding on to each other. Elizabeth tries to comfort them but they pull away. The children on the other side, directly opposite now make no sound at all. Both rafts, rider-less, spin in the eddies, catch the current and drift down the river, flags still flying.

Elizabeth sinks to the ground. "How could this happen?" she asks.

But before this question can be addressed, a

mirror in the hand of one *avisador* is telling the story to another, how the river took the boy who won the race, how the sheriff tried to save him, how the clever *La Pájara*, who saw everything from the bridge, could do nothing at all, except bring bad luck, even death to the people she pretended so cleverly to care for.

≋

Lalo Bernal would never have thought his death would give him immortality, that he would be remembered in song, and that his likeness on the raft would be painted upon the wall in the Alcazar, a place he often came to. The river has been rendered a bluer blue than it really was. The true color of the water that day had been a rusty brown from a recent flash flood as the river extracted its toll on the territory it passed through. Elizabeth includes the flag of Mexico, red, white and green. In the palm of Lalo's hand she paints a silver star, as if he's just caught it falling from the sky.

Only *La Vieja* comes to see her and only to report that Tito will not be returning for lessons. He has begun composing by himself, not at the Alcazar, but at the Allianza Mexicana, with his father and the others.

All *La Pájara* can do is hold a place for him. For all of them. Here in the Alcazar, Elizabeth paints the river. It flows beyond the frame and would stop at the corner of the room if she had not allowed it to take its own course along the floor in front of the stage. It continues up the aisle, out the door to the very edge of the sidewalk. This blue ripple on the sidewalk of Clifton serves as a pathway in. It might one day bring the people back.

In the meantime, rock fights have subsided, the burros are left alone, and no one at all goes near the now-quiet river.

A week goes by and still no one comes to the

Alcazar. She misses giving Tito his lessons. She has been hoping Ignacio will come again, if only to stand behind her in silence, but he has taken both his silence and his music elsewhere.

Only Sheriff Parker follows the blue line inside the Alcazar one August evening as a monsoon drenches the town. He's never set a foot inside, at least not since Elizabeth has been here. The rendering of the river might have brought him in, fortified by the steam the street has become. He walks halfway down the aisle, wet boots squeaking, and stops. He follows the blue line until he finds Lalo holding his star. He stops in front of him.

From where Elizabeth stands at the far end of the stage she can only see his back. He takes off his hat, looks at the painting a long time. Why didn't she see it before? He is missing from the picture even though he is an integral part of the story. It's as if he is the one who drowned. But to put him in could be an insult. After all, he is the man responsible not only for law and order but punishment. Only on the wall of the Alcazar he can be any man diving into dangerous water to save a life.

"Sheriff," she says, "would you like to be included?"

He turns around, following her voice.

Everyone on the wall stares at the unlikely scene before them. *La Pájara* is asking *La Ley* a question.

"That's not something I could ask," he says to her. "You'll do what you like, with or without permission."

Without another word the sheriff is leaving, putting his hat back on as he goes. *La Pájara* is walking to the wall. She gets her paint brush from the can. She dips the brush in color and paints the shape of a man from the back with no hat, no shoes, no gun, diving into the river. If one does not know the story he could just be going swimming. His body is an arc in air, aiming toward the water on a day without death and the boy just beyond him stands, balanced, the river flowing gently around him as he holds the star aloft in offering.

Ezra
1932

On the maiden voyage of the Model-A Ford, Ezra drives Samuel south of the city limits of Dalhart. As a counterweight to this new-found freedom, a heavy chain drags beneath the car to manage the ever-present static electricity.

"This," Samuel says, leaning forward in his seat, looking out on the dry plains, "was the heart of the west. My ancestors came out here in a wagon, before a railroad tie had been laid. There were still buffalo. They were standing well ahead of the full brunt of rampant westward expansion."

"And now it's all shrinking."

"Too fast. Back then you could stake your claim just by stamping your foot and saying 'Right here.' But now, for a lot of people, right here is back there as they look over their shoulders or ahead, to California. Some look further back, east, across the ocean. So I'm saying 'Right here' like my father did. Full circle. I'm done. And it surprises me. For so long I couldn't get far enough away."

"So why don't you go all the way back?"

"I insist on protecting my heart while I still can. This is close enough."

"You're lucky. You have a place. You've probably got pictures somewhere to prove it. You have a 'right here' and always will have. I want to see it, Samuel. With you."

"Take me back to the hotel."

"We're not that far…"

"You said we were going to Amarillo!"

"I took a wrong turn."

"The hell you say. You've kidnapped me. It's not fair at all."

There is no playfulness in Samuel's voice. A desperate edge has taken hold of him and a tone just short of pleading breaks the certainty of his speech.

"But how long do you think you can keep secrets from me?" Ezra asks.

"I was doing fine until you grew up and started asking questions."

"That's something *you* taught me to do."

"Then I should be exempt."

Fence posts tilt in drifts of dirt, leaning away from the wind. A lone cottonwood tree barely stands, little more than a stick of driftwood stuck in the ground. Ezra wonders how clearly Samuel can see any of it. Maybe poor eyesight is a blessing now.

"Turn here," Samuel says dully. "Take the second left. We've come this far together, we may as well go all the way and you can revise everything you know about me when we get there. Let's get this over with."

A long driveway slopes down to a low water crossing, the creek dry as the proverbial bone. It only holds a place for rain. Ezra fights the urge to turn around and drive away.

"That," Samuel says, his voice breaking, "was Rita Blanca Creek. It was deep enough after a good rain to reach my horse's withers."

Ezra stops the car. "We don't have to go any farther if you don't want to."

Samuel turns to him. Ezra expects to see the beginnings of tears but his eyes are as dry as the creek bed. "Oh, yes we do. Because *you* do. You're the writer, now. I never dreamed I'd be a subject of one of your stories. Maybe it's only fair you get the last word."

Ezra holds onto the steering wheel with both hands as a gust of wind rocks the car at the top of the rise. The sky grows darker to the north. "Another duster," Samuel says. "Maybe I'll be buried here, too."

"Who else is buried here?"

"Everyone but me."

A two-story ranch house rises out of an undulating, treeless plain. From a distance it looks solid enough, enduring. Closer, the house shows its true face, as if it had turned away in great shame and now, with visitors approaching, must reveal itself, unprepared, its windows blown out, the door ripped from hinges, the whole structure near collapse. The weather got in long ago with a warrant for this house's arrest.

Ezra stops by the porch, turns off the ignition and they both sit, not moving, looking into the open door, straight through the house and out the other side. In between the two doors, something partially blocks the view. Ezra gets out of the car, climbs the two short, broken steps onto the ravaged porch, balancing on the joists. He gets to the doorway and stops. An immense carcass of a longhorn barricades the hallway. Having gotten into the house, no doubt for shelter, it could not turn around or back out. It collapsed and died right there, its horns like an enormous bow, its rib cage like the hull of a ship, its massive spine prehistoric in scale. Resting on its right side between the horns, a skull stares at the wall with eye sockets big enough to put a fist through. And surrounding this animal, a silence so weighted it's as if even the wind, out of respect, stops to whisper, "Hush. Look. Remember."

Ezra hears the car door close. He doesn't want Samuel to see this but Samuel is walking past the house toward the foundation of what must have been a barn, at the kindling of a broken corral, and Ezra follows as he climbs a small hill. Samuel stops by what looks like a wire cage, enters through a gate.

Ezra stands outside the gate but he can see the names and dates.

Emory	1841-1889
Ida	1845-1891
Robert	1872-1917
May	1873-1918
Matthew	1869-1889
Samuel	1869-

Samuel stands at the foot of what should have been his grave, his head unbowed. "My father," Samuel says and stops, as if these two words took everything out of him.

Ezra waits for the rest.

"My twin brother, Matthew," he says this time, "was in the barn. Very late one night." He stops again as if he has to take a full breath before he can go on. "He had a sweetheart. Jane. She'd ride a bicycle here and leave it behind the corral." He stops again, as if remembering something about Jane that almost makes him smile.

"My father heard the calf bawling, and thought a wolf had gotten in—the barn door was halfway open. The calf was new and we put it in the barn because we'd already lost one to a wolf the week before. My father called out. Matthew and Jane didn't answer.

"My father saw something moving toward the stall and shot. My brother was killed instantly.

"Samuel," Ezra says, reaching for him. "You don't

have to go on. Please stop."

"No," he says, pulling away. "You wanted me to start, now let me finish. It was my girl he was in the barn with. I heard them." He looks at Matthew's headstone. "I left that barn door ajar." He turns to look at Ezra now. "On purpose. It wasn't Jane, like everybody thought. It was me. There was no wolf. The calf had gotten a leg stuck in the stall fence and was bawling its head off. My brother went to the stall to free that calf. I didn't pull the trigger, but I was the one that killed him."

Ezra watches Samuel, waiting now for the release that must surely come from telling such a story. Samuel stands straight. His shoulders do not shake. "Are you satisfied now, now that you know the facts? Tragedy isn't mysterious at all, is it? And what's happening out there now," he says, sweeping his arm wide to indicate the whole of the Great Plains, "is just more of the same. It even seems right, somehow, that I came back after all this time and I find devastation. There's a curse here. Things shouldn't grow on this ground, not after what happened. But I'm sorry for all the innocent people suffering. I've made my living writing about them. I never have to look very far. All of that seems fitting. Except you."

"I didn't have to go with you that day from the station," Ezra says.

"Then why did you?"

"Because you didn't ask me anything about where I came from and why. And now I've forced you to tell. I'm so sorry, Samuel. I didn't mean...."

"One never means to. We do what we do. I left this place. I should have stayed to take care of it, of *them*. I was the eldest. Everyone thought it was an accident. It was. And it wasn't. I *ran*. After years of running, I ran into you. You changed everything." Samuel turns toward Ezra now. "I did not come to the station for any child that day. But I saw you, sitting on that suitcase, writing. What did *you* have to write about? I was moved. I still am. But I've dishonored you."

"You saved my life."

"No. I took it from you. Or at least borrowed it without permission. Do you really want to hear the truth now? Do you?"

Ezra doesn't say anything. He has no choice and knows it.

"I kept the letters the Children's Aid Society sent to you. I didn't open them. I was afraid to. Afraid that I'd have to send you back to New York. And so we stayed in Terlingua, long after I got the story about Perry I was after. I thought that was the last place in the world anyone would look for you. And I was going to make things right. At least with you."

The truth twists inside of Ezra like a snake only wounded by a blade. He doesn't know whether to laugh or cry in outrage, *How could you?* There's still far too much to say about Samuel's story. Now that's upstaged by what Ezra never knew about his own.

Samuel turns and heads down the hill toward the car. Ezra stays where he is. He'll stay right here with these graves, by this family abandoned by their son. They left a headstone for his return. It isn't until he sees Samuel standing in front of the passenger door, pulling on it without being able to open it, that he begins to move. He watches Samuel struggle with the door, his strength all but gone.

Samuel gives up. He looks back at Ezra. Heat shimmers in the barren fields. The wind is still, for once. No bird flies anywhere near. There's not even the sound of insects. Nothing can break through the stultifying air.

Ezra goes to him. There is nothing to be done now but open the door. Help him in. Get them both away from here.

≋

Ezra finds Samuel in his reading chair, a folder of papers and a magnifying glass on his lap. He shakes him gently. Samuel opens his eyes and grabs Ezra's hand. Ezra is close enough to see the blue clouds of cataracts and his own reflection in them, and as Ezra watches, Samuel's face changes right in front of him, the muscles on the right side forgetting how a face is supposed to go. He opens his mouth but no words come out, just an almost inaudible moan. Samuel's looking at him, still. His hand goes slack; Ezra doesn't let go.

"You *can't* go now. Samuel. *Please.*" Ezra, still holding Samuel's hand, sits down in a chair right next to him, leaning close. "I'm taking you to California with me. I don't know how to go *anywhere* without you." Ezra feels Samuel's pulse quicken, then slow. "Can you hear me? You have to take me with you!" Ezra's heart is racing, his voice louder than he means it to be. Samuel's pulse slows and Ezra finds himself counting each erratic beat, farther and farther apart. Samuel takes a long, shuddering breath. Ezra waits and waits for the next one. There isn't another.

He feels the heat leave the hand he's still holding and feels himself shrinking, as if Samuel's soul is pulling him away from his own body until he's a child, sitting on a suitcase again, writing, as if the words filling the page could crowd out the emptiness flooding into him. He does what he didn't do then. Open his mouth to speak, but all that comes out is a child's wail from so far inside him it's taken all these years to become a sound. It's fighting to get out and he has nothing left to hold it back with any more.

Minutes or hours go by. It takes a very long time to stop weeping, but finally he draws one long breath and lets go of Samuel's hand. The wind, which must have been blowing somewhere all along, returns. The panes in the windows rattle. Ezra wonders if it's

Samuel's soul trying to get out, or the wind trying to come in.

He opens the window. In the street below he expects to see clouds of dust moving through town, but there's only the street, a dog trotting, a man with a handkerchief held over his face, a gesture more suited to grief that protection.

Ezra takes the folder from Samuel's lap. He sits down and opens it. It contains several letters. He looks at the return address: "Children's Aid Society of New York." Postmark on the top letter: July 23, 1923. There are four in all, the first postmarked Oct. 1, 1922. They're all addressed to Ezra Duval. All unopened.

He'd given up writing to them long ago since nobody bothered to write back. He sits and looks at the letters, several emotions churning like cats in a sack. Shock. Fear. Curiosity. At the bottom of the list is dread. He's not sure these letters should be opened, to have to revise the story he had pieced together on his own, the one he has learned to live with.

October 1, 1922

Dear Ezra,

Several of our annual letters to you have been returned. We here at CAS received your last letter from Terlingua with great relief and also great interest at the events so vividly described. We are so grateful to hear that Mr. McPherson has made a good recovery from his recent bout of pneumonia. It seems that those stricken with influenza never fully recover their former robust health and are prey to all manner of infection. Desert climes must aid in such remissions. On damp winter days here when smoke is so thick I have often dreamed of desert skies. Perhaps one day I will visit you in Terlingua.

As for recoveries, you seem to have made yours since we heard from you last, though such losses are never assimilated, nor should they be. Perhaps there is some consolation in knowing your father made a significant contribution to the century's greatest discovery. Some of the findings were given to the Brooklyn Museum where a permanent exhibit will be made in his name. I would pay no mind to the stories of "The Mummy's Curse." As a young journalist you know the tendency the reading public has to be lured to the sensational. The fact remains that your father died of a recurrence of scarlet fever and is buried in Cairo. Several years after Carter. We can add to that the recently known detail that Lord Carnarvon paid all expense.

You must wonder. How could you not? Did he intend to return? It is only fair now that we tell you what we have long withheld since you have come of age. We have kept too much secret for too long. When nothing else can, death engenders acceptance, even forgiveness, at least we hope that it will be so with you.

Your father signed surrender forms the day he took you to the orphanage at St. Anthony's. They transferred the documents to us when they brought you here. Samuel McPherson was informed about these documents when he took you from the train. When my own grandfather died—thirty-three years ago now—I felt at first I could not bear the loss. But I took up his cause, a great cause in the name of children. You are testament to the success of his vision. Your story puts to rest the fears I may once have had about placing out children to the West. Of you, I'm sure, my father would be proud. As would your own. Fathers do not forget their sons though they sometimes leave them, either in body or mind. But sometimes people who step in from left field, as it were, turn out to be the most loyal of all.

Please, Ezra, feel free to call on me if I can be of any help to you. Your well being is, will always be, our concern.

I remain ,respectfully yours,
Charles Loring Brace III
February 25, 1925

January 18, 1928

Dear Ezra,

We have not heard from you for many years and trust that this letter finds you well. It is with a heavy heart and the deepest of all regrets that I must inform you of the death of your uncle, Michael Duval, on January 20 of this year. He was in a coma when he was brought to the hospital following a fall.

We hope Mr. McPherson can help you find solace, once again. Time does eventually heal even multiple wounds.

Sincerely,
Charles Loring Brace III

The next envelope, opened and addressed to Samuel, is a Last Will and Testament filed with the county clerk in Alpine, December 30, 1924, stating that all his worldly goods would go to his legal heir, Ezra Duval.

The fourth letter contains a section of land in Sutcliffe, Nevada, and savings bonds totaling $650.

The power of the pen cuts him clean in two. Reading about his own life, it's as if someone else had lived and recorded it for him. But someone else has— the Ezra who was chosen, who changed everything for Samuel McPherson because he was simply writing. From that point on, someone else held the pen. All that waiting for his father and the whole time Ezra never knew he was surrendered. All the things he could have, should have shouted out loud boil up in his throat, nearly choking him. The people he could blame are gone, buried with the artifacts of their professions and the remnants of their secrets. How little he knew no matter how much he paid attention. One man gave him away, the other took him in. More than took him in. Claimed him. And perhaps the greatest irony of all of this secrecy is that if Samuel had opened the envelopes he would have known Ezra had become an orphan. No one was looking for him at all.

~~~

It's almost more than Ezra can stand to watch Samuel buried in the naked ground in the family cemetery by Rita Blanca Creek. There's so much more to say and no time left to give the word "father" to him.

There is no grass to overturn, no shade tree nearby. The mourners are few. Even the minister seems worn down from saying the same service so many times. The grave is one more of many, back in town, markers of those who stayed, who would go no farther, even if it never rained again. The final date is filled in. 1932. It took forty-three years for Samuel McPherson to come back home.

Ezra wonders how he can leave now. How can he *not* leave? He has never been anywhere on his own.

Elizabeth
1932

Elizabeth hears the news in the street, from Lalo's father who was going from house to house selling wood. He heard it from an *avisador*. Another *avisador* heard it from the foreman. They could all be deported, even those who were born here. *La razzia*. The price of copper is not good now. Be ready to leave your homes. *La Migra* is coming.

When Elizabeth returns to the Alcazar the women and children are standing outside in a cloud of confusion. Elizabeth opens the door and *La Vieja* enters first, goes straight to the wall, and pleads with Santa Teresa. A great many candles are lit. Tito follows her and sits down at the piano. He does not play.

Soon, the seats are filled like they once were. But babies are crying and some of the mothers start to cry with them. Elizabeth walks down the aisle—so many people she doesn't recognize. The musicians she knows have brought all these new people, the ones who were too shy or could not bring themselves to trust this *gringa* who does not teach at school, who has no husband, who casts a spell upon the men in the town. Who can save no one.

Concepción says, "They have already taken many to the depot."

"Ignacio?"

"Especially Ignacio."

"They can't do that," Elizabeth says.

"They can. Why didn't you know? Why didn't you tell us?"

Elizabeth had heard the rumors. But that's all she thought they were. Ever since Black Tuesday people were looking for someone to blame. But sitting in Clifton reading the paper about the rest of the country in soup lines, the appalling Hoovervilles jumbled by the side of the road, she couldn't help but feel that all of that was very far away.

Noise from the street reaches everyone inside the Alcazar. The miners are gathering, herded by a posse on horseback. Elizabeth watches helplessly as the women swarm toward the door, beckoning their husbands inside. *La Vieja* has to pry Tito's fingers from the piano.

The men have come to get their families. Pandemonium follows. Who's going in? Who's coming out?

The sheriff pushes through the crowd. "I don't want anyone to get hurt. The train's waiting and you all need to walk in an orderly fashion down to the depot." He looks at Elizabeth coming through the crowd now. *"Por favor,"* he adds. *"Quieto."*

Elizabeth pushes through the swarm of women who have fallen silent with the news.

"What, exactly, is going on?" she asks the sheriff.

In the time it's taken her to get outside he has been joined by two deputies. Their hands hover over their guns and an immigration agent in a green uniform she's never seen before gives her a warning look.

"They're being repatriated," the agent says. His

skin is light brown. He could easily be Mexican.

"On whose authority?"

"Mine. And Uncle Sam's."

"But they haven't done anything! A lot of these people were born here. Many of the children have never even been to Mexico."

"Haven't you heard? The hospitality in this country has been tapped out. They're taking jobs from Americans. Foreigners need to go home. And the ones that have legal right to stay here, well they can sort it out in Mexico."

"*I'm* one of those *foreigners*," Elizabeth says vehemently. She doesn't know why *this* man is here, ordering everyone around.

"No ma'am. You're not a Mexican."

"I came from Ireland!"

"You're a naturalized citizen, a resident alien. They're just aliens. Now I've done all the explaining I'm going to do. I need you to move aside and let me finish my business. Official business."

She looks at the sheriff. "I want to speak to John Tyrone," she says.

The agent answers instead. "He's got no say in this anymore. He just washed his hands. Phelps Dodge held the basin for him."

"What kind of country is this?" Elizabeth says, frightened now.

The agent has a ready answer. "It's an American country. For Americans. That's what it's supposed to be. Now step aside."

Elizabeth doesn't move. "I'm not going to leave these people."

"I'm going to ask you once more. Step aside. Or I'll have to arrest you for obstructing justice."

"Is that what you call this? Then I'm going to find the judge."

Elizabeth walks down the street, past the women

too shocked by her defiance to say anything at all but willing to follow her again, the only white person speaking for them.

They're flanked now that they're in the open, by the deputies. The men fall in behind. A wave of people moves slowly down Chase Street to the depot as if it's a citadel about to be stormed.

What had been a drizzle turns into hard rain. At the top of the street, white women with umbrellas stand close together. Behind them, husbands with guns. A train whistle blows in the canyon. The Frisco River roars alongside. On the other side of the river, the large white house of the mine owner has all its windows locked and shuttered.

At the depot there is no courtroom, no jury, just a tired man in an overcoat, the rain dripping through his collapsing umbrella.

"Miss Farrell," he says, studying her. He looks surprised, as if he'd been expecting someone else.

"They've broken no law."

"Laws change," he says. "Changed," he adds.

"No," she says. "It's the times that have changed. That's all."

The long column pools up at the depot, husbands and wives frantically searching for each other, children wailing, all kept in check by men on nervous horses that nearly jerk the reins from their riders' hands. Wagons overloaded with belongings only add to the confusion. Thunder doesn't help, adding a rumbling so deafening it's as if the very mountains these men mined are protesting their departure.

"*Tengo papeles!*" It's Ignacio, shouting, waving papers in the air. "*Diez años.*" The immigration official takes a look at the documents. He says something to the sheriff and Ignacio is pulled aside. He's holding a baby. Tito's new sister, born only a few weeks ago.

"*Mi familia!*" Ignacio cries.

"Do they have *papeles?*"

He shakes his head.

The sheriff looks down, his face a frozen mask of divided loyalties. He knows many of these people, knows they've been here long enough to qualify for residency. But there's a government man here he obviously cannot argue with.

Here is *La Vieja* now, aged in less than the hour it's taken her to gather her things. And Tito, shivering in wet clothes even though his grandmother wraps herself around him. *La Vieja* had to pry him from the piano at the Alcazar before they left and now he's holding on tight to her as if she's the anchor, or together, they make a heavier weight that will keep them in Arizona.

Ignacio holds on hard to his baby daughter, his papers crumpled now in his fist. The baby was born in Mexico, earlier than she was due. His wife was trying to get back to Arizona in time but the baby wouldn't wait. Ignacio calls to Tito and *La Vieja* from the edge of the crowd, trying to push his way through the boiling herd to be near them. The train whistle blows long and loud, drowning out the thunder, drowning out everyone, even Ignacio who is shouting, reaching for his daughter, his mother, his wife. All are being swept farther along toward the train.

Father Corrigan stands helplessly, nearly trampled until someone takes his arm. The crowd surges toward the railroad cars and Elizabeth, along with everyone else, is pushed from behind by the men on horses closing in. Ignacio keeps plowing through the crowd toward his family and they, in turn, try to push back against it and finally they're swept toward the train and literally thrust up the steps.

The seats are filling; everyone is opening the windows. Tito tries to crawl out and there's a moment when he hangs halfway, when *La Vieja* holds his legs on the inside, Ignacio tries to at least touch his hands. And then Ignacio, with a look of total anguish, tries to hand the baby to his wife. She's leaning from the next window, arms out. Of course the baby must be with her mother; her mother may not be able to come back. But the train is starting to pull away.

Elizabeth, just behind Ignacio now, grabs the baby and runs alongside the moving train. She manages to get on as the immigration agent grabs hold of her skirt, shouting for the brakeman to stop the train. But the brakeman doesn't hear above the thunder and the engine and all the wailing.

Elizabeth hands the baby to her mother who has made her way to the front of the car. Ignacio runs alongside the train making sure she's safe as the train finally pulls away. Elizabeth stands in the open space between cars, leaning out, holding one arm out to him. He cannot reach far enough. He stops running. He stands, his papers still in his hand, watching the train take everyone he knows away.

≈

Elizabeth returns from Lordsburg a week later. Ignacio has gone to San Carlos to try to get the necessary papers to bring his family back. John Tyrone has left town abruptly.

The sheriff serves Elizabeth with a document stripping her of her right to ownership of the Alcazar. The accompanying letter from a Tucson lawyer states that her actions are suspected of "willful incitement" of mine employees and that she, herself, could be deported as an anarchist because of it.

She could fight this. But she has no fight left in

her. She stands in the Alcazar, empty of everything.

She can almost see it: one day, people from Arkansas to Oklahoma will move into the abandoned adobes; they will know nothing of what happened here. Not unless they come to the Alcazar, which is never locked, where *La Pájara* tried to tell the story on the wall—the train that once brought Irish orphans to Clifton left with other children on board who had no choice in leaving part of their family behind.

She goes to work with her paintbrush. First, a railroad car. "Arizona and New Mexico" written on the side. Inside, looking out the many windows, she paints faces. *La Vieja.* Tito. Ignacio, his daughter in his arms. Elizabeth never even knew her name.

The flashes from the last *avisador's* mirror signal to no one now. They say the mine is closing.

In the Alcazar, words are written on the wall in English:

La Pájara is gone.
She closed the cover of the piano.
She locked the door.
She left the key.
She did not fly.
She left on a train. Alone.
She said goodbye to no one.

--Ignacio Torres

Ezra
1935

Ezra sits at the bar in the DeSoto Hotel looking at the "Last Man's Club: Sign Up Tonight" poster. The bar is crowded, smoke adding to the ever-present dust. McCarty, the editor of *The Texan,* bangs on the bar. Someone from MovieTone pictures stands cranking a camera on a tripod.

"Fellow Spartans!" McCarty cries. "Let's show the rest of the country what we're all about. We're not quitters. Who's going to be brave enough to join the Last Man's Club tonight?"

Several men step forward to sign their names next to the available numbers. After they've signed, McCarty turns the book around, reads the names out loud with the numbers: 63, 64, 65.

"Who's going to be lucky 66? The number of the Mother Road where all those Exodusters are deserting us for California. Who's going to take 66 and *stay?*"

Silence. No takers. McCarty's schills have done their job. But then a voice says, "I will." Everyone turns. The MovieTone man turns the camera, searching for the face that goes with the voice.

Except for the ticking of the camera you can hear a pin drop. Everyone in the room knows Ezra Duval, the reporter who stayed after Samuel McPherson died.

"Well, sir," McCarty finally says. "We're all duly honored to witness."

McCarty picks up the pen himself and hands it to Ezra. For once he doesn't say a word as Ezra bows his head to sign the book. He signs Samuel's name.

≈

From the second story window of the DeSoto Hotel Ezra watches the dark cloud looming, a thick, black skirt sweeping down from Oklahoma across the Panhandle Plains. Just ahead of it, like a hem unraveling, another cloud of birds tries desperately to out-fly the wind. From a distance, the end of the world is almost as beautiful as it is terrifying: God is almost finished erasing everything, Ezra thinks, as if the six days of creation had been but a disappointing sketch for the final work of art.

Ezra takes one last look around the room he has lived in for the last seven years. It seems like a room in Miss Haversham's house in Great Expectations. A thick film of dust lies over everything and when he lifts the suitcase off the bed there's already a darker rectangle where it has lain for less than half an hour.

Yesterday he sent the small suitcase, all but empty now, that once held all he had from that other life in New York: a shirt, a pair of socks, notebooks filled with stories and messages. The suitcase will travel on a mail train east and south. In a few days, that suitcase and the notebook will belong to the Children's Aid Society of New York. He had thought only briefly of taking it there himself, of staying at the Chelsea Hotel to see who was still there who remembered him. But that Ezra can't go back. Not east. There is still the West, where he always meant to go.

He starts up the black Ford, the car he saved for,

that Samuel helped him buy. Samuel rode with him proudly up and down the dusty streets of Dalhart.

The black cloud rolls closer, down from the Oklahoma plains, a curtain closing on the dustbowl and one car caught in it now, trying to break away. The headlights don't cut though even five feet of the roiling dark. Ezra drives as fast as he dares, which, by the speedometer, is a mere six miles per hour. He veers off the road several times. He turns on the wipers but they only smear the dust around. Things thud against the windshield and he doesn't realize they're birds until one catches its wing in the blades. It's dragged twice across the bloody glass until it tears free, leaving half its feathers behind. They're dropping dead right out of the sky, their miraculous plumage useless against the bully shove of wind.

Ezra can't see ahead or behind. The tachometer sweeps back and forth from three to four. Last night Ezra was hunched beneath the green-shaded lamp at the desk, typing at the black Remington. But it was as if he'd forgotten the pattern that his fingers had always known by heart. He felt powerless over the most basic tool of his trade, trying to wrest more from it than a hesitant tick, tick, tick of the keys. He'd been working on a piece about the Last Man's Club and stopped. In joining that club he'd committed to "stay until hell freezes over." Well, it just did. He'd stayed because he was carrying on for Samuel but it was as if Samuel himself had signed his own name to stay. As if he'd leaned close and said, "Ezra, it's time for you to go now. It's time."

Ezra's fists are on the wheel but he isn't driving, he's kidnapped by the wind, braking against it. He knows only that he's pulled west like half the people in the Great Plains who've given up on the ground they fought so hard to keep. Ezra is no farmer but he feels that bone-deep defeat now as if he is looking out on his own empty, uprooted field. Unlike the others on the road, he might have something specific to go toward.

He's heard the WPA is hiring writers for something called Life Histories, to interview people in different walks of life making it through hard times. His plan is to find a story en route to California, to write it up and send it to the San Francisco office of The Federal Writers Project as a sample of his work. Samuel would approve, he's sure. He wishes Samuel were with him now so he could ask his advice, receive his encouragement. But it just goes on and on, this slow crawl out of Texas. He never gets any closer to the junction at Route 66. There's only the road, and even that seems ephemeral now.

≈
≈

There is no breakthrough from the storm into the sun, only an incremental lessening of midday dark. The real world, or what's left of it, slowly materializes, emerging from a grimy fog. Ezra takes in the details, starved for tangible things. At last there's a real barn, a landmark that means he's coming back to the world. But in front of it a gray horse runs in crazed circles, counterclockwise, as if it's trying to turn back time. Then there's the main street of a town, but the sign that names it has blown away, and its buildings stand shuttered, hunched in the wake of the storm, their false fronts leaning toward the street as if they only want now to be allowed to fall. Finally, he sees a sign that still stands, that says Route 66, Samuel's Last Man number, scoured and worn. It's missing a 6, Ezra thinks, wondering if whoever wrote The Book of Revelations knew the Beast had already reared up and roared down that very road.

The wind is dying down but the dust is everywhere: in his eyes, his mouth, like a film of mud now on his sweating palms.

Ezra reaches behind the seat. Next to a thermos of coffee and sandwiches wrapped in wax paper is a leather-bound notebook, a map of the United States carefully cut out and pasted inside—a gift Samuel had given Ezra when he first started writing his own column. There's nothing written in it yet. He sets the notebook beside him on the seat, glancing at it every now and then, unable to imagine how it will begin. He unwraps the sandwiches and eats without really tasting them. He drinks the coffee a sip at a time though it's barely warm.

He pulls back onto the highway again. Less than a mile up the road he comes upon a solitary tree. There's a car parked beneath it, tilted on the shoulder, leaning toward the ditch. As he drives closer he can see both front doors are open. An ungainly load has been tied to the roof: a mattress, two chairs and several boxes. It's lucky it managed to roll this far down the road. The license plate says Arkansas - "Land of Opportunity."

Several people sit on the ground beneath the tree, their heads bowed. Above them, a crow roosts in the uppermost branch, uncharacteristically quiet for a crow. Ezra thinks maybe the car has overheated so he pulls over in front of it to see if he can help. They came through the storm just like him, after all.

He puts the notebook in his pocket along with a fountain pen and heads for the tree and the people still seated there. This could be his first story for the Life Histories project, a tale of hardship and perseverance and the will to survive. Their heads are no longer bowed, but all of them, even the children, stare at him as if he's the devil incarnate come to haul them off to hell. A young woman in a sun-faded blue dress sits stiffly beside a cardboard box. She pulls it closer to her as if she thinks Ezra might steal it. A man who could be her husband or her brother stares warily from under the small shade of a once-black hat.

"We're just leaving," the man says, but makes no move to leave. Even the children, a boy and a girl whose ages together might add up to five, press close to their father. The little girl, in an oversize shirt safety-pinned together hides her face in her father's coat. The boy holds a stick, ready to defend them all.

"We'll be going now," the man says, as if Ezra is one more person about to tell them they have to keep moving on.

"No, wait—I'm just like you, going to California." As soon as he says it he wishes he hadn't. He's not just like them. His car is extravagant next to theirs. They all look hungry and dazed, like people who had understood long ago that things happened *to* them, not for them. They aren't headed for California by choice; they're pushed from behind.

The man stands up. He touches his forefinger to his hat and makes his way toward the car. The children run ahead of him. The man calls out to the woman to hurry; she calls back to him to wait.

The woman lifts a cloth draped over the cardboard box and reaches inside. Her hand comes back out of the box empty.

"Please wait—I only wanted to ask—Could you tell me," Ezra says, taking out his notebook, "what it was like for you and your family—the duster today and driving through it—in your own words."

"What it was *like?*"

The man calls out to her again but she ignores him this time.

"What it was like..." she begins again. "It wasn't *like* anything. It *was* the end of the world." When she speaks again the words came from deep down, not from her head, but angry and low like a long-rehearsed verdict from a bitter heart. "I used to think I was a good woman," she says, "but I went into that cloud, and I came out different, bad different." She cuts her eyes at him, daring him to question or contradict. "Something happened in there and now I have to leave this baby behind."

"What baby?" Ezra whispers. Then he knows. There's a baby in the cardboard box.

"You can't just leave..."

"My own milk's gone and we have no money... what we have to feed is the car now, not her..."

He's relieved that the baby, evidently, is alive but then the real horror comes to him. This mother is going to leave her living child by the side of the road. "What about a hospital...a church!" he cries.

Her eyes widen as if he's said a completely crazy thing. "They arrest you in town. Everybody out on the road knows that. Someone will come along."

None of it seems real to him until he lifts the piece of cloth. The baby can't be more than a few months old and she looks up at him, more like some well-traveled soul than an abandoned infant. Pale as a cloud. Her almost-translucent blue eyes fix on him.

"How can you have so little faith?" he asks, turning to the woman again.

"Faith? You're asking *me* about *faith*? How much have *you* got left? Mine didn't leave me all at once. I was picked apart for years." She's on her feet, shifting from foot to foot as if the ground is too hot to stand on. Her words come faster now with no spaces to break in, as if Ezra is the first and last person in her life who might take the time to listen.

He writes feverishly to record her words. "I used to have it, I tried to protect it. It was something my Daddy had plenty of and he gave a lot of it to me. But all those nights after he died when the wind beat up the house I lost sight of it--what he'd tried to pass on to me. I couldn't feel it anymore. He took it with him. Then I married Carl. We had the other two right off, then waited a few years. Then *she* came and it seemed like a miracle at first, that anything could still grow inside of me the empty way I felt. She took what she needed and somehow there was plenty. Then there wasn't enough to keep her even though I swore I'd try. We left our land—it was all we ever dreamed of having. Scratched to get it, stole from ourselves to keep it and then finally we couldn't give it away. Then that black cloud came and it sucked the soul right out of me. We were in it for days, for years, and it wanted whatever was left. It couldn't be satisfied until it had everything, like the banker that took our farm. I couldn't see anything to believe in except that we'd finally gotten to the "dust to dust" part in the prayer. I can't hold on to her. She doesn't have a chance with me. Now here you are." She stops, looks him up and down. "I can't explain it to you," she says. "I don't know why I'm trying to." She puts one hand on her hip, pushes a stray strand of hair away from her eyes with the other. "God doesn't understand it either—how the devil got the better of Him, but he did. You write *that*." She jabs at the notebook with her forefinger. "You're a writer? Write *that*. Maybe you got the words to make sense of this. Mine just sound crazy to me."

Ezra stands there, the pen poised above the blank page. She's done. The baby, quiet up until now begins to cry, softly at first, barely more than a whimper, then it works its way up into a full-throated wail. The true punctuation at the end of the storm.

He doesn't have to think about what to do next. He gives her $600 of his inheritance from Samuel, leaving $50 for gas for himself.

She looks at the money he just put in her hand, then at him, in disbelief. "I can't pay you back."

The baby is cried out now, too hungry to cry. He takes her out of the box—she weighs next to nothing. He hands the baby to her mother.

The woman turns quickly, clutching her baby, as if she thinks Ezra might change his mind, then moves quickly to the car. She doesn't look back once.

Ezra walks back to the tree. It's then that he sees faint writing on the flap of the empty box, something written in pencil, misspelled. "Som-body pleas take this baby girl. Her name is Jane." Jane is crossed out, and next to it written, "Rose Louise," as if the more elegant name would have helped her get a home.

≈

He stops at the first building he sees in Glenrio. He doesn't know why it happens to be a church—he hasn't set foot in one in twenty years. "New Morning Meeting House" is painted in block letters on the door and when Ezra pushes the door with his shoulder and steps inside he doesn't know whether to stay or leave. An Indian in a clerical collar, his dark hair tied back with a red string, stands at the front of the church stacking hymnals on a bench next to a pump organ. Behind him, a blue cross hangs on the wall. Two white feathers dangle from the crosspiece on strings, twisting in the wind that comes into the room with Ezra.

"Can I help you?" the man says.

Ezra walks halfway down the short aisle, just ten rows of pews in all. "I found a baby, by the side of the road. These people...I gave them money..." he says, but can't finish.

At first the minister just looks at him as if this is the most incomprehensible confession he's heard. But he says, "Hatbox babies. Newspaper calls them that. Second one this week."

Hatbox babies. The baby had been in a box that has never held something so fine as a hat. Ezra can see the minister has no doubt about the existence of hatbox babies at all. His suspicion is about whether or not Ezra is telling the truth about finding her.

Ezra wants to say that he never, that he's not the kind of person, to do such a thing. But he knows that it's just the circumstances he can't imagine, not any more than the mother did when she decided she had no choice but to leave her child down by the side of the road. Not any more than his own father did when he surrendered him. Not any more than Samuel could when he took Ezra with him that day and in every way possible, made him his secret son. He feels only his own heart now, loud, complicit, giving everything away and then he hears it grow even louder as if some of Rose Louise had slipped inside back there and taken hold of him.

Ezra stands there, just five feet from the door, unable to move in either direction. Slowly, the minister walks down the aisle toward him.

"Your baby girl..." the minister finally manages to say to him.

Ezra backs away. He stumbles out the door and leaves it open, expecting the minister to follow him, or forgive him. The minister stands in the doorway and goes no farther. He watches Ezra get in his Ford. He stands there until Ezra is out of sight.

The sky is dark in all directions, the few stars in unfamiliar places. He can't tell which way is west anymore.

He crosses the state line into New Mexico. "Land of Enchantment," the sign says. Why did he, of all people, have to find her? The sight of her still haunts him, there, in the box looking up at him. Beyond Tucumcari and Santa Rosa where he stops for gas there are no more lights, just black country and black, star-shot sky. He could be the last man alive. He feels he's left earth altogether. And it's Samuel, not his father, he thinks of. Samuel's determination through years of drought always held him in awe. "How can you keep ignoring the signs?" And then there was Samuel's answer, "Signs can be misleading. Faith is not a debate, blind or otherwise. It's not a second guess; sometimes it's the only answer." What would Samuel say now? Neither of them had been looking for children when they'd found them. One of them tried to become a father. The other was just mistaken for one.

〰
〰

On the other side of the Rio Grande Bridge past Albuquerque he pulls off the road, unable to go any farther. He finds a dirt track that follows the edge of a high bluff above the river. He picks a place and stops. He rolls out a bedroll, lies down on the hard ground. He can hear the river below pushing north. Hypnotized by the sound of so much water, he falls into a fitful and restless sleep.

He can't tell where his thoughts end and the dream begins anymore. He sees the tree again. The box beneath it. But the writing on it says "Ezra Duval" in his own childish handwriting. Not Jane or Rose Louise.

He wakes with a start. He raises himself up on one elbow and looks around. Dawn isn't far off. There's another car parked about fifty yards away. He can make out the shape of a man leaning over a cooking fire, stirring it with a stick, and feels relieved to see another human being doing something so ordinary. He crawls out of the bedroll and stands up, and when the man sees him he waves Ezra over. At least that's what it looks like. He could just as easily be warding off an intruder.

"Ezra. Ezra Duval," he says as he approaches, his hand out.

"Wesley," the man says. "Johnson," he adds after a time. He finally shakes Ezra's hand.

"Pleasure," Wesley adds, a little uncertainly, taking

back his hand, touching his hat. The brim is slightly curled upward as if it's been wet and dried that way, as if he never took it off, even to sleep. He looks to be about fifty, though his weathered face has already pushed him well into the next decade. But his eyes are clear and getting bluer, reflecting the rising sun in the desert sky.

"Coffee?" He speaks in single words for the most part, like a foreigner getting the most out of nouns, or a man who doesn't believe in squandering whole sentences on strangers.

Wesley pours the boiling black liquid into two tin cups. "Alone?" He looks behind Ezra toward the car as if somebody else might still be in there sleeping.

"Just me," Ezra says.

"Did you leave your family behind, in the ground, or did they go on ahead?" He asks this carefully, as if the dustbowl has unleashed an army of wandering fathers, their wives and children six feet under the dirt of failed farms they finally found a way not to leave.

"I had a wife," Ezra says carefully, surprised at himself. "Elizabeth," he adds, even more surprised that a real name could surface in such a fiction. "She left with the baby." And what is the truth, anyway? The minister mistook him for a father. The truth or what's left of it doesn't seem to apply to him any more.

"Shame," Wesley says. After a long silence broken only by intermittent sips of coffee he continues. "I buried my wife and little boy back in Kansas. Dust pneumonia, doctor said. I say they died because they couldn't stand the wind anymore. I was afraid it would dig them back up again. You're lucky you still got people alive, even if you don't know where they are."

Ezra doesn't want to think about Wesley's buried family, the wind scratching at their graves. He wants to think about Elizabeth in Arkansas. But he's having trouble growing her up from an orphan girl on the train with him to a woman who took his name. He wouldn't recognize her if she was standing in front of him now. More than anything he wishes she were here. She, of all people, would know what to say.

"Where, exactly did you come from?" Wesley asks.

"Dalhart, Texas."

"What's your wife still doing in Arkansas?"

"That's the last place I saw her."

"You make it sound like she disappeared." Wesley looks at him as if he isn't sure of Ezra's sanity. "Quite a thing," Wesley says, trying another tack, "young man like you traveling all alone." He's warming up now, sentences stretching out as he feels more at ease. Or maybe it's out of nervousness. "Any children?"

"I tried to take care of her," Ezra says defensively.

Wesley sits on the bumper of his car to sip his coffee, motions Ezra to sit down. "You sound like you think you didn't try hard enough."

"Maybe I didn't. Maybe I shouldn't have let her out of my sight." Ezra waits. No bolts of lightning come down. But he can't keep this up. His imagination isn't big enough for what a life with her could have been like. She might have helped him see. But he has to tell someone about Rose Louise. A father, any father will do. This man Wesley had been one, at least for a little while. "What if I told you that was a lie? I have no wife. The baby wasn't mine. The truth is, I found her-- the baby," Ezra says, barely above a whisper, not sure this man will believe anything he says now. "By the road. The mother was about to leave her when I stopped to help."

Wesley narrows his eyes at him, sifting through the stories. "I'd say that's the saddest thing I ever heard," he finally says. "I don't think you would make a thing like that up." He pulls half a cigarette out of his shirt pocket, gets up to pull a stick from the fire to light the frayed end.

He offers it to Ezra. Ezra thinks about taking it. Does. Draws on it. Hands it back.

Wesley takes a long pull on the shared cigarette. "So what'd you do when you found this baby girl by the road?" He exhales and a grey cloud blooms in the air between them.

"I gave her mother everything I had. So she would keep her."

Wesley is staring at Ezra now, smoke curling from the cigarette like a long drawn out thought, heated and rising. He speaks slowly, evenly at first, emphasizing the words as if he wants to make sure Ezra hears every one. "That farm, my wife...the child...was all I ever wanted." His voice changes, the words coming closer together, harder. "But you--you've got guilt written all over you. You show up with a story about a mother and a baby you helped and you don't know why it happened or what it means." He holds out his hands, cracked and calloused as if he's begging for the weight of a child to fill them again. He gets up off the bumper abruptly, shakes his head as if to clear it. "The whole world is blowing away to nothing." Wesley coughs and swipes his hand across his mouth. "Good God," he says.

He drops the quarter inch of cigarette in the dirt, grinds it slowly with his boot.

"It's not your fault," Wesley says. "It's no one's fault." The smoke from the fire shifts as competing breezes meet above it. "We tried."

Ezra sets his coffee cup down. Wesley turns away, begins to pack up his car. Ezra doesn't know how to move, how to go on from here. He hadn't asked for absolution. Wesley had simply given it to them both.

Trucks and cars are moving west along the highway in a steady stream. He walks to his car. He can't feel his body anymore. He sits in the front seat, the door open. He looks back to Wesley's camp, sees the wisp of smoke from the fire, the shape of a man with the ten o'clock sun behind him.

Ezra watches a hand, his hand, isn't it?--reaching for the key and turning it, watches that same hand release the brake, shift into gear, take the wheel and steer it toward the road. Somebody's driving, somebody who must have someplace to go. In the rearview mirror the silhouette stands and watches, growing smaller, shrinking to a single punctuation point against the bright blue sky.

≋

Ezra is stopped like everybody else at the California border by a sleepy guard in a government shack. The car is checked for fruits and vegetables, some hidden contamination that could taint the golden crop in the valley beyond. He's waved on through to the Promised Land.

Ezra drives into the Mojave Desert until he sees mountains ahead. On the other side, he knows, is the ocean. He stops the car at the junction of US Highway 395. It's so late no other car comes from either direction. After a while, he pulls back onto the road.

He turns north. The desert enfolds him as it once did. He lets it do so again.

All night he drives alongside the long spine of the Sierra Nevada on his left, its jagged ridgeline visible in cloud-covered moonlight. He passes Mono Lake, black as onyx without sun to brighten it. Past Bridgeport he leaves California, crosses into the far edge of Nevada. At Sparks he sees the road sign pointing north to Pyramid Lake.

He follows the river on his right through brown hills until he crests a ridge, and on the other side his first glimpse of Pyramid Lake stops him in his tracks. He has to pull over. Set in the desert hills, a vast body of water as blue as a turquoise stone stretches a great distance before him. A pyramid-shaped island emerges in the growing light.

He drives the entire length of it, some thirty miles until he reaches the north end where he finally stops right at the shoreline. Strange limestone formations like stalagmites thrust from the bottom of the lake. Fumaroles of steam from some deep place within the earth release their heat into the cool air. Pelicans glide above the water, weightless. It's so beautiful he doesn't dare try to describe it in words. He feels that gouged-out place inside him, widening until he's empty of everything he thought he knew. He takes out his new notebook, turns to the first page. "Dear father," he writes. He isn't sure which one he's writing to. The water laps at the wheels. The ink dries in the air.

He feels for the marble. Still there. Always still there. Somehow he expected it would disappear, like gifts in fairy tales that aren't wisely used.

Ezra sees himself in the marble's green pupil—a child huddled in a seat on a train to Texas. He sees himself the way he is now: a young man getting out of a car in the piece of this Nevada desert he has inherited, standing, knee-deep in improbable blue water. "Father," he whispers. "It's me. I'm here."

Elizabeth
1985

If Elizabeth could watch from the height of the hawk she just caught a glimpse of, she, too, would see a pickup filled with people, a family sitting in back, black hair whipping their faces. Red shirts. Turquoise. A bit of bright yellow. And one elderly white woman looking up at the sky.

Now that the destination is out of her hands, she can pay attention to the journey itself, think about where she's going, what will happen when she gets there. It began with a letter from Mai, an invitation to her granddaughter's coming of age ceremony. They've kept in touch all these years. Mai had written to Elizabeth about Tiba's funeral in Ganado five years ago. If Elizabeth hadn't been teaching at a reservation school, she would have gone. Now it's summer; she didn't hesitate to make this trip. She took a bus from Farmington to Klagetoh. There, Mai met her with her family in a pickup. They embraced, laughing, both women gray-haired, dressed in long skirts, Levi jackets. Mai held Elizabeth's wrinkled hands and looked—still no wedding ring. Elizabeth insisted on riding in the back of the truck.

The pickup plows slowly through a drift of oncoming sheep that materialize out of nothing; they part for the wide prow of the truck. The sheep come alongside Elizabeth now, a wake of wool, bells clinking different notes, a few baas, a wild-eyed face pressed momentarily right up against her. And then they're gone, swallowed in the dust, rippling southeast where the two halves of the herd join again. A man on horseback rides by, looks at her curiously without stopping, then he hurries to catches up with the herd. A black and white dog races past him; they all disappear into the pink mist of the dust they came from.

The truck comes to a stop and when the dust subsides she sees a small corral fenced on three sides, the fourth side a solid wall of rock that rises straight up toward the blue, cloudless sky. Inside, a jumble of pickups, even a wagon, and horses and mules tethered to the ground. A round hut with smoke curling from a hole in the top crowns the top of a low hill. A man comes out of the door, his hand raised in greeting.

A conversation, brief, between Mai and the man. A nod in Elizabeth's direction. An agreement of sorts is reached. Still, she feels like an intruder.

"You," Mai says, smiling. "Will come with me. My granddaughter, Ajei, is in the hogan, waiting."

She feels a twist of panic, not knowing how to respond. To ask how long this is all going to take would be an insult and besides, Mai had invited her. But a hogan? Elizabeth worries she'll get claustrophobic.

Mai turns as a man in a straw cowboy hat, new jeans, and a red shirt comes out of the hogan. Other people come out and follow him.

All attention is on the man in the straw hat standing at the edge of a shallow pit the size of a bathtub. It's been lined with coals burned down to a gray ash.

"That man," Mai whispers, "is going to cook a

cake made of corn. Not what you thought, eh? You were expecting bones and rattles, a real medicine man. My daughter has been grinding corn for days to make the flour. Probably a hundred pounds of it. And she's been running all week in each of the four directions. It's part of what has to happen."

She knows next to nothing. Being a teacher gives her no quarter here. She teaches English, not anthropology. She feels foreign and frightened, something she hasn't felt since Ellis Island. All she can do is watch, listen. Try to learn.

The man in the hat shovels coals out of the pit and when the pit is clean Mai and Tiba help the other women line the pit with wet corn husks stitched together. Baskets are brought from the hogan and handed to the man who pours the thick batter inside them into the pit. More husks are placed on top. Finally, the men cover it with dirt and shovel the coals on top.

"It'll cook all night. Tomorrow we'll eat," Mai says.

Elizabeth turns, incredulous. "Tomorrow? What happens tonight?"

"We sit." She points to the hogan.

Before Elizabeth can think of what to say, she's following Mai and everyone else into the squat, round hut, bending her 5'8" frame through the slit of a door, entering the cave of an eight-sided room. A single lantern hangs from the ceiling. Blankets line the perimeter. In the center, almost like an animal, an oil-drum stove waits to be fed the wood waiting at its feet.

Elizabeth shares a mattress with Mai. They lean their backs against the mud-chinked logs of the wall. Elizabeth hugs her knees and wonders how she'll survive the night. She's never done well in small, enclosed spaces.

Mai's granddaughter Ajei enters the hogan, her arms banded with silver and turquoise, her neck almost pulled forward by the heavy squash blossom necklaces around it. A long skirt flares from her waist; her feet are bound in knee-high, laced deerskin boots. She sits down alone, her back against the wall, her feet straight out in front of her facing the door. The man in the straw cowboy hat tells her in Navajo and English (for Elizabeth's benefit?) that she must sit straight or she will grow crooked, that she must not fall asleep. The girl looks willing, not the least bit uncertain. She sits perfectly still and straight.

The man in the hat sings. Elizabeth listens to the strange words and begins to hear certain ones over and over. Sometimes other people join in and gradually their voices fall away as the man carries the song through the night. After a while, the world, or what's left of it, dissolves. There is no longer any floor or roof, no aching spine, just sound. Elizabeth slips into the river of it, lulled and borne along by syllables that have no meaning to her. No one translates for her now. At times, she flails, resists, comes back, sees the room, the girl fighting sleep, the man in the hat nudging her awake. Somewhere in the night rain adds its hard percussion on the roof, nearly drowning out the song. Rain comes through the smoke hole and slithers down the black stove pipe, hissing. Someone built a fire in the oil drum when she wasn't looking and she's glad because she realizes now that she's cold. The wind comes roaring and the man keeps singing and Elizabeth falls in and out of sleep as she feels Mai shifting next to her. Each time Elizabeth wakes, she looks at the girl in the center who seems oddly alone despite all the people surrounding her.

The singing draws Elizabeth back into the world and the world is the hogan and the song, nothing else. At dawn, the singing stops and the sudden silence envelops her, huge, deafening. The man in the hat helps the girl to her feet. She looks like someone taking her first step—so tentative—then the other foot follows. She steps outside and they all follow. She faces toward the rising sun and, as if released from a taut bow, she begins to run toward the place where the sun will show its full face on this part of Arizona.

Elizabeth remembers Mai telling her Ajei has been running all week in each of the four directions. Now she will run again, farther than she has ever run before. The man in the hat says that anyone can run with her if they wish, but they must follow behind.

Elizabeth follows. She's well behind the girl, but keeps her in sight. Others run ahead, but soon fall behind, turn and go back to the hogan. Elizabeth keeps going. She wonders how far the girl will go. She tries to keep up. She doesn't want to let her make this journey by herself.

She walks along a canyon wall. The growing light throws itself against the wall creating a red boundary between her and the open range beyond. The girl is slowing down now. Elizabeth feels her own second wind coming, thinks maybe she can walk forever, that she could even pass this girl. But she paces herself, lets the girl choose her own finish line and cross it first.

At the first place where the entire sun can be seen rising through a gap in the mountains the girl stops, bends forward, her hands on her thighs. It takes a while for Elizabeth to catch up—she quickens her pace. Ajei is still breathing heavily when she gets there. They do not speak; they only breathe together until separately their breath becomes private and almost silent again. Without a word, they walk back, side by side, where all Ajei's relations wait for her.

The cake is unearthed, cut and eaten. Elizabeth takes the piece Mai offers her and on the first bite feels sand cracking between her teeth. Sometimes she bites sand, sometimes her teeth meet the soft give of raisins studded in the cake. The man in the hat gives a piece back to the earth and the pit is covered again.

Elizabeth thinks it must be over now but the man leads everyone back into the hogan again. New blankets are laid down on the dirt floor this time, their bright patterns blending. Everyone is asked to put something of value onto the pile of blankets. The only thing she has is the spiny oyster shell ring she helped the soldier in Belen pick out for his sweetheart, the same ring he sent back to her just as she left. And it was Carter that stepped in front of the train just before he mailed the ring. She'd looked it up and found it on microfiche from the *Los Angeles Times*. She's had the ring so long and can't imagine her hand without it. But she takes it off and places it in the pile with keys, watches, bracelets. Mai looks at her and nods. The men put a final blanket on the valuables and help the girl lie down on it, face down, arms out. The man in the hat blesses her and everything beneath her body. She rises and everyone retrieves their belongings. Elizabeth takes her ring back. It seems strange to put it on again; she'd thought she was giving it away, had been prepared to do so.

Gifts of food—candy and fruit, pillows and blankets—are distributed to everyone. Tiba steps forward and begins to gently comb her granddaughter's hair with a bundled sheaf of long, dry stalks. Everyone listens to the sound of the dry stalks softened and slowed by the girl's shining, thick hair. Finally, Ajei stands facing the door and everyone moves clockwise in a circle. As each person stops before her she closes her eyes and passes her hands in an upward motion over them. When it's Elizabeth's turn Ajei looks her straight in the eyes, something she hasn't done with anyone else. A sudden, dizzying turnabout takes place and Elizabeth feels herself somehow smaller, much younger, the girl before her taller and older, though they are almost the same height. Ajei takes Elizabeth's hand and presses something into it. When Elizabeth opens her hand, there's a tiny, carved raven with two turquoise beads for eyes.

This girl has something more than a talisman now, something forged in fire and song and long history. Elizabeth things the poverty of the visitor before her must seem like a hollow space the wind rushes through. She must know from her grandmother that Elizabeth has no family. Now, the upward motion of her hands, inches from Elizabeth's body draws something up from deeper down. Something artesian and staunched and stricken. And as quickly as it flows through her and from her, it dissipates into the eight-sided room, then out through the hole borne on smoke into the abundance of blue above.

Outside, a group of men have gathered. From where Elizabeth stands she can clearly see they're releasing a foal into the corral. It can't be more than a few days old, a week at most, and tilts on its unwieldy legs toward a mare. It thrusts it head under her belly and begins to nurse. To Elizabeth's horror the mare lashes out with its sharp hooves, knocking the foal to the ground. The foal's front legs splay out in two directions. Elizabeth moves toward the corral and grips the fence with her hands as the foal struggles to its feet and goes a second time to the mare. Again, the hind hooves lash out, this time opening a wound in the foal's shoulder. The foal gets up a third time, falls, then gets up again and heads once more toward the mare.

Is this part of the ceremony? Elizabeth looks around. Mai and Ajei are now nowhere to be found. Elizabeth climbs the fence and immediately feels a hand on her shoulder pulling her back but she can't stop. She swings one leg over the top just as the foal is kicked a fourth time, a bright wound opening on its foreleg. The foal stands, shaking, and does not try again.

Elizabeth's over the fence now, moving toward the

foal, trying not to run, trying not to frighten it. But the foal lets her come. Her hands stretch, trembling toward the wound; blood covers her palms as she closes her hand over it and holds on. She hears voices behind her, the man who led the ceremony louder than the rest.

She turns, her hands still on the foal's leg. "Can't you do something?" she says to the line of men sitting on the fence.

"It will be all right," one of them says.

"No. It won't."

"The foal's mother died. This is her new one. It takes time."

"Get a bandage. You have to get a bandage. Please."

She turns toward the foal again, sits down in the small corral holding tight, feeling a little of the warm, sticky blood that the pressure of her hand abates. She looks out through the fence.

Hats bob as the men talk among themselves. How little they understand.

She tears a strip from the bottom of her skirt and, with great difficulty, ties it around the leg.

Hats bob along the fence. The foal wobbles toward the mare. Stops as if waiting to be kicked, but somehow more certain, as if the covering of the wound has given it something it didn't have before. It approaches, slowly this time. The mare watches then bends to eat some hay on the ground. The foal nudges closer and the mare does not kick the foal away.

Elizabeth sits in the dirt at the center of the corral, hears the mare chewing grain. She feels the blood on her hand, feels the skin on her palm tighten, pull as if shrinking.

She has no daughter or granddaughter to honor, to draw the stalks through their dark red hair. She has no gifts to bless and give away. She sits alone, a spinster with no one singing for her. But the blood of the brand new foal, a tattoo for courage, dries to a darker color on her hand.

Ezra
1985

The sun breaks soundlessly through the east window. Light stakes a claim on the bed and red gradually spills over the shape of a man beneath a yellow quilt. But it is not the light that brings Ezra back to the world; it's his own voice, speaking from a dream. He opens his eyes with a start and immediately closes them. He feels the heat on his back and is grateful for it, the fact that he can feel it at all. He moves the fingers on both hands. The left hand is working, the right not so well. Images come flooding back. A child standing between the cars of a train, the only passenger. As he watches, it happens all over again. The couplings separate, the train pulls away from him and the car he's on rolls for a while then slows, stops dead in the middle of Texas.

Ezra opens his eyes, still himself in his own house in Nevada, still seventy-nine years of age.

He sits up with great difficulty, bracing himself. He looks out the window. Red sky at morning, sailors take warning. The sun rises into a gray wall of clouds and disappears. Snow, maybe.

Something's coming, to be sure.

Next to the bed, his black Lab, Buffalo, assembles his arthritic legs beneath him, lurches upward and tilts his face to within an inch of Ezra's. Buffalo breathes on him, and it is a foul but friendly greeting; he thumps his tail on the wooden floor.

Buffalo shambles toward his dish to wait for the dry kibble that, once again, he will revel in, and this is what Ezra appreciates about dogs and Buffalo in particular, because what he has hoped for has come to pass and each and every time it does it's worth celebrating. He's still trying to learn from the dog. He saw a cartoon in a magazine once, a man with a bubble above his head and an idea inside it: Please God. Let me be as wonderful as my dog thinks I am. Ezra tries to live by it.

He begins his own ritual, paying particular attention this morning. His right hand is compromised since the last small stroke. The hand seems to be in another world, waiting for the rest of him to follow. Now everything takes more patience, especially learning to use his left hand more as if he has to clumsily translate a language the other hand knows by heart. But the strange thing is that with the loss of feeling in his hand, he's feeling the loss of other things. He has no wife and never did, no children. An unfinished book in a drawer. A silent hermit, that's what he's become. A hermit with an elderly dog.

He continues his rituals, hoping the details will take over, push back the dream and other nagging thoughts where they belong. He fills the percolator with water, shakes the last of the coffee from a yellow can into the metal basket, spilling some on the cracked Formica counter. He'll have to make a trip into Sutcliffe to get some more. He bends to turn the flame on under the propane burner. While the coffee is brewing, he looks out the window at the lake. Buffalo is down by the water wagging his tail at nothing in particular. Maybe he's grateful for the familiar this morning, too. There's a row of sticks by the shoreline, markers for the changing water level. From where Ezra stands, it looks like the spine of a huge fish, a prehistoric Lahontan cutthroat trout excavated a bone at a time. He wishes it were such a fish. He was witness to their extinction. Diversion of fresh water that feeds the lake from the Truckee River cut the fish off from their spawning grounds. The lake evaporates, a bit at a time. The pyramid for which the lake is named, Anaho Island, actually, has another name, which Ezra prefers. The Paiute call it Stone Mother, who cried an entire lake full of tears for her lost children, hoping to bring them home again.

Buffalo is only halfway up the path by the time Ezra passes him on the way down. It doesn't seem that long ago that the dog ran ahead of him and made several trips between the lake and the house in the time it took for the coffee to brew. Now they are like old watchmen changing shifts, not nearly as punctual as they used to be.

Ezra sits in a rusted metal chair and watches the gulls wheel and rise in a column above limestone outcroppings. There's a notebook on his lap. A fountain pen, uncapped, ready. There are a few gulls and white pelicans circling above Stone Woman. They're arriving the same way they've been arriving for the last fifty years; they're coming all the way from the California coast, nesting in their own private continent. He sits with a ledger on his lap, ready to record numbers no one cares about. Words are malleable, but numbers don't lie. He'd participated in the Audubon count of 1976, netting and releasing. There were 46,000 gulls, 2,000 avocets, 22,000 red-necked phalaropes, 93,000 Wilson's phalaropes, 750,000 grebes and 200 snowy plovers, give or take, and a mere handful of mallards. There were millions of ducks when he first came here. He keeps track now, not for Audubon, but for himself. Nothing else is going to go extinct on his watch if he has anything to say about it.

Flora and fauna flourish and disappear. But water—now that's the next thing a war will be fought over, he's sure of it. He hopes he's not around to see it come to pass.

A cloud is coming down the dirt drive, a whirlwind moving fast. The red, white, and blue jeep inside the cloud emerges, seems to gallop more than drive. Cowboys, Ezra thinks. Mailmen are all cowboys these days, old bronco riders off the rodeo circuit still needing to feel their asses slam down on a saddle. It doesn't occur to him that it's coming to his house until it skids to a halt in his drive.

"Looks like we've got company," he says to Buffalo, who's barking now.

The cowboy in a blue uniform jumps from the van, a Special Delivery folder in one hand, a clipboard in the other. A summons from the Sierra Club, Ezra thinks. Honorary membership. Or a one-way ticket from St. Peter, C.O.D. The driver sees Ezra and waves. As he comes closer Ezra is surprised to see he's a she with her long black hair pushed up beneath a cap. Paiute, most likely.

"You look like Moses at the Red Sea." She frowns. "Or was it the Dead Sea?"

"Moses didn't have a dog."

She notices Buffalo for the first time.

"Does he bite?"

"He'd probably like to, but it takes everything he's got just to breathe."

"Well," she says, bringing her eyes back to Ezra, a hint of an indulgent smile showing. "I just need you to sign for this. Special Delivery."

He takes the large envelope and sets it on his lap. She holds out a pen. "Next to the X," she says gently, staring at his shaking hand, as if he might need reminding, as if his hand might need to be guided to write the letters of his own name.

He peers at the paper she's handed him on the clipboard. "Which name do you want?" he asks. "My real one or my alias?"

"Doesn't matter," she says, "as long as an actual person accepts it."

Ezra signs 'Moses McPherson' and hands it back to her. She looks at it and laughs. "Nice touch," she says with admiration.

She stares at the envelope as if she might see through the cardboard into its contents. "Aren't you going to open it?"

"How long have you been at this job?" Ezra asks. "You act like you're at a birthday party instead of delivering mail."

"Just curious," she says, her face flushing.

"Whatever it is, it can wait."

She stands there for another moment slapping the clipboard on her thigh in a steady, rhythmic way. She waits. But something in Ezra's face must have told her it will be a long time before he opens it and that it's something he'll probably do alone in the dark, late at night, or not at all. "Well," she says, "I guess I'll leave you to it, then."

"Thank you," Ezra says. She starts to walk away. "For everything," he calls after her. After all, her people were pushed from this land a long time ago. Some are in the courts right now, fighting to get it back. The least he can do is try to take good care of it.

"FROM," it says, in capital letters. "The Children's Aid Society of New York." Like he told her. It can wait. He hasn't heard from these people in years. What's the rush now? He's surprised they still exist. They're probably soliciting donations from alumni. Special Delivery, indeed! Nobody does anything regular anymore. Everything is Extra Strength, New & Improved. Ultra. 10% More for the Same Price! The latest in American expansion.

He puts Buffalo in the house with a bone. Gathers up his keys, a pocket knife. And the cat's eye marble, which he never leaves home without.

Clouds composed of alkaline dust drawn up from the east shore hang like sheets, undulating weirdly over the water. Foam boils up on the lake from the friction of the wind. Suds and suds, but nothing comes clean. Cold rain comes down hard and fast as Ezra runs, or tries to, to his Studebaker truck parked in the shed out back. He heads up the dirt road to the highway toward town to buy more coffee. At least he has an errand today.

The fact that he signed for the envelope has set something else in motion now. Nothing's the same. He used to have a quiet life, counting birds, writing their numbers down, picking up his Social Security check once a month, bothering no one. Now, something else will probably have to be done. Now, at this eleventh hour, the past comes knocking.

February 1, 1985

Dear Mr. Duval,

Your name was found on an original passenger manifest in the annual report of the Children's Aid Society of New York dated September 20, 1918. We have traced you with the help of Social Security records. We are writing to all Orphan Train Riders and their descendants to invite you to the first reunion to be hosted by the Heritage Society in Fayetteville, Arkansas, at the depot, April 16, 1985, at 2 p.m. After a brief train ride of approximately one hour on the Arkansas & Missouri Railroad's original 1912 Pullman car there will be a reenactment of the placing out of the children at the Van Buren Opera House followed by a reception with the press. We very much hope you will be able to participate in this historic event.

R.S.V.P. by April 1
Ethel Worthington

Was he that easy to find? They followed the money, so to speak. It's called Social Security now, but it's still Relief. And now it's made him find-able, through some kind of computer, no doubt. How times have changed.

And what's so important now, seventy-two years later, that such a reunion take place? Forty-seven children were scattered across America. Some budding history student probably found an obscure newspaper clipping in a library. They should have left well enough alone. And the RSVP date: April Fool's Day. On the basis of that, he'll reply.

∿∿∿

Ezra drives straight through the Great Plains, his dog Buffalo curled on the bench seat of the truck. He's

amazed to see everything so green once again. Route 66
is now an interstate with a different number. He passes
all the places where he could make a detour, the
crossroads at Amarillo for the road to Dalhart or
Terlingua and the Big Bend. He doesn't have enough
time. Maybe on the way back. Right now he just wants
to get to Arkansas.

The only reason he's on this trip at all is because
it's in Arkansas. Elizabeth might be there, if she's still
alive. Would he be able to recognize her? Does she still
wear an eye-patch? The closer he gets the more he's
afraid she might not remember him at all.

Arkansas is nothing like Oklahoma. Dark green
hills rise up outside of Fort Smith breaking the mantra
of the Great Plains. The road to Fayetteville follows a
ridge and at the bottom of this steep ravine, the White
River works its way slowly through the Ozarks. "The
oldest mountains in America." Ezra reads from his
WPA guidebook. It may be out of date, but mountains
don't change, at least not in his lifetime. These hills are
smooth and flowing, the valleys cut deep into them.
They're fringed with oak, laced with dogwood, whose
white blossoms are like small, curious clouds that came
down for a closer look.

≋

The depot in Fayetteville, Arkansas, looks like it
hasn't seen a train in years. The building is boarded up,
the windows shuttered from the inside with yellowed
newsprint. But the door is propped open with a lawn
chair and a hand-made sign taped to the brick building
says "Orphan Train Reunion Here!" in black letters and
an exclamation mark and an enormous arrow pointing,
a little crookedly, inside.

Ezra steps tentatively across the threshold of the
depot with Buffalo right beside him on a leash, as if he

might need the dog's protection. They enter a bare waiting room. Ezra can make out a small group clustered around a table in the back of the room. A few are seated in metal folding chairs. Their voices mix and murmur, echo from the bare walls, the concrete floors. A few are looking up at a swallow that darts back and forth across the high-ceilinged room. A few turn as Ezra and Buffalo come closer. One tall man stooped over a walker openly stares. He's probably never seen a man Ezra's age with long hair, at least in this century. A woman creeping along with an oxygen tank strapped to a carrier stops in her tracks when she sees them. Smiles. "Wild Bill with a beautiful Handi-dog!" she says. "I'm going to get one, too."

Other faces turn to him, searching his for some recognizable feature. They look a little bewildered, a little hopeful. Their scrutiny, though gentle, is almost unbearable.

Ezra searches each face now that their attention has shifted to him. A loose arrangement of dried flowers--white heads on delicate stems--that's how they look to him. He doesn't recognize anyone. They all wear nametags. If a wind were to come through the room he would expect a faint rustling. These people are like rice paper, their blue veins a ropy script written on their skin. Sepia light coming through the windows drapes a gold shadow on everything.

A train whistle cleaves the air. The swallow shoots across the eaves and back again as if propelled, ricocheting rather than flying of its own volition. All heads turn toward the sound of the train, to a woman with a clipboard coming through the door to the platform on the side of the building. They begin murmuring again. They begin to move.

The man with the walker goes first and emerges onto the platform in the lowering sun, blinking. The others follow. If Buffalo hadn't tugged on the leash

Ezra doesn't think he could have taken a single step.

On the other side, just ten feet in front of him Ezra can see a massive, black steam locomotive sliding to a laborious, shrieking halt. Behind it, two Pullman cars with "Arkansas and Missouri Railroad" painted in gold letters stops in front. The first car is full of children, their faces pressed to the windows. Some of them open the windows and lean out wearing costumes from the turn of the century. Boys in caps, girls in enormous bows. Tags on strings with their names flutter in the breeze.

"There we are," the man in the walker says. His nametag says Colonel Winger. Missouri 1922.

Buffalo is leading Ezra into a cloud of steam. It boils from the engine, obscuring the view. It clears, boils back again. Faces appear and recede within it and now he can read their nametags. Dates and places: Nebraska 1912, Missouri 1918, Ohio 1910 and one, incredibly, Pennsylvania 1899. This isn't the class reunion of 1918, it's an entire era without a name. He had no idea, no idea at all there were so many and for so long. He feels like a citizen of a country no longer on the map. The entire population is about to be reunited, their common heritage one he never knew he shared until this afternoon.

Ezra watches another member of this motley population climb up the steep step, pulled by a conductor's hand. How many of us are there? A multitude? This handful? Nobody from the WPA came looking for us to write our stories down. All his hermit life he's shared so much with people he's never met. Of all the stories he ever wrote, his own may have been the most remarkable.

Buffalo needs help getting up the two steep steps. So much for the Handi-Dog disguise. Ezra lifts him with difficulty, then climbs up the two steep steps himself. The woman with the clipboard asks him,

"Your name?"

"Duval," he says. "Ezra."

She looks down her list, smiling. "I was hoping you'd come," she says. "But I don't see your name here."

He's feeling a little desperate now that he might be refused admission.

"Did you pay your registration?"

"Registration? You people sent me to Texas. Isn't that enough?"

She touches his hand. "I just meant, do you have a ticket for today?"

"Of course not!" he cries. He hadn't thought an RSVP was all that important. He doesn't tell her kept changing his mind up until the last minute to decide to come at all.

"Well, I happen to have an extra." She hands a ticket to Ezra, looking at him kindly, stooping to pat Buffalo on the head.

He starts to relax a little as she writes down his name. Ezra puts his tag on his jacket pocket.

"He's already got a tag," he says, pointing to Buffalo. "And a rabies shot, too."

Ezra makes his way down the narrow aisle. The rows of green plush seats are filled now. He feels their eyes on him all over again, reading his tag first, then his face. Some look excitedly out the windows, others stare straight ahead in a polite state of shock. There is too much remembering going on. He feels like his knees are going to literally buckle as he makes his way past the rows of elderly passengers. In the last seat before the empty ones two men clutch each other's hands. But they don't look frightened at all. "He's my brother," the man by the window explains as Ezra looks at them in concern. "I just found him." The other man looks up at Ezra, his chin trembling as he smiles through his tears. "You wouldn't be Jim, would you?" he says trying to focus on Ezra's face.

"No," Ezra says, looking back up the aisle. There isn't anyone he recognizes. She isn't here. He turns back to the brothers. "But I think I'm one of you," he says, his voice breaking. "All of you."

Ezra collapses in the seat behind them.

The platform slowly slides by. The clang of the crossing bell comes through the open windows. They all look out the window on the left side as the train inches across the street. And they all see her, a woman in a long dress and feathered hat running into the front door of the depot. She's got a beaded handbag over one arm; the other arm is flung outward, sweeping the air as she tries to flag the train down. Colonel Winger stands up clutching the seatback in front of him. "Stop this train immediately!" he commands. The woman with the clipboard runs forward through the car, finds the conductor who pulls some handle on a chain. A terrific screech comes next and they're all thrown forward, then back as the train comes to a shuddering halt. There's silence in the car but the crossing bell still clangs wildly. They're in the middle of the street. People stopped in cars at the crossing stare through windshields at them.

Then, incredibly, the train begins to move backward. A few seconds of stunned silence. Then everyone applauds. The platform slides back into view, the depot and the open door. The woman is standing there, the expression on her face very pleased that the train is actually backing up for her. In another moment she emerges at the front of the car, out of breath, wiping strands of long gray hair that had come loose from underneath the feathered hat. Her high-collared burgundy dress has at least a hundred buttons from neck to toe. A few of them are missing. A single peacock feather in her hat floats through the air behind her as she makes her way down the aisle.

The woman with the clipboard hurries up behind her, hands the woman a nametag. "You just scared me half to death! You're supposed to be *on* the train, not running after it! Never mind—I'm so glad you made it."

She takes the nametag and pins it on. She sits down in the seat across the aisle from Ezra, putting her beaded bag on the empty seat beside her. She looks at Buffalo and smiles. She says to him, "Are you going west to find a new home, too?" Buffalo thumps his tail in answer. Then she turns to look out the window.

Ezra's almost afraid to speak. It's her, isn't it? Doesn't she recognize him? He leans toward her to get a better look at her nametag. Maud Farrell. His hope falters, a bird shot out of the air, trying to keep flying. She's definitely not wearing an eye patch. "Is that your real name?" he asks.

"Sometimes," she answers. "We should have suitcases, shouldn't we? Just a small one, for the journey." She looks out the window. "All I had in mine was a night dress and a hand-rolled cigarette. A few odds and ends, I suppose."

Surely, it's her.

"What's your dog's name?"

"Buffalo."

"Of course it is. He should be on the nickel."

Ezra leans forward. Of course it's her.

Someone in one of the cars stuck at the crossing starts honking their horn. Several others follow suit.

"Obviously," she says, "they don't know who they're honking at."

"Maybe they'll have our real parents bussed in from heaven and see if they can pick us out again," Ezra says.

She looks at him cautiously, as if ascertaining his mental acuity, but still smiles at his joke.

The train whistle cleaves the air. "There's so much I don't remember. Maybe I don't want to remember.

But that's a sound," she says, "I will never forget."

Ezra looks at her eyes, can't tell if there's a difference between them but then he doesn't see so well these days. Is he wrong about her? Has she changed her name?

Flustered by such scrutiny she changes the subject. "I never thought I'd be running to get *on* one of these trains. An *orphan train*, they're calling it." She moves her hand in a wide arc, a theatrical gesture to match the emphasis in her voice.

The train slowly picks up speed as they leave the last of Fayetteville behind. The whistle is almost constant as it blows at every crossing—dirt roads and narrow pig trails—every hundred yards, it seems, there's another blast. It's almost impossible to talk.

Maybe words are beside the point anyway. Ezra takes the cat's-eye marble out of his pocket. Holds it up between his thumb and forefinger so the light behind him shows through.

She sees it, he can tell. She leans across the aisle, closer. She stares at the marble, then at Ezra.

A blur of green outside the window. Another blast of whistle.

"What happened to your eye?" Ezra asks when the noise subsides. It has to be her. Everything depends on her answer.

She looks at him. "What?" she says, cupping her hand around her ear, "What did you say?"

"Your eye," Ezra says, "What happened to your eye?" He can't stand it, this yelling across the aisle over the noise.

He looks right at her, still not breaking his gaze. Here she is across the aisle like some queen from an obscure but influential principality whose favor he has to gain once more. He's not sure what he wants or where to begin. He's afraid he'll make a fool out of himself. He should have stayed at Pyramid Lake, counting birds. He's out of his league here, but then he always was, with her.

"What an impertinent question!" she says. "I didn't think it showed," she adds more quietly.

The sound of wheels on the tracks changes from syncopated trotting to galloping as the train enters the unbroken hills south of Winslow; the whistle blasts grow less frequent as they leave the towns and their crossings behind.

Still flustered, he says, "I was worried that I'd dreamed all of this...." he says. "Even you."

"It might make a better story," she says.

The woods streak by, green broken only by the white of wild dogwood just beginning to blossom, now that they're traveling south. She leans across the aisle trying to say something quickly before the next crossing. "Sometimes I think some things are better left alone." She looks down the aisle at the other riders turning around in their seats, introducing themselves to each other. Their voices begin to fill the car, high-pitched, excited. They almost sound like children on a school field trip.

The train crosses a long trestle bridge and the sound of the earth drops away as the train rumbles through the air.

A roar as the ground comes back again. The sound of wheels on the tracks is so familiar, those nights when he wrote in his notebook by match light, when he could not sleep, after she was taken. He burned his fingers so often. He had too much to say.

Now Elizabeth breaks the silence. "I almost didn't make it here. But when I looked at myself in the mirror earlier I saw an interesting character in a costume with the kind of guts I admire. That woman in the mirror kidnapped me, you know."

Ezra leans across the aisle, completely confused now. "She saved my life."

"I doubt that."

"She sang," he says, prompting her. "She stopped a nightmare for a whole three minutes back then. She stopped a train this afternoon."

"Did she?" She pauses, as if trying to get back to her original script but she's groping now.

"I never," Ezra says, "should have let you out of my sight."

She looks at him, surprised, very surprised, as if she didn't expect this at all, as if she had been prepared for polite conversation, a little monolog about his life, maybe pictures of his grandchildren, not this eleventh hour declaration.

Her hands twist together her lap. She looks out the window. The train is out of the mountains now, coming into a town. She doesn't turn his way again.

The train pulls into Van Buren station. There is no crowd to meet them, no band. No ticker tape parade. No mayor with the key to the city. The children in the car behind them get off first.

Ezra doesn't know what else to say. She doesn't seem to know who he is; maybe she has no memory of him whatsoever. He puts the marble back in his pocket, wonders if he should find a bus station. Get the hell out of here. But when he helps her off the last high step of the train she doesn't let go of his arm. Buffalo takes a flying leap onto the platform and nearly falls flat. Colonel Winger is holding things up getting the walker down the steps. Hazel Conners, her name tag says, with the oxygen tank, isn't much faster. The brothers, Jeremy and Elliott move slowly, gladly shackled together, never letting go of each other's hands.

A news team arrives belatedly, hurriedly setting up to film them as they come down the steps. Ethel Worthington is being interviewed by a reporter. Ezra finally recognizes her, astonished that she's here. Is she going to line them all up again, tell them to put their best foot forward? But Ethel is directing all attention to another woman, introducing Mary Ellen Johnson to the press, who started the Orphan Train Heritage Society of America, not because she was ever on an orphan train, but because she thought it was high time people knew about it. She had stumbled upon it in a microfiche of a newspaper in Rogers announcing the arrival of a company of children and learned that a brother and sister were separated. She didn't understand how such a thing could happen. She's the real reason they're all assembled here today.

When they're all assembled they head down the street together to the old opera house, renovated just in time for the occasion. Ezra holds onto Maud Farrell. Whoever she is, she's not letting go of Ezra's arm.

They all file into the opera house, their steps softened by thick burgundy carpet on the aisle. Still passing as a Handi-Dog, Buffalo is waved through. They take their seats. Buffalo collapses on the floor in front of Ezra's feet, as if exhausted by his new responsibilities. The house lights go down. The curtain slowly opens.

An American flag the size of a billboard stretches across the screen. In front, twenty-three children of varying heights stand in a long row, overwhelmed by the stars and stripes looming behind them. They look straight out into the darkened theater. Mary Ellen Johnson has changed into a costume to play the matron in charge. She addresses the audience. "We're here today to honor you all. There are many more of you. So many more. Two hundred and fifty thousand," she says. "At least."

Maud Farrell gasps, grabs Ezra's hand between both of her hands and holds on tight.

Ezra's thinks he's going to pass out, right here in the theatre. A quarter of a million. One of them is holding his hand right now. But it's too late. She doesn't even know who he is.

Mary Ellen calls the name of the first child, Leroy Hickens. A small boy steps forward. "This little boy is eight years old. He's really good at geography and baseball and what he wants more than anything in the world is a puppy of his own. He says he's sure he could learn how to take care of chickens." She holds out her arm, presenting him. "Who would like to take him?" she asks. Leroy looks like he's trying really hard not to laugh out loud.

Someone in the front row raises his hand right away. He comes to the steps at the side of the stage. Leroy takes his hand and smiles. They sit back down together.

Mary Ellen continues. Several more are given away.

A toddler named Susie is next. Age three. Birds and finger painting are her specialties. Her parents' hands shoot right up when Mary Ellen asks who'd like to take her, but Susie just stares at them when they step forward. Susie hides in Mary Ellen's skirts. Finally, her father finds a piece of candy in his pocket, a roll of Lifesavers, and holds it up. Susie steps forward, hand out. Everyone laughs, grateful for comic relief.

A little boy is next. "Sammy may look small for ten years old but he has some grand ideas. He wants to travel around the world, she says. "He knows how to ride a bicycle now but wants to be a captain of a ship." When she asks who would like to take him nobody answers. Mary Ellen shields her eyes, looks out into the crowd. His parents must be late. Sammy looks out into the audience, too. He looks anxious, as if he's afraid he's spoiling everything. A minute or more goes by. It must seem like a lifetime to him. He steps forward, looks straight at a man in the front row, leans down over the edge of the stage. "I promise I'll grow bigger if you take me," he says. "I promise." The man looks embarrassed and more than a little shaken; he's not sure what to do, but Sammy's promise hangs there in the air, begging to be answered. The man stands up. "I'll take him," he says and practically runs to the side of the stage, up the little set of steps, to get him out of here to find his real father.

Finally, Mary Ellen comes to the last one, an overweight girl in a calico dress. She stands alone on the stage. Clara. Age eleven. Sewing. Arithmetic. Spelling. Her hands are clasped tightly together. Her nametag hangs crookedly on its string. "Would anyone like to take her?" A long silence. Clara looks like she's about to cry. Are her parents not here, either? Ezra wonders if this one was thrown in for accuracy of the reenactment, to have at least one child that won't be taken. Like he was through most of Texas.

He thinks they've gone too far. He thinks about this happening many times over, an endless parade of children torn between wanting to be chosen, hoping they wouldn't be.

"Would you like to hear her sing? She's a real good singer," Mary Ellen says. But Clara doesn't want to sing. She shakes her head, a most definite "no."

"For God's sake!" Maud Farrell cries, standing up. "Don't make her if she doesn't want to!"

Utter silence except the creaking of seats as everyone turns around slowly, stiffly, to look. Mary Ellen peers out into the darkened theater.

"Is that part of the script?" Colonel Winger shouts.

"It is now," Ethel Worthington, turning around, says to them all.

〰

Maud Farrell holds onto Ezra even tighter as they leave the opera house. She looks bewildered in the bright light, confused, especially since the girl, Clara, was claimed in the opera house lobby by her parents.

A man who must be the mayor holds an oversized key to the city of Van Buren. He stands next to the refreshment table talking to a lone reporter with a camera slung over his shoulder on a strap. A different Instant-Eye news team from Fort Smith is just arriving. A few innocent bystanders—two librarians and one elementary school teacher—come to hear the stories of the riders in the windowless, fluorescent-lit conference room and to look at the letters and pictures brought from the archives in New York.

Maud Farrell lets go of his hand and wanders through the room as if searching for someone. Mrs. Worthington guides Ezra to the table. "I believe that's your notebook there," she says, "inside your suitcase."

The suitcase is open. It's definitely his. The notebook looks so thin and fragile that it would fall apart if he picked it up. Ezra wonders if anybody ever read it. He looks around for Maud Farrell. She's moving slowly toward the table. He steps away quickly, curious about what her reaction to the suitcase will be. He wants to watch her from a distance.

She stops in front of the table and looks at his open suitcase. He sees her hand turning pages, one at a time. She stops on a particular page. She looks right and left but doesn't see him. She reaches in her bag for something and finding it, places it inside the suitcase. She closes it and then she leaves.

Ezra returns to the table. He opens the suitcase. On top of the notebook, she's left the nickel. The same one, he's sure. The page on which it rests has only two words: *Elizabeth. Elizabeth.*

How much has she really forgotten? If she does remember, why won't she say?

He reaches in his pocket for the cat's-eye marble. He sets the marble down, next to the nickel. He closes the lid of the suitcase on these two tokens, the only actual evidence that he and Elizabeth had even met on that September day.

A loudspeaker summons everyone to a buffet table. They settle at round tables with their cake and coffee, stretching to see the person across from them through the two-tall centerpieces of artificial flowers. One by one the riders step up to a small stage and stand behind a podium. A single microphone sits on a stand. They look surprised anyone is interested to hear their stories after all this time.

One by one they speak, timidly at first, un-accustomed to the microphone and its occasional shriek of feedback. This one was an orphan, taken from the streets where he'd always lived, sent to a farm in Nebraska where he saw a cow for the first time. That one was surrendered by her mother and lived two years in an orphanage waiting for her to return and was finally sent to Missouri to work on a farm. The two brothers who were separated in St. Louis spent their lives looking for each other. The man from New Jersey only found out years later when he wrote to the Foundling Hospital to try to discover his name that he was left in a basket in a department store. One woman said her life began the day she got off the train; another man says he thought his ended. All of them tried to find their birth parents. Many failed. Most of them were grateful, they said, for the chance to have new homes, but it was the train and the lining up to be chosen and losing their brothers and sisters that was so hard. Several said the hardest part was that they weren't allowed to talk to each other. The matrons didn't want them to make friends on the train that they would probably have to leave in the very next town.

Mrs. Worthington hadn't exactly forbidden them to talk. They whispered, for the most part. They were lucky. He was lucky. If he and Elizabeth had been forbidden to talk, he would not have had her voice inside him his whole life long. A song that lured him here. A song she no longer remembers singing.

The reporter, sitting down next to Ezra, makes a few notes. Ezra can see them: cryptic hieroglyphics, a lot of history boiled down in such a short time to fit such a small page. Ezra can't contain himself any longer. He whispers vehemently to the reporter. "You're never going to get a better story. You couldn't make this up even if you tried," he says. "We'll soon be gone. Write it down—the whole truth, not just a one-line caption for a photo on the back page with the obituaries."

The reporter, speechless, nods his head.

Colonel Winger finally stops pacing the perimeter and gets up to speak. For all his bravado on the train he looks now like he can hardly open his mouth. When he does, people have to strain to listen. "We don't know who we are or where we come from. We have to believe we've got more than bad blood, that there's something good in us, someone worth knowing."

He stands there a moment longer, coughing, covering his mouth. He walks, with dignity, nonetheless, off the stage.

The reporter's just listening now. He puts the pencil down. He looks like he's trying not to cry.

Ezra reluctantly lets go of Maud Farrell's hand to take the witness stand. He has no idea what he's going to say. He certainly didn't know he was supposed to speak. He's absolutely speechless with all that he's heard and seen.

He looks out at their faces, their expectant faces. They really want to know. About him. His life. Who he is. Where he came from and why. So he begins at what he considers the beginning and the words come rushing out as if he's already written them. And in so many ways, he has.

"I ended up with a good home. I'm grateful for that. The man who chose me wanted me; it took me a long time to appreciate it. You see, I was put on the train because my father surrendered me. But at the time I didn't know about being surrendered and I kept waiting and hoping until the very last second as I got on the train that he'd come running down the platform to get me. I kept wondering how he could have forgotten me, what I had done or failed to do that made me so forgettable. If it hadn't been for her," he says, pointing at Maud Farrell, "I would have been invisible."

Maud Farrell stands up and walks toward the stage as if he's called her there. He isn't done yet, but maybe there is nothing more to say. It's her turn now.

He can see some of the Elizabeth he knew in her saunter. It's taken all these years to get here and she's not about to rush this last minute. But she doesn't stand behind the podium. She stands at the front edge of the stage and even though it's only raised a foot from the floor, she looks as if she's poised on a ledge.

"You say you remember," she says, looking at Ezra who's leaving the stage but standing nearby. "But I don't really understand any of this. What it's supposed to mean, in the grand scheme of things. But listening to your stories I know I feel honored to be with you." She pauses, searching for the next thought.

"I once knew someone—I don't remember his name...." She pauses again, searching for that name.

Please, Ezra thinks. *Please remember.*

"He was going to build a pyramid. But not in Egypt."

Egypt. Ezra can't believe that word came from her. He has an urge to raise his hand. *How did she know about his father?*

"That man was going to put all kinds of things inside it: a printing press, among other things. A gyroscope. A book written for the people of the future so that when they found it they would learn how to make a better world than we did. I don't know if he ever built it." She scans the crowd, as if looking for him. Her eyes sweep the audience and she stops when she finds Ezra.

"He still believed in the future, after the war. I don't know how. The great war changed everything. And nothing."

Why is she looking at him when she says this? Two stories have become one, somehow. The suitcase—they had each placed something inside it on top of the notebook where he'd once written her name. For the people of the future to find and wonder how they came to be together.

"We may look like people of the past," she says, continuing again, turning toward the reporter. "But we have something to say to the people of the future. We were once somebody's children. They may not re-member, but *we* should not be forgotten."

The reporter is writing furiously. Ezra can hear the scratch of the pen across the page. Elizabeth, speech-less now, looks lost, as if she doesn't know how she has ended up in this room in Arkansas. Again.

Ezra holds out his free hand to her.

The applause startles Buffalo who's been asleep through all of this. He gets to his feet with great difficulty and limps toward the stage.

The news team is finally ready; the anchor is throwing up his hands, pointing at his watch. Then he points at a man reaching for a woman, and the team moves in for the shot of a man, weeping shamelessly. A woman, trying not to. A dog trying to lick both of their hands, tightly held together.

∿∿∿

The Ozarks stream by in the early evening light and except for the occasional glimpse of a house far back in the woods they could be traveling in virgin country. Everyone is tired, falling asleep or sleeping. Elizabeth leans back, eyes closed. Buffalo is snoring on the floor.

Ezra gets out of his seat and heads for the back of the Pullman car. He opens the door to the roar of the wheels on the tracks, the wind. He closes the door behind him. There's nothing as powerful as a train and he wants to feel it again—that rocking, that sense of being borne along, so small. But he is a part of something larger now, a tribe that claims him as one of their own. He has been recognized, but not in the way he hoped to be.

The sun is dropping down behind the hills. The sky is clear, a single star showing through. He isn't long by himself, five minutes at most. She opens the door, falls against him as she fights for balance. The sounds change abruptly as they reach the trestle bridge and a whole world opens up below them, an enormous cavern of air spliced by a long whistle blast the whole length across it. He opens his mouth. He goes ahead and does it—what he did back then, alone, what he wants to do now, with her. He howls. For the hell of it.

They reach the other side, laughing. The train slows to a crawl now. There's a truck stopped at a crossing where the train nearly comes to a full stop. The man in the cab is listening to country music that Ezra can hear clearly. He sees the driver smile as he watches them slowly pull away—a man and a woman, hair white with age, dressed in clothes from another time. They look out from the moving train, a blurred tintype from the last century.

〰
〰

They climb off the train, weary from the long day. The sun is completely behind the hills now. A photographer with a large format camera on a tripod awaits them and assembles everyone for a group shot before they leave. Each of them will receive a postcard of the photo in the mail in a week's time along with a list of names and addresses of all the attendees so they can keep in touch.

"I'll count to three," the photographer says.

The photographer focuses the camera. Every-one tries to hold on to a smile as long as they can, but Ezra looks only at Elizabeth.

"One!" the photographer says.

But Elizabeth is walking away from the group, distracted by some musicians outside the depot on the street corner. They're singing a song in a minor key accompanied by a mandolin.

"Two."

Ezra presses past the others. "Elizabeth!" he calls out to her.

She stops. She slowly turns around. She looks at him, at his hand reaching out to her.

"You're the boy in the photograph, aren't you? With the Indians. *The Vanishing American.*"

Before he can answer she grabs his hand. They step inside the picture just as the shutter clicks.

"You moved!" the photographer says. "I'll have to take another, just in case."

But Ezra wants the first one, the one where they're in motion, blurred. She *saw* him. Not just his future, but his past, as if the cat's-eye marble, even in his pos-session, afforded her a view from afar. How else could she have known about Egypt? About Indians?

Elizabeth looks like she's not sure what to do next, as if she's hoping someone will make a suggestion.

The music out on the street has stopped though Elizabeth is still listening. Ethel takes her by the arm and walks with her in the direction the music came from. Whatever it was, it's gone now. Ethel lets go of her arm. Elizabeth drifts a few feet farther and stops.

Ethel Worthington, as if she knows Elizabeth is on the verge of something, begins to hum what little she remembers from that day when Elizabeth sang and stopped the world. Elizabeth turns, startled, toward the source of the sound as if she's listening to an understudy in the wings but is having trouble hearing.

"Tristan and Isolde," Hazel with the oxygen tank says from the group. "I studied it in school long ago." She takes the music Ethel began, singing until Elizabeth can carry it on her own.

Ezra can see from where he stands, not ten feet away, the power this music has over her. Her face changes from confused, clearing to confident like a pane of glass caught momentarily between cool and warm. Her mouth moves, her muscle memory strong, and her eyes seem startled that this is so. Her voice falters but does not stop. She follows the thread of melody as far as it will take her.

Ezra still doesn't know what she's singing. It's in German, of all things, a language nobody sang in back then with the war on. He'll never know what planted this particular song, of all songs, in her. It doesn't matter. Nothing else matters. Elizabeth is singing.

This kind of brightness cannot help but fade as it does now, the look on her face darkening as the world rushes to meet her with all its clamoring details. The last note of her song hangs there, suspended, now falling, now gone. If he could he would hold on to everything, move closer, feel the heat of her hand, look once more at the eye that was never glass, only scarred with the single cloud of a darker time. But all he can do is look at her from ten feet away and wonder.

Free and lost—he feels it once again in this moment that, so vivid, already begins to become memory. But no matter what she calls herself, Elizabeth is, was, here. With him.

He'll leave tonight, before the morning, ahead of

the mundane logistics of transportation to the airport, the farewells, the promises to keep in touch. He cannot say goodbye. He still wants to believe in that most American idea: a limitless future.

He can only slip away, get behind the wheel, the dog beside him on the seat, and head west the way he came. He has one hand on the wheel, the other buried in Buffalo's fur as the moon rises heavily behind him.

The lights of the cities, the towns of the Great Plains appear on the horizon as distant galaxies. By the Panhandle of Oklahoma, the old Indian Nation, the towns wind down to villages, like smaller constellations, farther apart. The desert enfolds him once again.

A crossroads in Kansas looms and is quickly contained in the circumference of the rear-view mirror. He goes north now to meet highway 50 across the Great Divide, and the sun rises as he ascends and descends all the mountains of Colorado and Utah. Crossing the state line into Nevada, the highway becomes The Loneliest Road, or at least a sign declares it so, and, as if to prove it, there are light years between towns, between the times and places of his life, the people he loved and tried to love. The ones he lost. And found. He did not know he had a heart that did anything but beat until he feels it breaking open. It's because of her. Again. Rise and fall, basin and range—it all matches the changing topography of memory. He opens the window and Buffalo catches the scent of home long before Ezra gets his first glimpse of the blue gem of Pyramid Lake.

Elizabeth. Elizabeth. That was her name. Ezra's heart is emptied now of everything but her song.